ONI PRESS PRESENTS   **BRYAN LEE O'MALLEY'S**

SCOTT PILGRIM

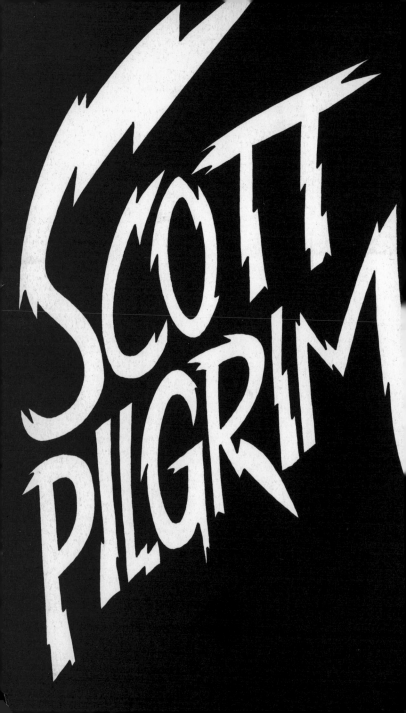

IN HIS
FINEST
HOUR

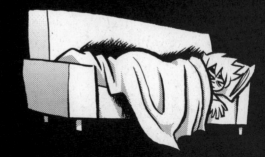

John Kantz art assistant

Aaron Ancheta junior assistant

Ben Berntsen back cover art

Dylan McCrae cover colors

Bryan Lee O'Malley and **Keith Wood** book design

James Lucas Jones editor

First edition: July 2010
ISBN: 978-1-934964-38-5

Published by **Oni Press, Inc.**

Joe Nozemack publisher | **James Lucas Jones** editor in chief
Cory Casoni marketing director | **Keith Wood** art director
George Rohac operations director | **Jill Beaton** associate editor
Charlie Chu associate editor | **Douglas E. Sherwood** production assistant

2 3 4 5 6 7 8 9 10
www.onipress.com | www.scottpilgrim.com | www.radiomaru.com
PRINTED IN THE U.S.A. by Lake Book Manufacturing.

ONI PRESS, INC.
1305 SE Martin Luther King Jr. Blvd.
Suite A
Portland, OR 97214
USA

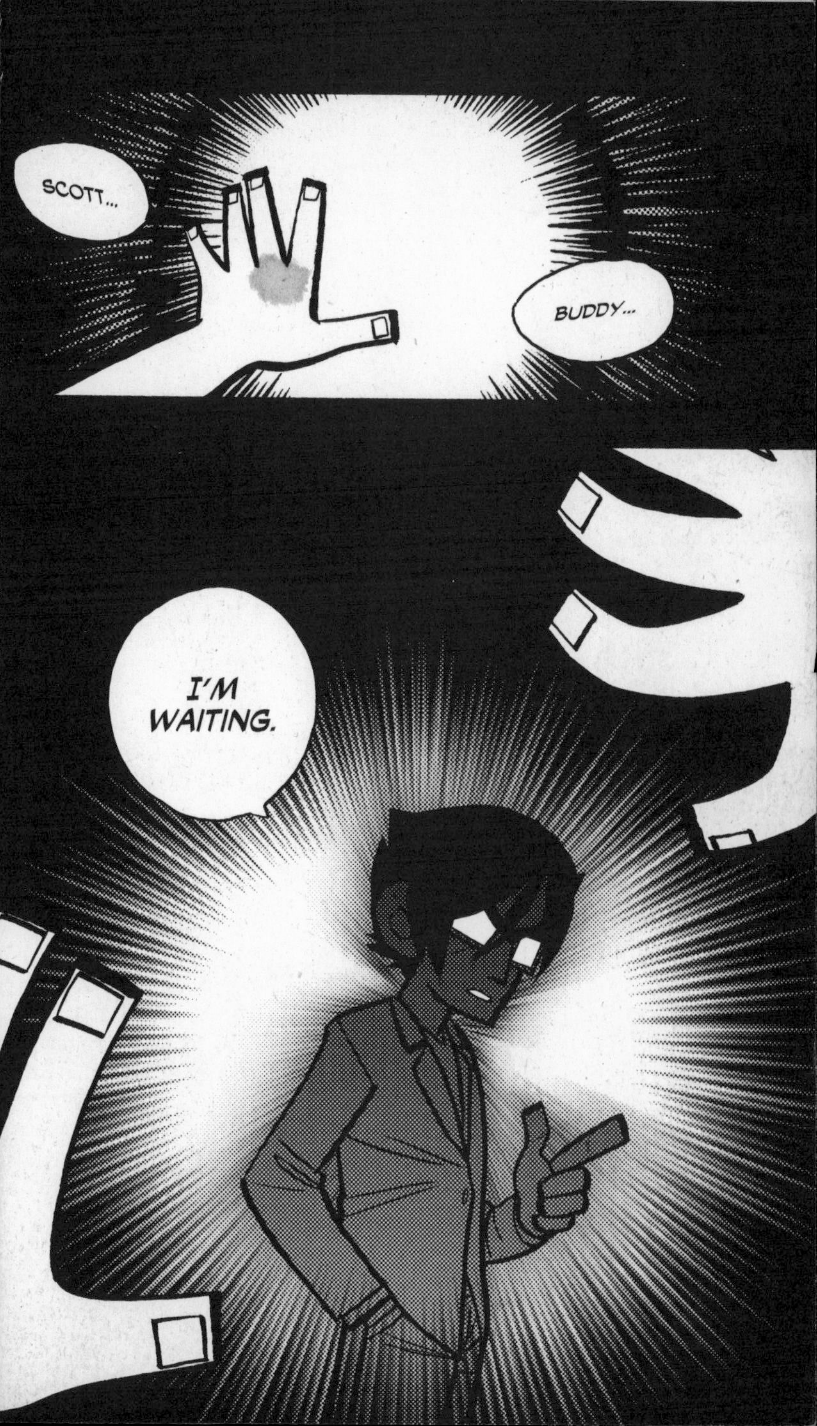
SCOTT...
BUDDY...
I'M WAITING.

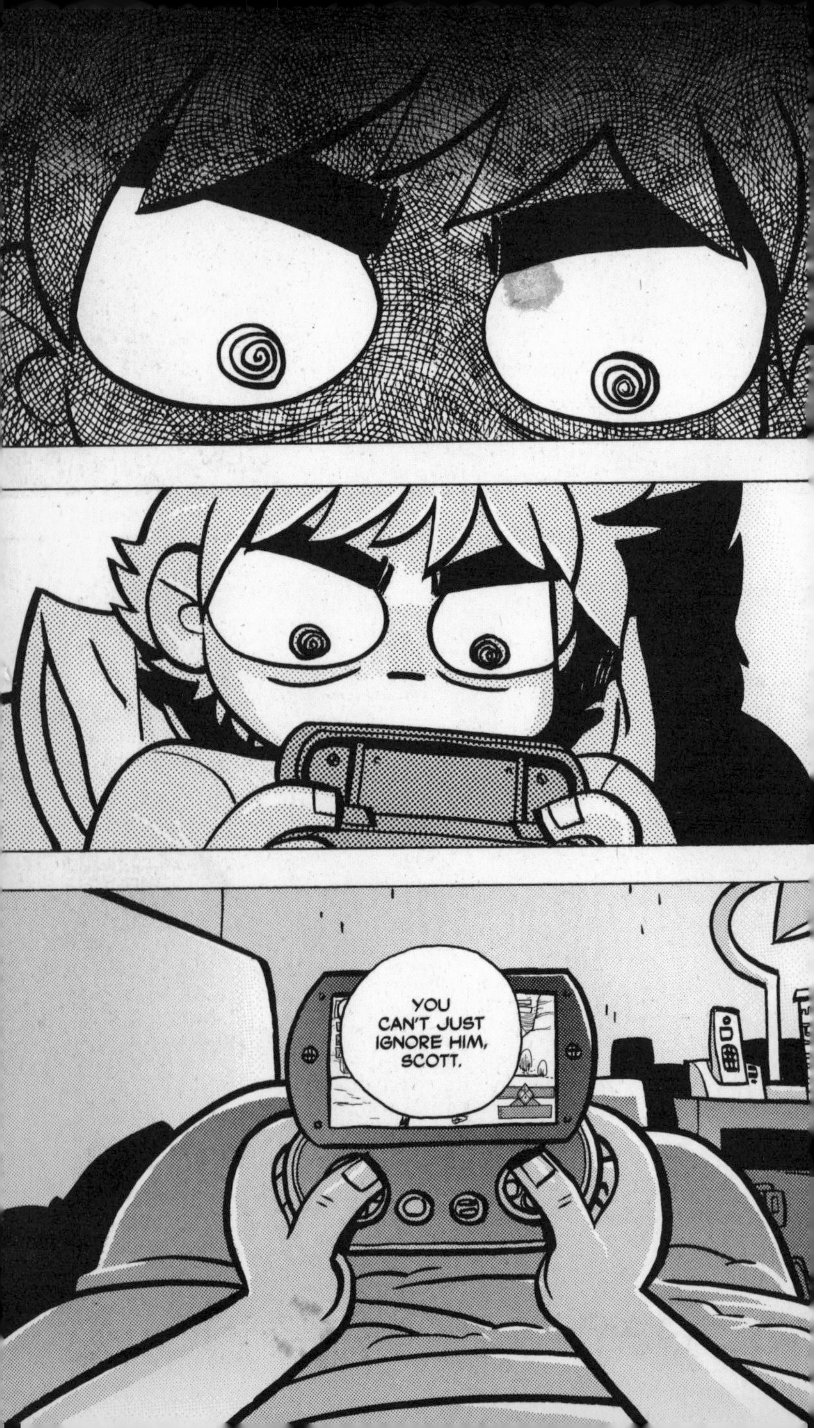
YOU CAN'T JUST IGNORE HIM, SCOTT.

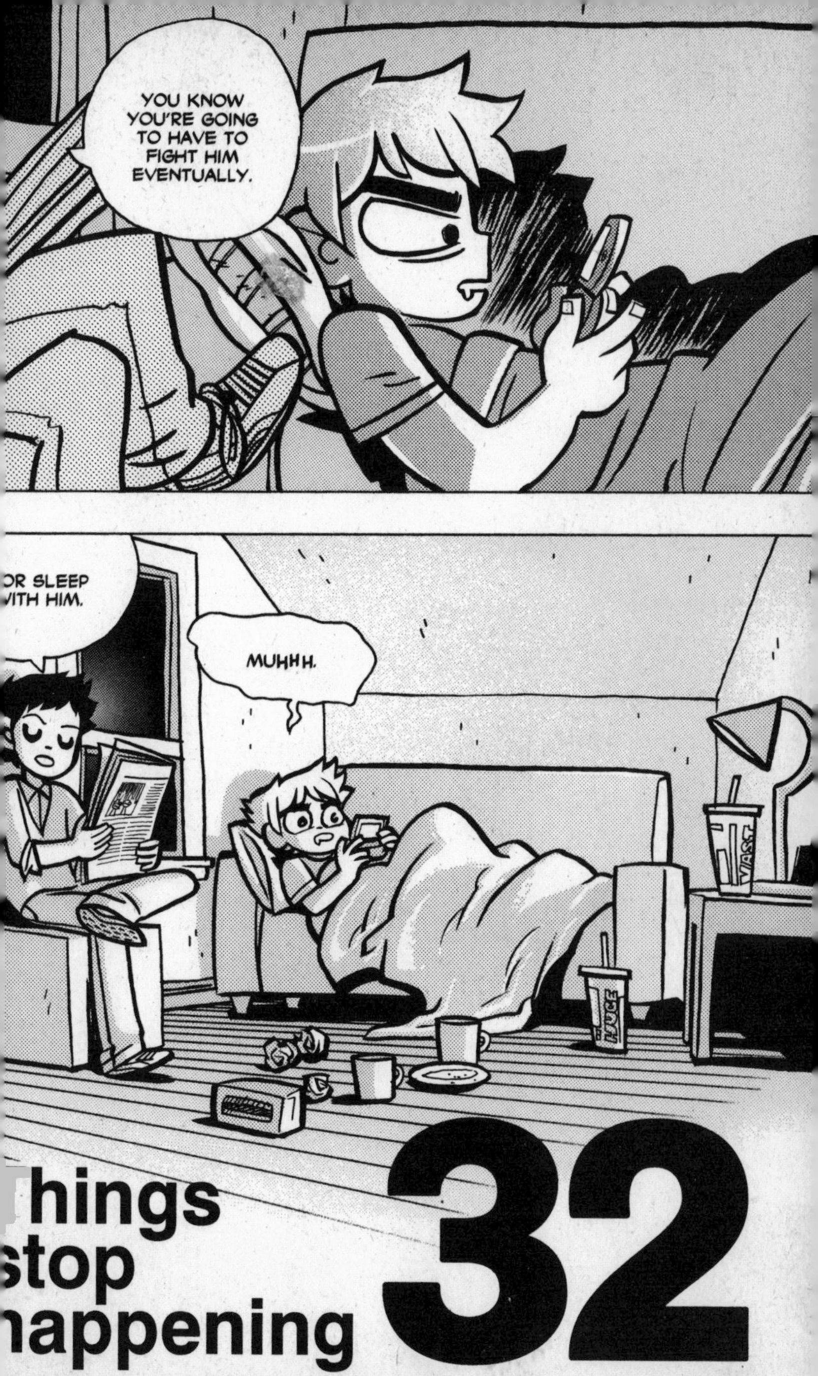
YOU KNOW YOU'RE GOING TO HAVE TO FIGHT HIM EVENTUALLY.
OR SLEEP WITH HIM.
MUHHH.
VIASA

hings
stop
appening
32

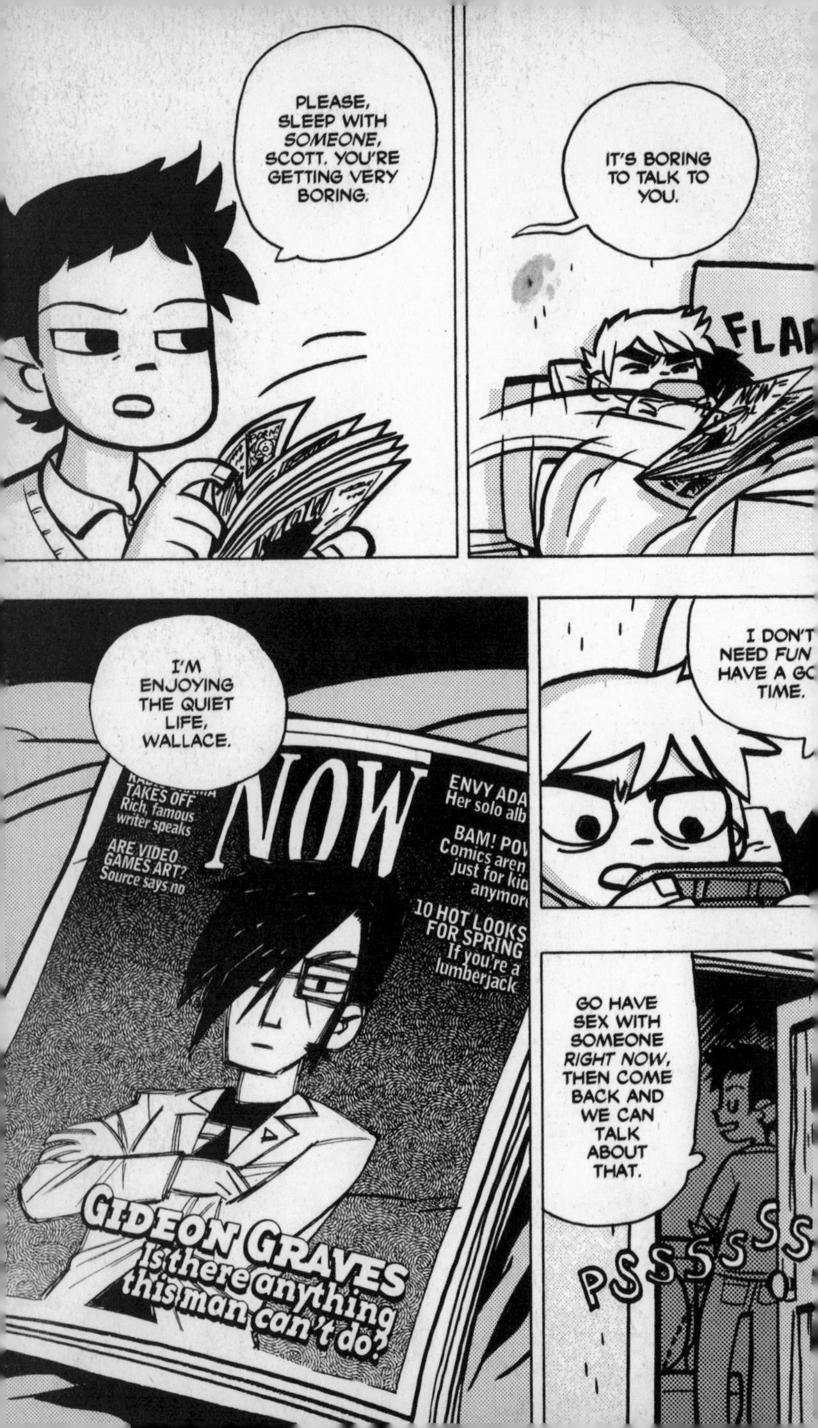
PLEASE, SLEEP WITH SOMEONE, SCOTT. YOU'RE GETTING VERY BORING.
IT'S BORING TO TALK TO YOU.
FLA
I'M ENJOYING THE QUIET LIFE, WALLACE.
NOW
TAKES OFF
Rich, famous writer speaks
ARE VIDEO GAMES ART?
Source says no
ENVY ADA
Her solo alb
BAM! POV
Comics aren
just for kic
anymor
10 HOT LOOKS FOR SPRING
If you're a lumberjack
GIDEON GRAVES
Is there anything this man can't do?
I DON'T NEED FUN HAVE A GO TIME.
GO HAVE SEX WITH SOMEONE RIGHT NOW, THEN COME BACK AND WE CAN TALK ABOUT THAT.
PSSSSSS

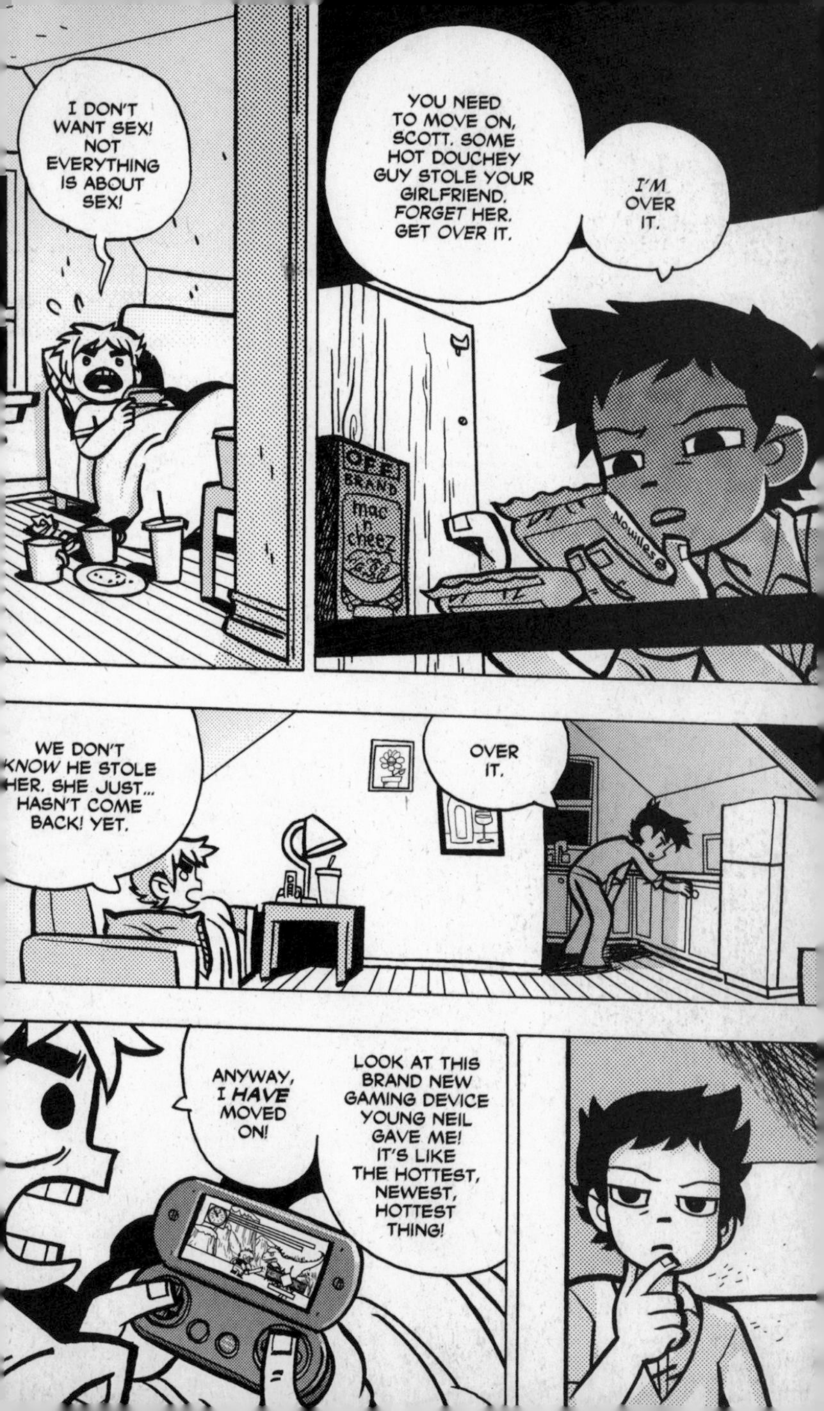

I DON'T WANT SEX! NOT EVERYTHING IS ABOUT SEX!
YOU NEED TO MOVE ON, SCOTT. SOME HOT DOUCHEY GUY STOLE YOUR GIRLFRIEND. FORGET HER. GET OVER IT.
I'M OVER IT.
OFF BRAND mac n cheez
Nowilles
WE DON'T KNOW HE STOLE HER. SHE JUST... HASN'T COME BACK! YET.
OVER IT.
ANYWAY, I HAVE MOVED ON!
LOOK AT THIS BRAND NEW GAMING DEVICE YOUNG NEIL GAVE ME! IT'S LIKE THE HOTTEST, NEWEST, HOTTEST THING!

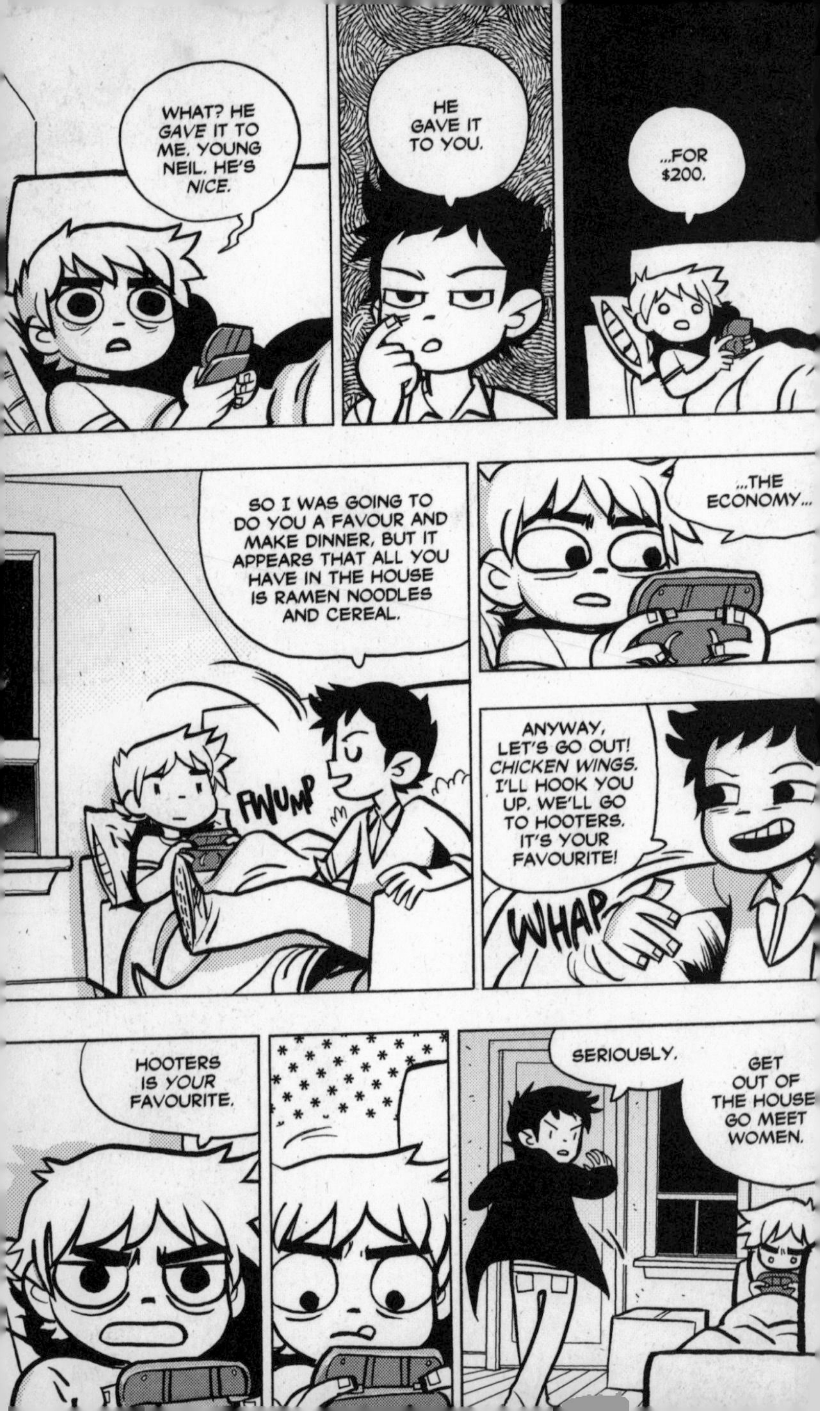
WHAT? HE GAVE IT TO ME. YOUNG NEIL. HE'S NICE.
HE GAVE IT TO YOU.
...FOR $200.
SO I WAS GOING TO DO YOU A FAVOUR AND MAKE DINNER, BUT IT APPEARS THAT ALL YOU HAVE IN THE HOUSE IS RAMEN NOODLES AND CEREAL.
...THE ECONOMY...
FWUMP
ANYWAY, LET'S GO OUT! CHICKEN WINGS. I'LL HOOK YOU UP. WE'LL GO TO HOOTERS. IT'S YOUR FAVOURITE!
WHAP
HOOTERS IS YOUR FAVOURITE.
SERIOUSLY.
GET OUT OF THE HOUSE GO MEET WOMEN.

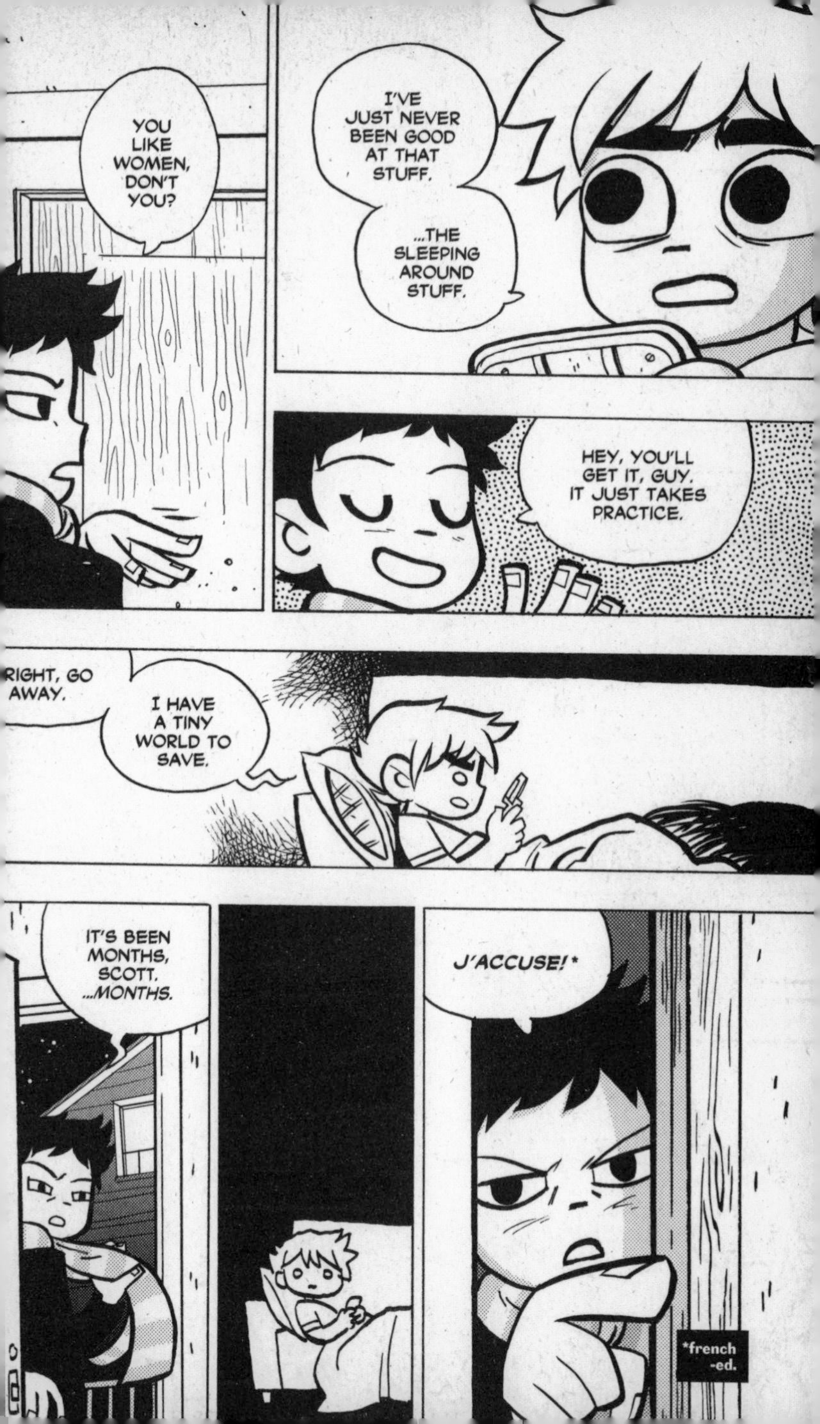
YOU LIKE WOMEN, DON'T YOU?
I'VE JUST NEVER BEEN GOOD AT THAT STUFF.
...THE SLEEPING AROUND STUFF.
HEY, YOU'LL GET IT, GUY. IT JUST TAKES PRACTICE.
RIGHT, GO AWAY.
I HAVE A TINY WORLD TO SAVE.
IT'S BEEN MONTHS, SCOTT. ...MONTHS.
J'ACCUSE! *
*french -ed.

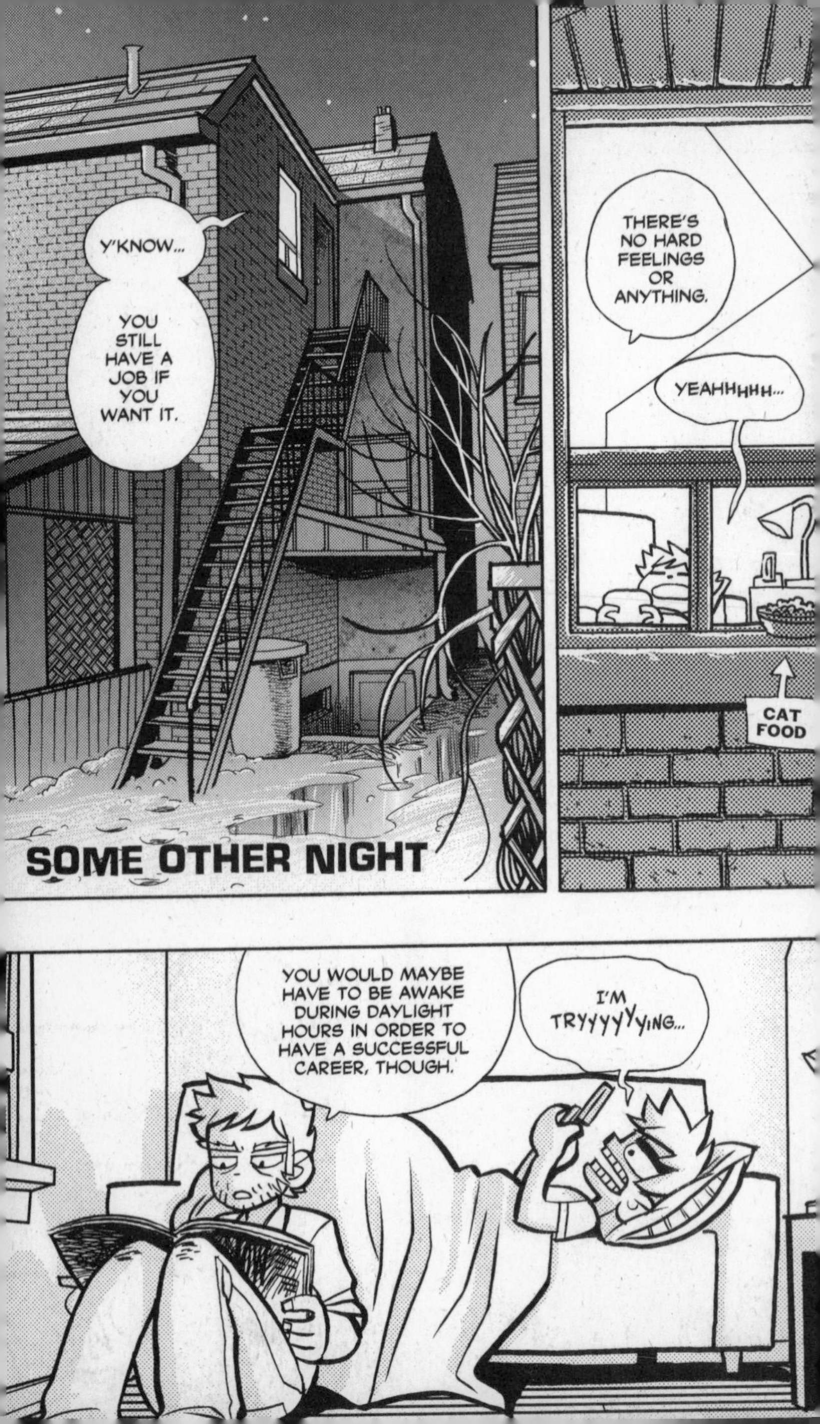
Y'KNOW...
YOU STILL HAVE A JOB IF YOU WANT IT.
SOME OTHER NIGHT
THERE'S NO HARD FEELINGS OR ANYTHING.
YEAHHHHH...
CAT FOOD
YOU WOULD MAYBE HAVE TO BE AWAKE DURING DAYLIGHT HOURS IN ORDER TO HAVE A SUCCESSFUL CAREER, THOUGH.
I'M TRYYYYYYING...

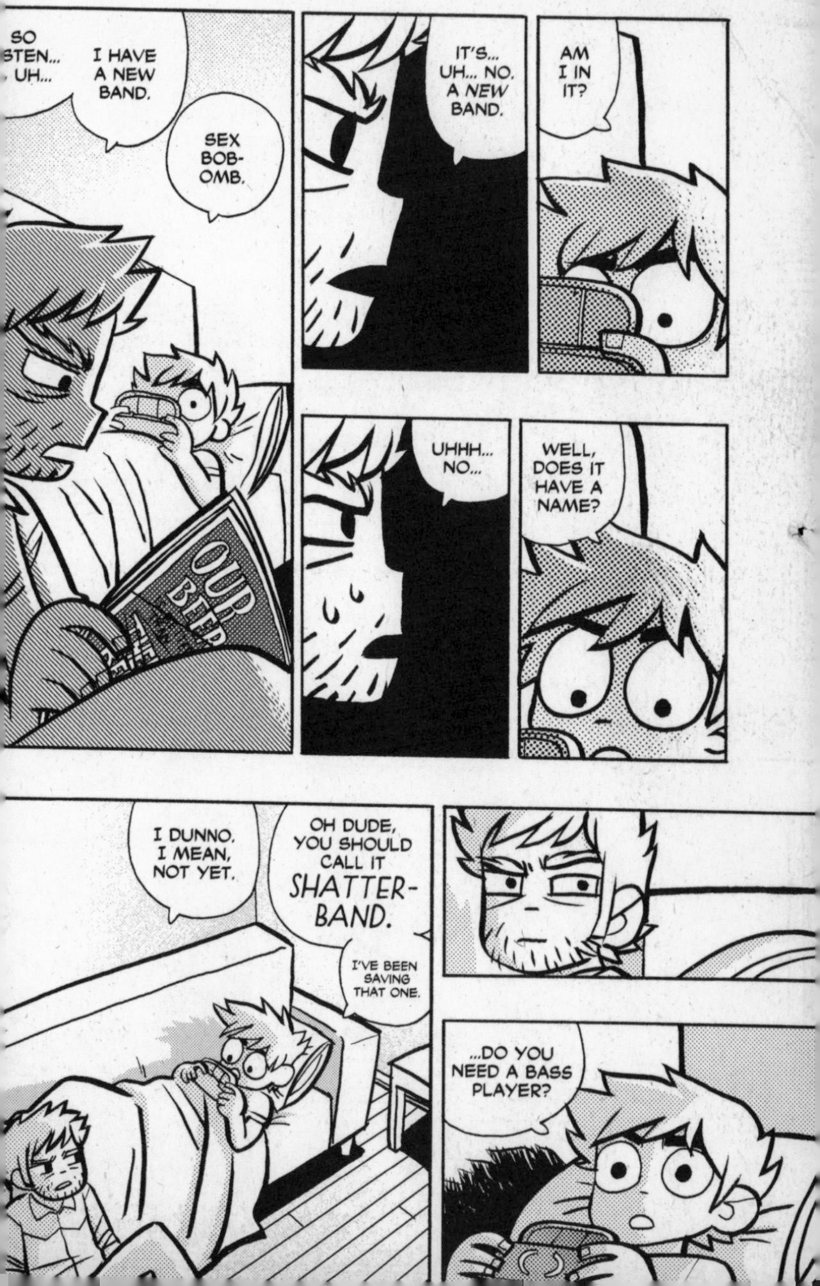
SO
STEN... UH...
I HAVE A NEW BAND.
SEX BOB-OMB.
OUR BEEF
IT'S... UH... NO. A *NEW* BAND.
AM I IN IT?
UHHH... NO...
WELL, DOES IT HAVE A NAME?
I DUNNO, I MEAN, NOT YET.
OH DUDE, YOU SHOULD CALL IT SHATTER-BAND.
I'VE BEEN SAVING THAT ONE.
...DO YOU NEED A BASS PLAYER?

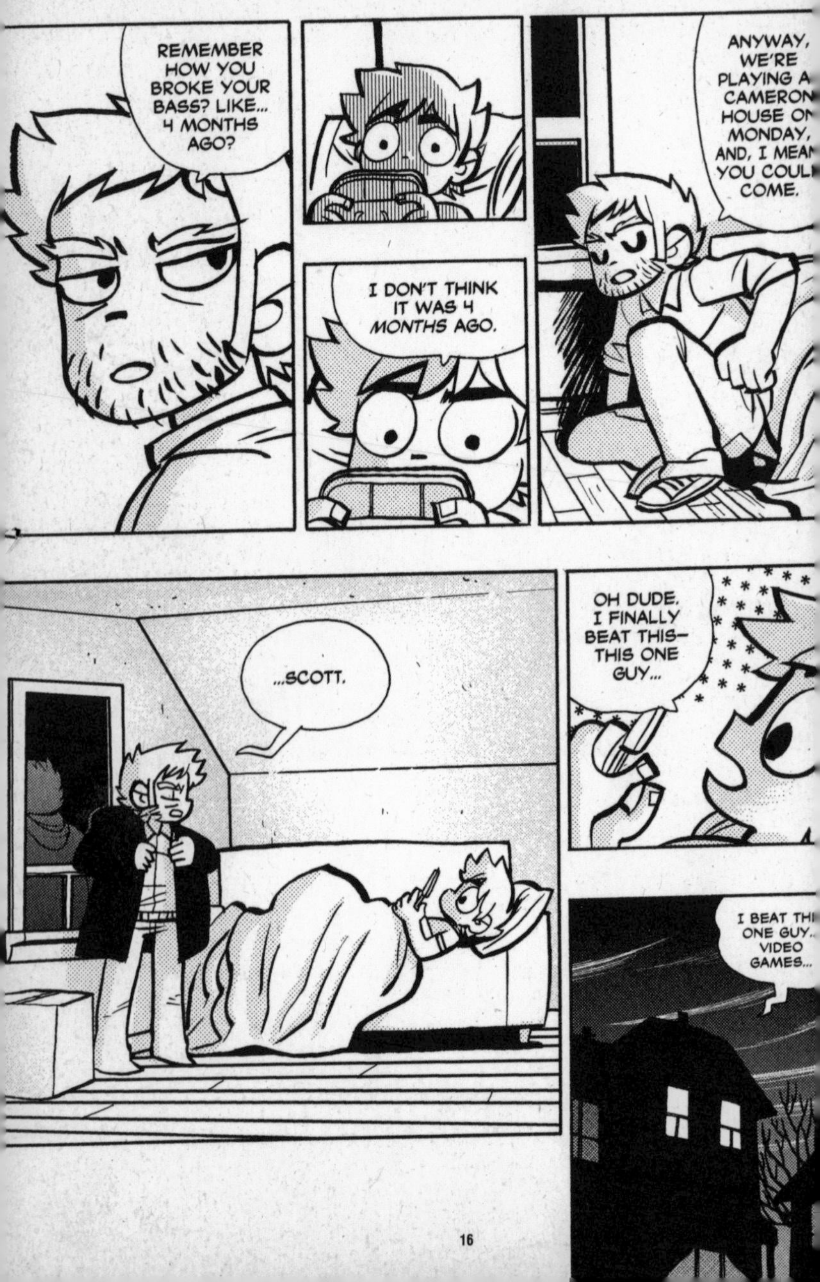
REMEMBER HOW YOU BROKE YOUR BASS? LIKE... 4 MONTHS AGO?
I DON'T THINK IT WAS 4 MONTHS AGO.
ANYWAY, WE'RE PLAYING A CAMERON HOUSE ON MONDAY, AND, I MEAN YOU COULD COME.
...SCOTT.
OH DUDE, I FINALLY BEAT THIS— THIS ONE GUY...
I BEAT THI ONE GUY.. VIDEO GAMES...

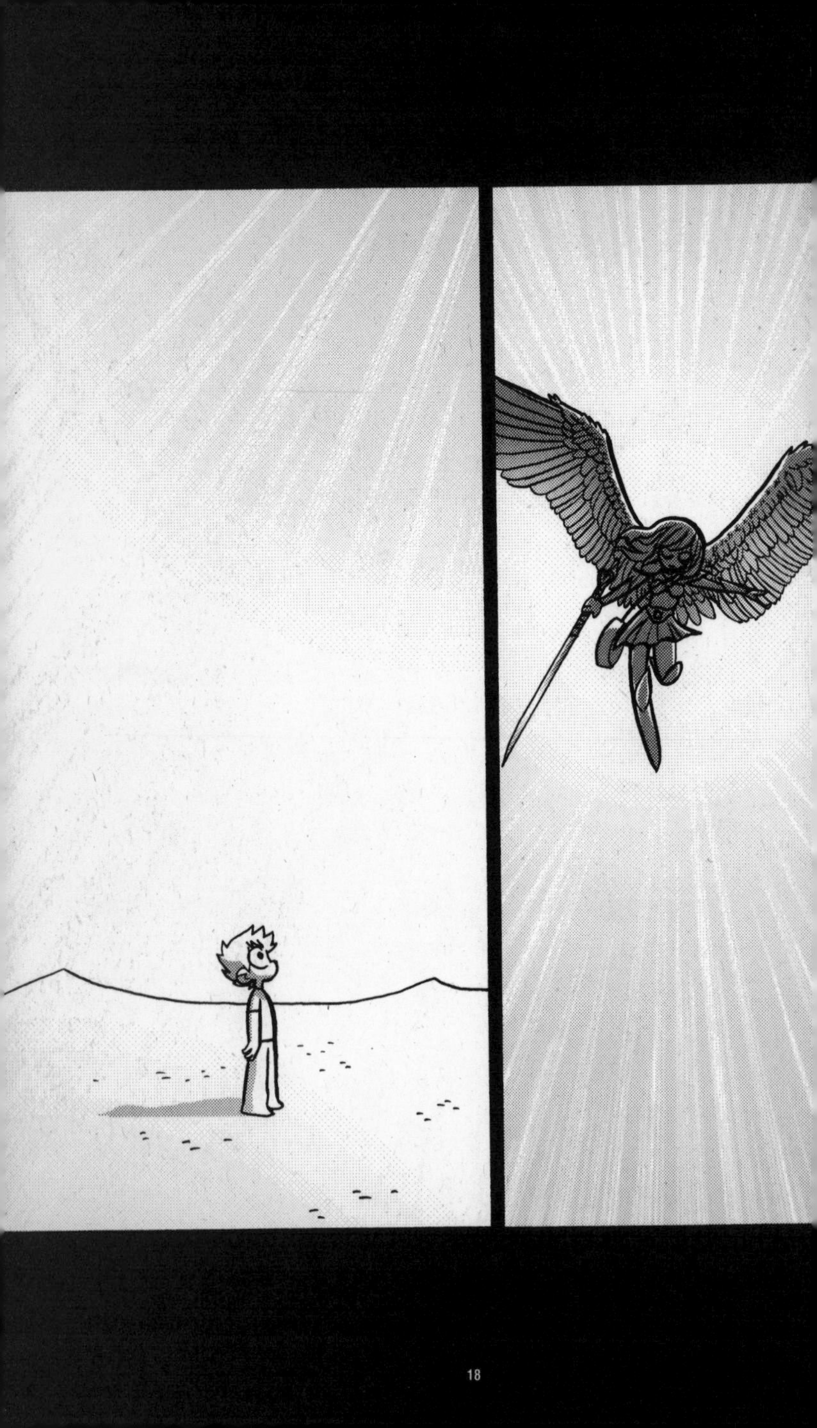

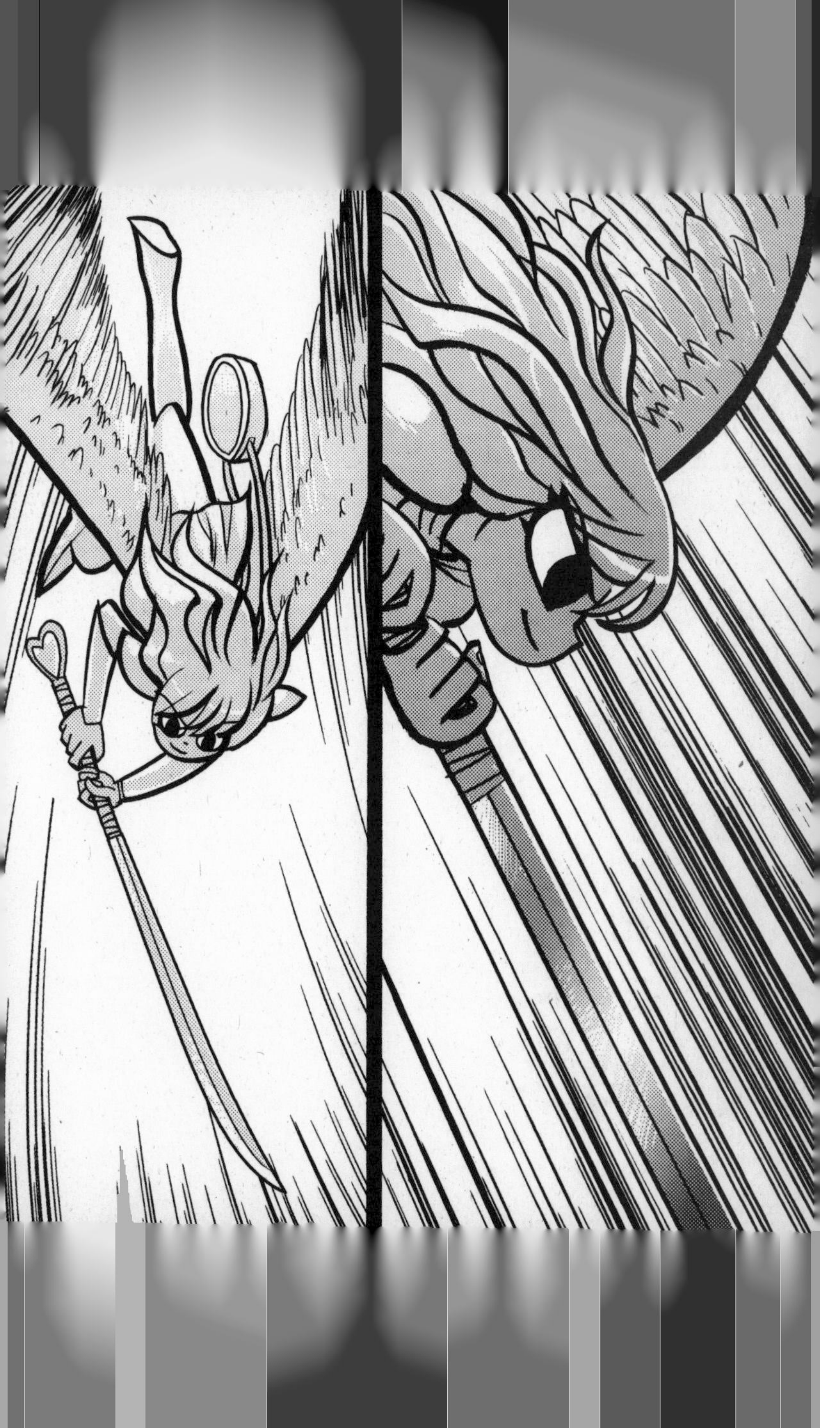

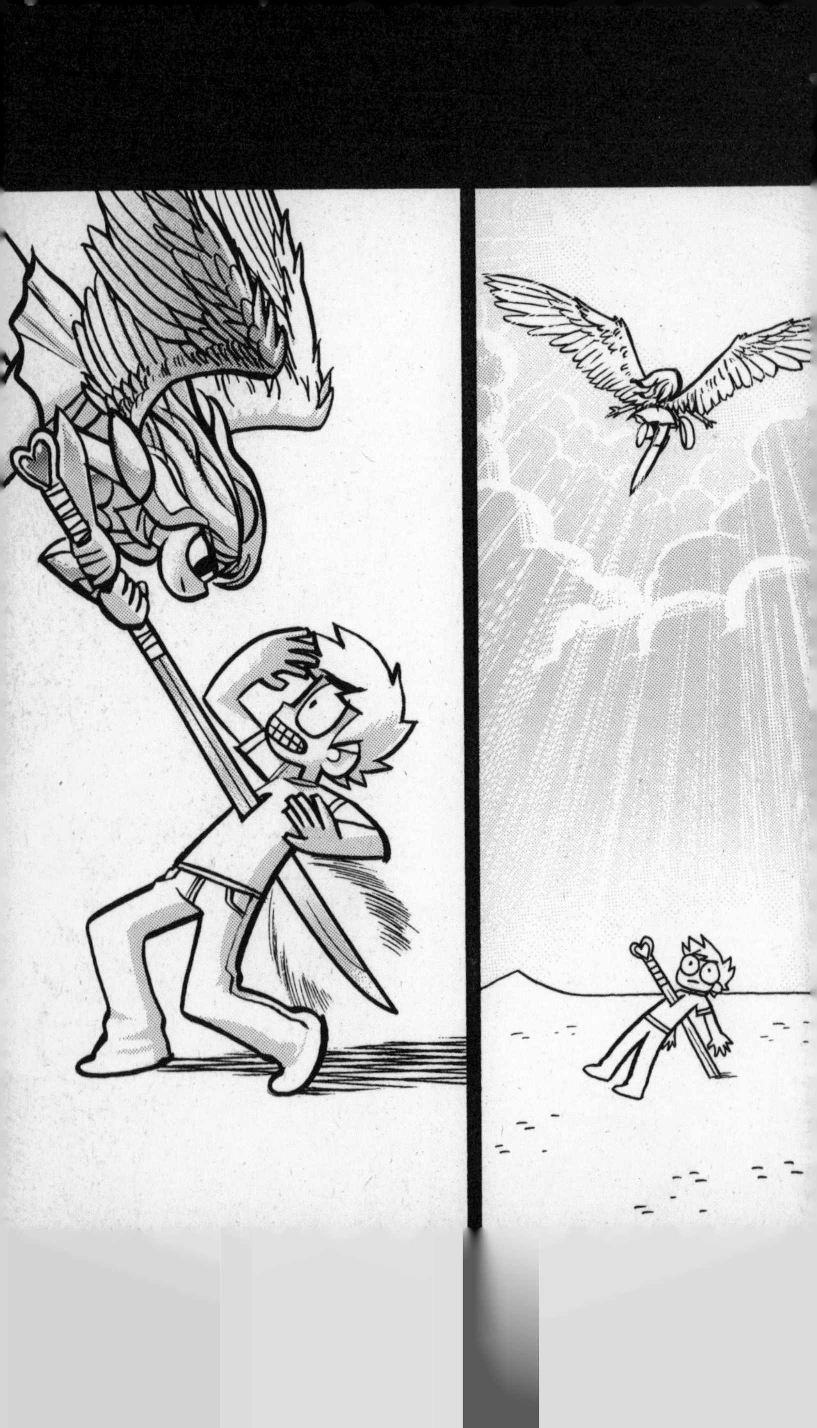

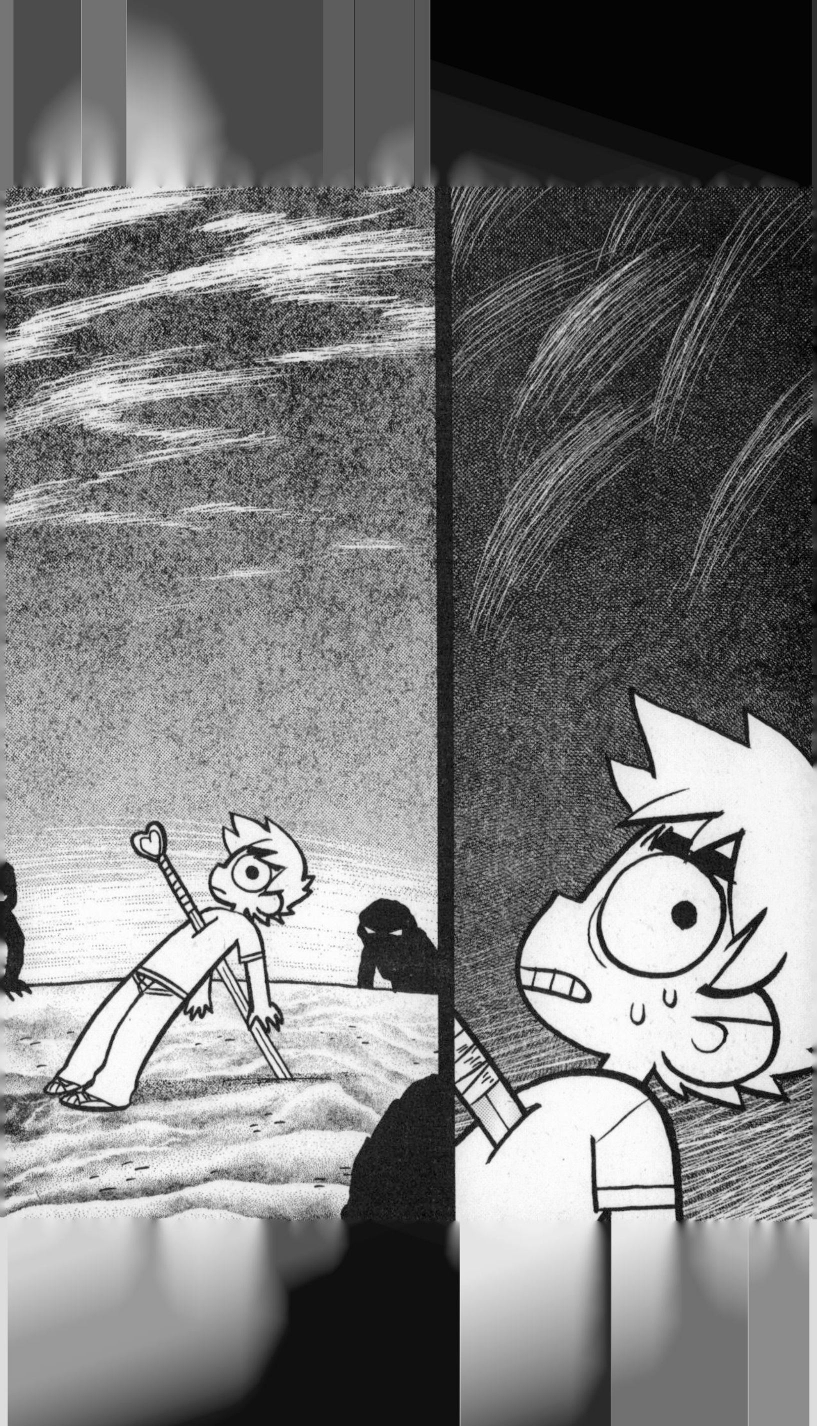

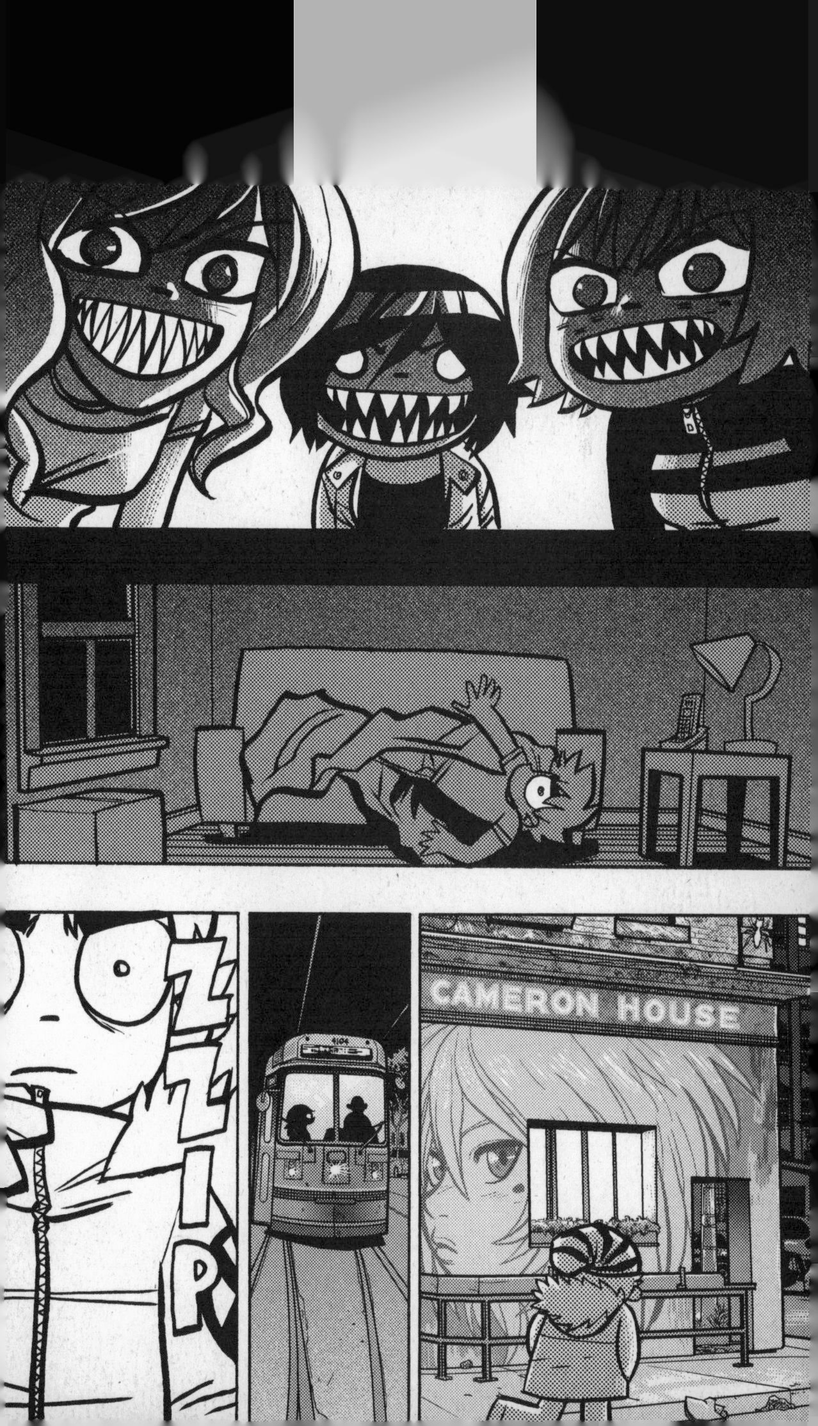
CAMERON HOUSE

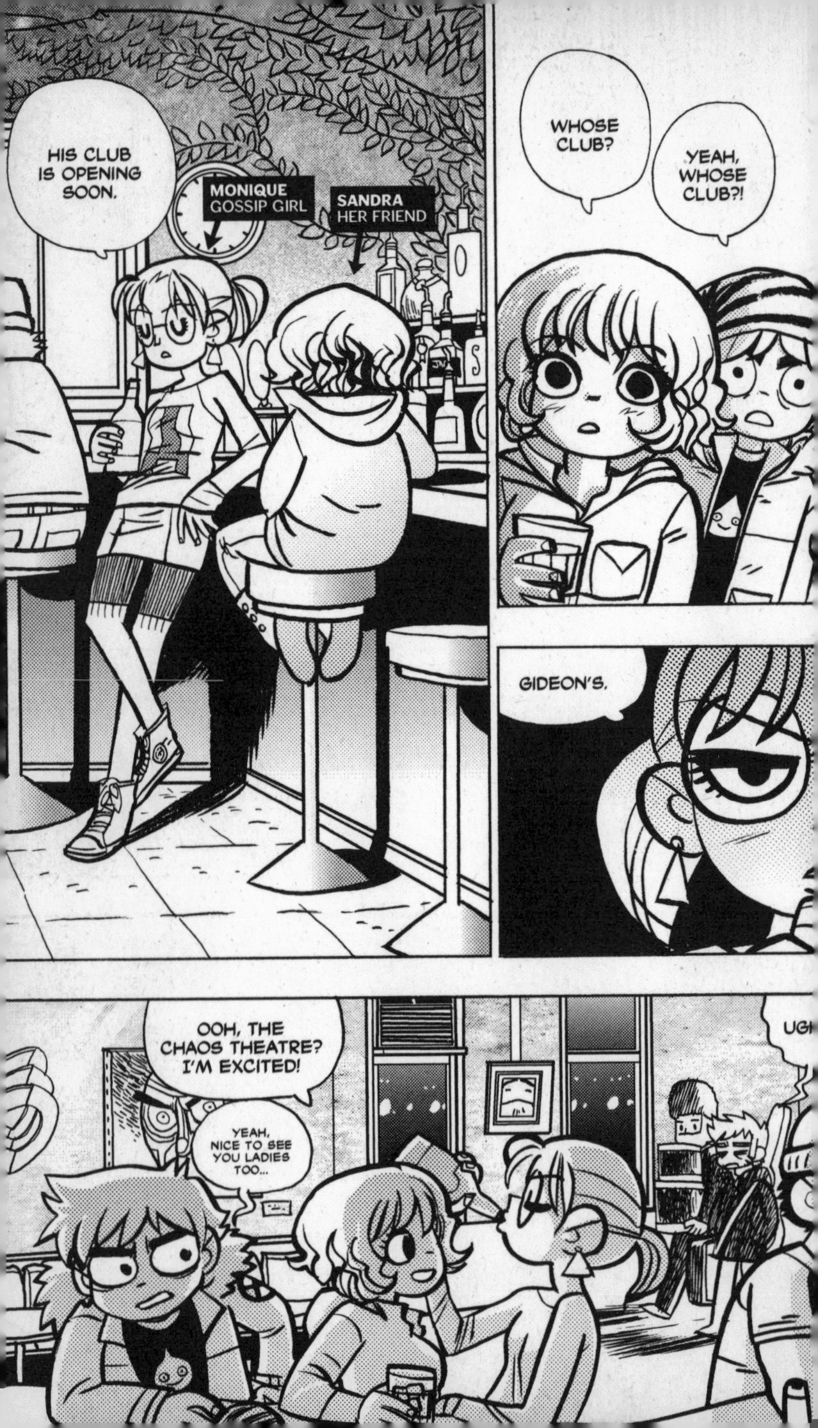
HIS CLUB IS OPENING SOON.
MONIQUE GOSSIP GIRL
SANDRA HER FRIEND
WHOSE CLUB?
YEAH, WHOSE CLUB?!
GIDEON'S.
OOH, THE CHAOS THEATRE? I'M EXCITED!
YEAH, NICE TO SEE YOU LADIES TOO...

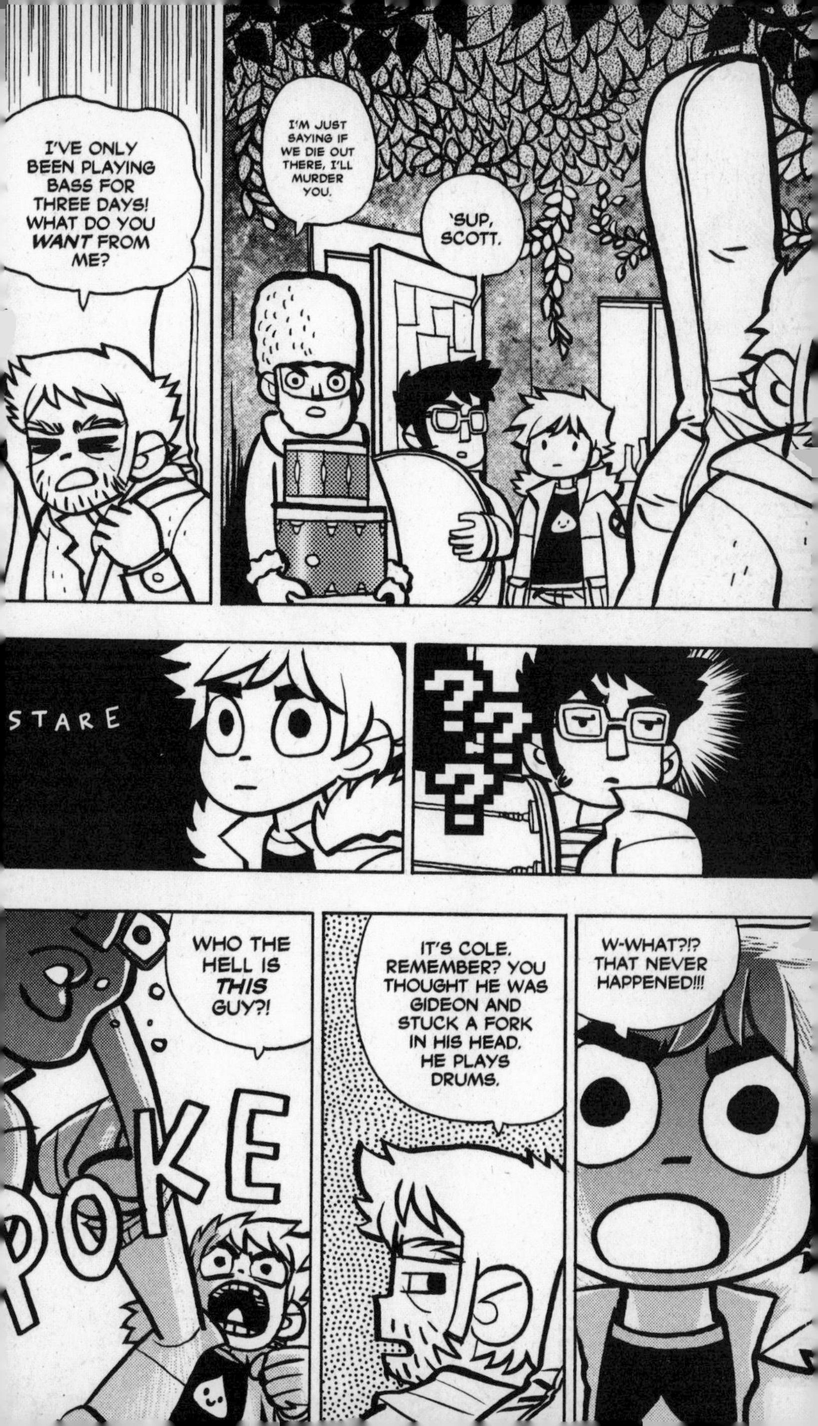
I'VE ONLY BEEN PLAYING BASS FOR THREE DAYS! WHAT DO YOU WANT FROM ME?
I'M JUST SAYING IF WE DIE OUT THERE, I'LL MURDER YOU.
'SUP, SCOTT.
STARE
WHO THE HELL IS THIS GUY?!
POKE
IT'S COLE. REMEMBER? YOU THOUGHT HE WAS GIDEON AND STUCK A FORK IN HIS HEAD. HE PLAYS DRUMS.
W-WHAT?!? THAT NEVER HAPPENED!!!

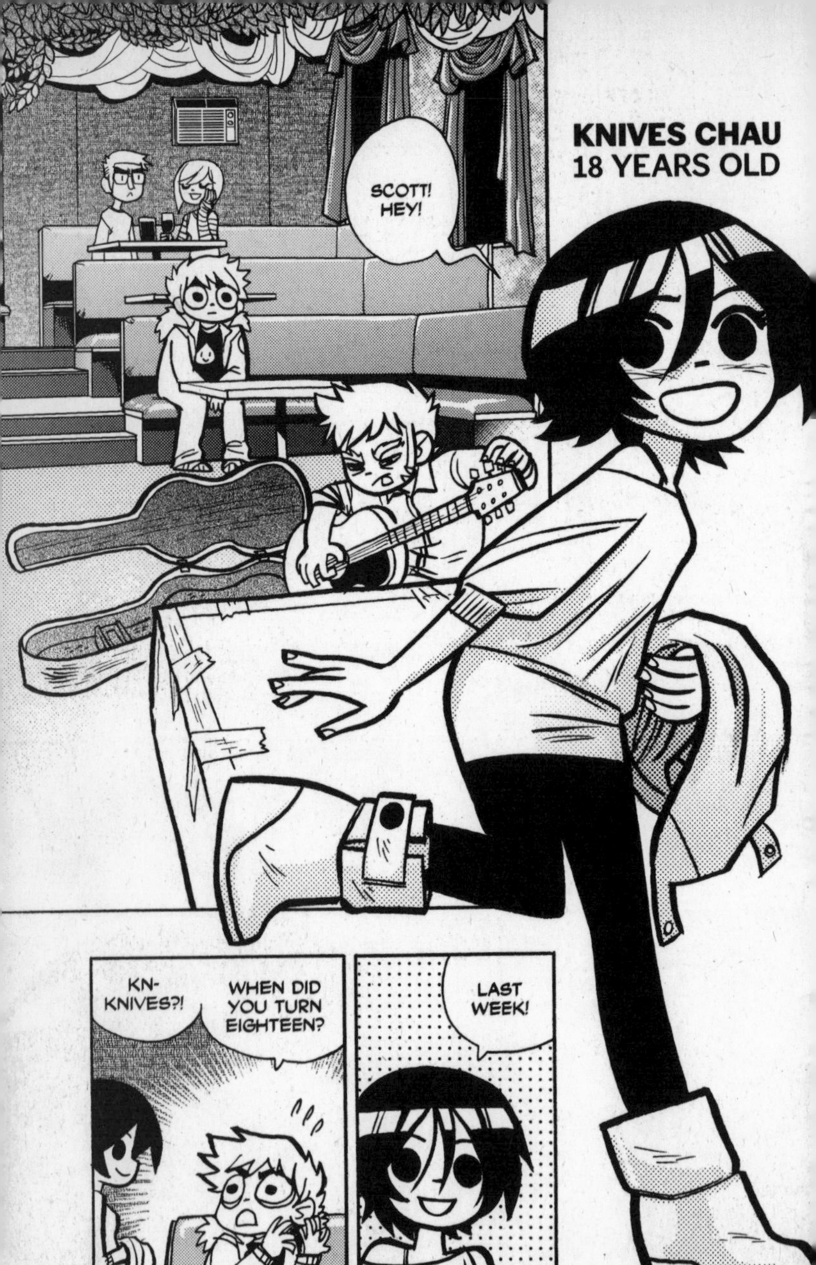
KNIVES CHAU
18 YEARS OLD
SCOTT! HEY!
KN- KNIVES?!
WHEN DID YOU TURN EIGHTEEN?
LAST WEEK!

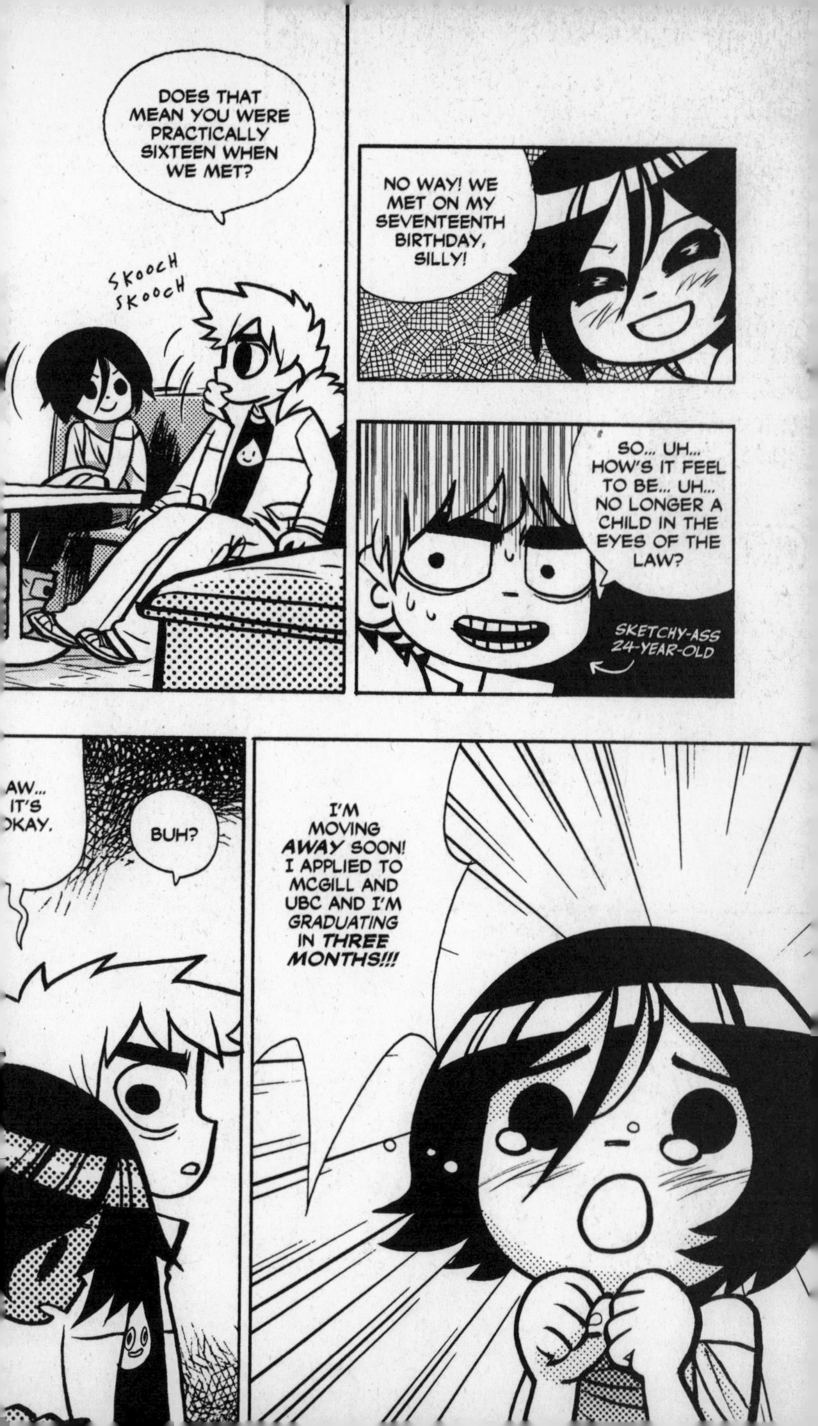
DOES THAT MEAN YOU WERE PRACTICALLY SIXTEEN WHEN WE MET?
SKOOCH SKOOCH
NO WAY! WE MET ON MY SEVENTEENTH BIRTHDAY, SILLY!
SO... UH... HOW'S IT FEEL TO BE... UH... NO LONGER A CHILD IN THE EYES OF THE LAW?
SKETCHY-ASS 24-YEAR-OLD
AW... IT'S OKAY.
BUH?
I'M MOVING AWAY SOON! I APPLIED TO MCGILL AND UBC AND I'M GRADUATING IN THREE MONTHS!!!

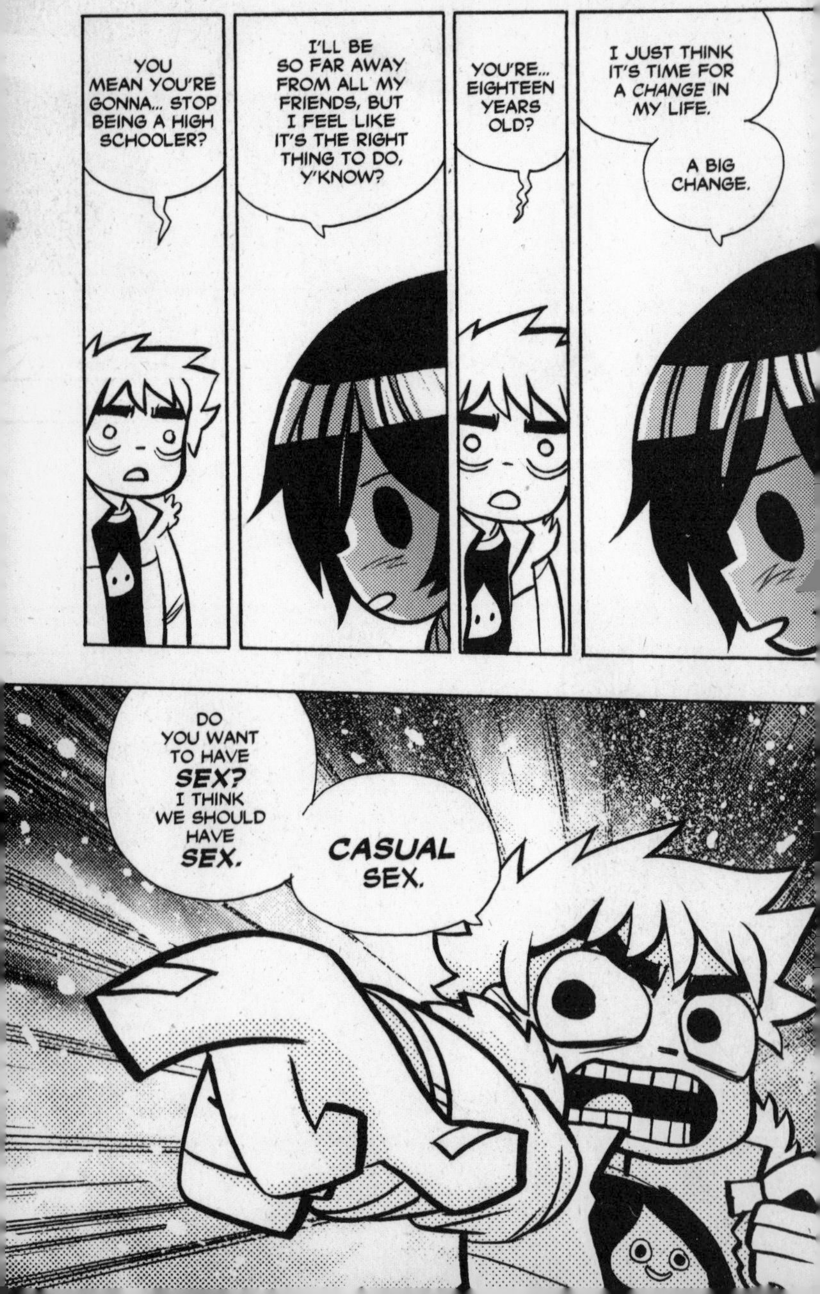
YOU MEAN YOU'RE GONNA... STOP BEING A HIGH SCHOOLER?
I'LL BE SO FAR AWAY FROM ALL MY FRIENDS, BUT I FEEL LIKE IT'S THE RIGHT THING TO DO, Y'KNOW?
YOU'RE... EIGHTEEN YEARS OLD?
I JUST THINK IT'S TIME FOR A *CHANGE* IN MY LIFE.
A BIG CHANGE.
DO YOU WANT TO HAVE **SEX?** I THINK WE SHOULD HAVE **SEX.**
CASUAL SEX.

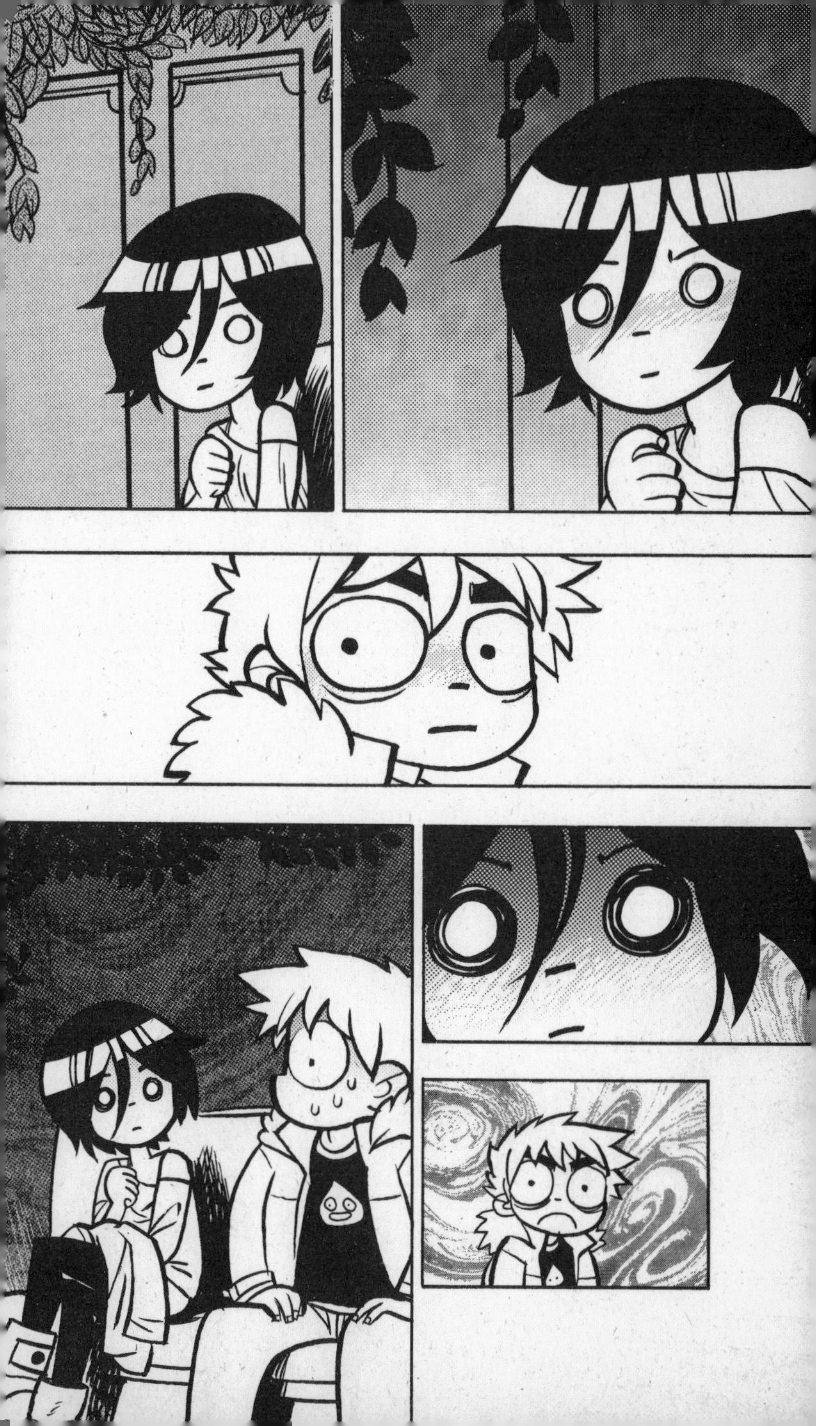

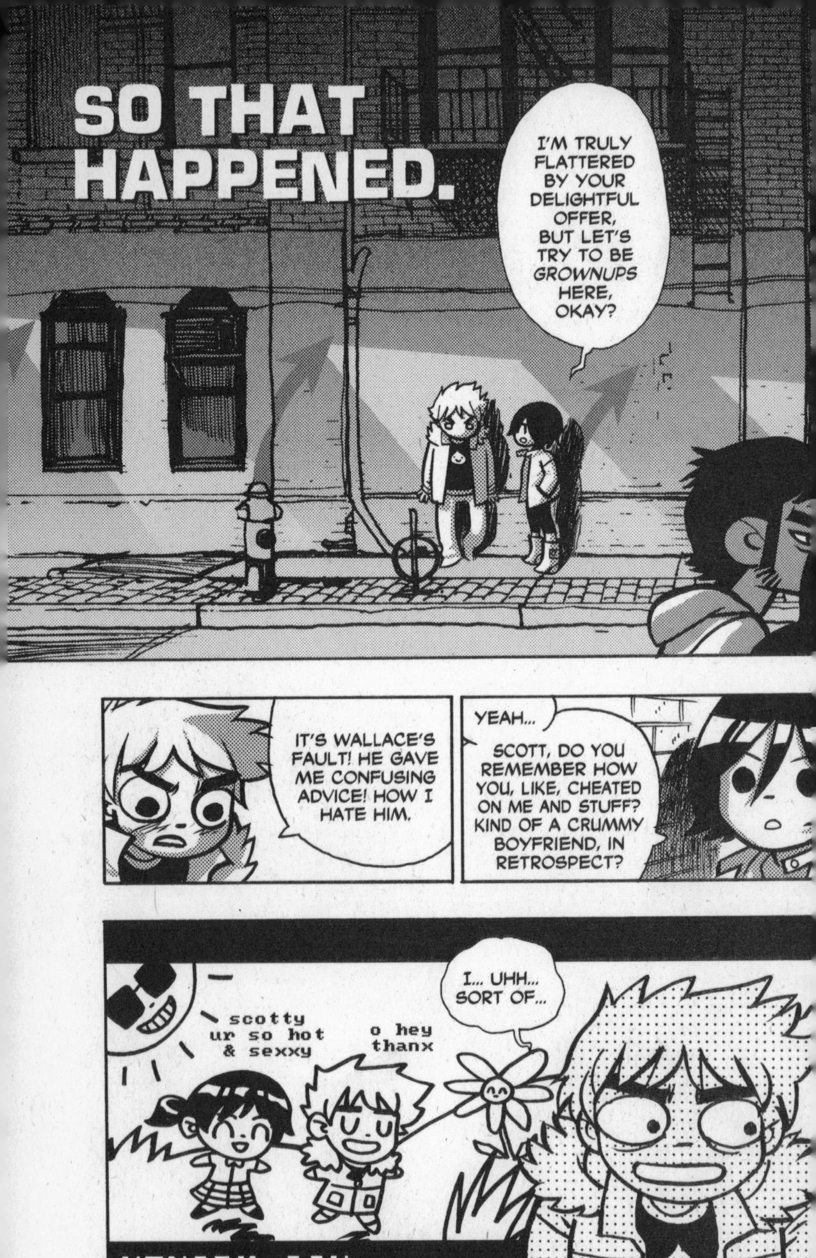
SO THAT HAPPENED.
I'M TRULY FLATTERED BY YOUR DELIGHTFUL OFFER, BUT LET'S TRY TO BE GROWNUPS HERE, OKAY?
IT'S WALLACE'S FAULT! HE GAVE ME CONFUSING ADVICE! HOW I HATE HIM.
YEAH...
SCOTT, DO YOU REMEMBER HOW YOU, LIKE, CHEATED ON ME AND STUFF? KIND OF A CRUMMY BOYFRIEND, IN RETROSPECT?
I... UHH... SORT OF...
scotty ur so hot & sexxy
o hey thanx
MEMORY CAM

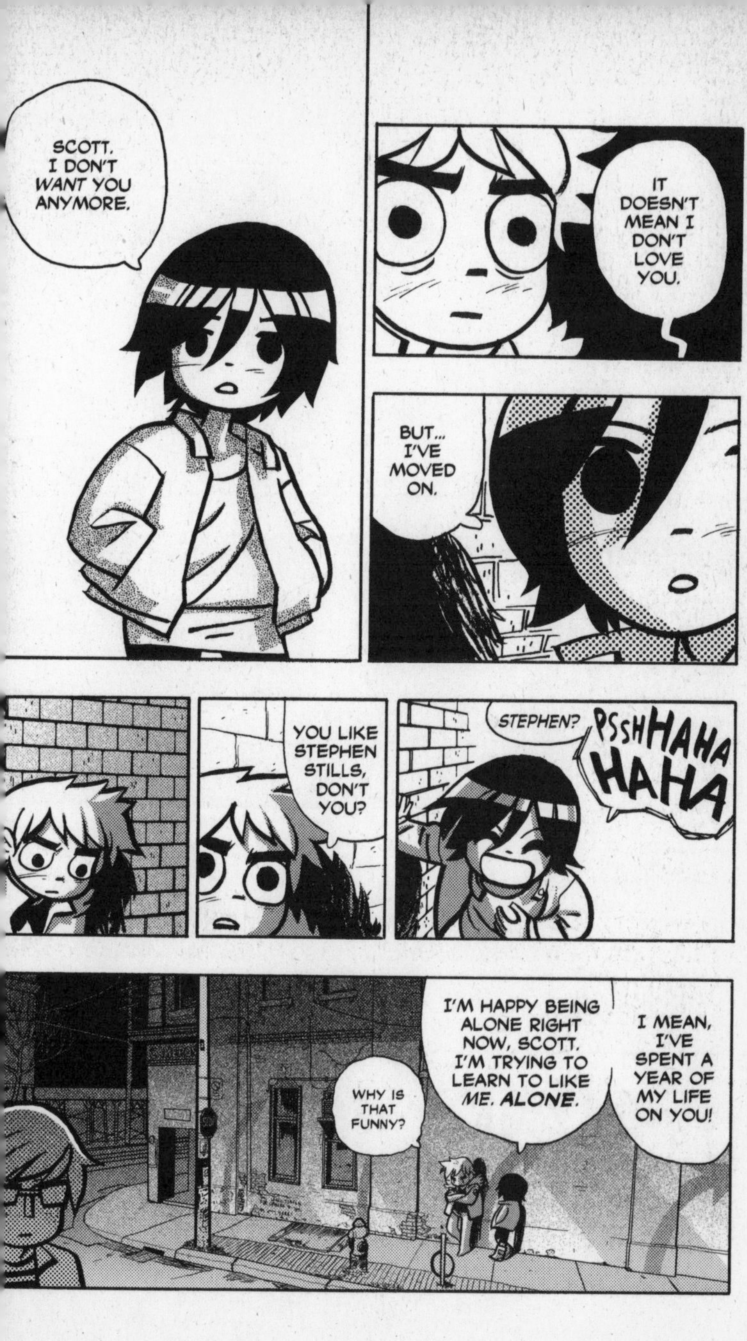

SCOTT. I DON'T *WANT* YOU ANYMORE.
IT DOESN'T MEAN I DON'T LOVE YOU.
BUT... I'VE MOVED ON.
YOU LIKE STEPHEN STILLS, DON'T YOU?
STEPHEN?
PSSHHAHA HAHA
WHY IS THAT FUNNY?
I'M HAPPY BEING ALONE RIGHT NOW, SCOTT. I'M TRYING TO LEARN TO LIKE *ME. ALONE.*
I MEAN, I'VE SPENT A YEAR OF MY LIFE ON YOU!

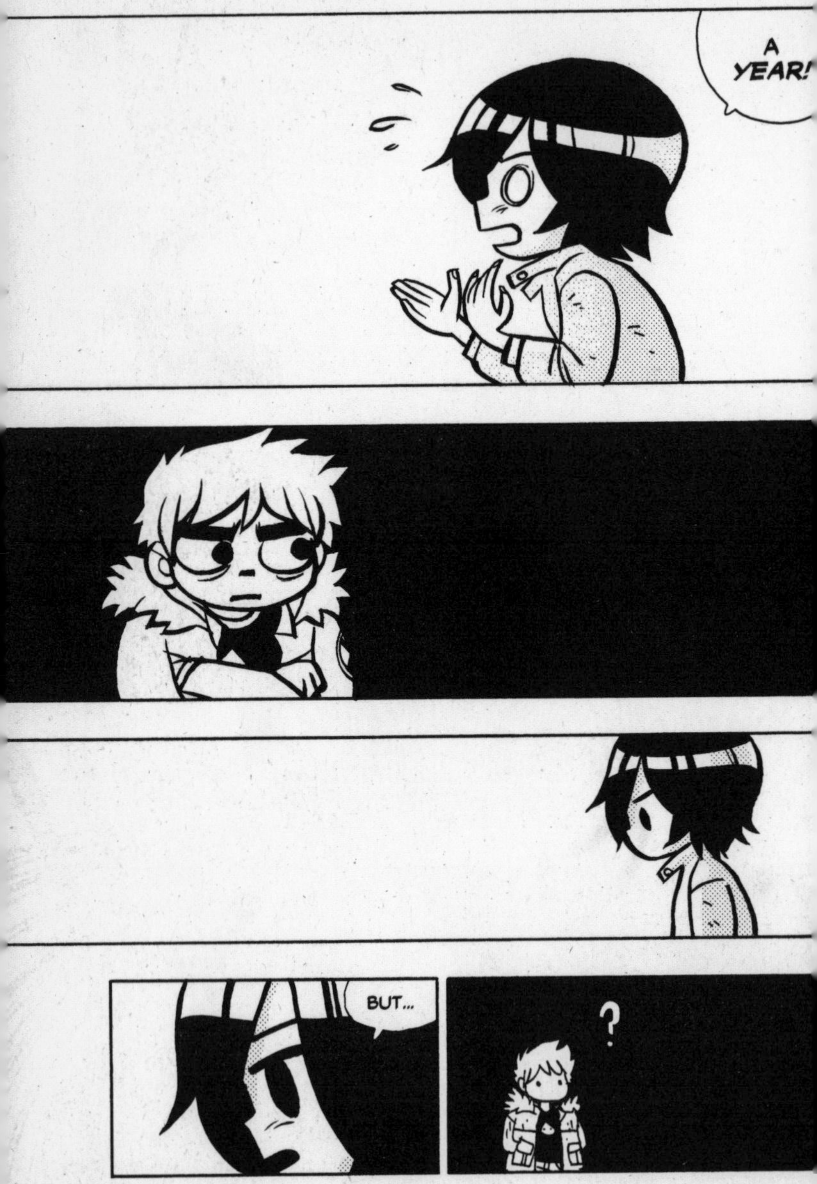
A YEAR!
BUT...
?

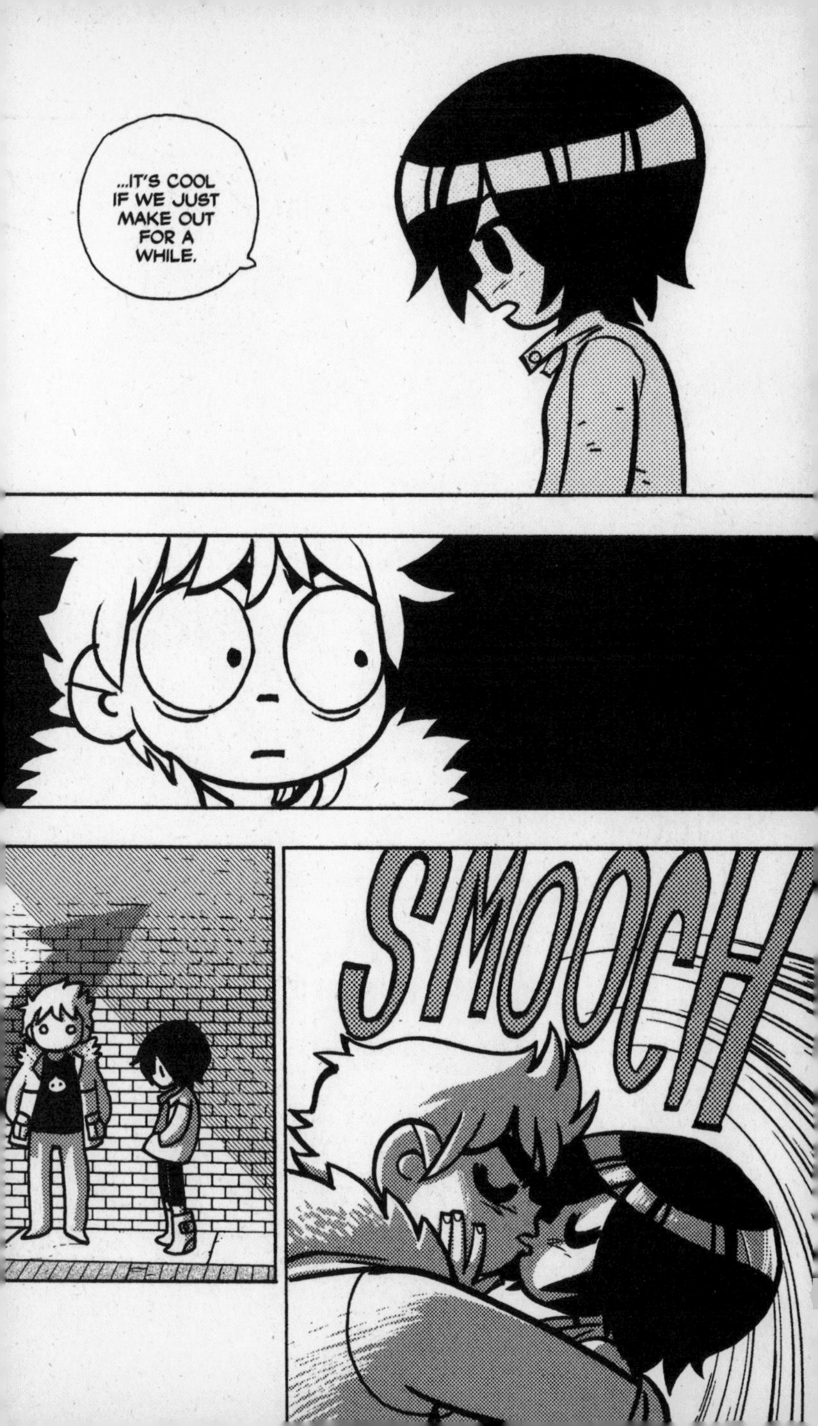
...IT'S COOL IF WE JUST MAKE OUT FOR A WHILE.
SMOOCH

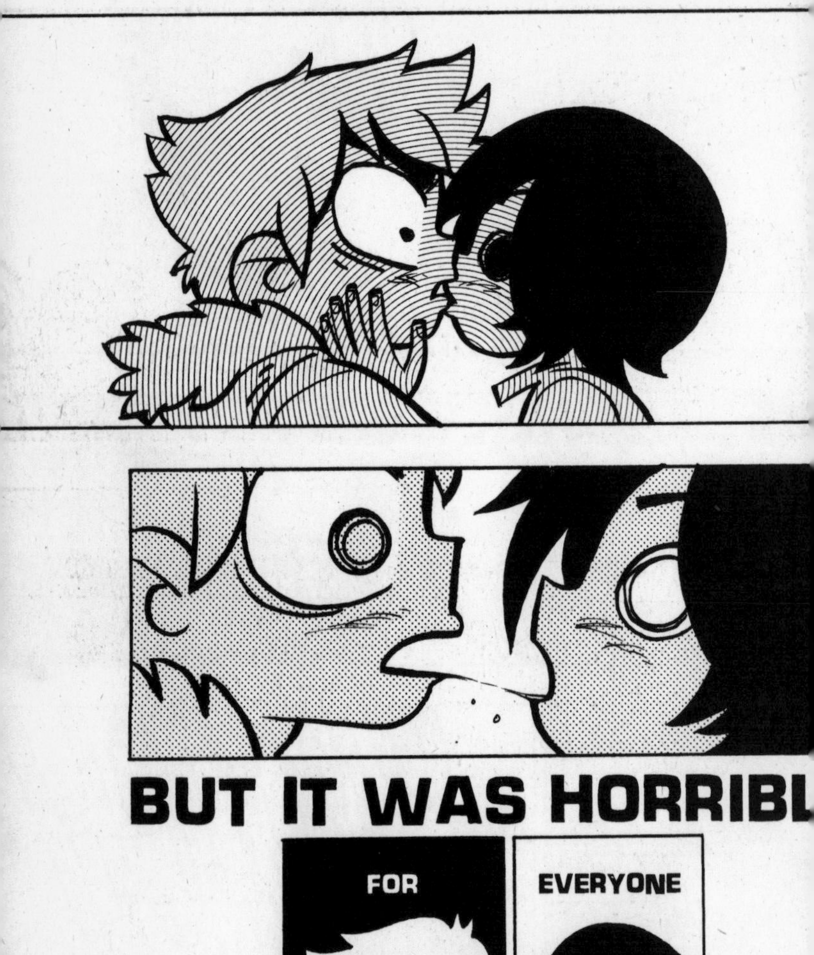
BUT IT WAS HORRIBL
FOR
EVERYONE
AND THAT INCLUDES YOU

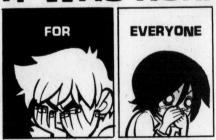

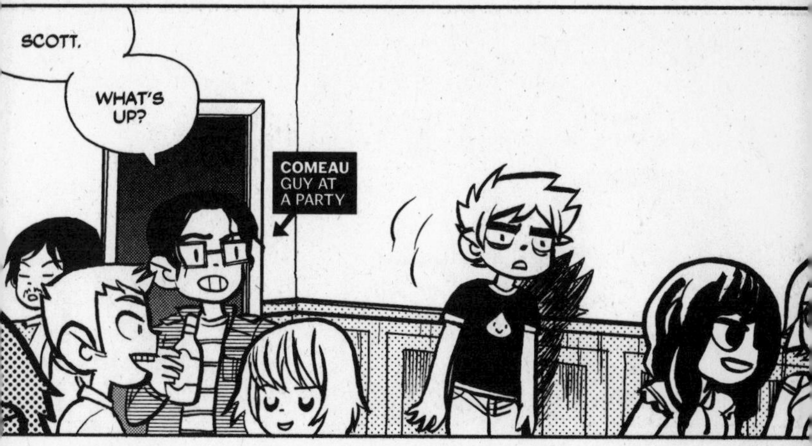
SCOTT.
WHAT'S UP?
COMEAU GUY AT A PARTY

33 She says what she means

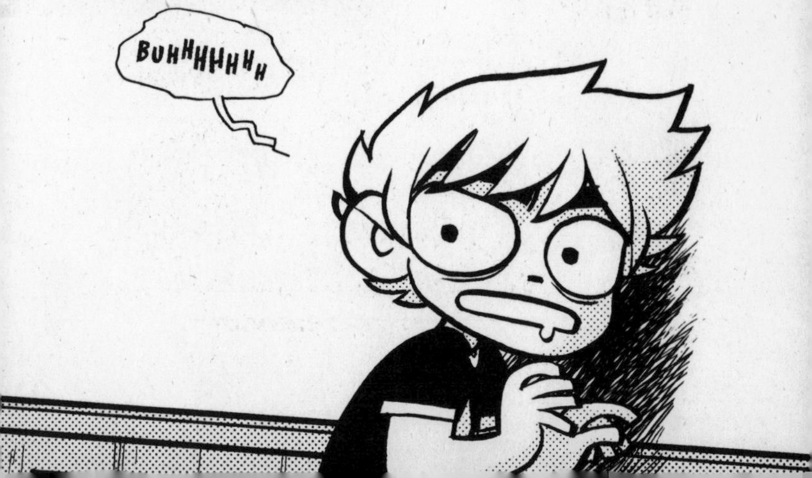
BUHHHHHHH

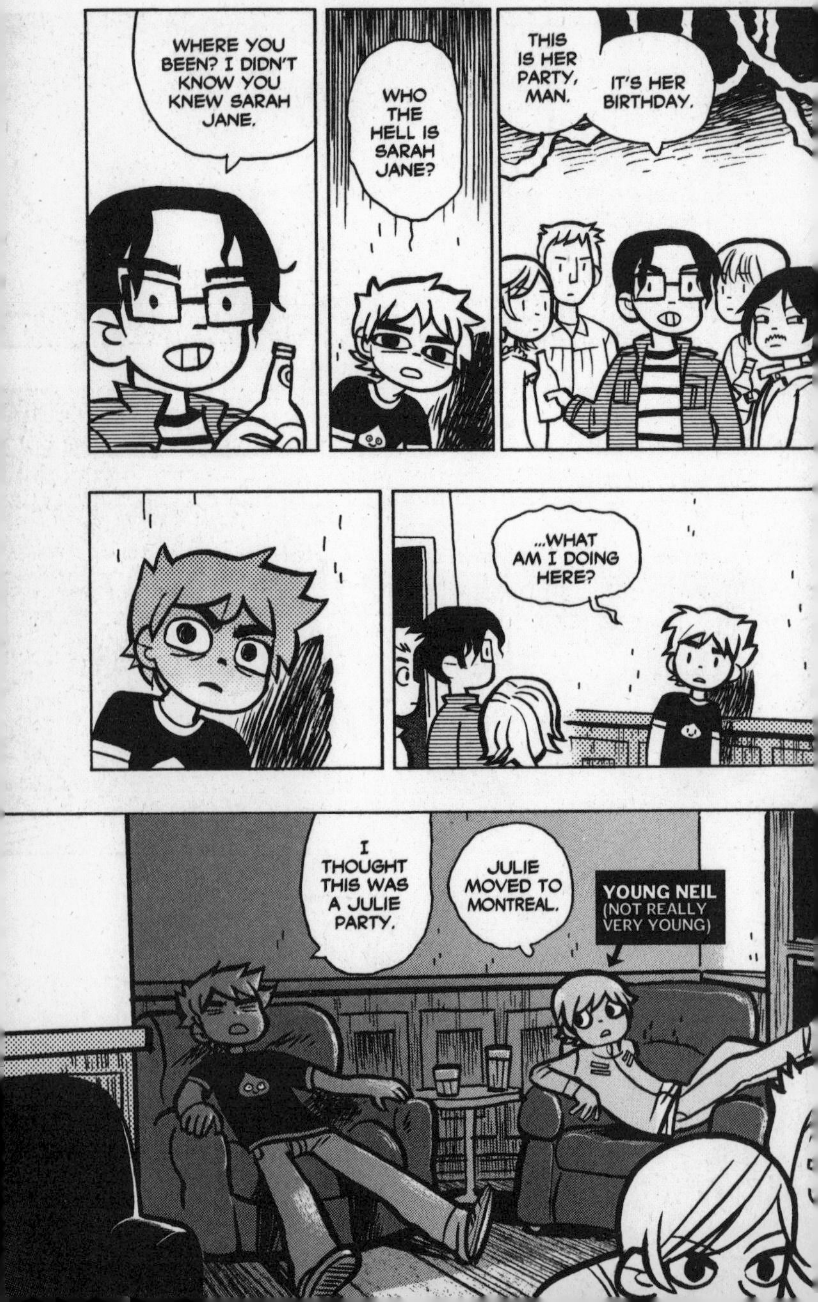
WHERE YOU BEEN? I DIDN'T KNOW YOU KNEW SARAH JANE.
WHO THE HELL IS SARAH JANE?
THIS IS HER PARTY, MAN.
IT'S HER BIRTHDAY.
...WHAT AM I DOING HERE?
I THOUGHT THIS WAS A JULIE PARTY.
JULIE MOVED TO MONTREAL.
YOUNG NEIL (NOT REALLY VERY YOUNG)

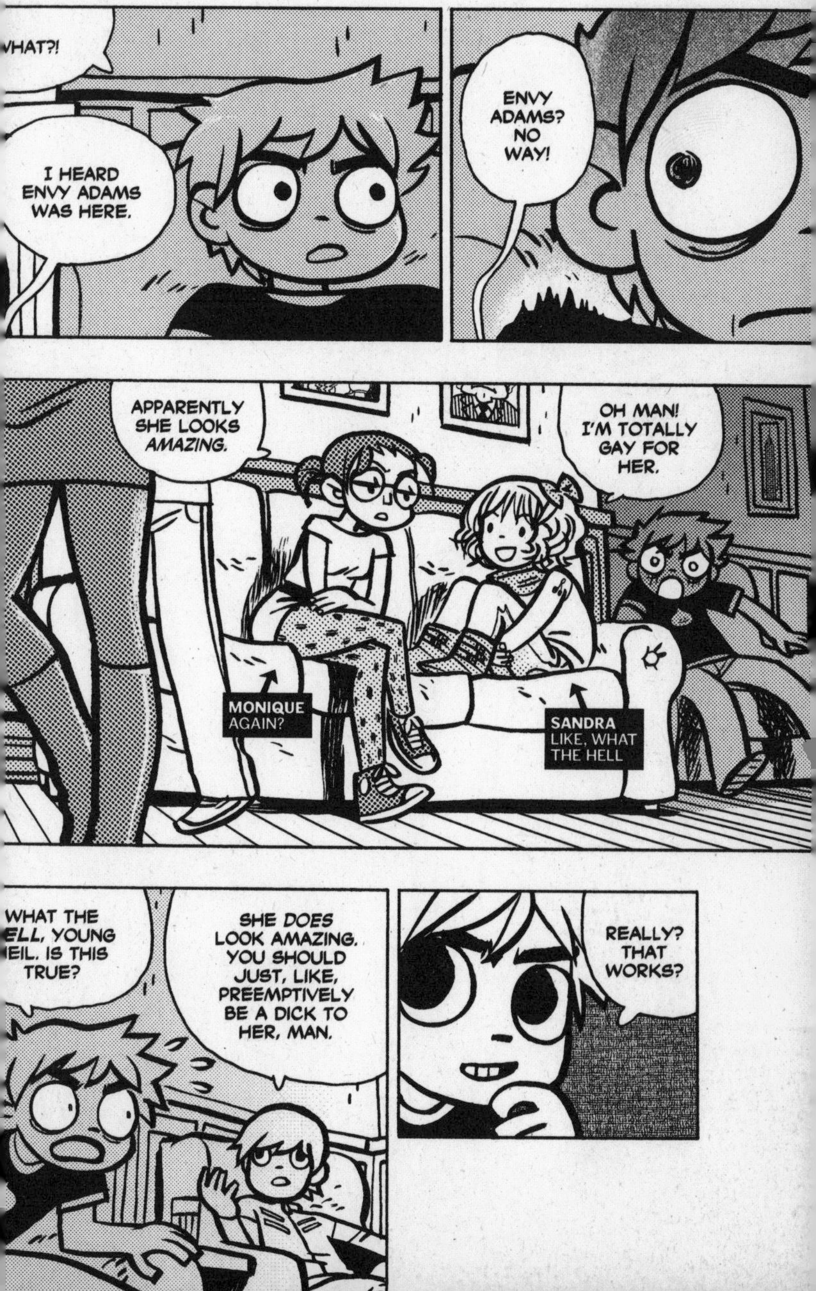
WHAT?!
I HEARD ENVY ADAMS WAS HERE.
ENVY ADAMS? NO WAY!
APPARENTLY SHE LOOKS *AMAZING.*
OH MAN! I'M TOTALLY GAY FOR HER.
MONIQUE AGAIN?
SANDRA LIKE, WHAT THE HELL
WHAT THE *ELL,* YOUNG EIL. IS THIS TRUE?
SHE *DOES* LOOK AMAZING. YOU SHOULD JUST, LIKE, PREEMPTIVELY BE A DICK TO HER, MAN.
REALLY? THAT WORKS?

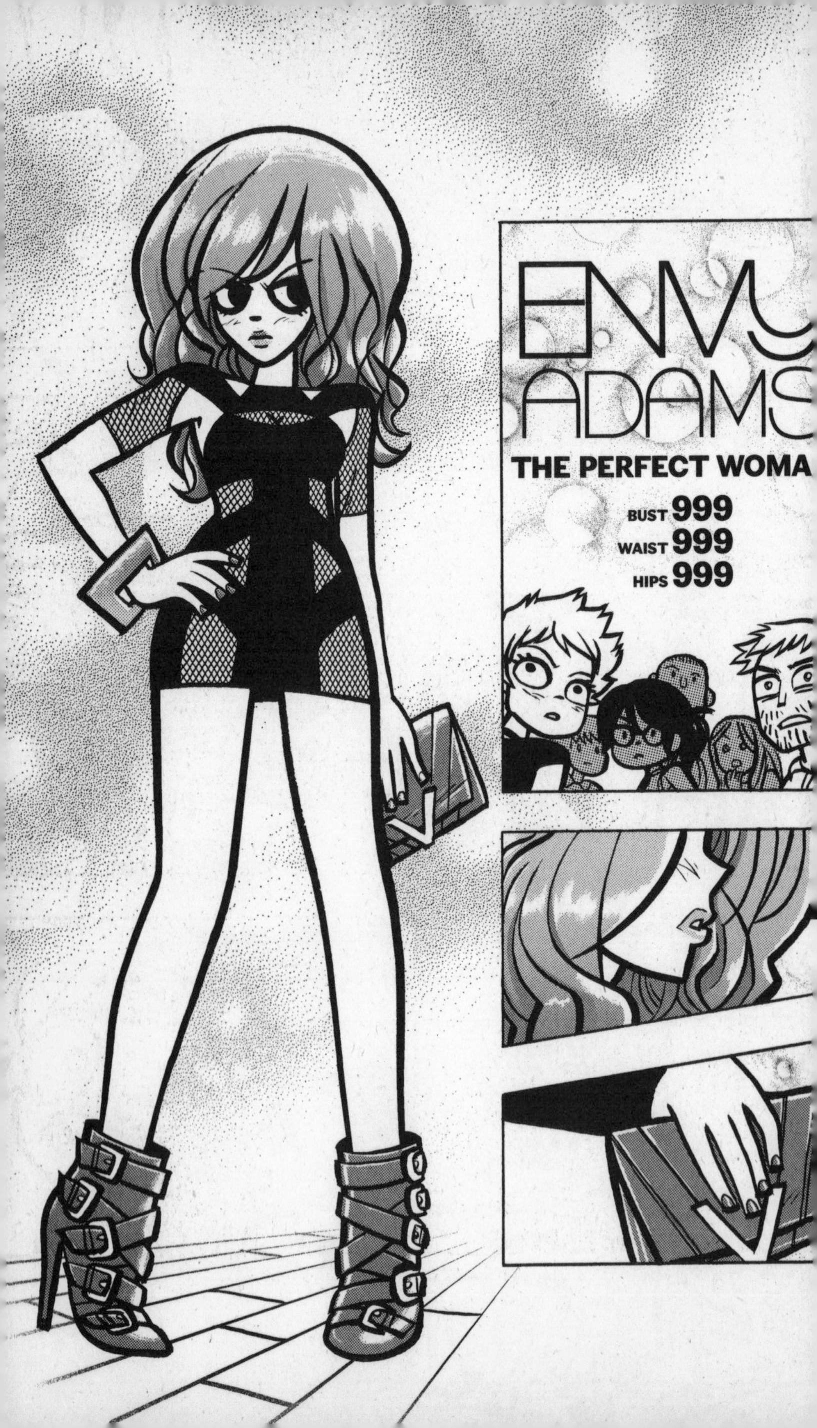
ENVY
ADAMS
THE PERFECT WOMA
BUST 999
WAIST 999
HIPS 999

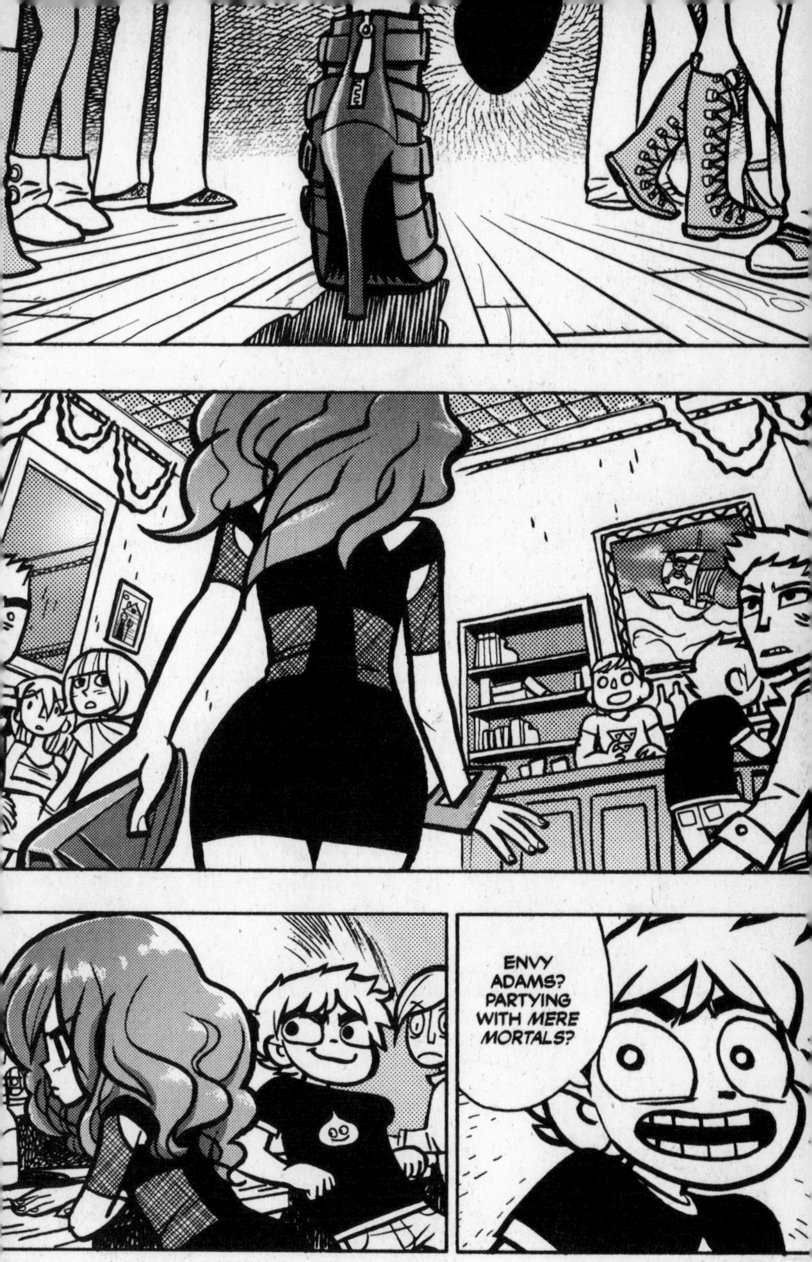
ENVY ADAMS? PARTYING WITH MERE MORTALS?

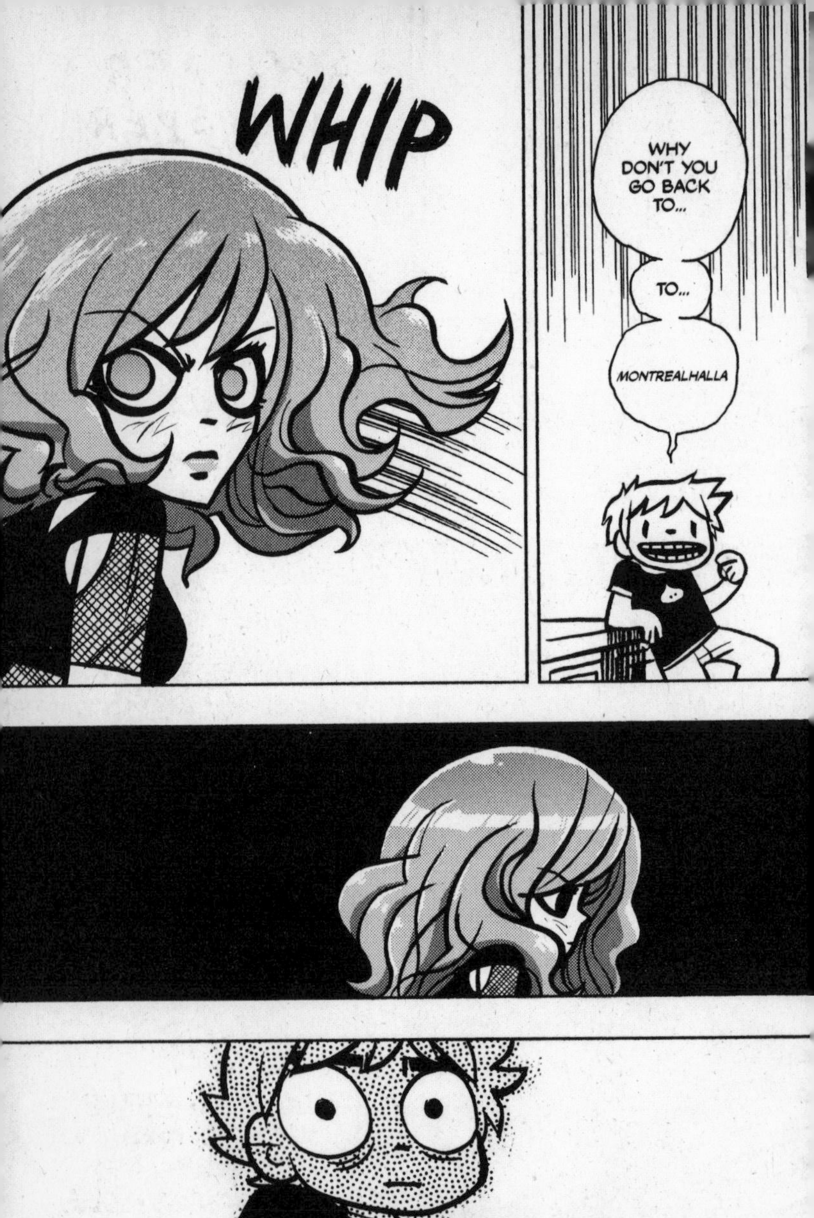
WHIP
WHY DON'T YOU GO BACK TO...
TO...
MONTREALHALLA

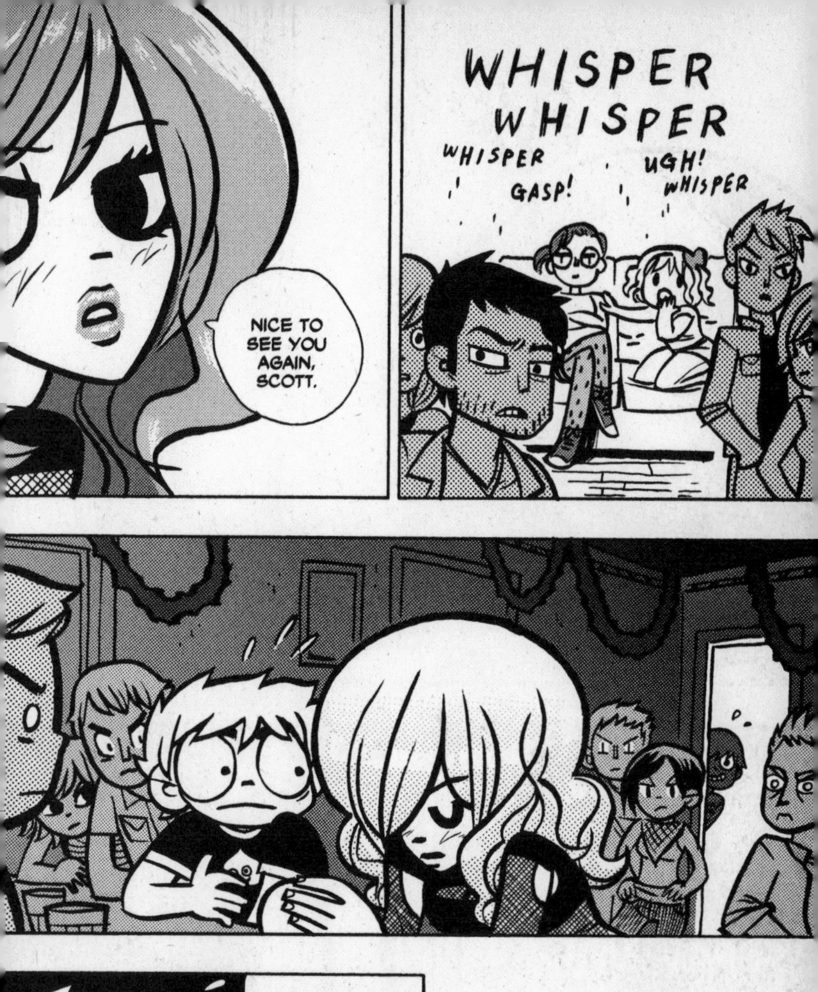
NICE TO SEE YOU AGAIN, SCOTT.
WHISPER WHISPER
WHISPER
GASP!
UGH!
WHISPER
UM... WHAT ARE YOU DRINKING? LET ME BUY YOU A...
JEEZ...
UM, I'M SORRY, I...
WE'LL SPARE YOU THE EMBARRASSMENT OF WITNESSING THE REST OF THIS AWFUL SPECTACLE.
(TURN THE PAGE)

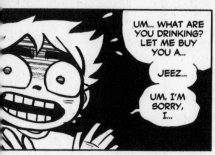

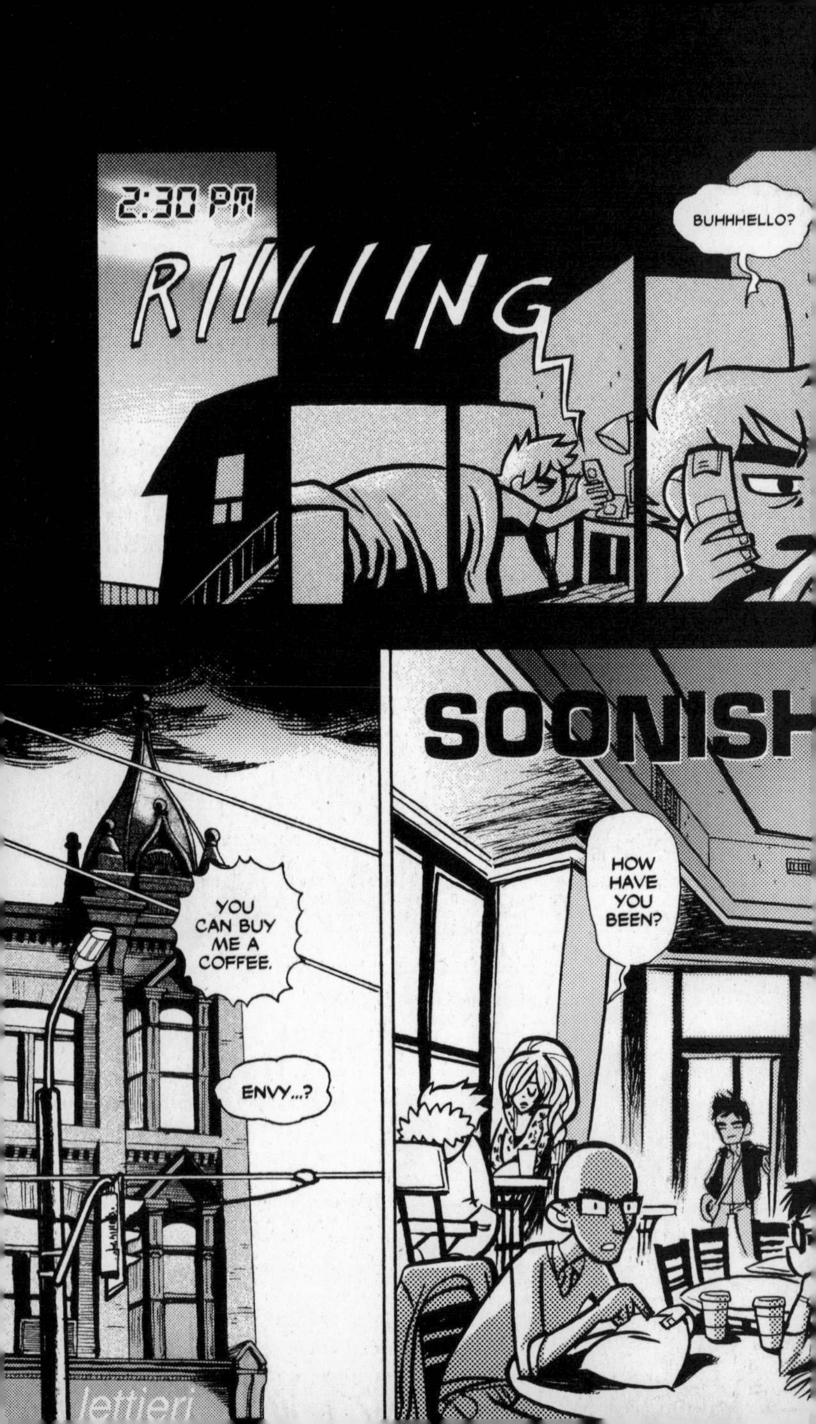
2:30 PM
RIIIIING
BUHHHELLO?
SOONISH
YOU CAN BUY ME A COFFEE.
ENVY...?
HOW HAVE YOU BEEN?

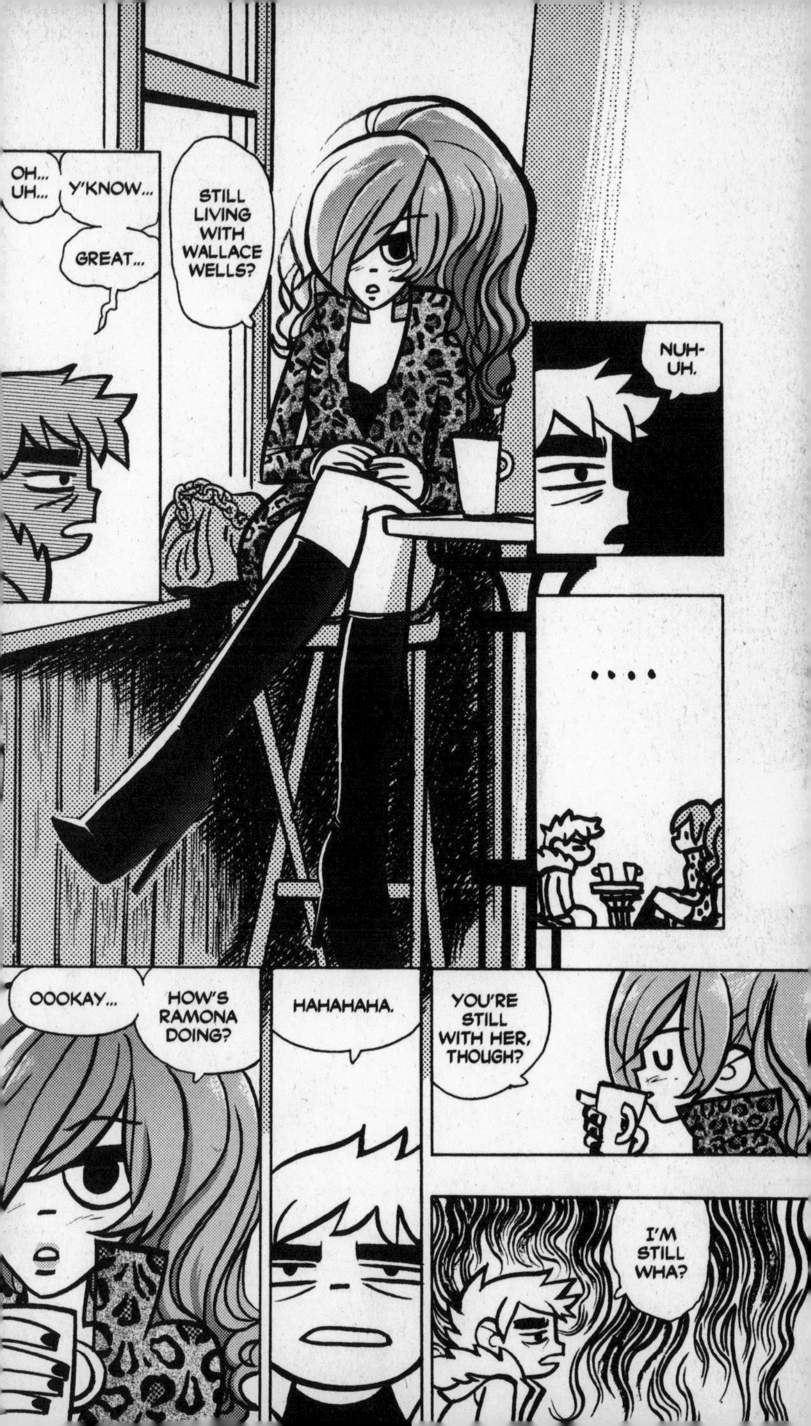
STILL LIVING WITH WALLACE WELLS?
OH... UH...
Y'KNOW...
GREAT...
NUH-UH.
....
OOOKAY...
HOW'S RAMONA DOING?
HAHAHAHA.
YOU'RE STILL WITH HER, THOUGH?
I'M STILL WHA?

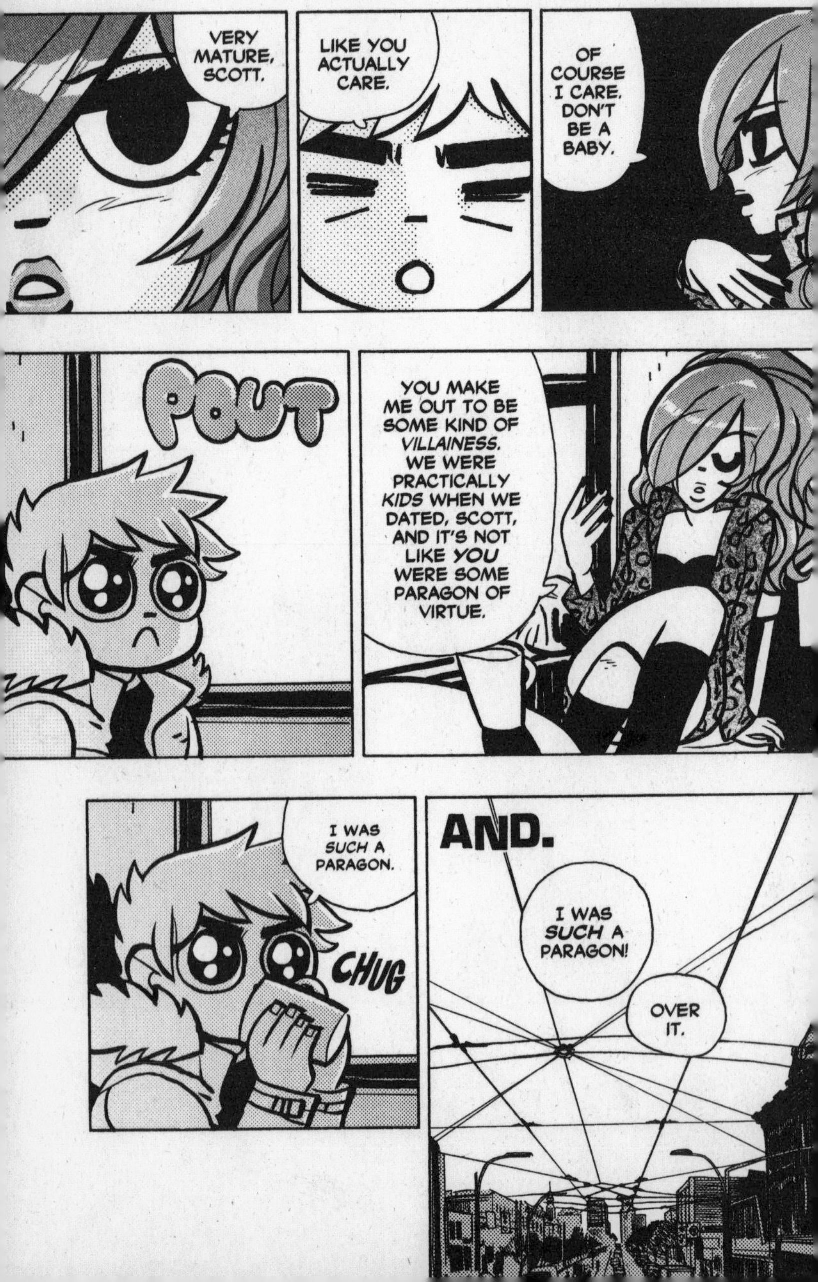
VERY MATURE, SCOTT.
LIKE YOU ACTUALLY CARE.
OF COURSE I CARE. DON'T BE A BABY.
POUT
YOU MAKE ME OUT TO BE SOME KIND OF *VILLAINESS.* WE WERE PRACTICALLY *KIDS* WHEN WE DATED, SCOTT, AND IT'S NOT LIKE *YOU* WERE SOME PARAGON OF VIRTUE.
I WAS *SUCH* A PARAGON.
CHUG
AND.
I WAS *SUCH* A PARAGON!
OVER IT.

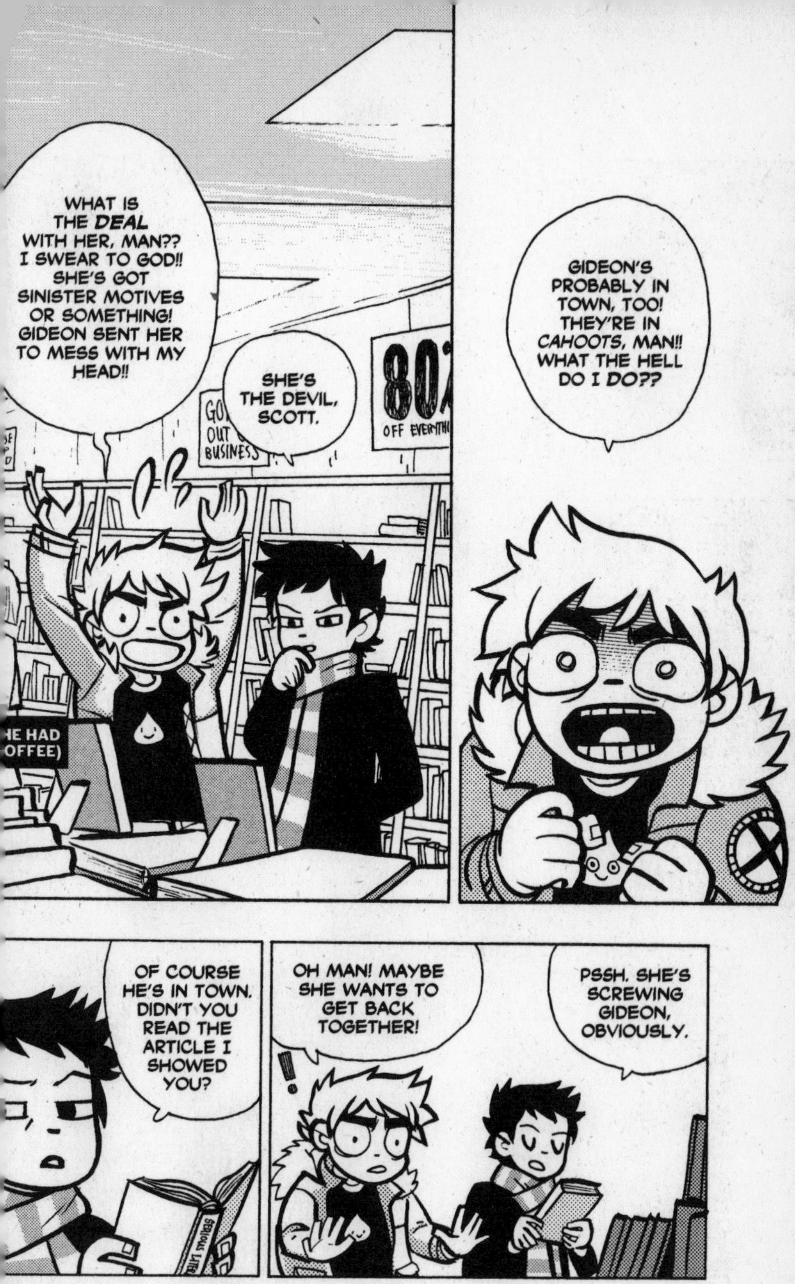
WHAT IS THE DEAL WITH HER, MAN?? I SWEAR TO GOD!! SHE'S GOT SINISTER MOTIVES OR SOMETHING! GIDEON SENT HER TO MESS WITH MY HEAD!!
SHE'S THE DEVIL, SCOTT.
BUSINESS
GIDEON'S PROBABLY IN TOWN, TOO! THEY'RE IN CAHOOTS, MAN!! WHAT THE HELL DO I DO??
OF COURSE HE'S IN TOWN. DIDN'T YOU READ THE ARTICLE I SHOWED YOU?
OH MAN! MAYBE SHE WANTS TO GET BACK TOGETHER!
PSSH. SHE'S SCREWING GIDEON, OBVIOUSLY.

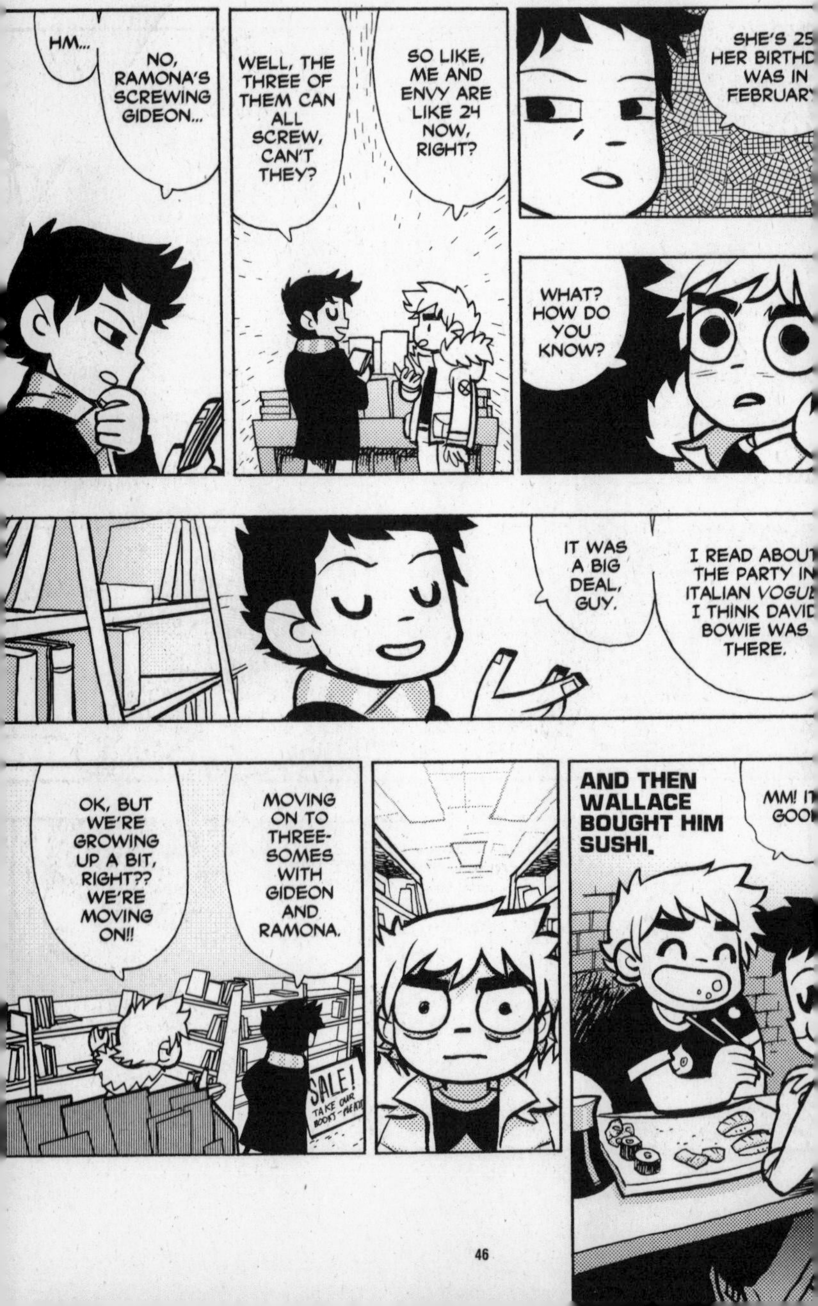
HM...
NO, RAMONA'S SCREWING GIDEON...
WELL, THE THREE OF THEM CAN ALL SCREW, CAN'T THEY?
SO LIKE, ME AND ENVY ARE LIKE 24 NOW, RIGHT?
SHE'S 25
HER BIRTHD
WAS IN
FEBRUAR
WHAT? HOW DO YOU KNOW?
IT WAS A BIG DEAL, GUY.
I READ ABOU
THE PARTY IN
ITALIAN *VOGU*
I THINK DAVID
BOWIE WAS
THERE.
OK, BUT WE'RE GROWING UP A BIT, RIGHT?? WE'RE MOVING ON!!
MOVING ON TO THREE-SOMES WITH GIDEON AND RAMONA.
SALE!
AND THEN WALLACE BOUGHT HIM SUSHI.
MM! I
GOO

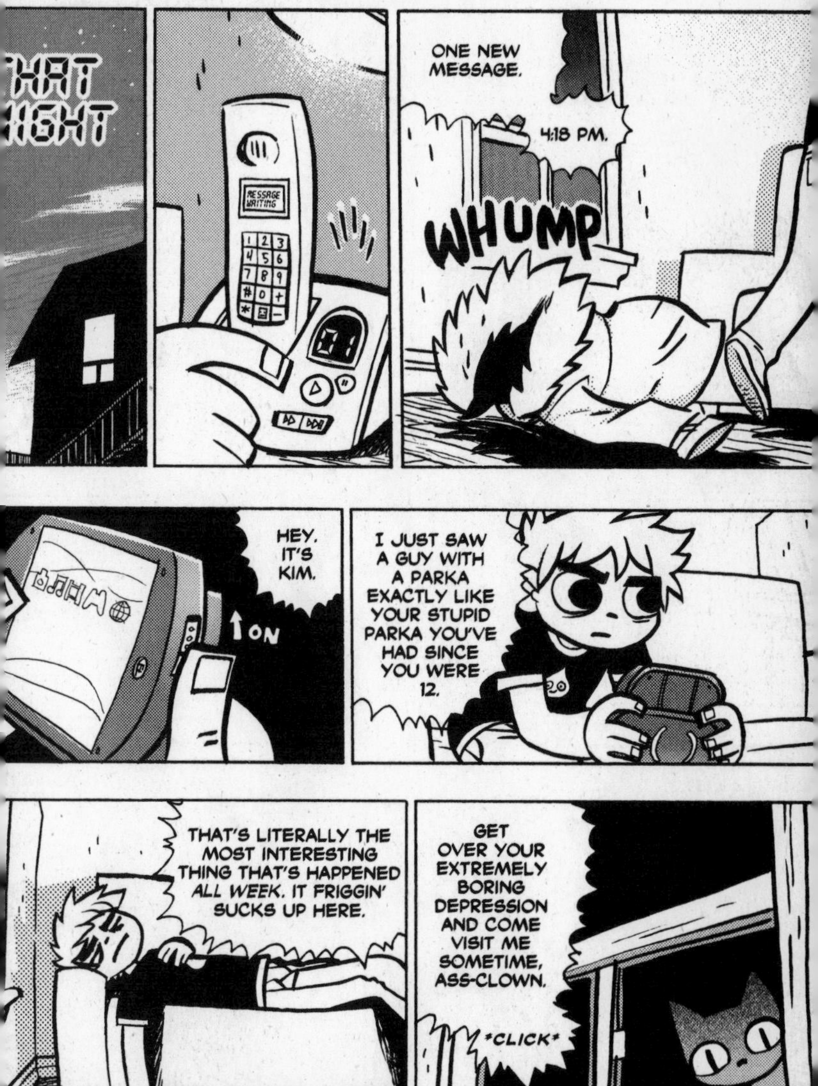

THAT NIGHT
MESSAGE WAITING
ONE NEW MESSAGE.
4:18 PM.
WHUMP
HEY. IT'S KIM.
ON
I JUST SAW A GUY WITH A PARKA EXACTLY LIKE YOUR STUPID PARKA YOU'VE HAD SINCE YOU WERE 12.
THAT'S LITERALLY THE MOST INTERESTING THING THAT'S HAPPENED ALL WEEK. IT FRIGGIN' SUCKS UP HERE.
GET OVER YOUR EXTREMELY BORING DEPRESSION AND COME VISIT ME SOMETIME, ASS-CLOWN.
CLICK

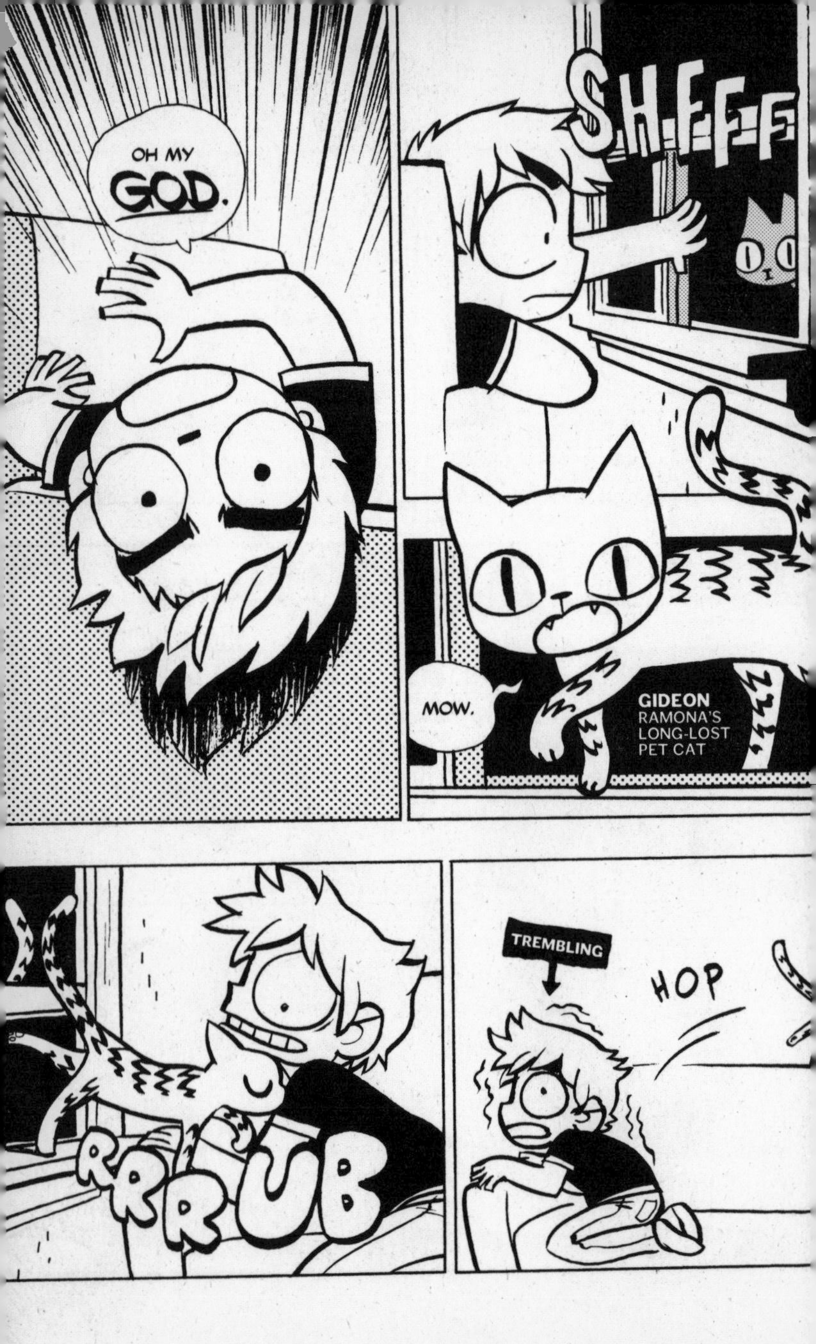

OH MY GOD.
SHFFF
MOW.
GIDEON
RAMONA'S LONG-LOST PET CAT
RRRUB
TREMBLING
HOP

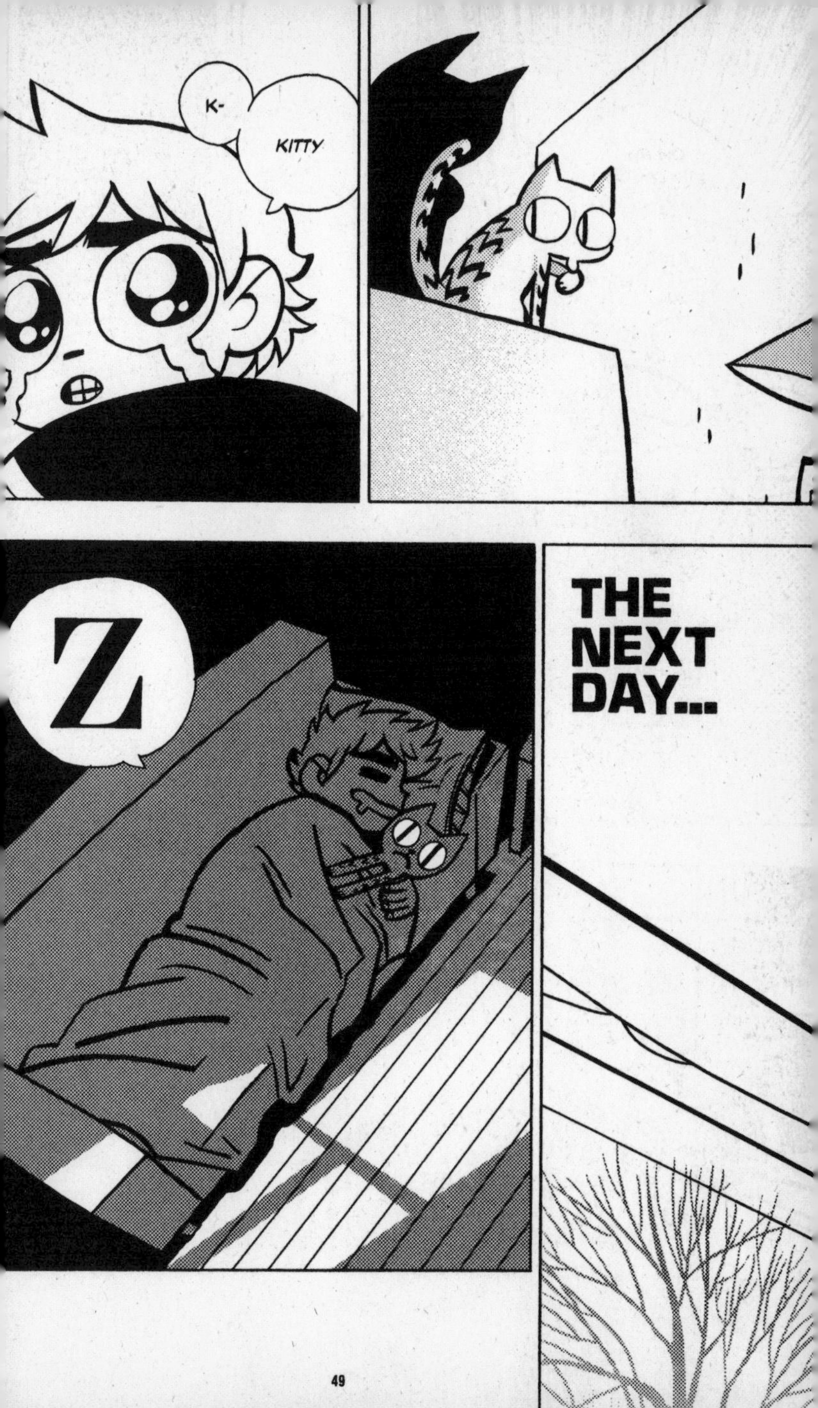
K-
KITTY
Z
THE NEXT DAY...

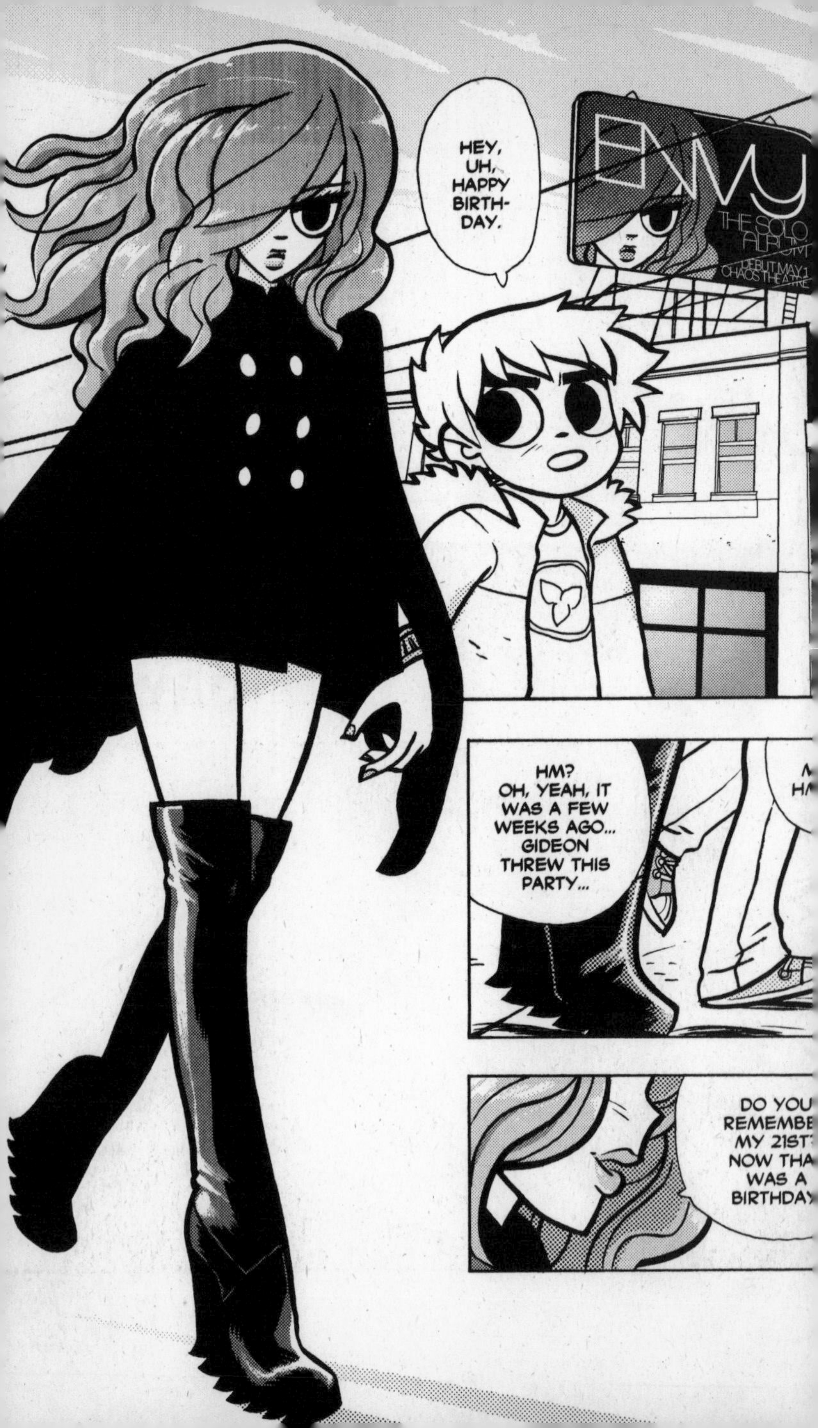
HEY, UH, HAPPY BIRTH-DAY.
ENVY
THE SOLO ALBUM
DEBUT MAY 1
CHAOS THEATRE
HM? OH, YEAH, IT WAS A FEW WEEKS AGO... GIDEON THREW THIS PARTY...
DO YOU REMEMBE MY 21ST NOW THA WAS A BIRTHDAY

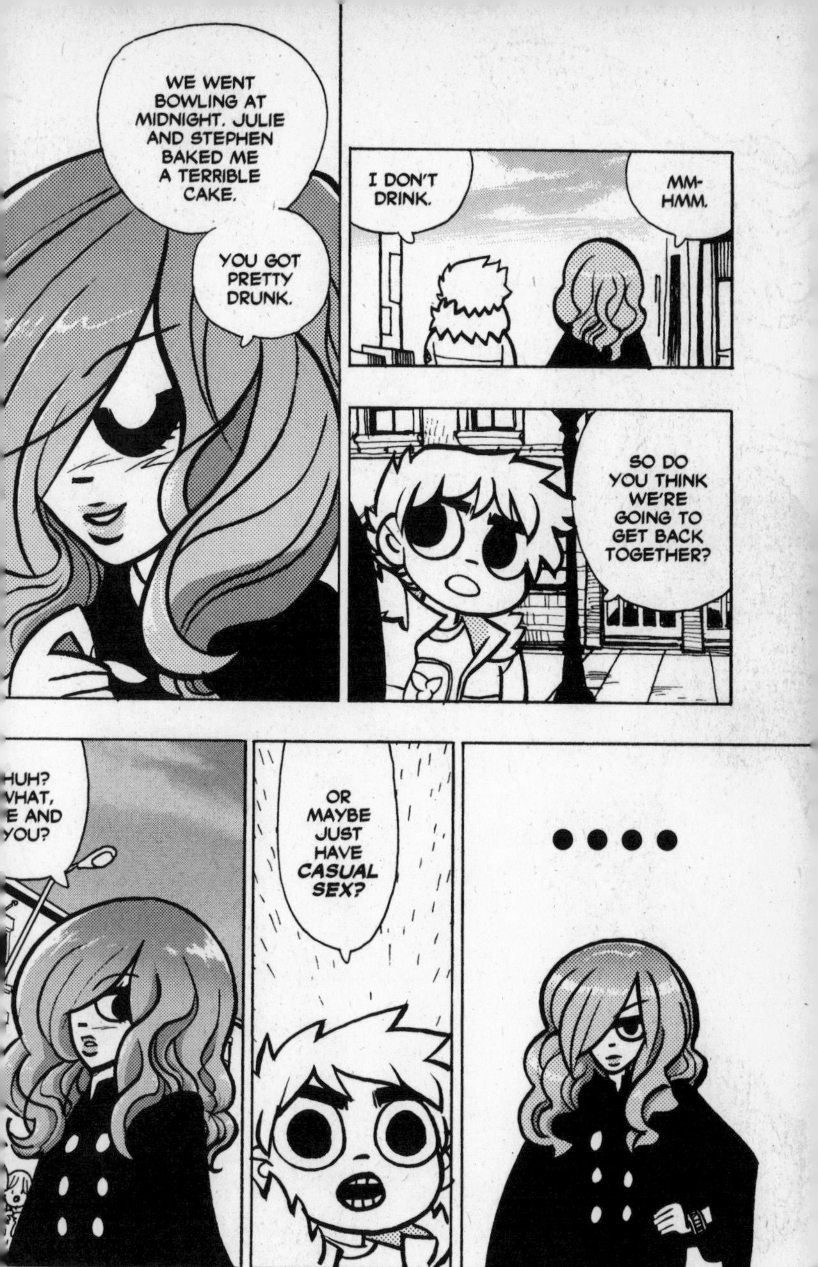
WE WENT BOWLING AT MIDNIGHT. JULIE AND STEPHEN BAKED ME A TERRIBLE CAKE.
YOU GOT PRETTY DRUNK.
I DON'T DRINK.
MM-HMM.
SO DO YOU THINK WE'RE GOING TO GET BACK TOGETHER?
HUH? VHAT, E AND YOU?
OR MAYBE JUST HAVE CASUAL SEX?
• • • •

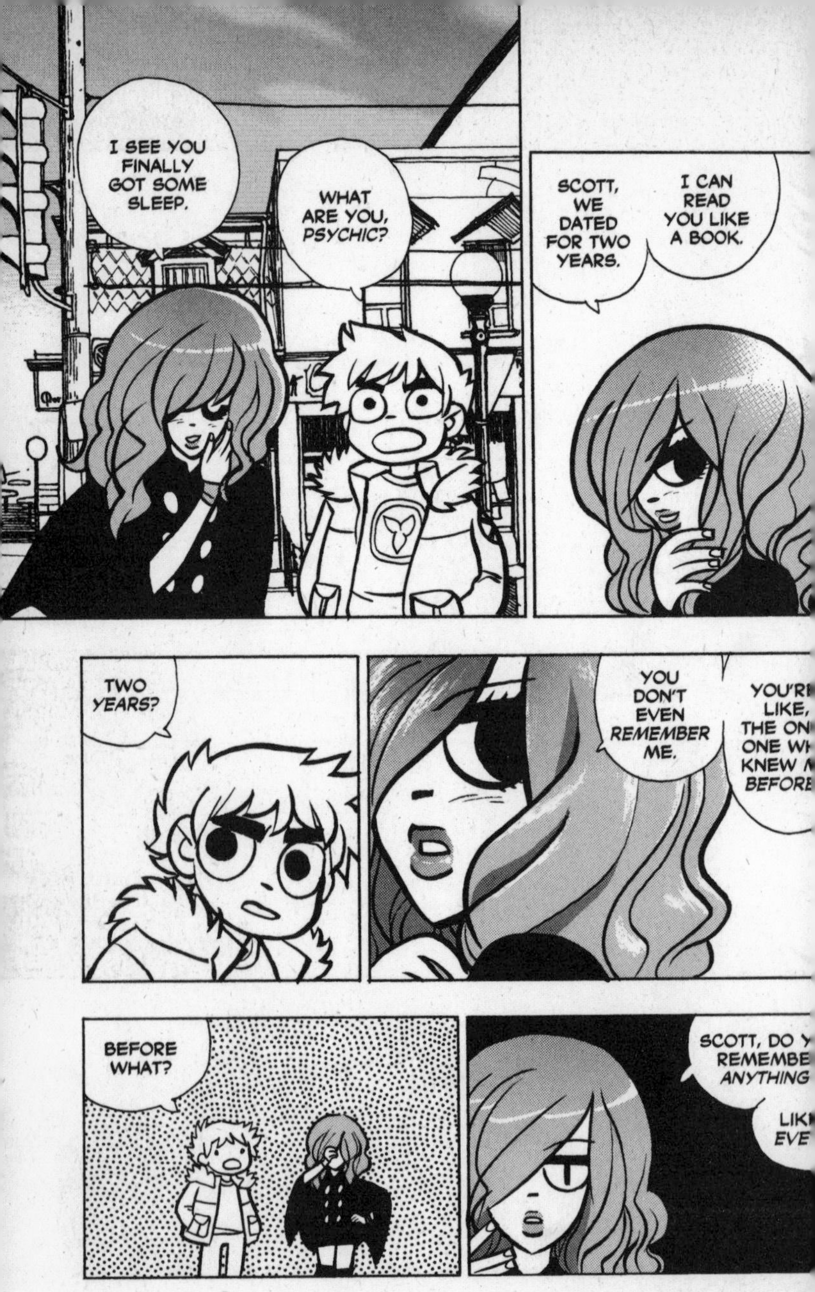
I SEE YOU FINALLY GOT SOME SLEEP.
WHAT ARE YOU, *PSYCHIC?*
SCOTT, WE DATED FOR TWO YEARS.
I CAN READ YOU LIKE A BOOK.
TWO *YEARS?*
YOU DON'T EVEN *REMEMBER* ME.
YOU'R LIKE, THE ON ONE W KNEW *BEFOR*
BEFORE WHAT?
SCOTT, DO REMEMBE *ANYTHING*
LIK *EVE*

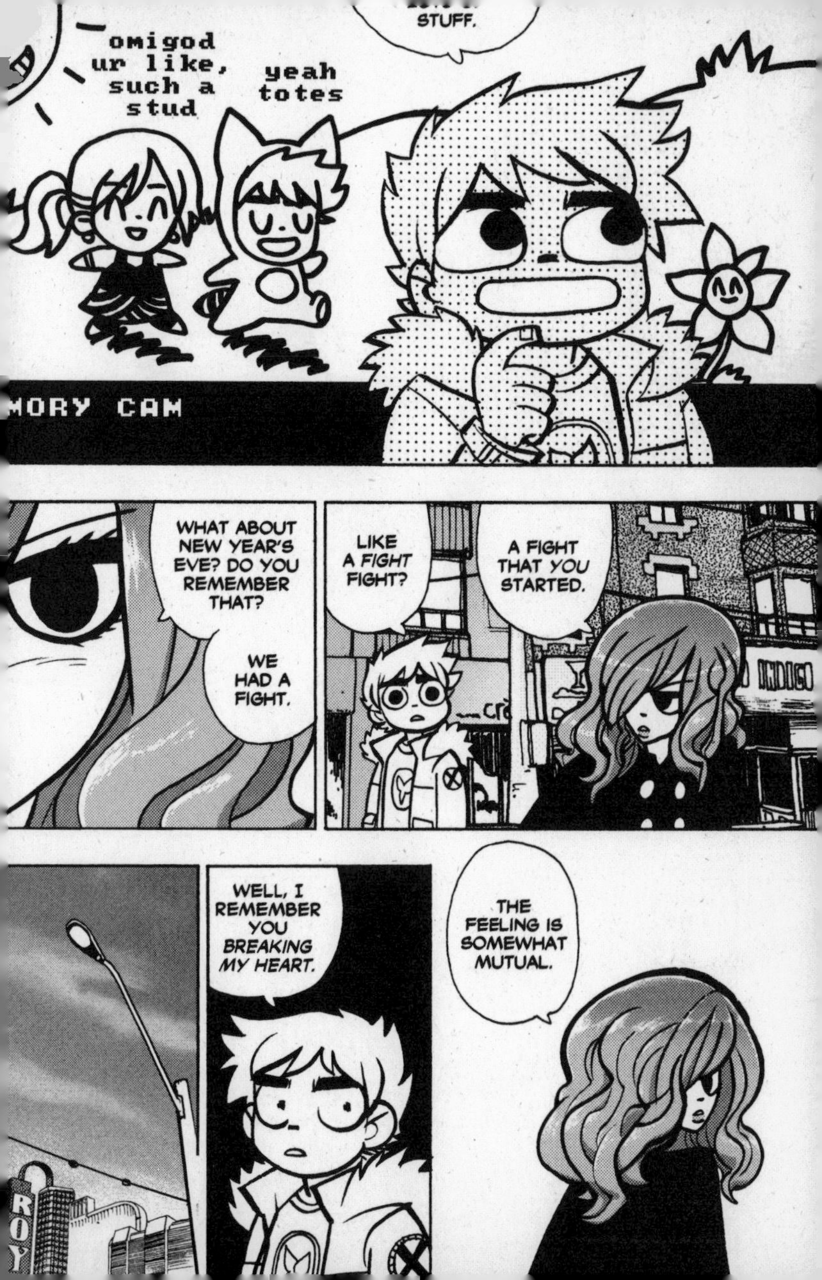
STUFF.
omigod ur like, such a stud
yeah totes
MORY CAM
WHAT ABOUT NEW YEAR'S EVE? DO YOU REMEMBER THAT?
WE HAD A FIGHT.
LIKE A *FIGHT* FIGHT?
A FIGHT THAT *YOU* STARTED.
INDIGO
WELL, I REMEMBER YOU *BREAKING MY HEART.*
THE FEELING IS SOMEWHAT MUTUAL.
ROY

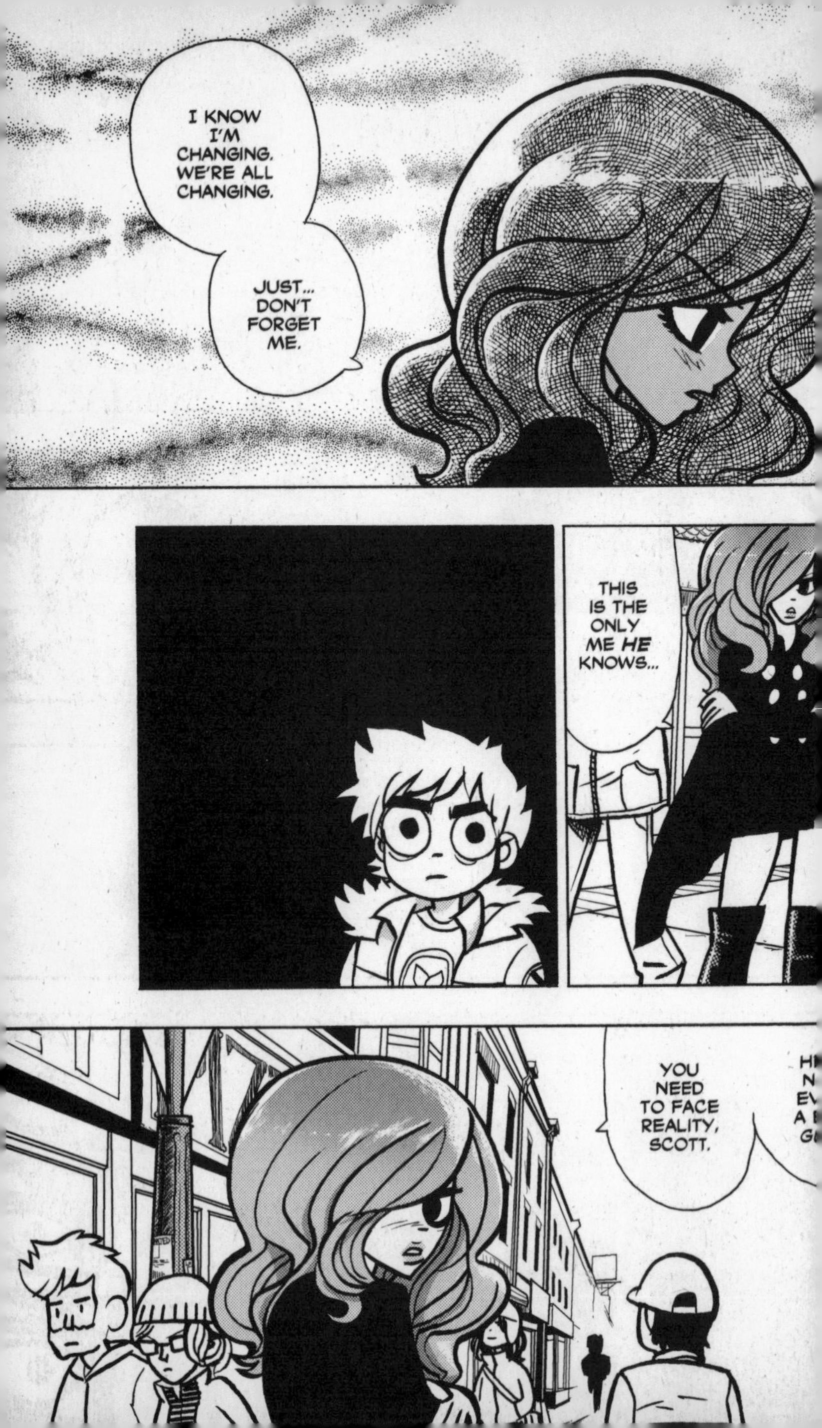
I KNOW I'M CHANGING. WE'RE ALL CHANGING.
JUST... DON'T FORGET ME.
THIS IS THE ONLY ME *HE* KNOWS...
YOU NEED TO FACE REALITY, SCOTT.

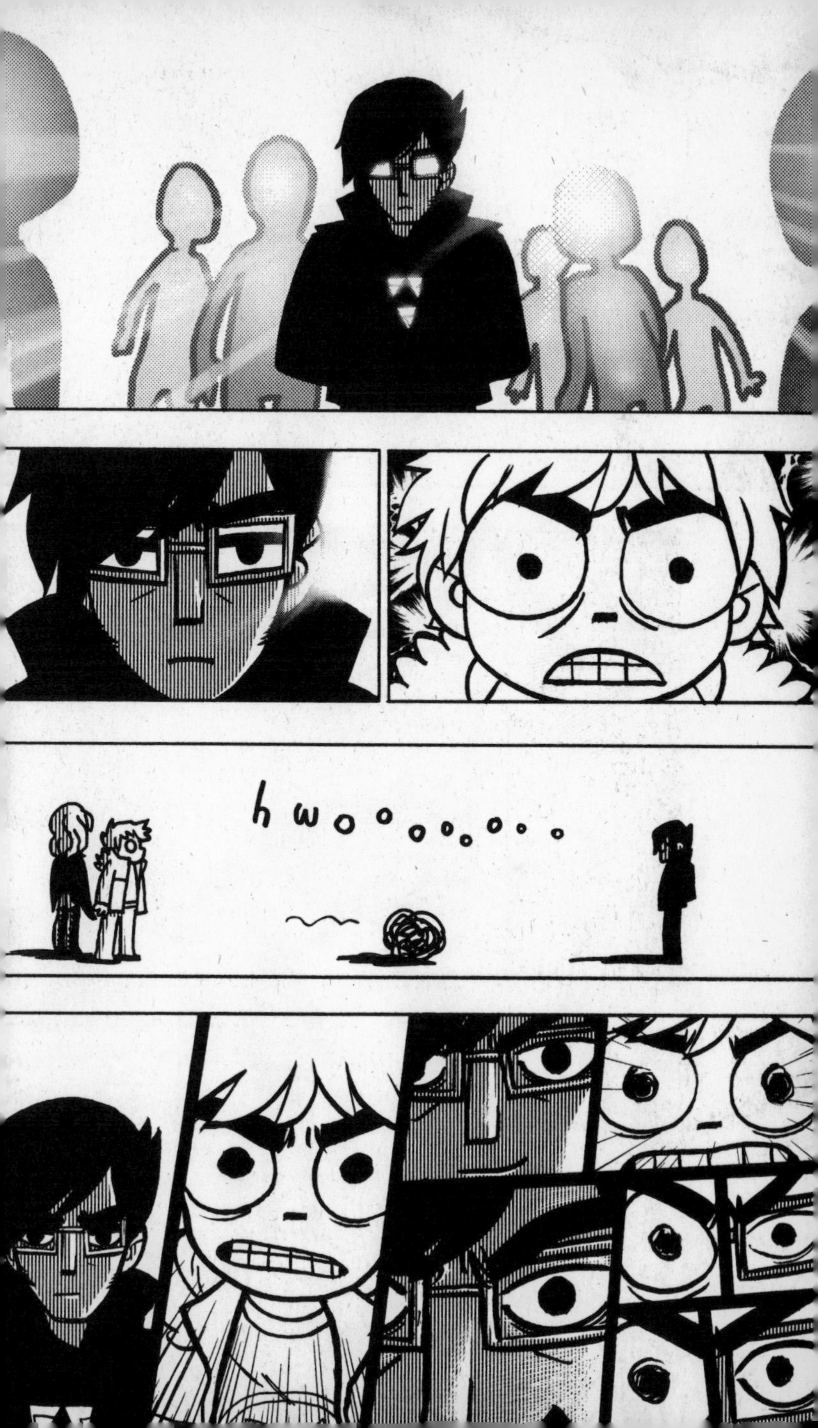
hwoooooooo

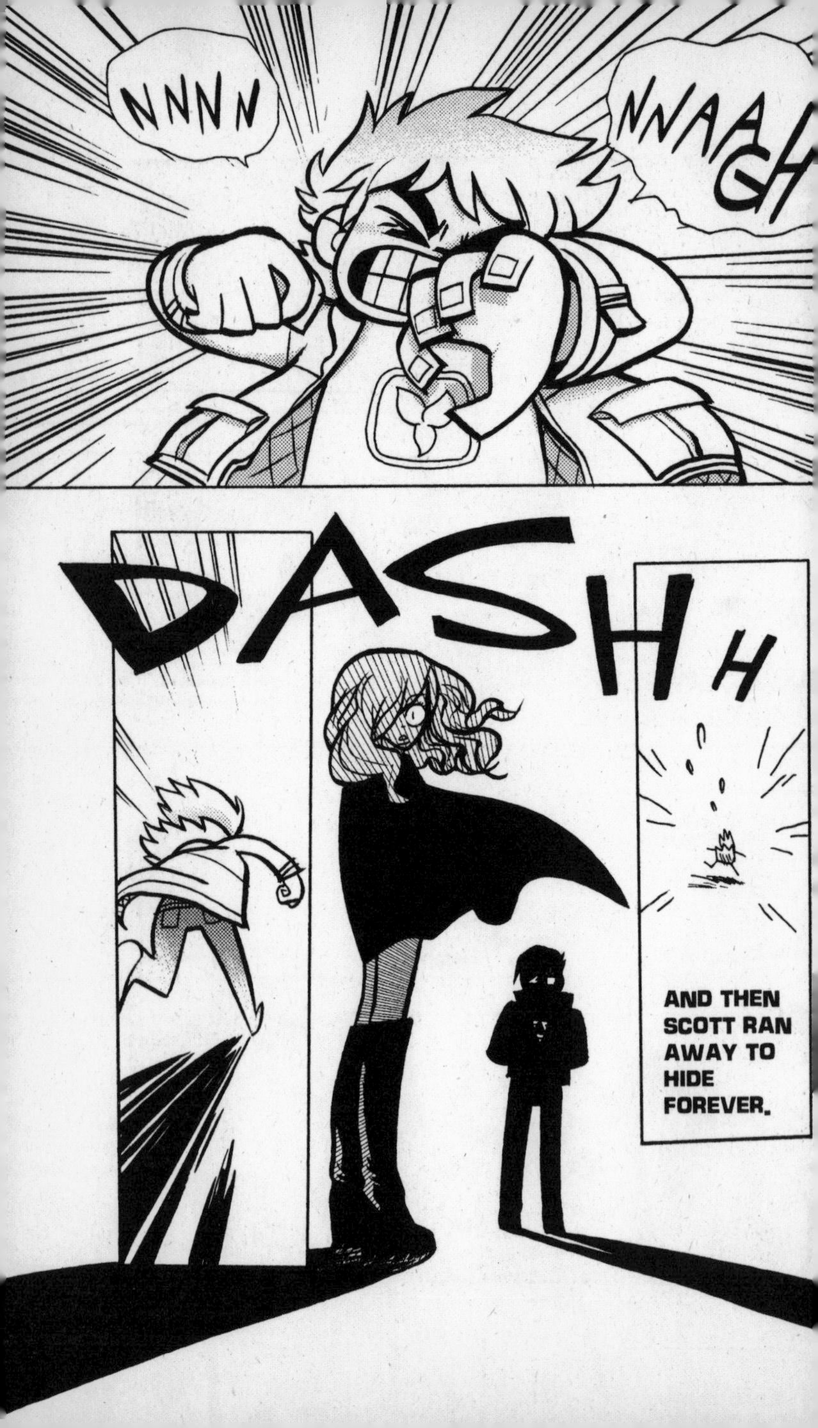
NNNN
NNAAGH
DASHH
AND THEN SCOTT RAN AWAY TO HIDE FOREVER.

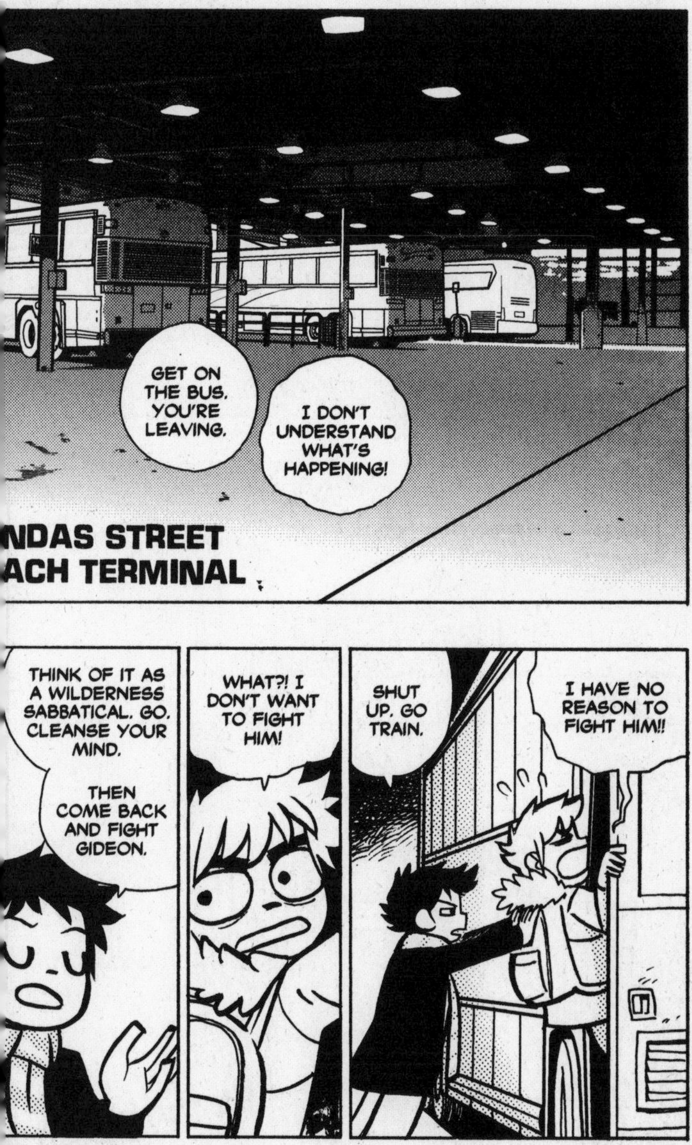
GET ON THE BUS. YOU'RE LEAVING.
I DON'T UNDERSTAND WHAT'S HAPPENING!
NDAS STREET ACH TERMINAL
THINK OF IT AS A WILDERNESS SABBATICAL. GO. CLEANSE YOUR MIND.
THEN COME BACK AND FIGHT GIDEON.
WHAT?! I DON'T WANT TO FIGHT HIM!
SHUT UP. GO TRAIN.
I HAVE NO REASON TO FIGHT HIM!!

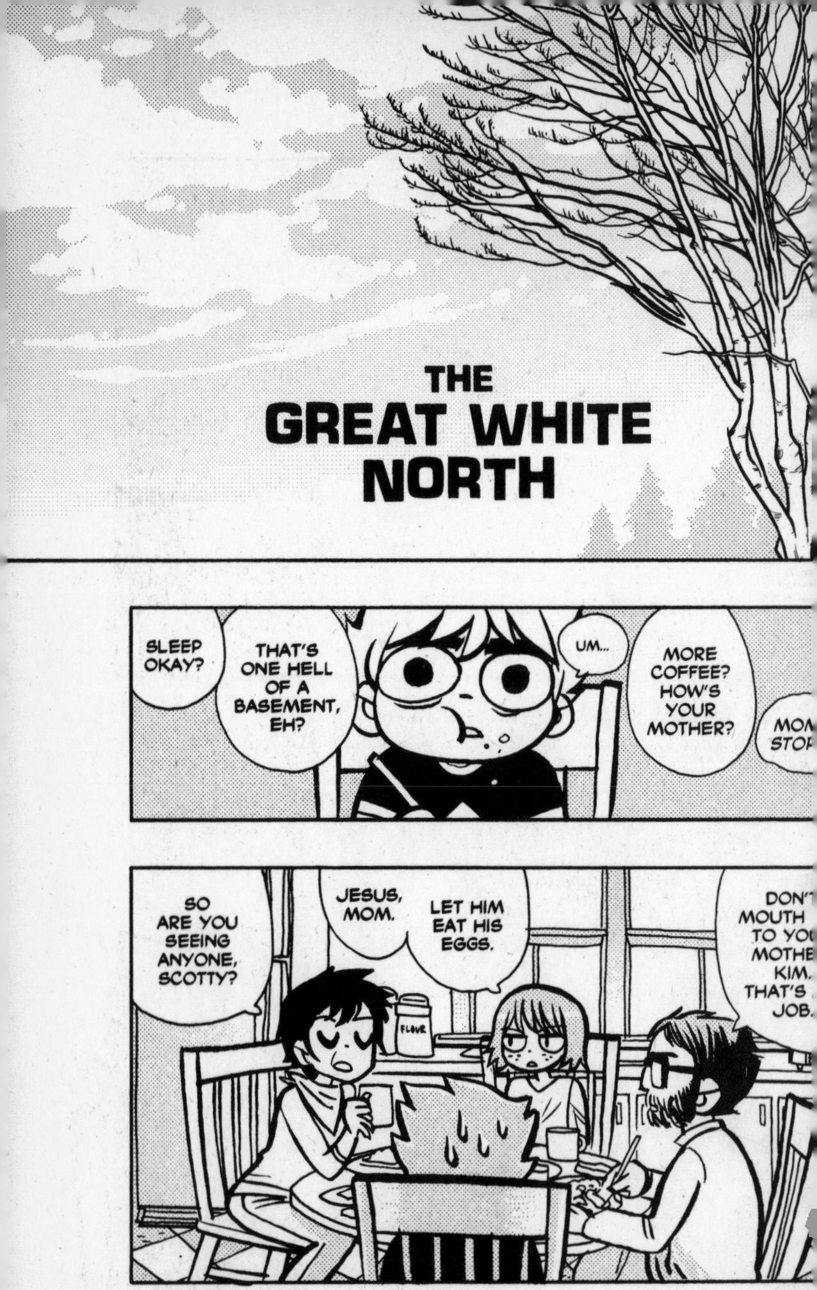
THE GREAT WHITE NORTH
SLEEP OKAY?
THAT'S ONE HELL OF A BASEMENT, EH?
UM...
MORE COFFEE? HOW'S YOUR MOTHER?
SO ARE YOU SEEING ANYONE, SCOTTY?
JESUS, MOM.
LET HIM EAT HIS EGGS.
FLOUR

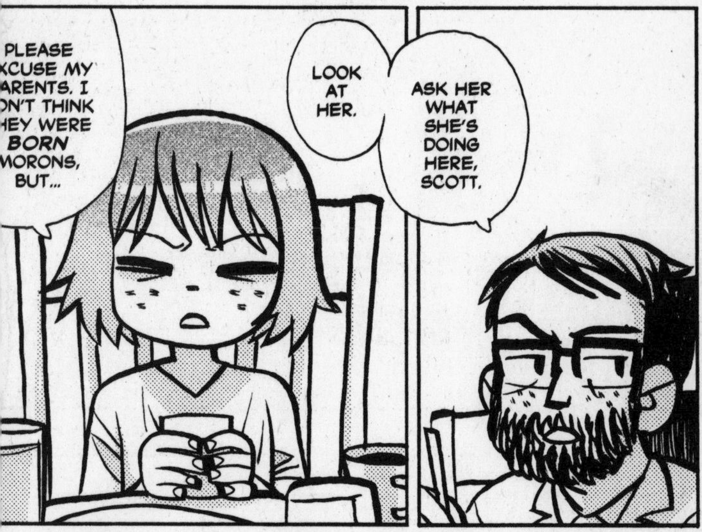
PLEASE XCUSE MY ARENTS. I ON'T THINK HEY WERE BORN MORONS, BUT...
LOOK AT HER.
ASK HER WHAT SHE'S DOING HERE, SCOTT.

34 A link to the past

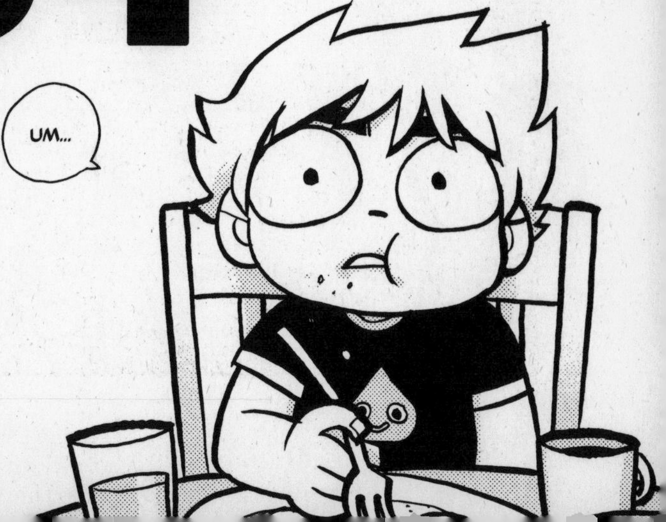
UM...

YEAH, SO, LIFE. THIS IS IT.

AMAZING, I KNOW.

S
W
A
Y
DO
HE

SCOTT.

LAST I CHECKED, CONTINUE NOT BE M MOM.

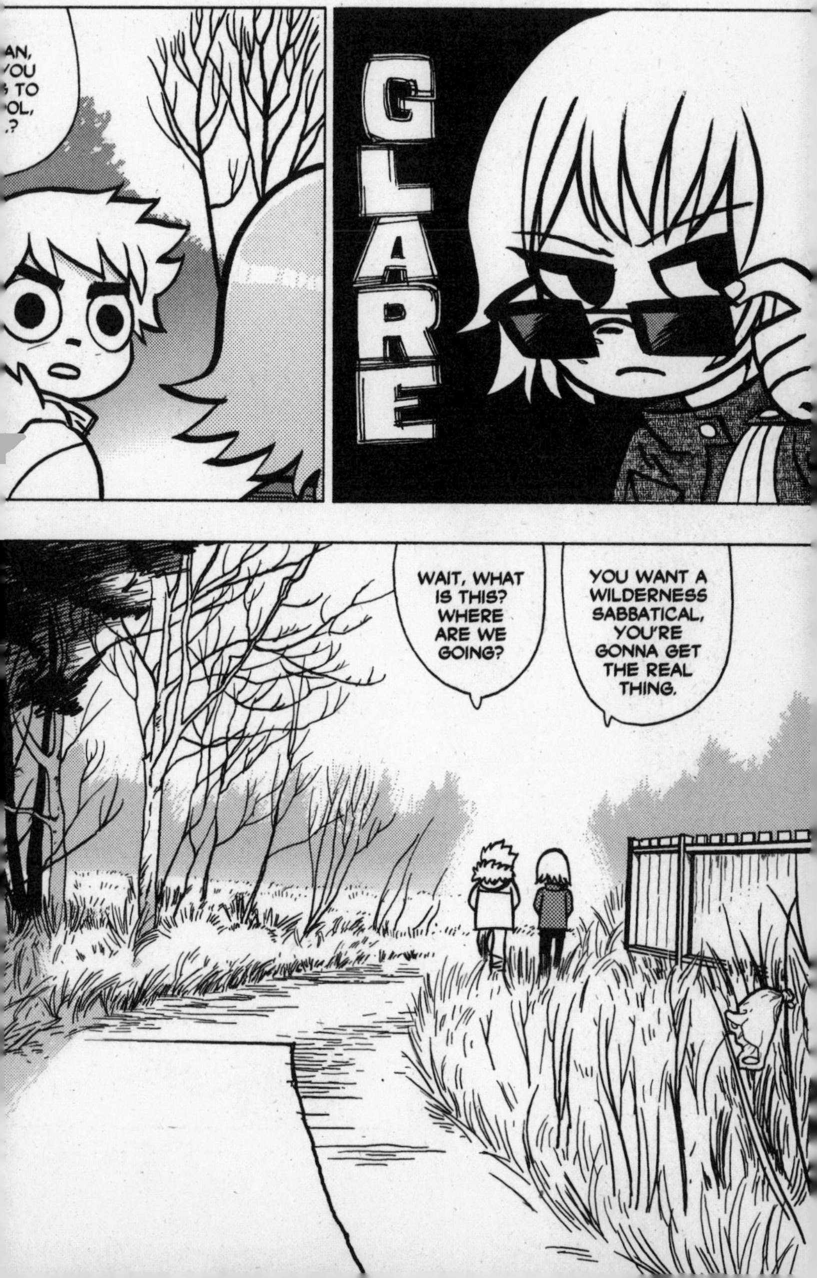
GLARE
WAIT, WHAT IS THIS? WHERE ARE WE GOING?
YOU WANT A WILDERNESS SABBATICAL, YOU'RE GONNA GET THE REAL THING.

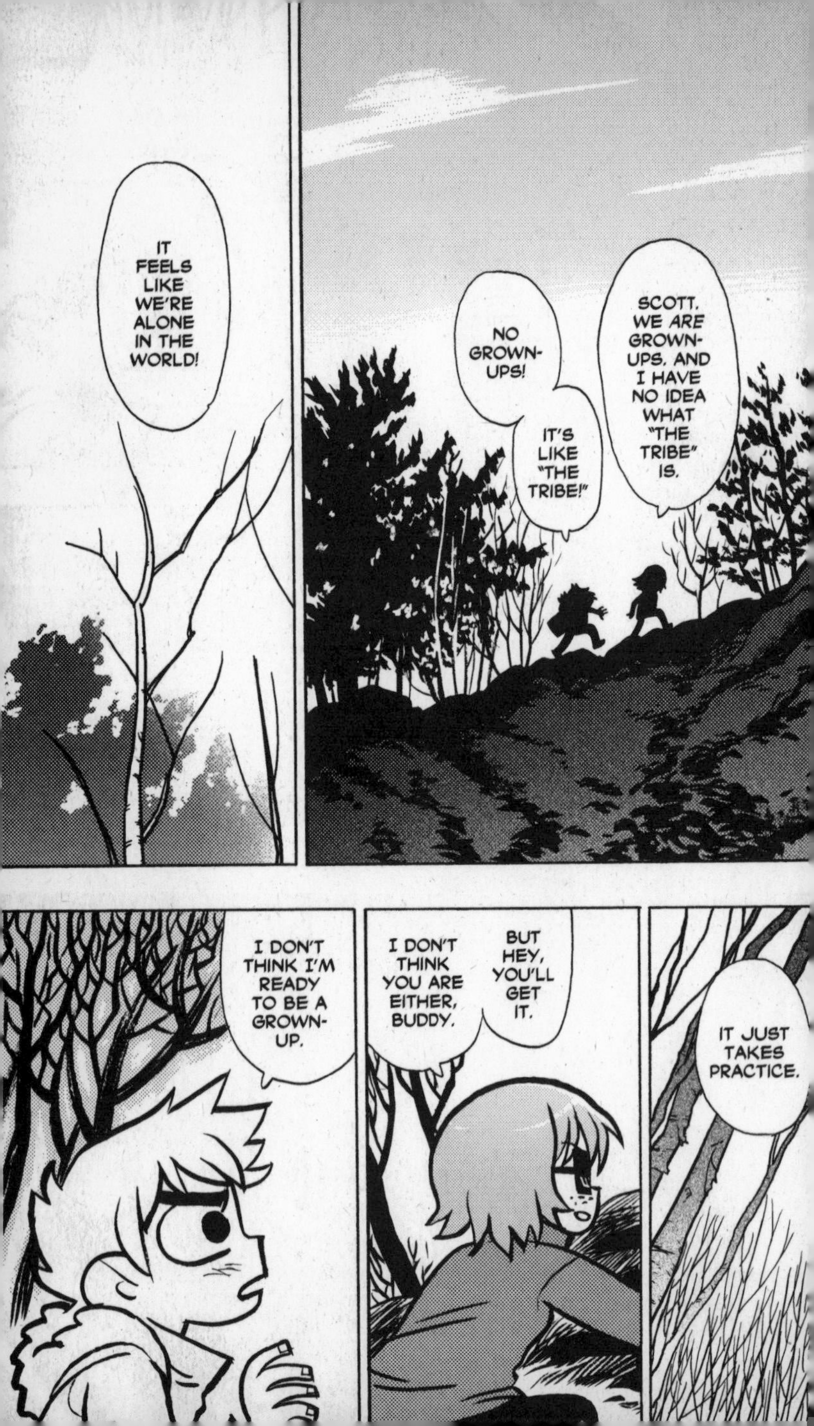
IT FEELS LIKE WE'RE ALONE IN THE WORLD!
NO GROWN-UPS!
IT'S LIKE "THE TRIBE!"
SCOTT. WE *ARE* GROWN-UPS. AND I HAVE NO IDEA WHAT "THE TRIBE" IS.
I DON'T THINK I'M READY TO BE A GROWN-UP.
I DON'T THINK YOU ARE EITHER, BUDDY.
BUT HEY, YOU'LL GET IT.
IT JUST TAKES PRACTICE.

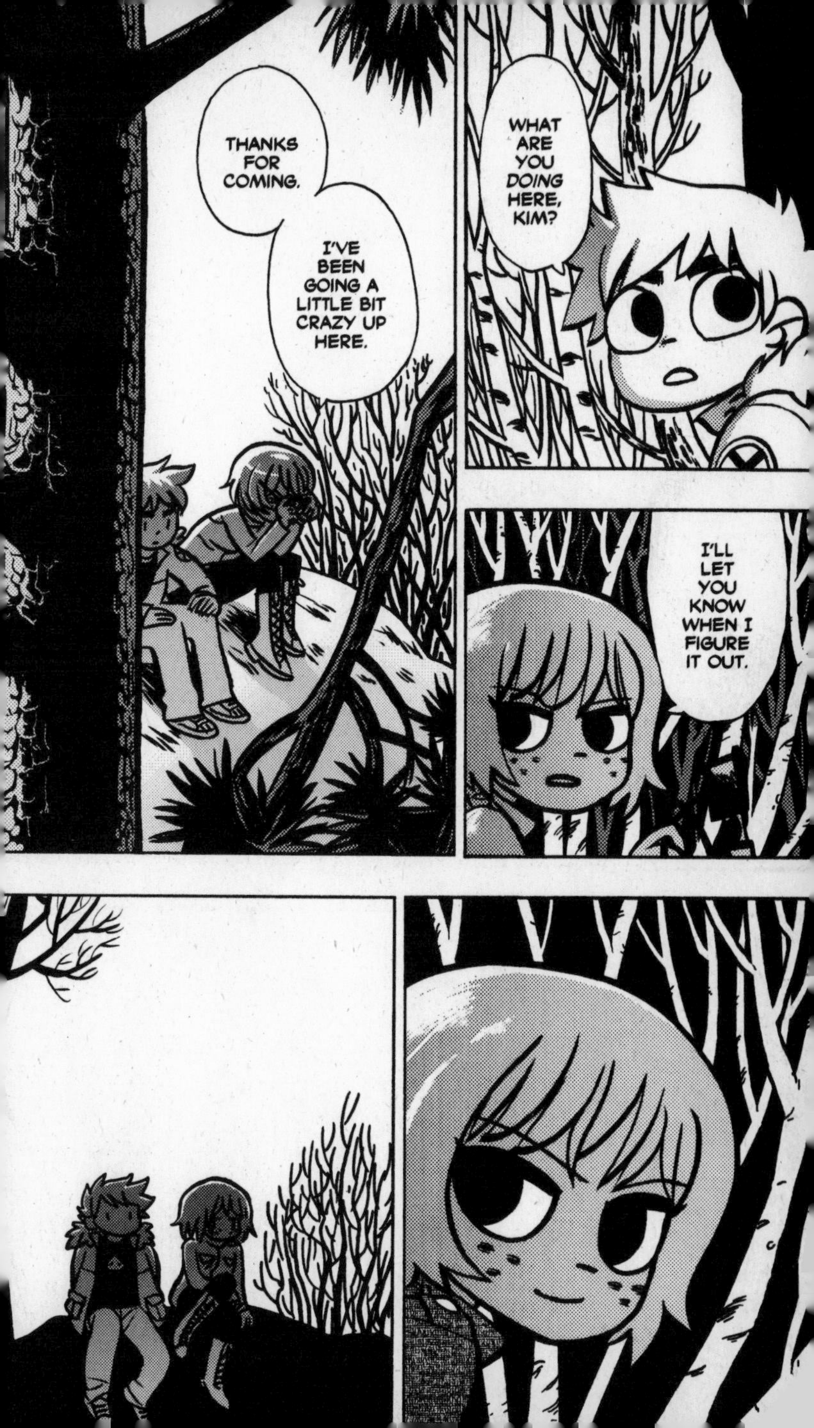
THANKS FOR COMING.
I'VE BEEN GOING A LITTLE BIT CRAZY UP HERE.
WHAT ARE YOU *DOING* HERE, KIM?
I'LL LET YOU KNOW WHEN I FIGURE IT OUT.

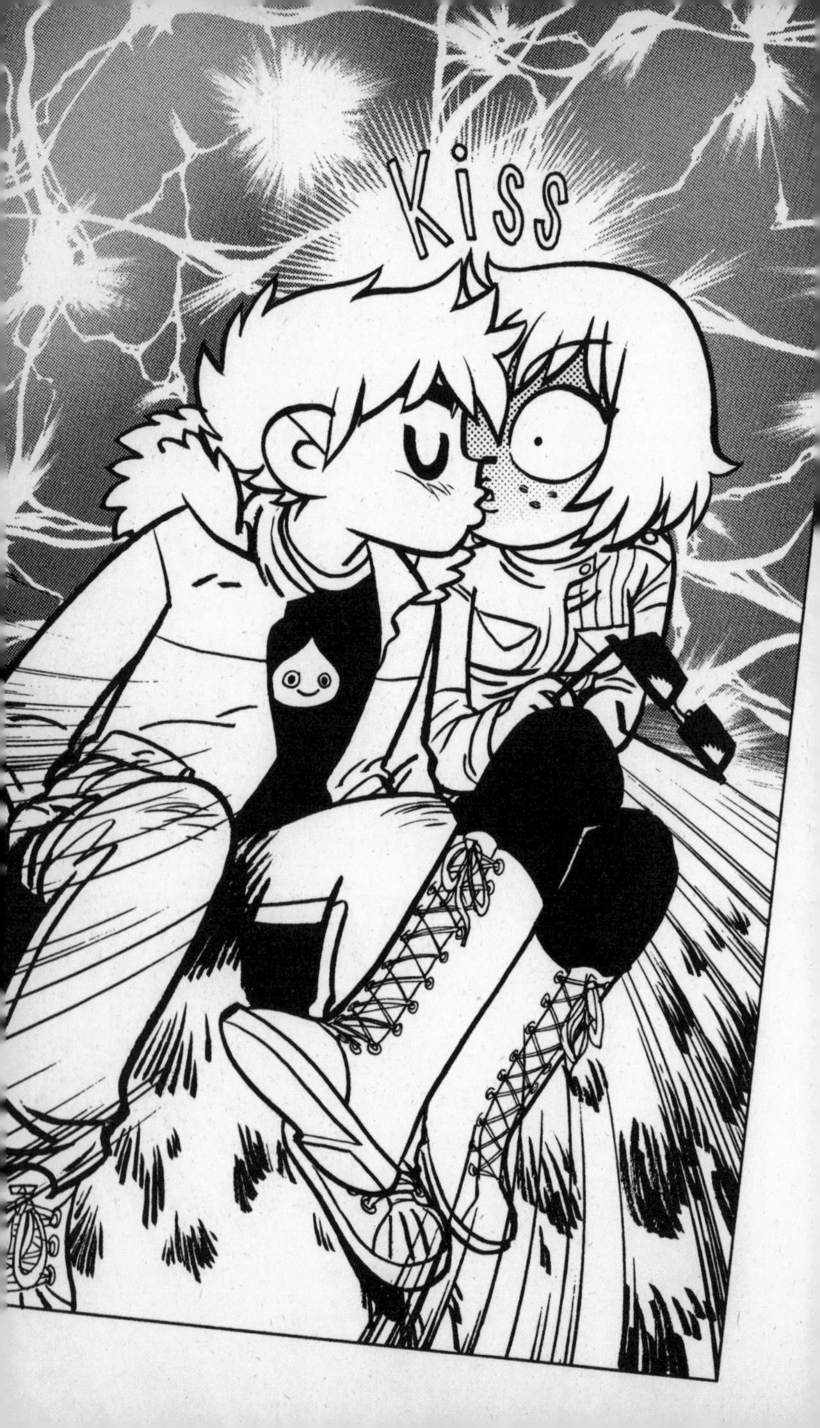
KISS

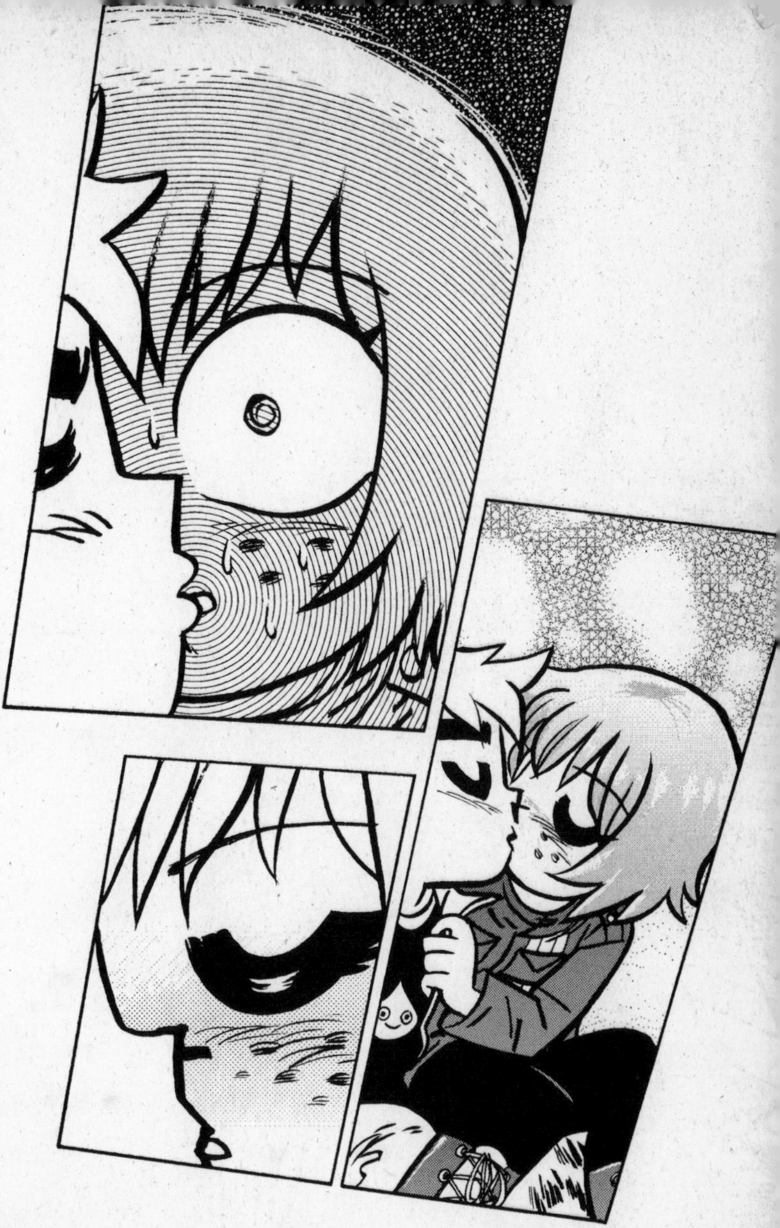

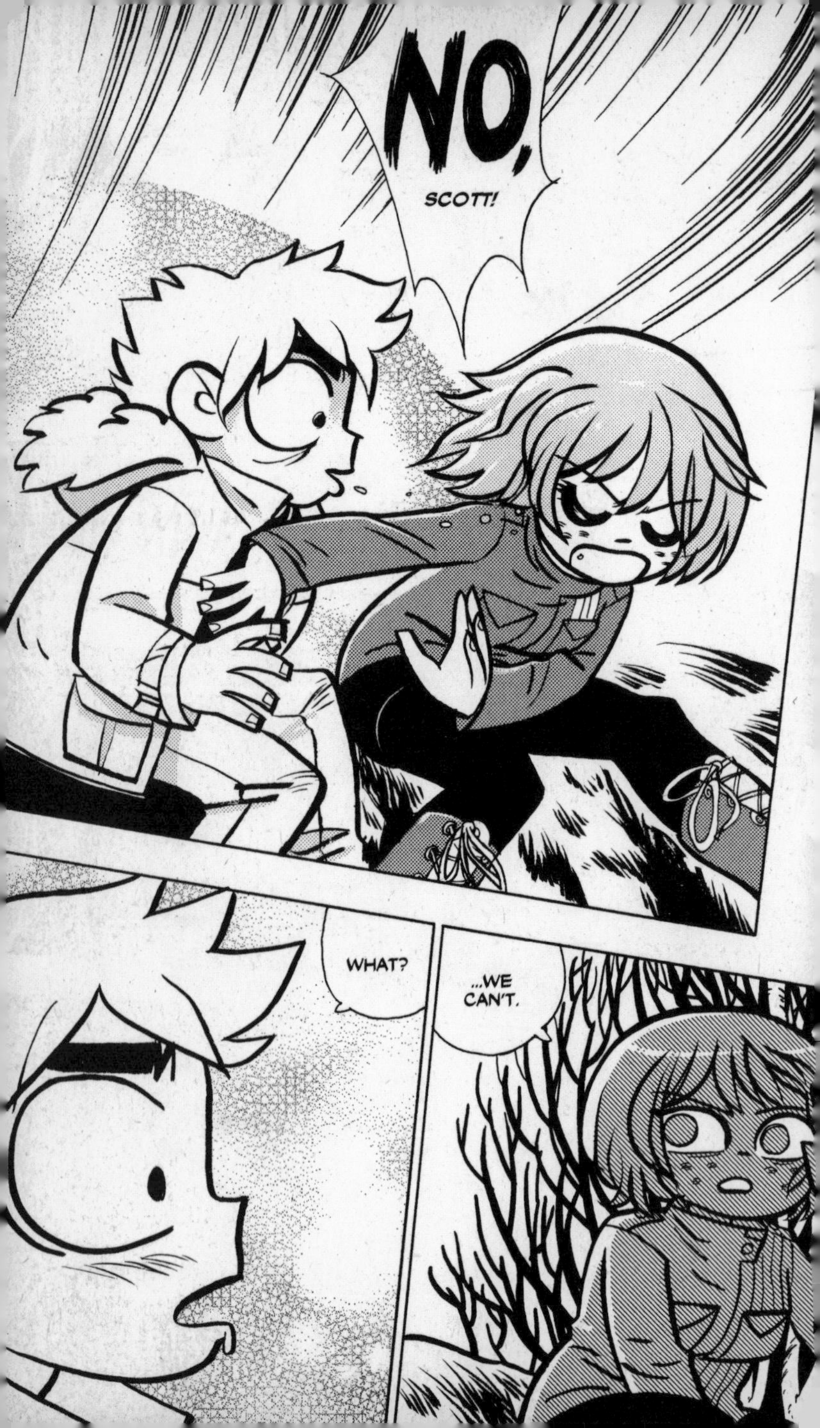
NO, SCOTT!
WHAT?
...WE CAN'T.

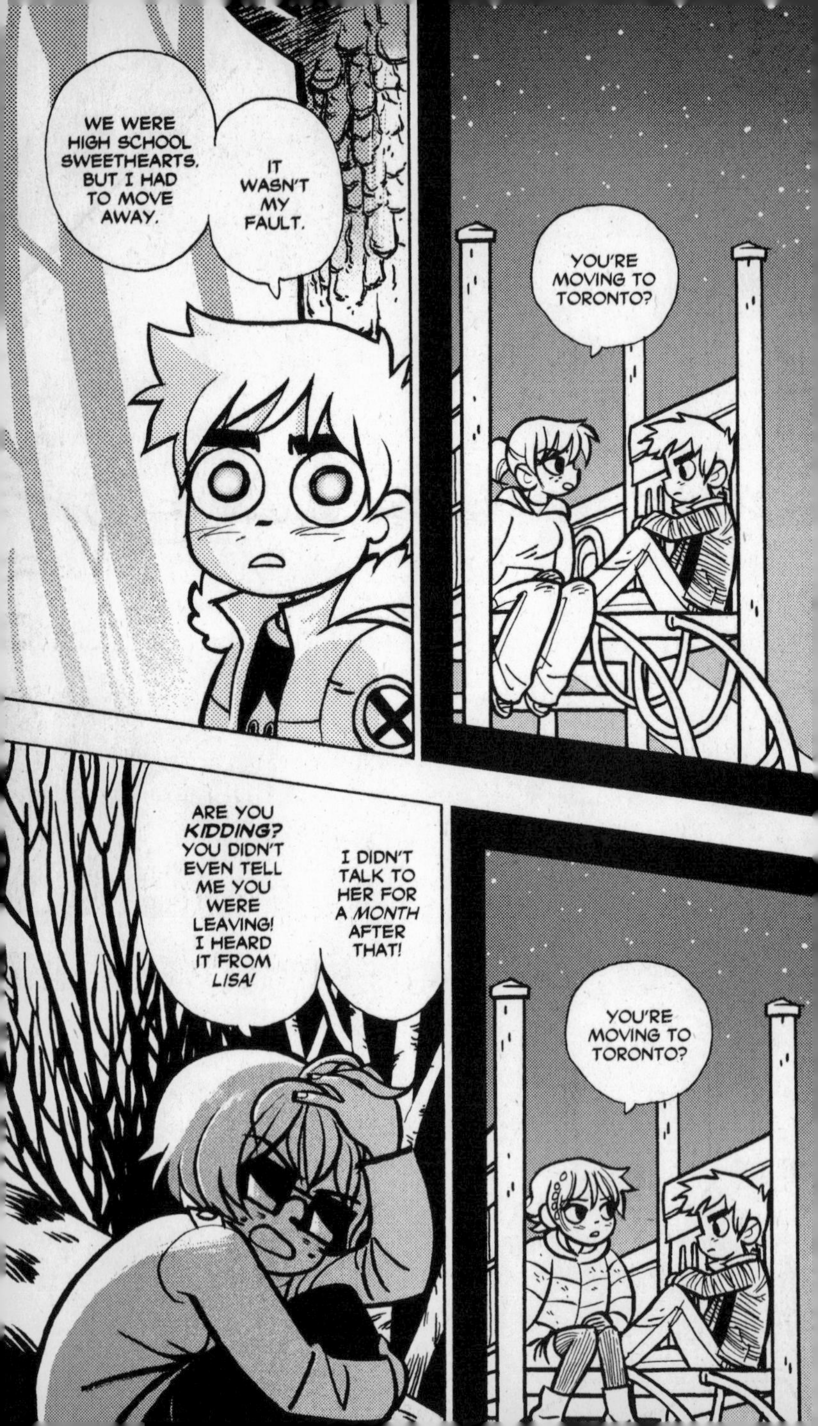
WE WERE HIGH SCHOOL SWEETHEARTS. BUT I HAD TO MOVE AWAY.
IT WASN'T MY FAULT.
YOU'RE MOVING TO TORONTO?
ARE YOU *KIDDING?* YOU DIDN'T EVEN TELL ME YOU WERE LEAVING! I HEARD IT FROM *LISA!*
I DIDN'T TALK TO HER FOR A *MONTH* AFTER THAT!
YOU'RE MOVING TO TORONTO?

NOT TO MENTION YOU CREWED OVER POOR SIMON LEE...

...WELL, WE BOTH DID, BUT THE LOOK ON HIS FACE...

RUB RUB

THIS IS THE BEST ST JOEL'S COULD MUSTER?

SIMON LEE?

BUT... HE WAS A BAD GUY.

I'VE BEEN A FOOL

YOU... NEVER CHANGE

SIMON LEE? THE CHINESE KID?

I WAS DATING HIM, SCOTT. I MEAN, I THINK HE HUGGED ME ONCE.

YOU'RE GOING DOWN, SIMON!!

SIMON

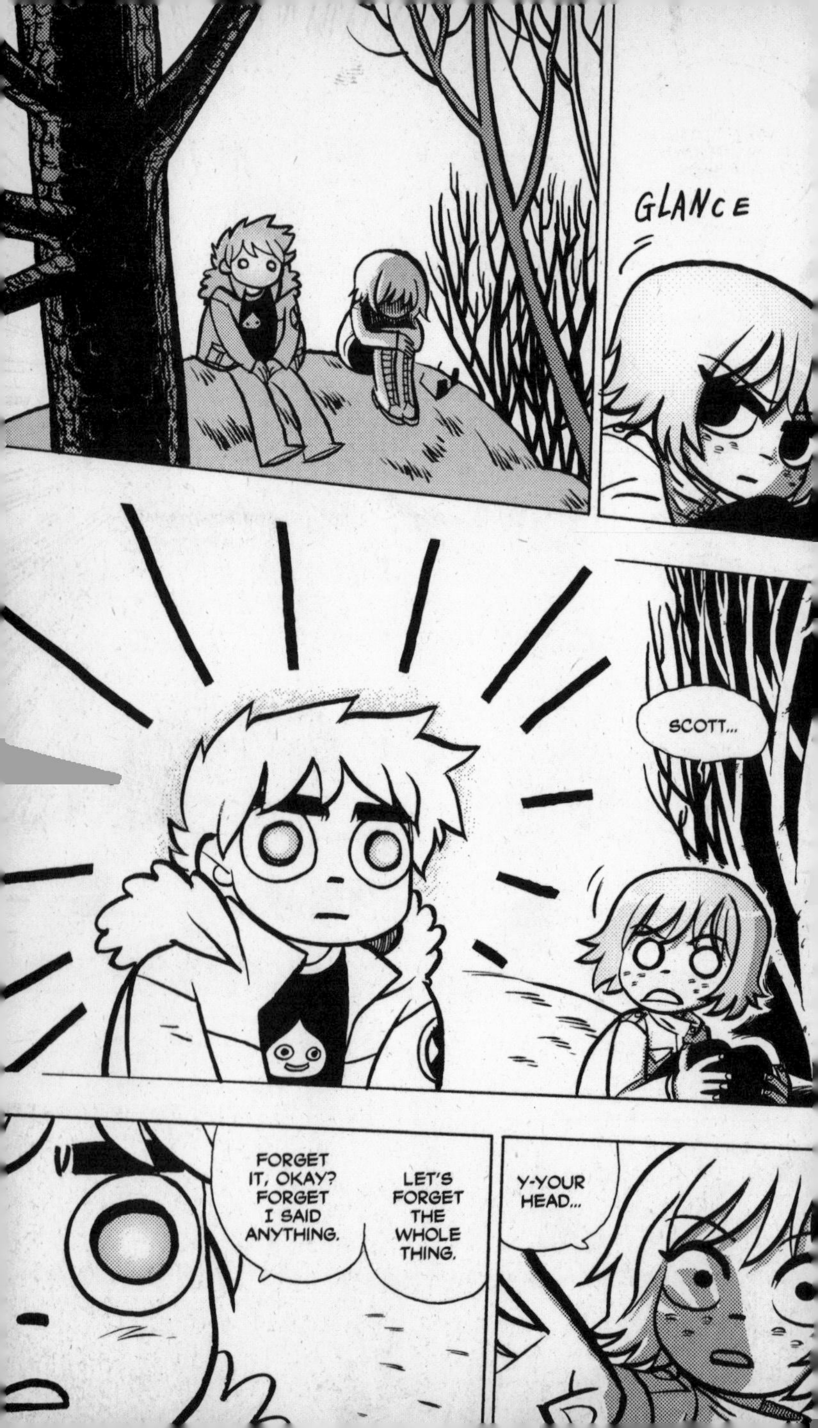
GLANCE
SCOTT...
FORGET IT, OKAY? FORGET I SAID ANYTHING.
LET'S FORGET THE WHOLE THING.
Y-YOUR HEAD...

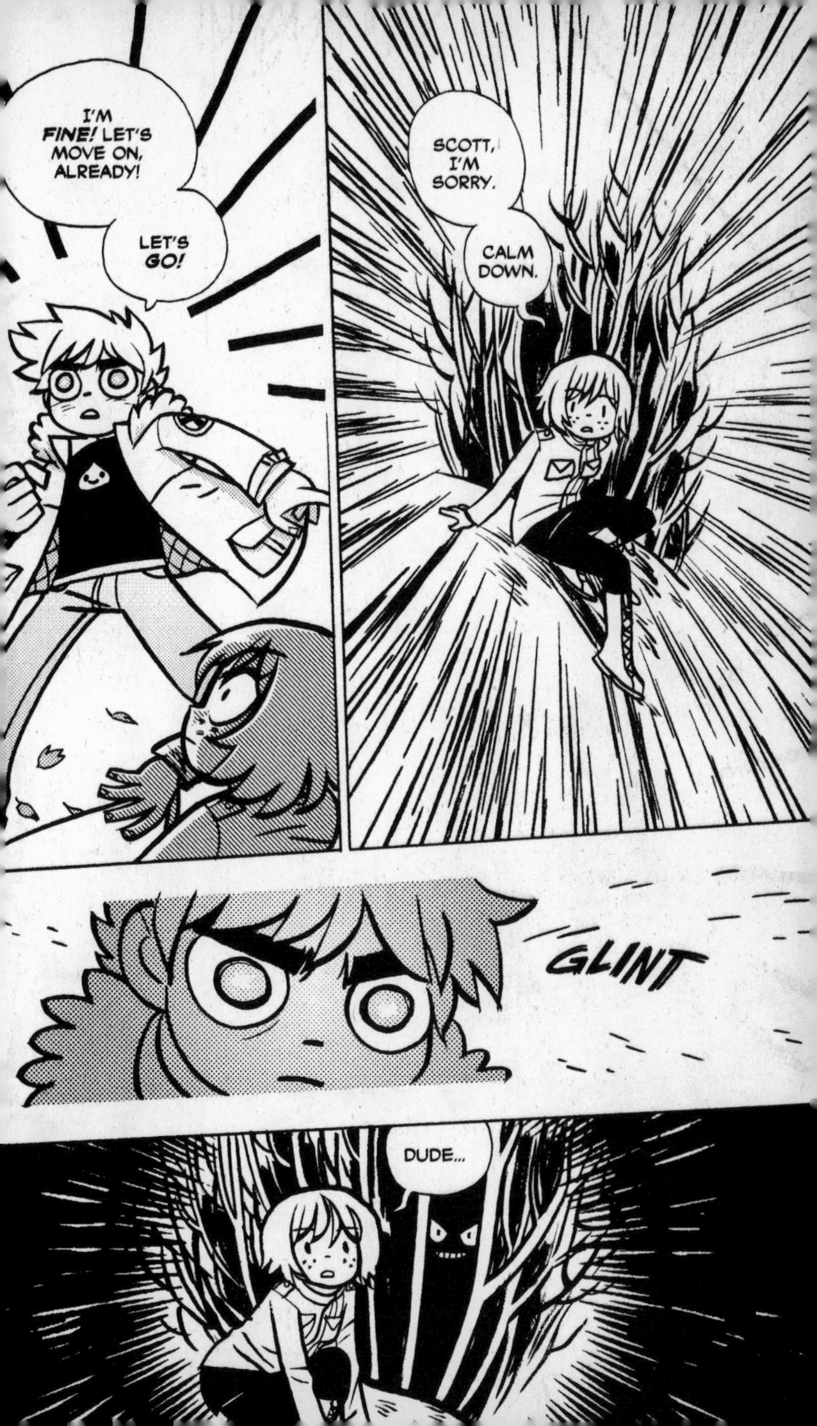
I'M *FINE!* LET'S MOVE ON, ALREADY!
LET'S *GO!*
SCOTT, I'M SORRY.
CALM DOWN.
GLINT
DUDE...

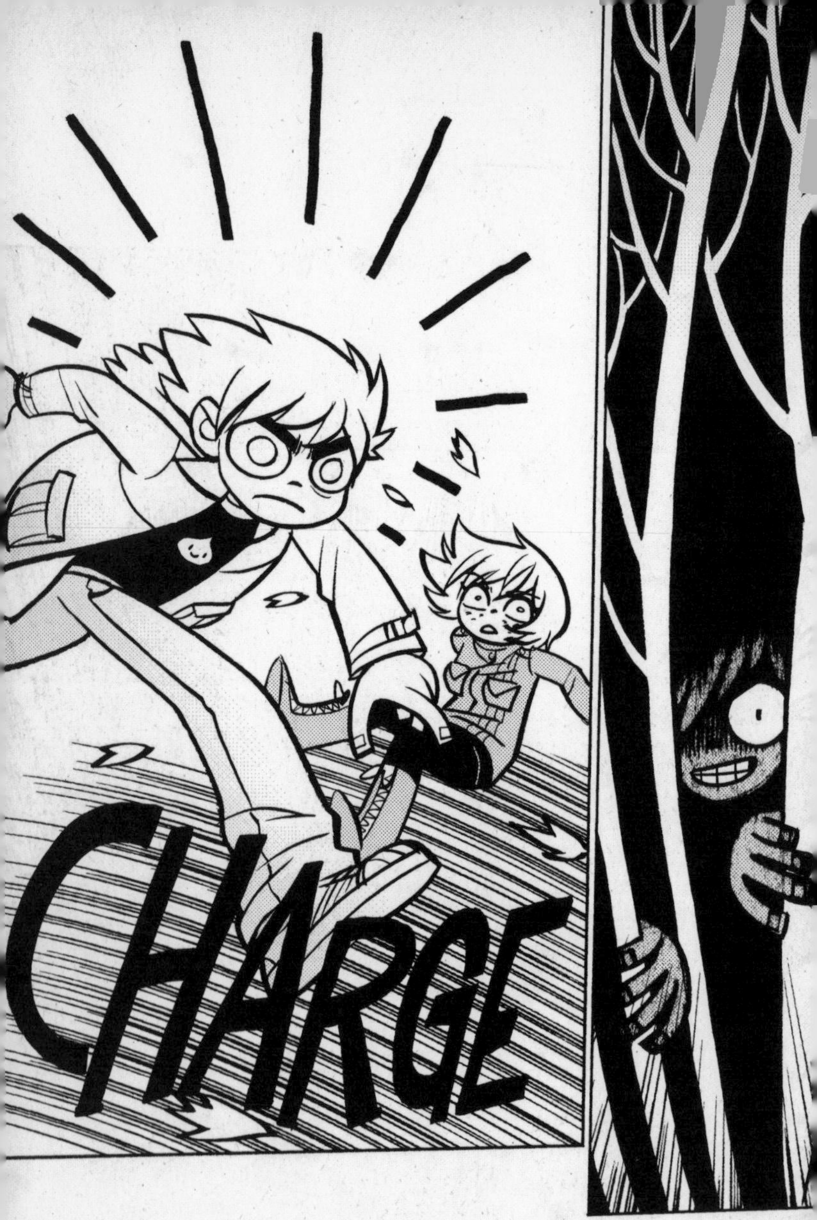
CHARGE

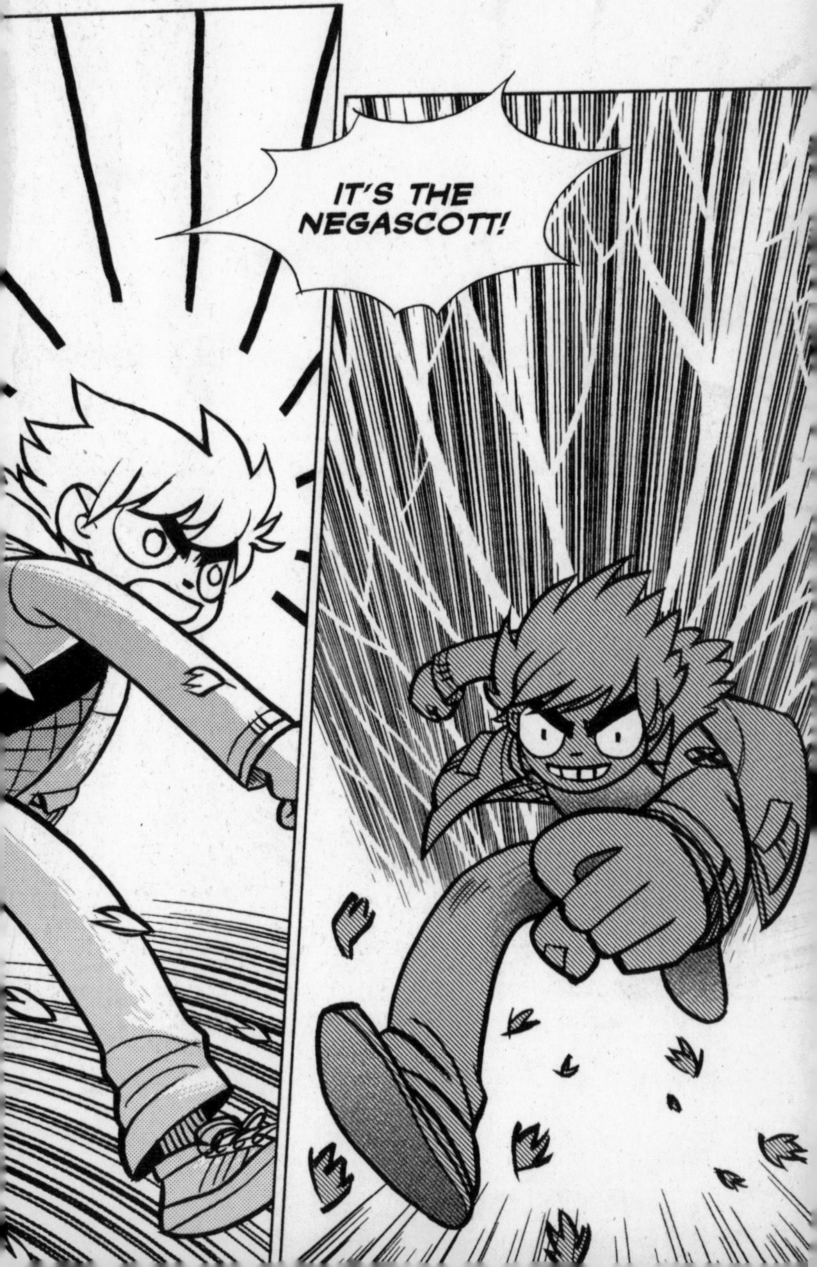
IT'S THE NEGASCOTT!

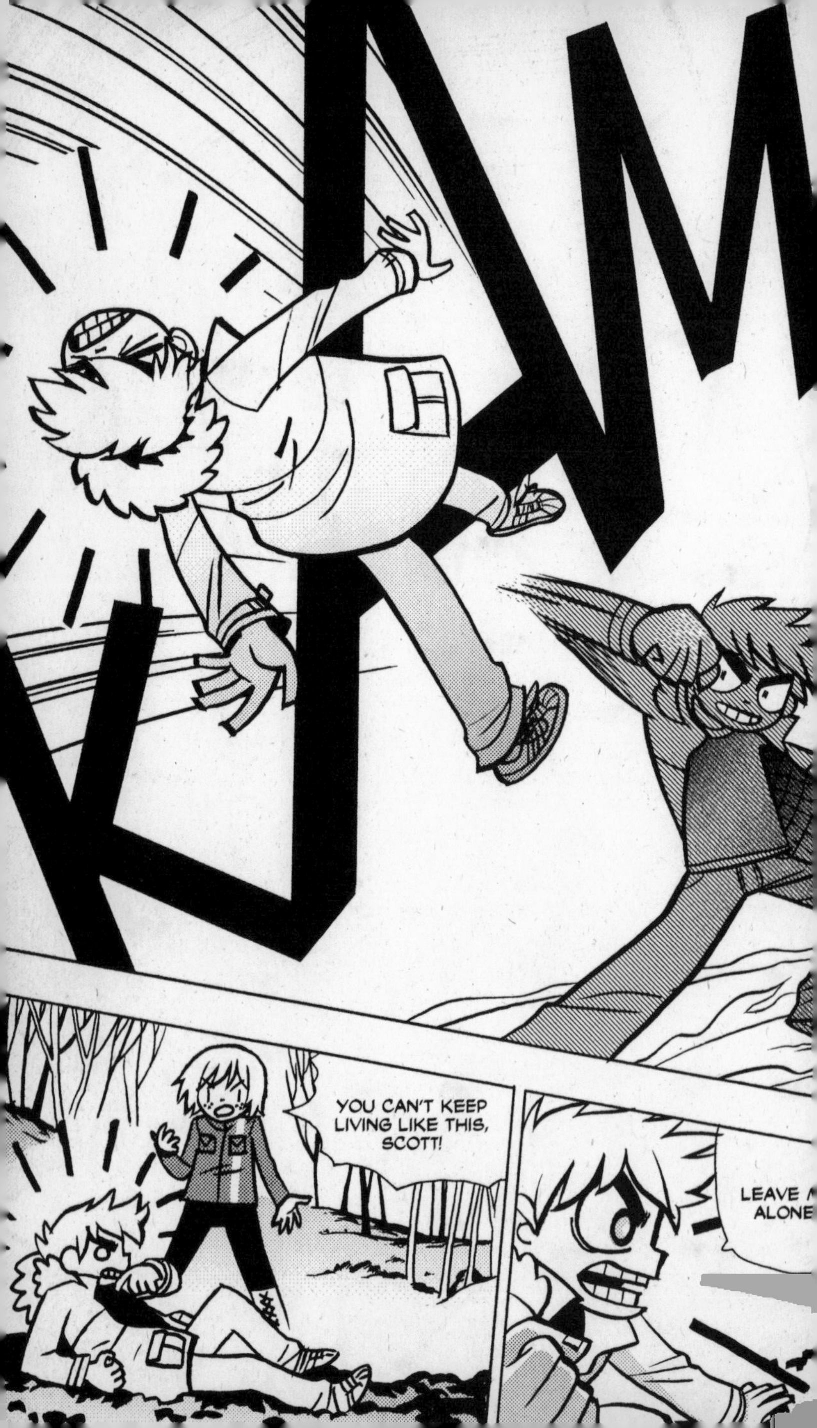
YOU CAN'T KEEP LIVING LIKE THIS, SCOTT!
LEAVE M
ALONE

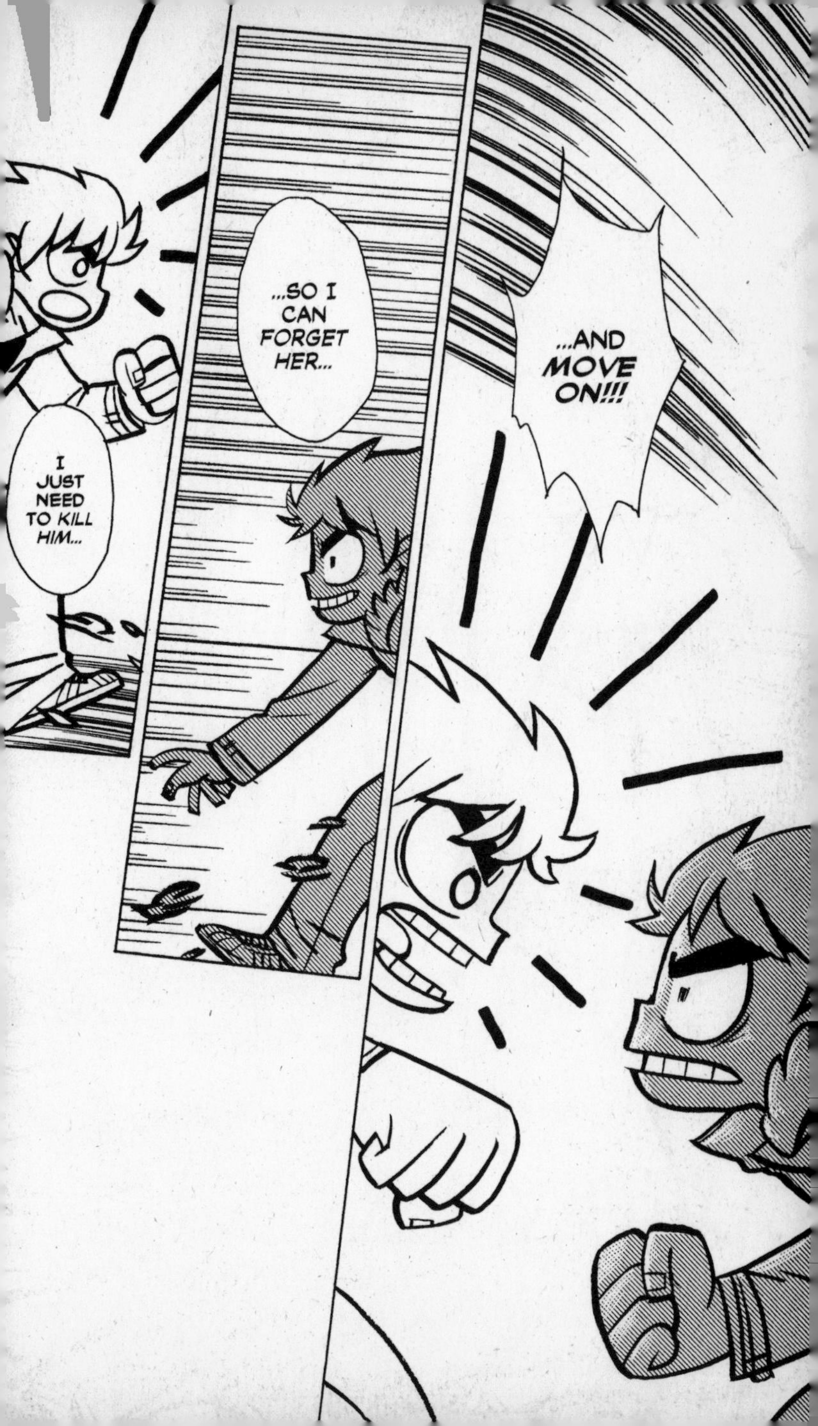
I JUST NEED TO KILL HIM...
...SO I CAN FORGET HER...
...AND MOVE ON!!!

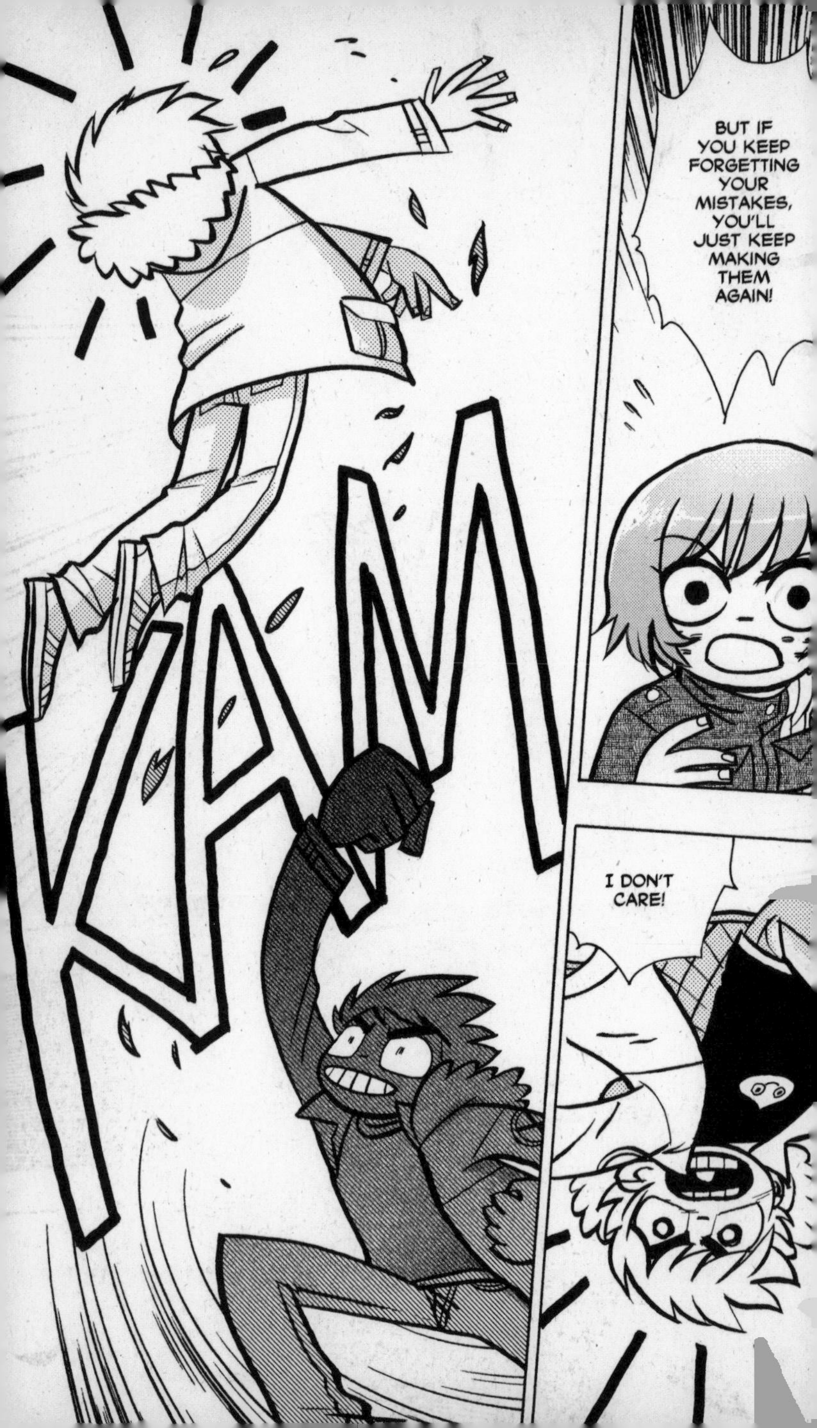
KAM
BUT IF YOU KEEP FORGETTING YOUR MISTAKES, YOU'LL JUST KEEP MAKING THEM AGAIN!
I DON'T CARE!

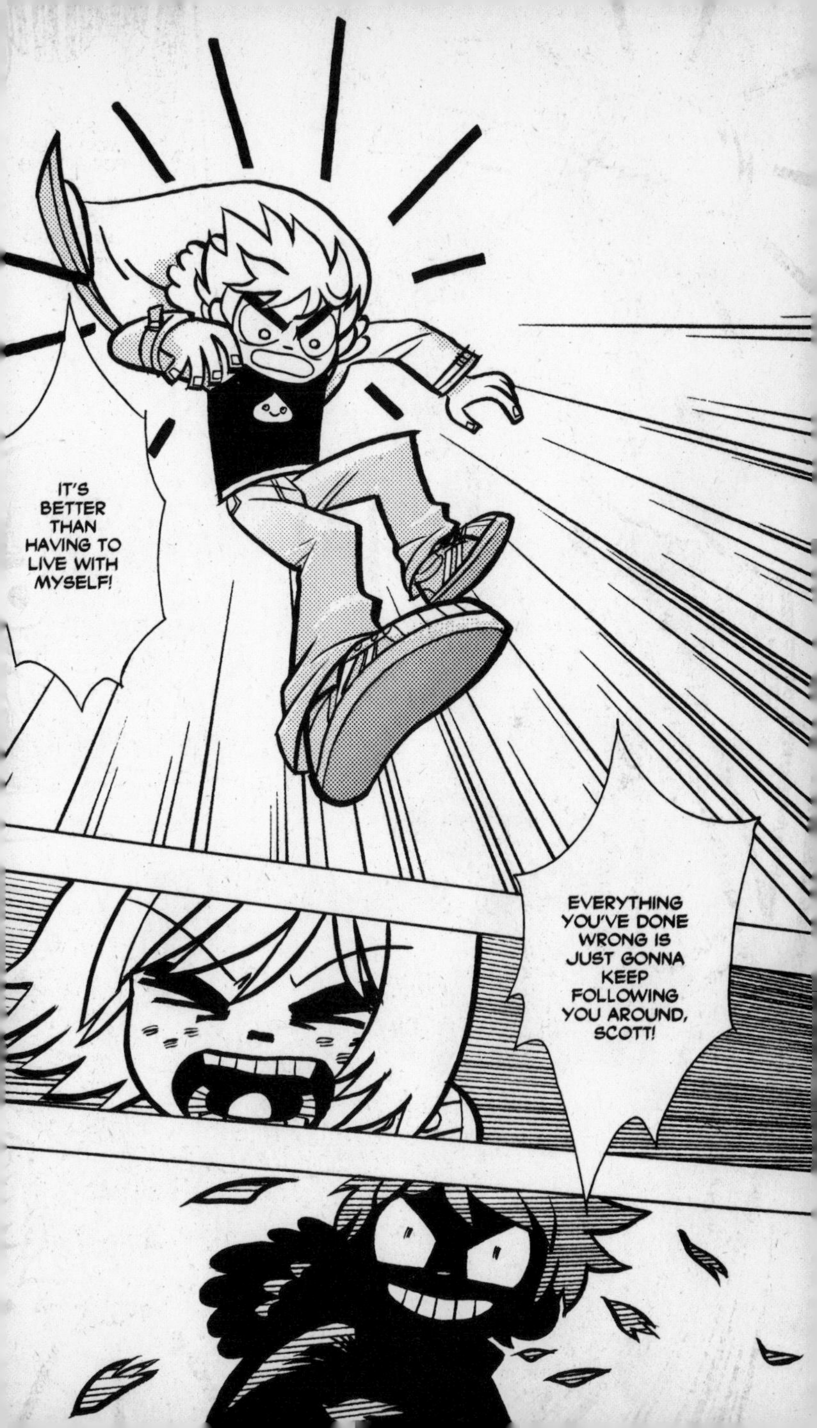
IT'S BETTER THAN HAVING TO LIVE WITH MYSELF!
EVERYTHING YOU'VE DONE WRONG IS JUST GONNA KEEP FOLLOWING YOU AROUND, SCOTT!

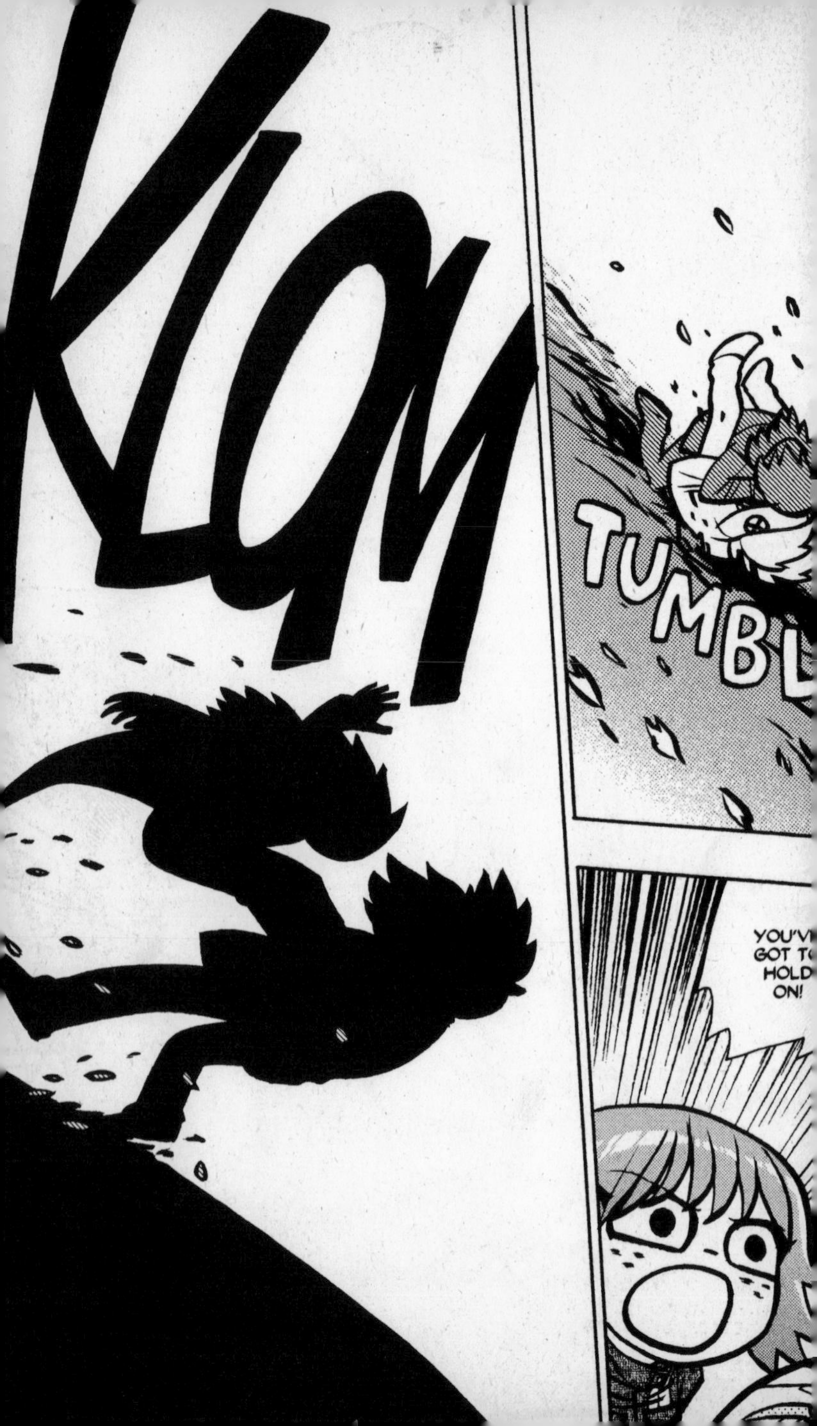
KLAM
TUMBL
YOU'V GOT T HOLD ON!

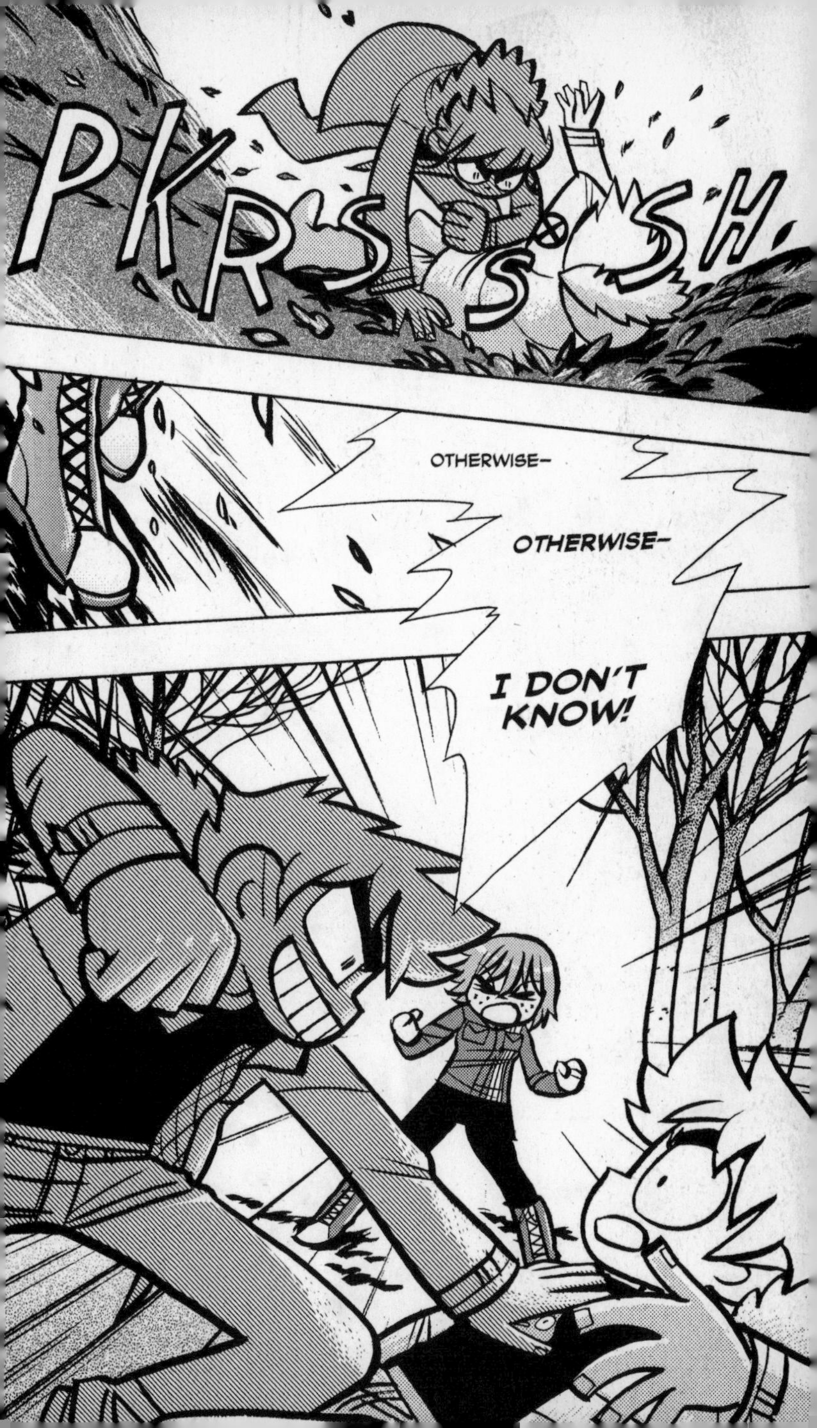
PKRSSSH
OTHERWISE–
OTHERWISE–
I DON'T KNOW!

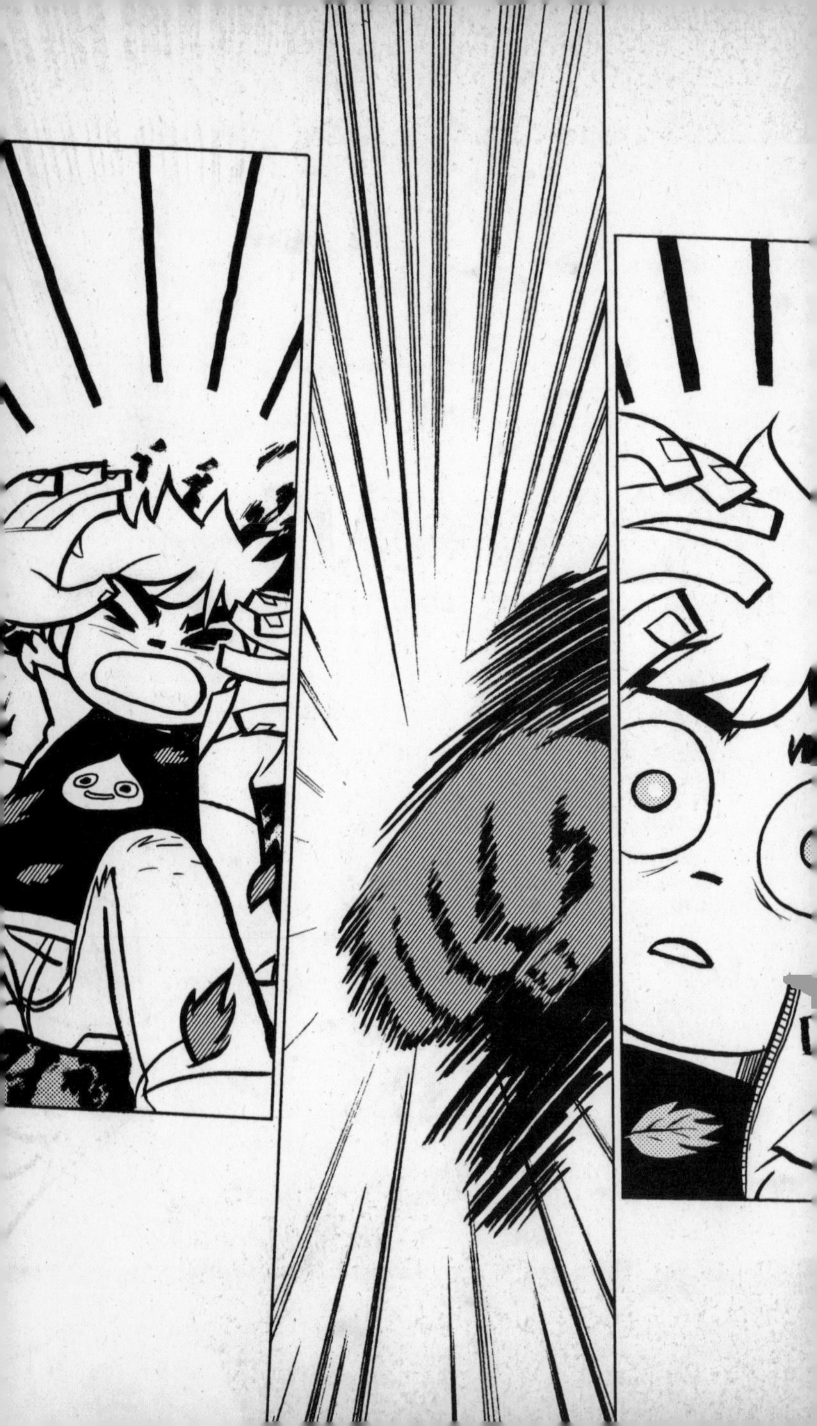

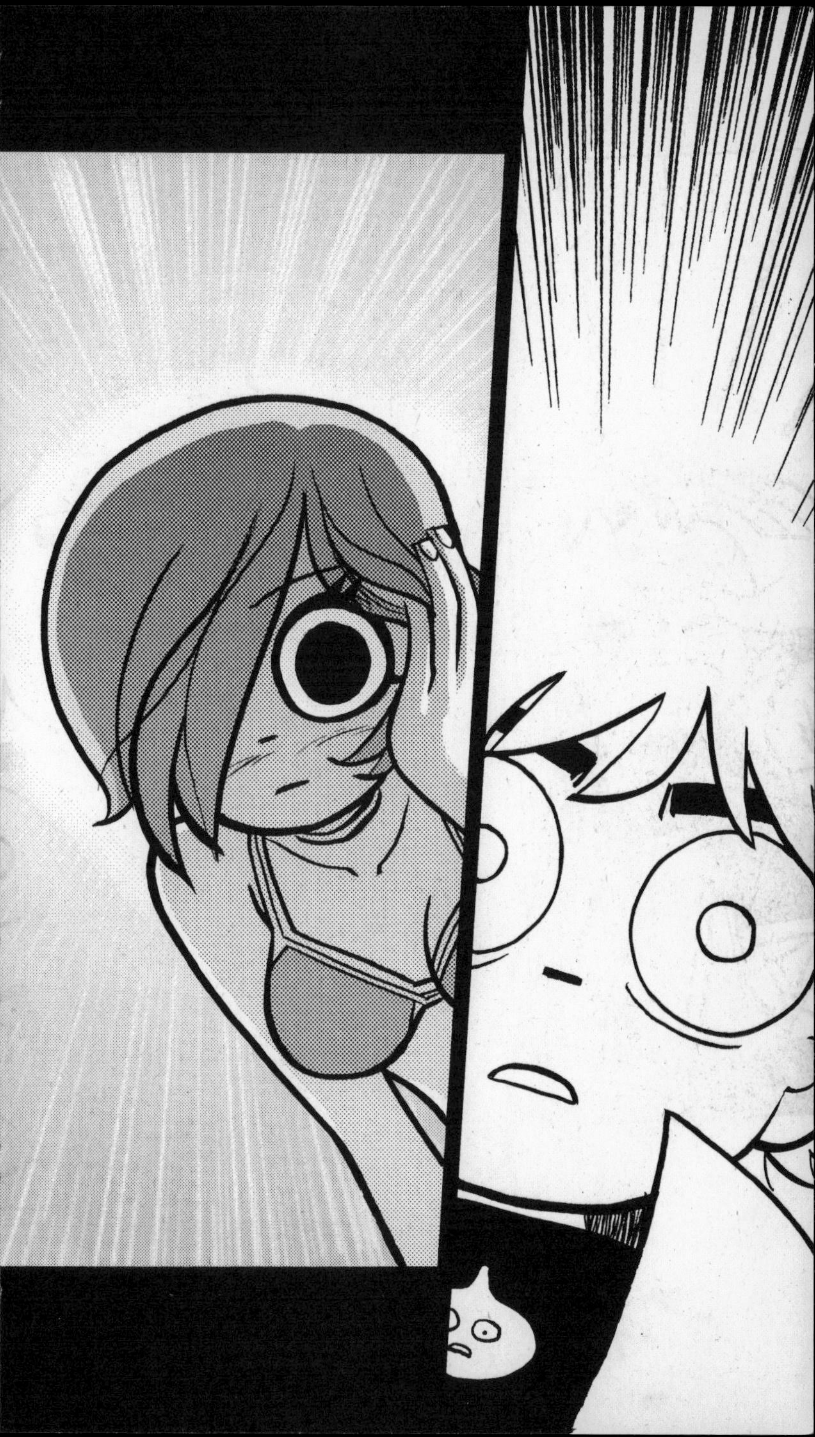

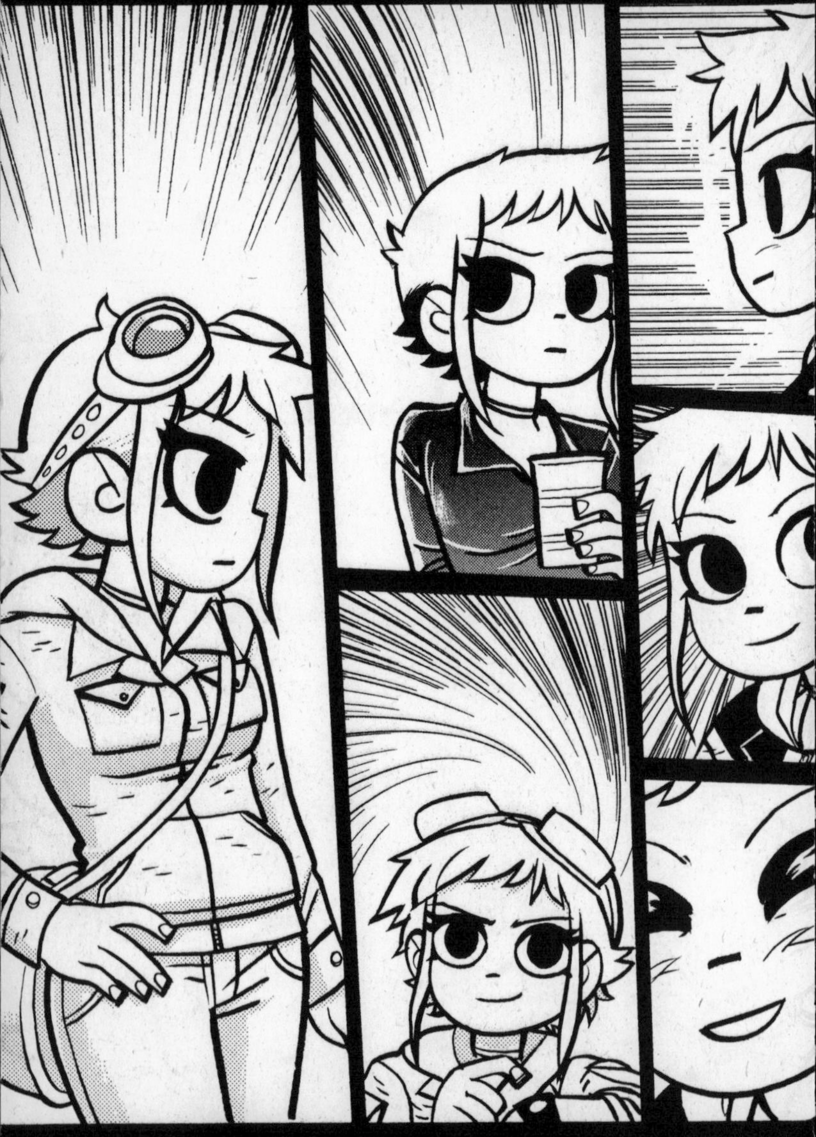

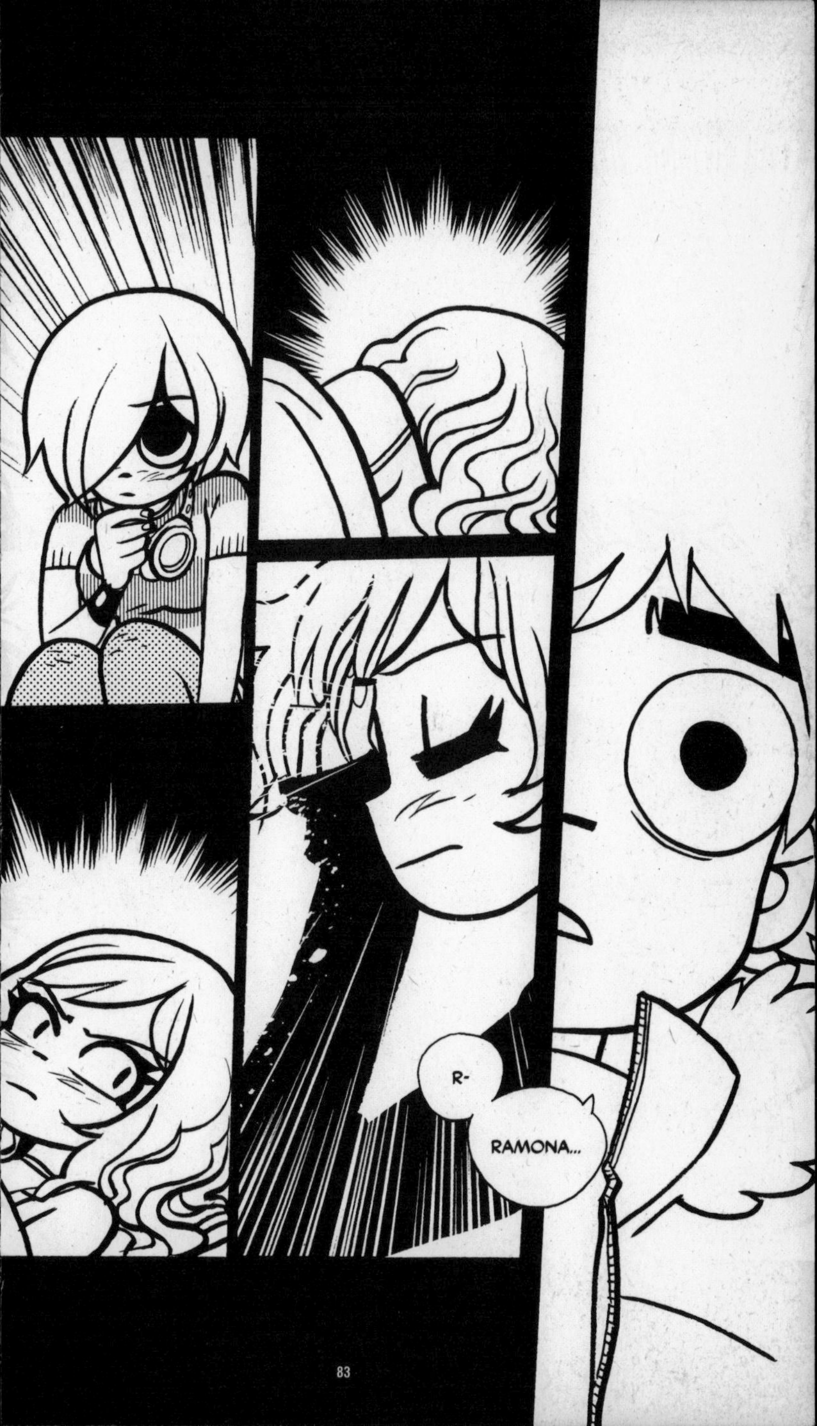
R-
RAMONA...

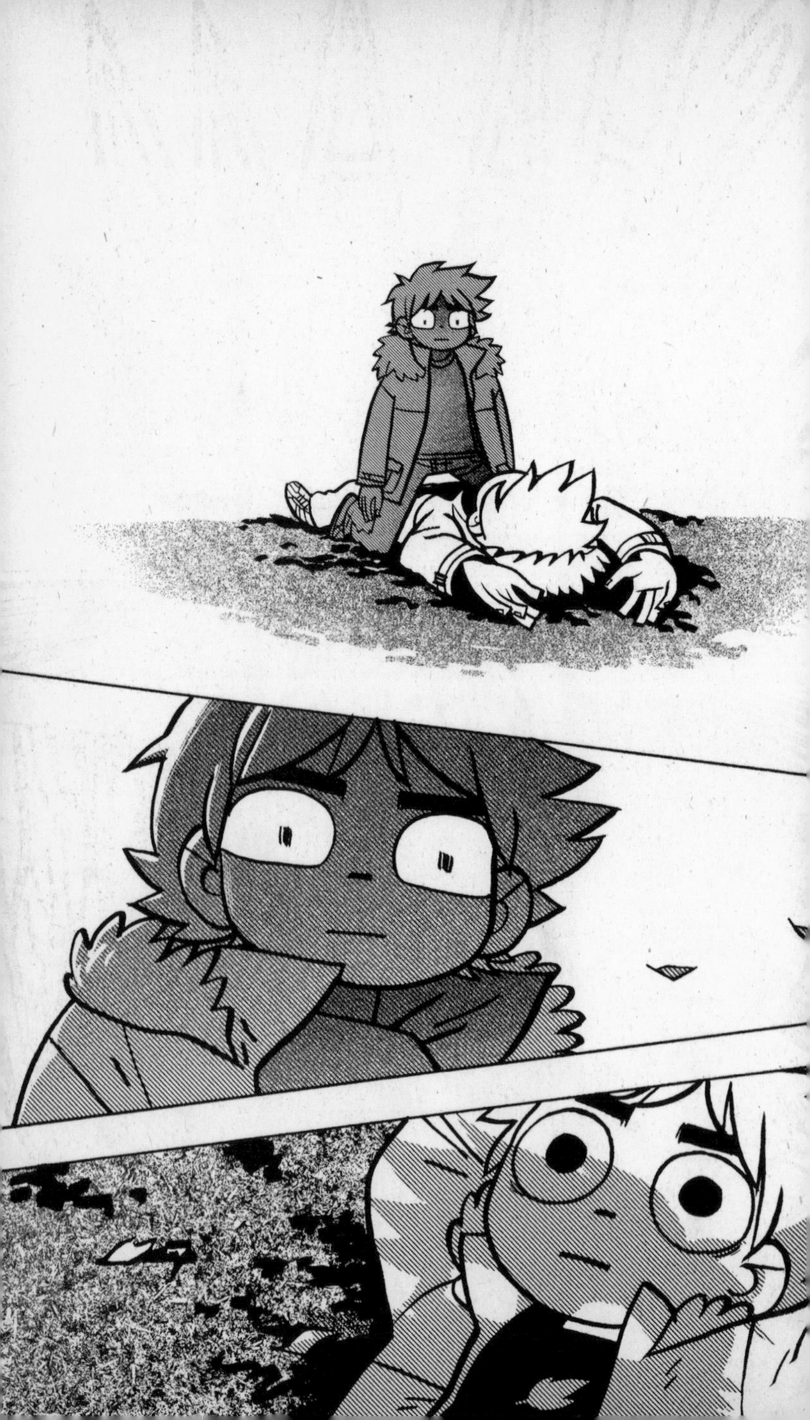

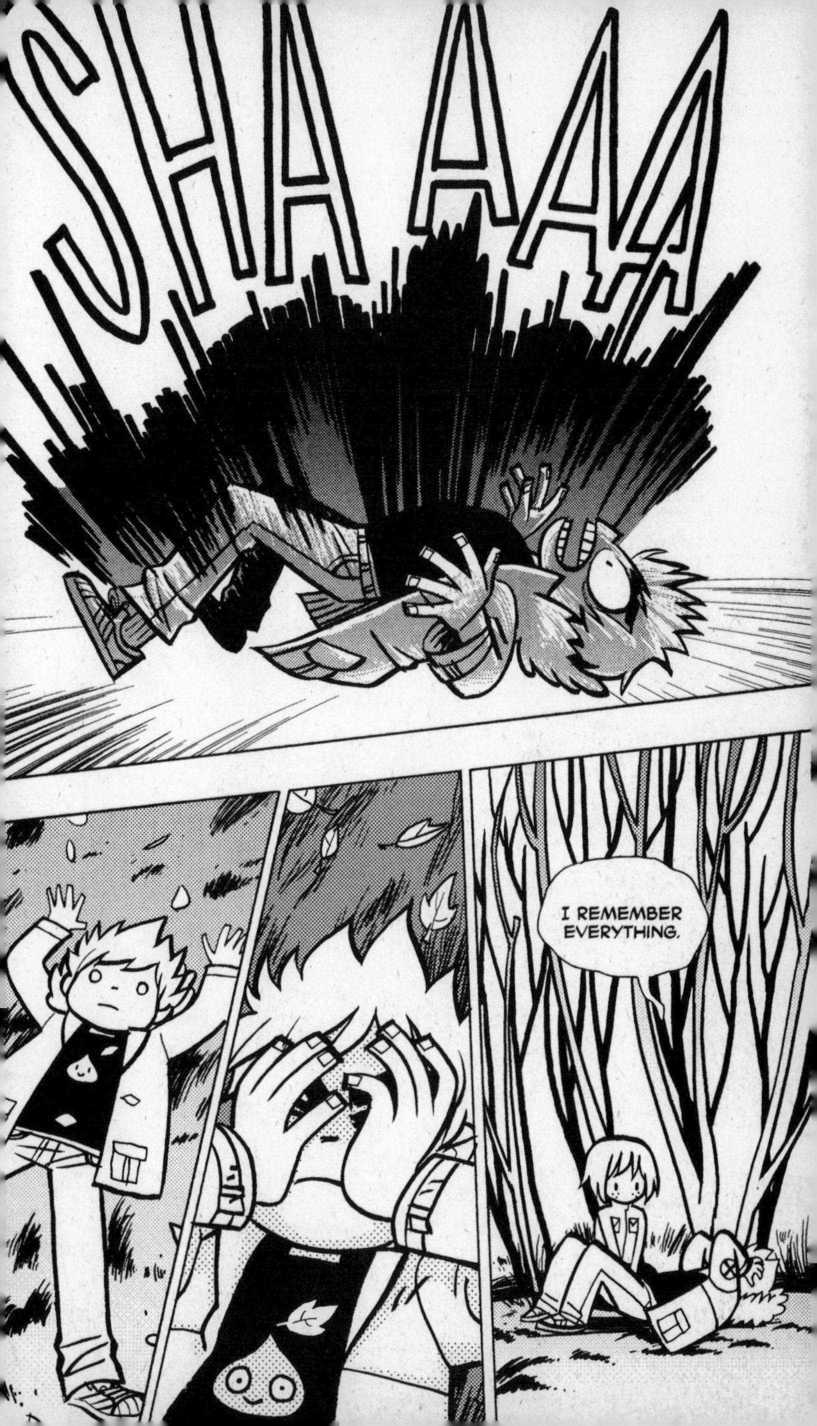
SHAAAA
I REMEMBER EVERYTHING.

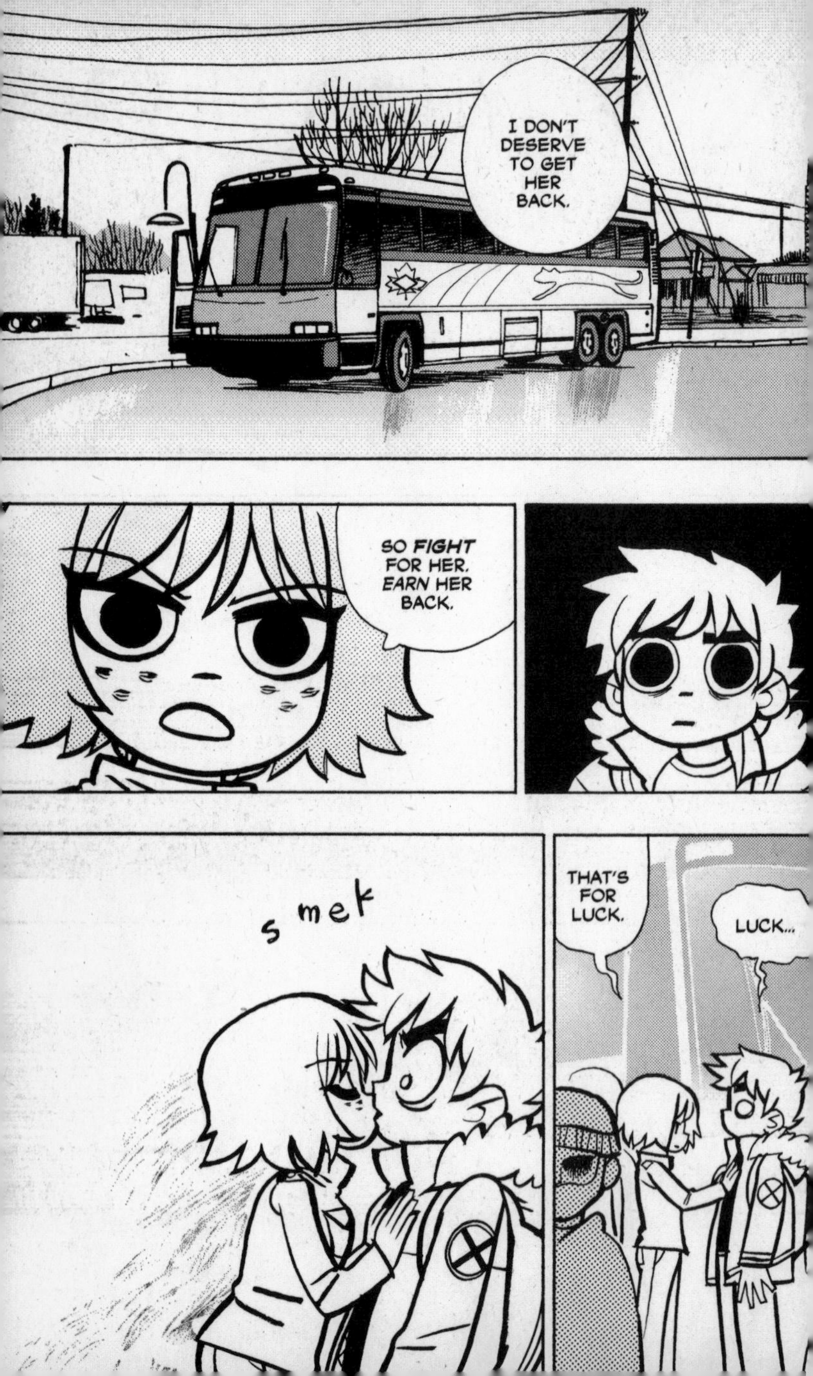
I DON'T DESERVE TO GET HER BACK.
SO *FIGHT* FOR HER. *EARN* HER BACK.
smek
THAT'S FOR LUCK.
LUCK...

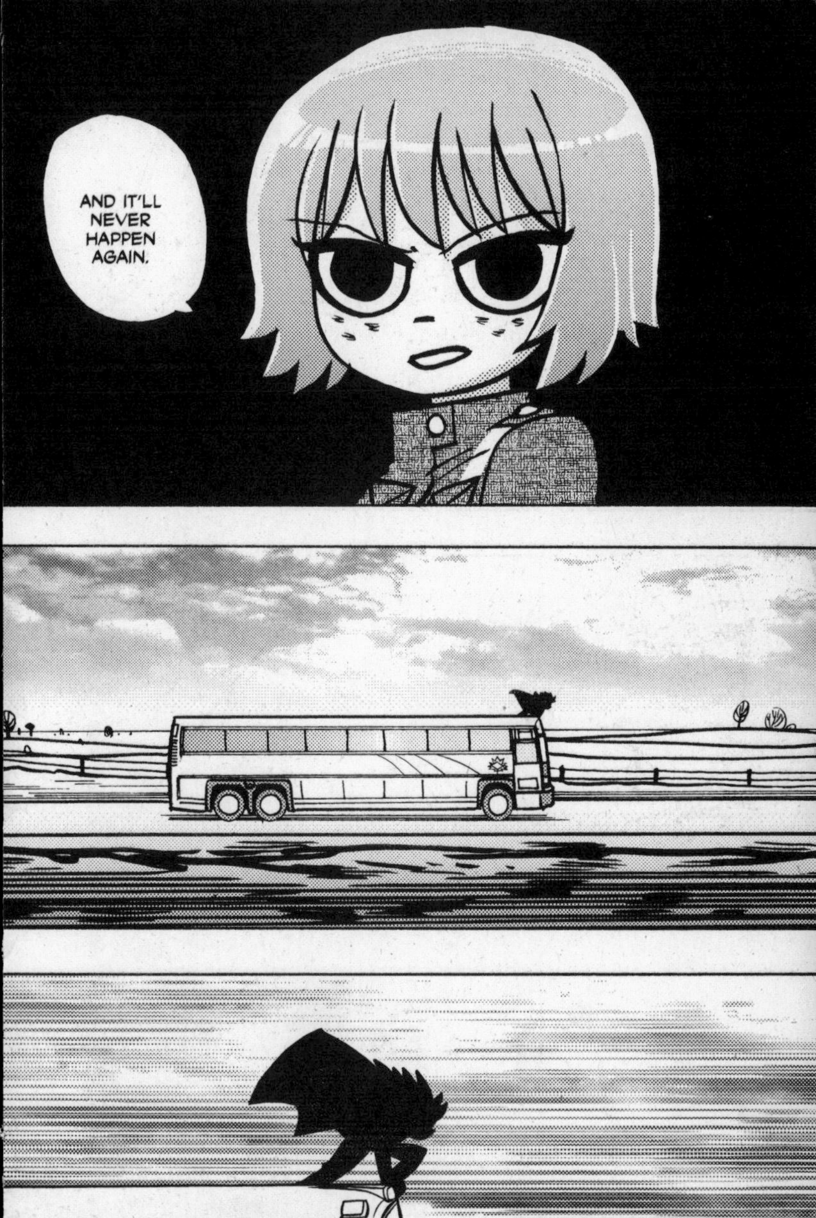
AND IT'LL NEVER HAPPEN AGAIN.

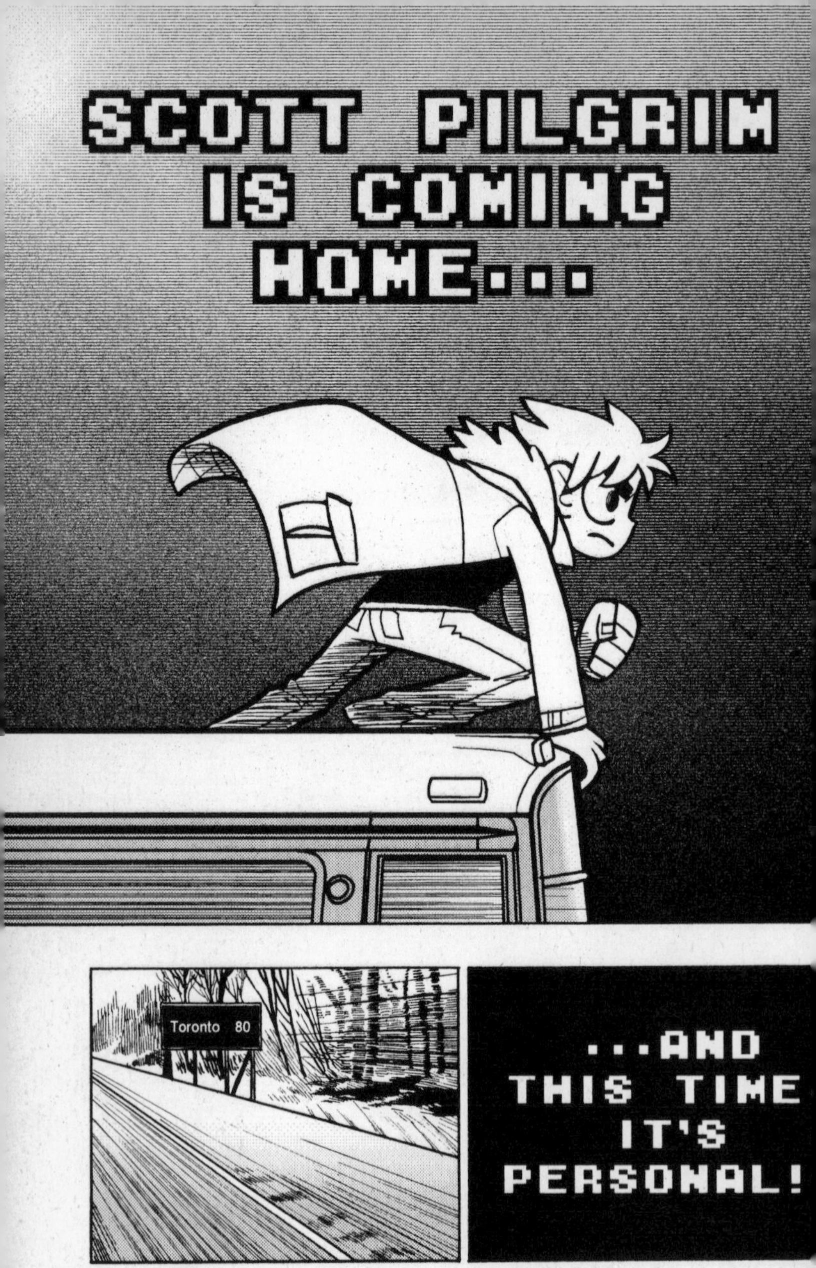
SCOTT PILGRIM IS COMING HOME...
Toronto 80
...AND THIS TIME IT'S PERSONAL!

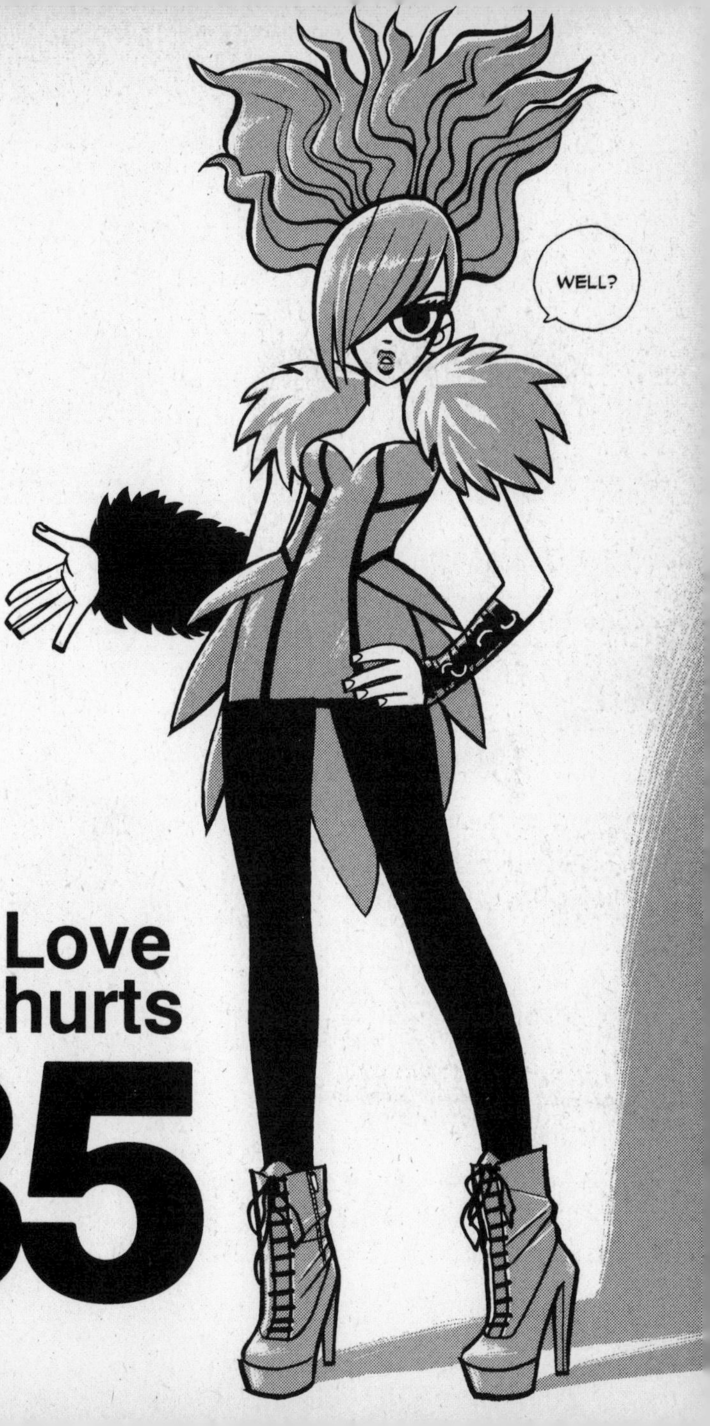
WELL?

Love hurts

35

MMM... I DUNNO.

MAYBE LOSE THE SHOULDERS.

GIDEON GRAVES
(31 YEARS OLD)

OCCUPATION:
ASSHOLE

I WANT SOME OPTIONS ON THE SHOES.

AND HAIR, PEOPLE, MY G PLEASE. I W YOU TO BUILD BONFIRE IN H HAIR. THAT IS METAPHOR

BACKSTAGE

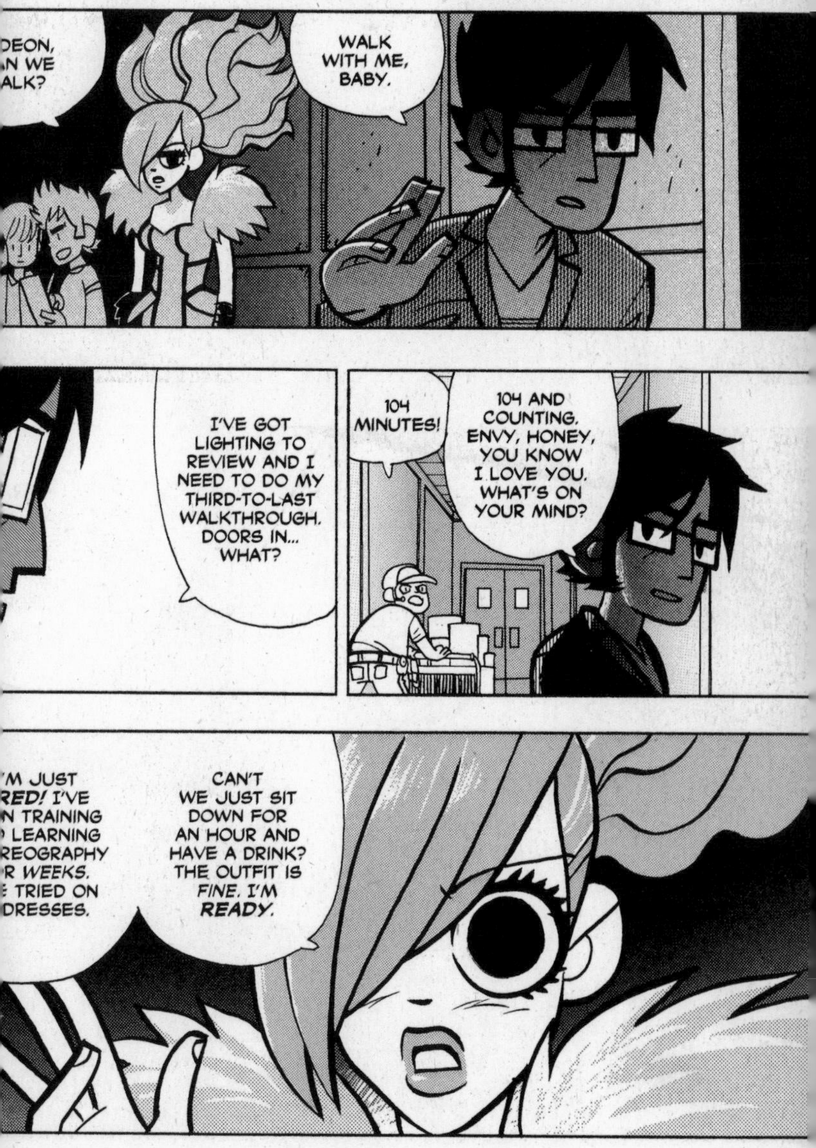

DEON, N WE ALK?
WALK WITH ME, BABY.
I'VE GOT LIGHTING TO REVIEW AND I NEED TO DO MY THIRD-TO-LAST WALKTHROUGH. DOORS IN... WHAT?
104 MINUTES!
104 AND COUNTING. ENVY, HONEY, YOU KNOW I LOVE YOU. WHAT'S ON YOUR MIND?
'M JUST RED! I'VE N TRAINING LEARNING REOGRAPHY R WEEKS. TRIED ON DRESSES.
CAN'T WE JUST SIT DOWN FOR AN HOUR AND HAVE A DRINK? THE OUTFIT IS FINE. I'M READY.

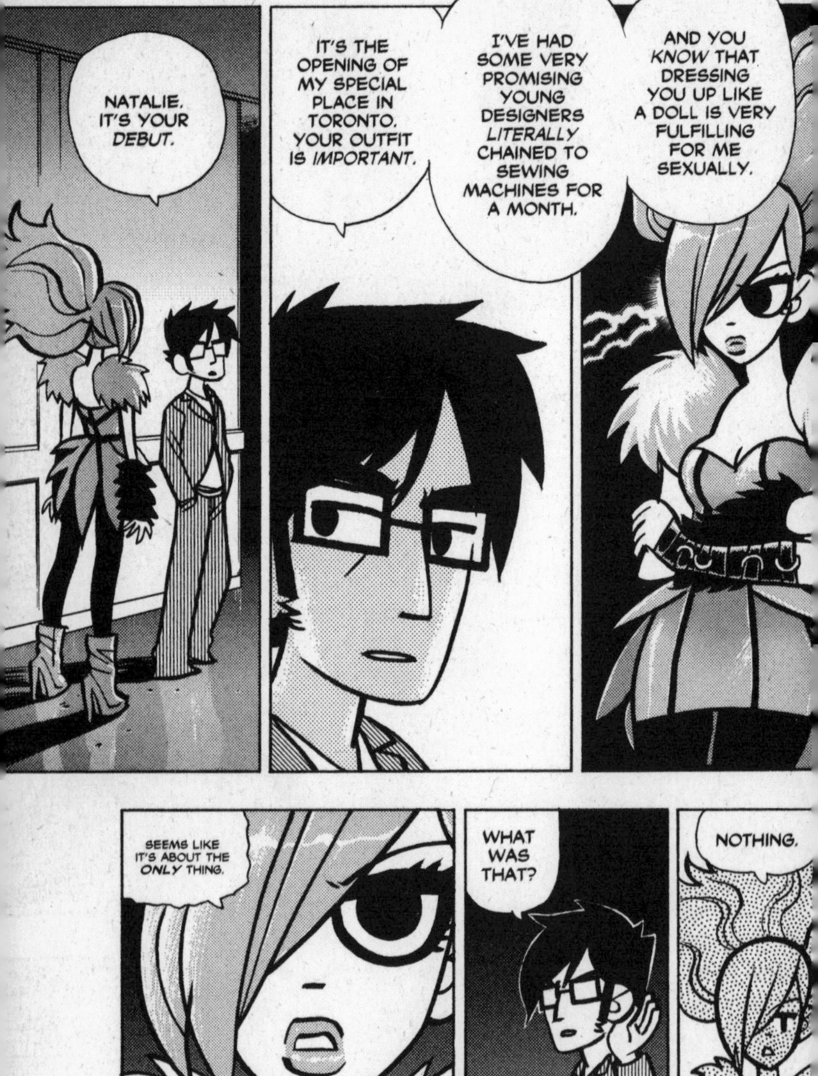
NATALIE. IT'S YOUR DEBUT.
IT'S THE OPENING OF MY SPECIAL PLACE IN TORONTO. YOUR OUTFIT IS IMPORTANT.
I'VE HAD SOME VERY PROMISING YOUNG DESIGNERS LITERALLY CHAINED TO SEWING MACHINES FOR A MONTH.
AND YOU KNOW THAT DRESSING YOU UP LIKE A DOLL IS VERY FULFILLING FOR ME SEXUALLY.
SEEMS LIKE IT'S ABOUT THE ONLY THING.
WHAT WAS THAT?
NOTHING.

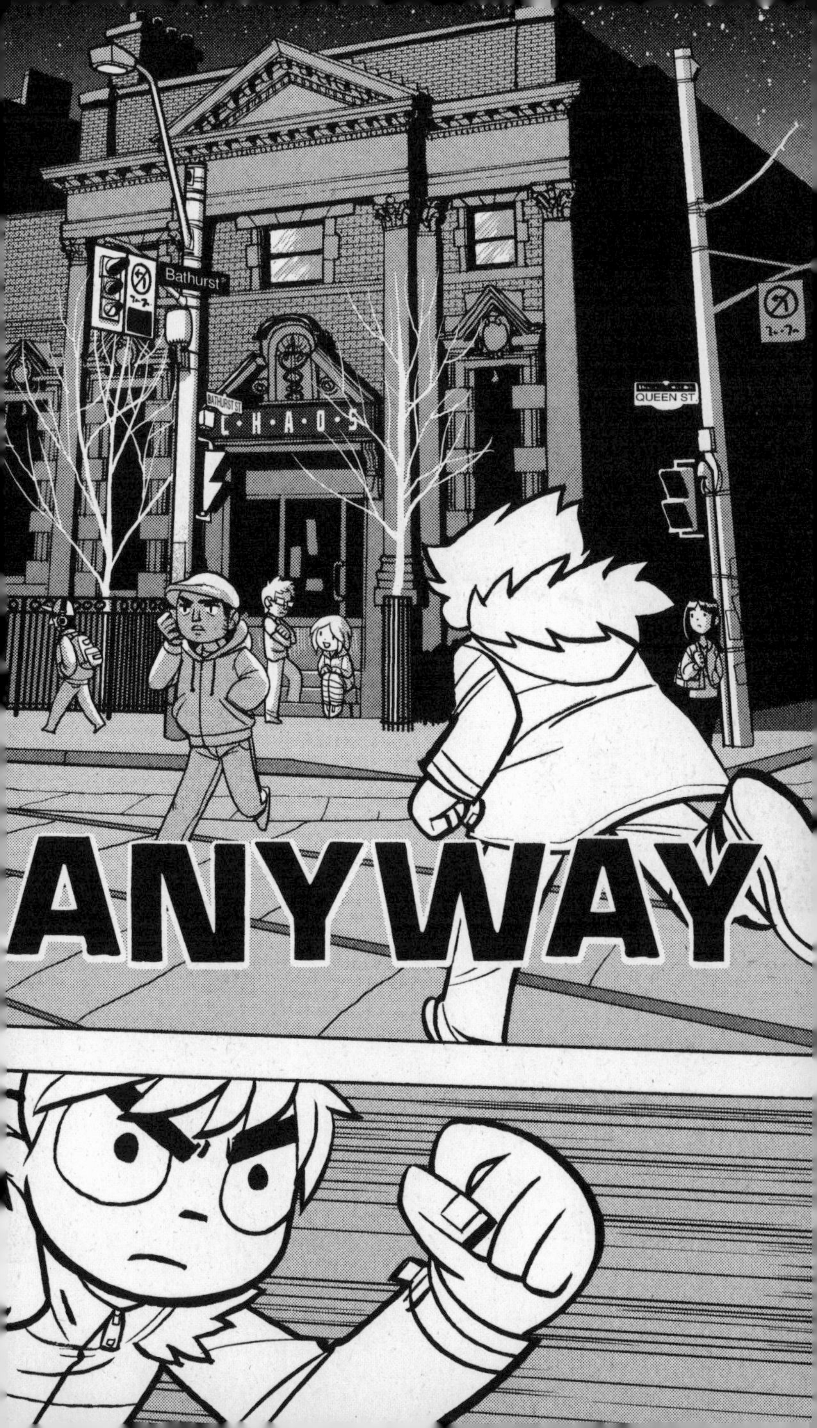
Bathurst St
QUEEN ST.
BATHURST ST
C·H·A·O·S
ANYWAY

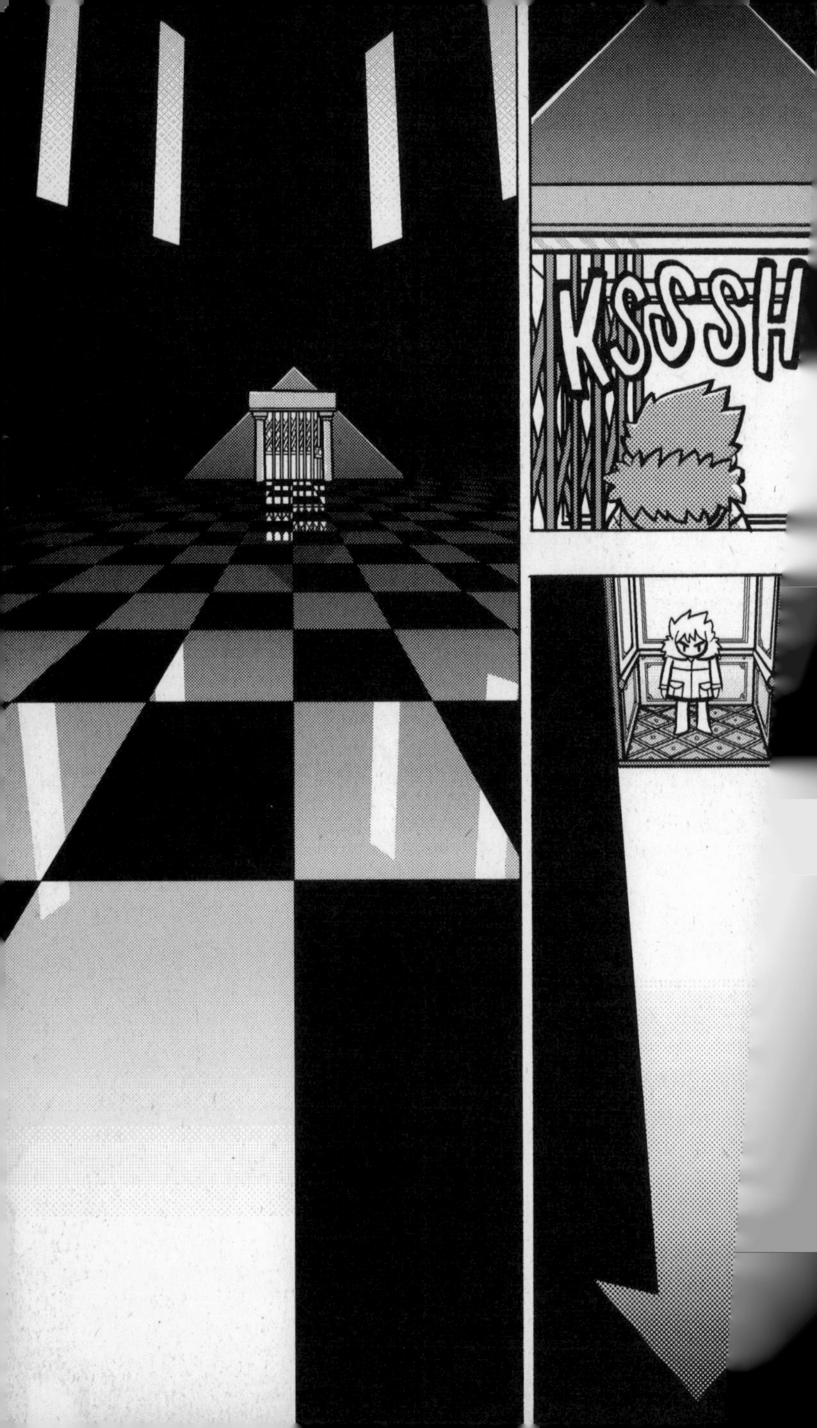
KSSSH

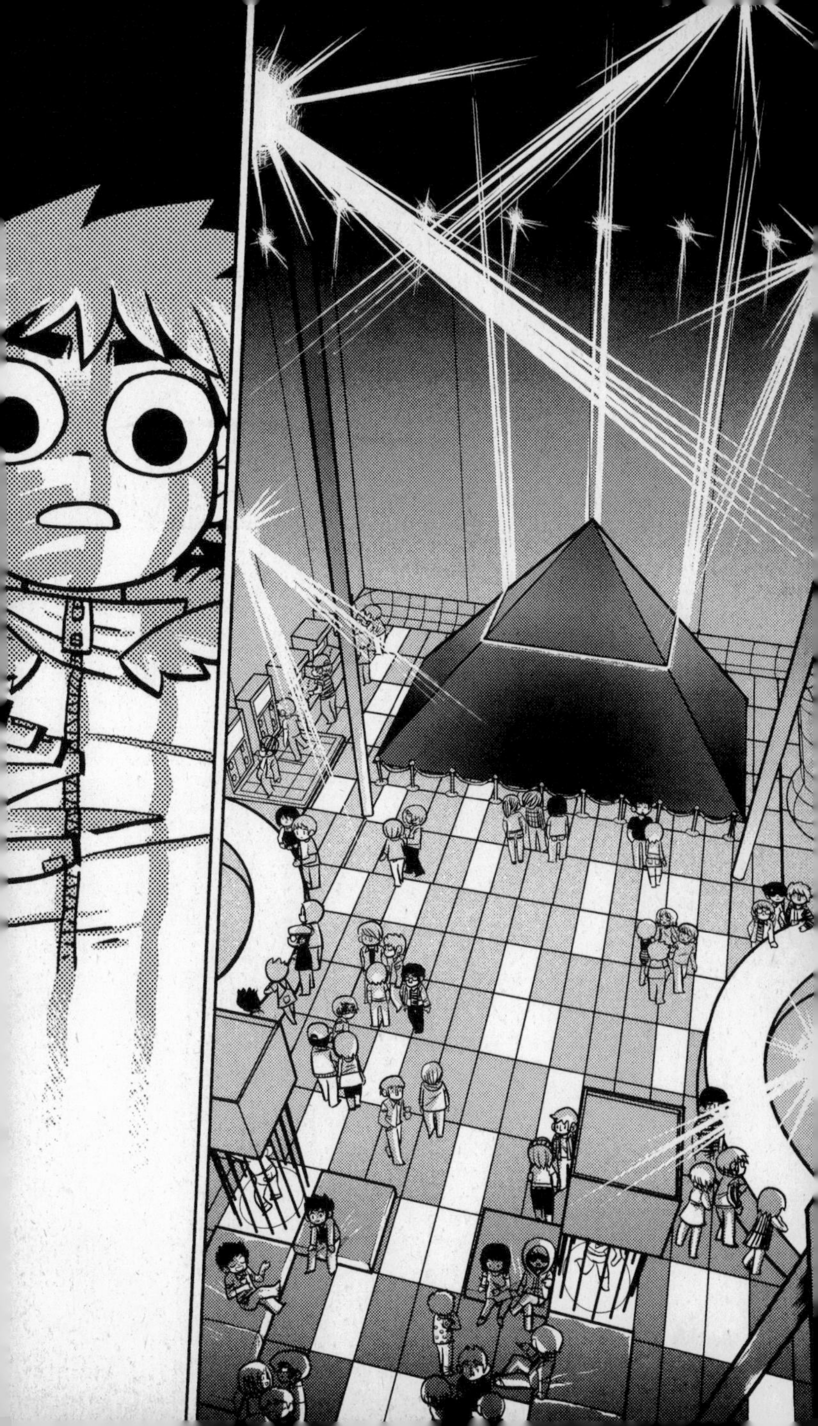

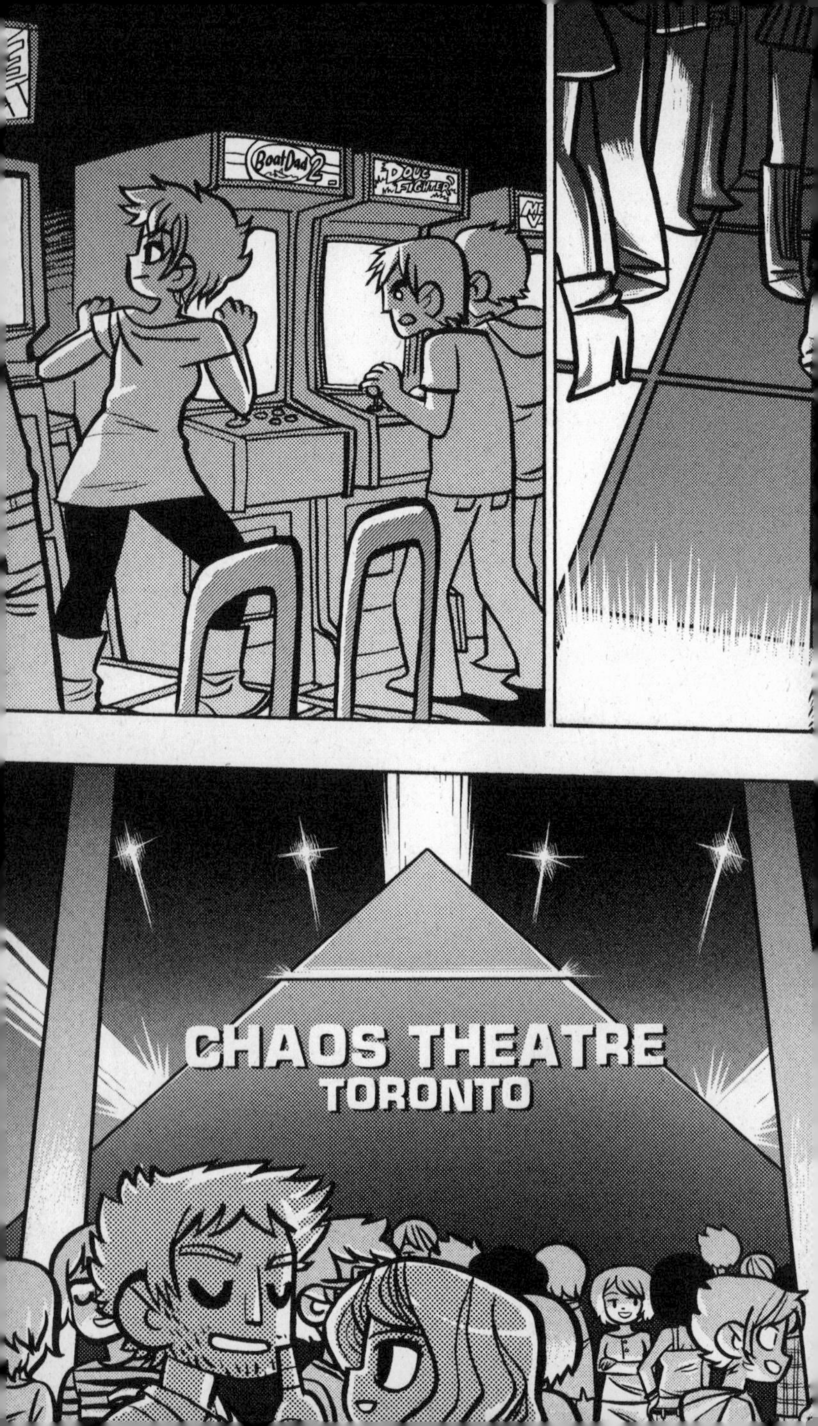

Boat Dad 2
DOUG FIGHTER
CHAOS THEATRE
TORONTO

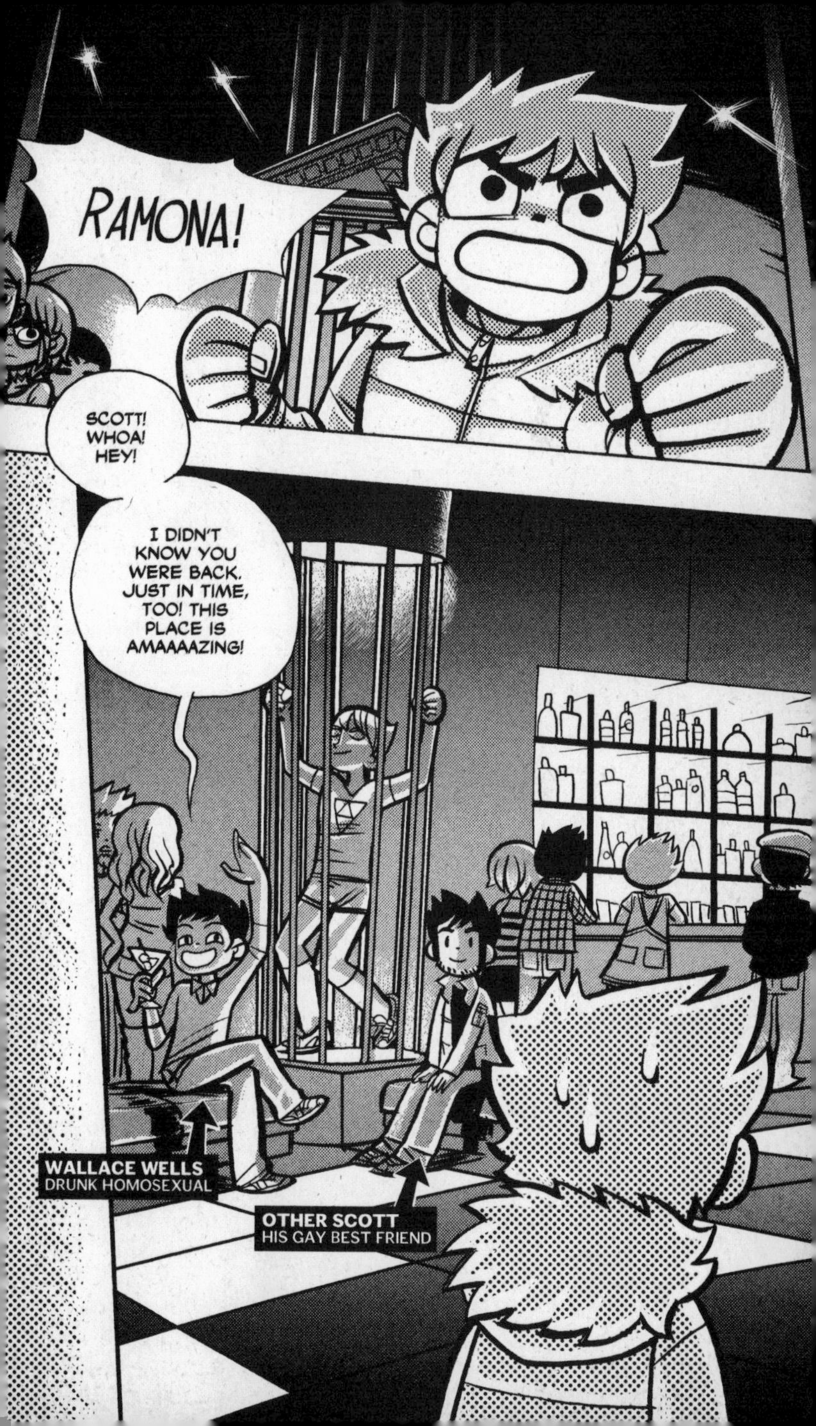
RAMONA!
SCOTT! WHOA! HEY!
I DIDN'T KNOW YOU WERE BACK. JUST IN TIME, TOO! THIS PLACE IS AMAAAAZING!
WALLACE WELLS
DRUNK HOMOSEXUAL
OTHER SCOTT
HIS GAY BEST FRIEND

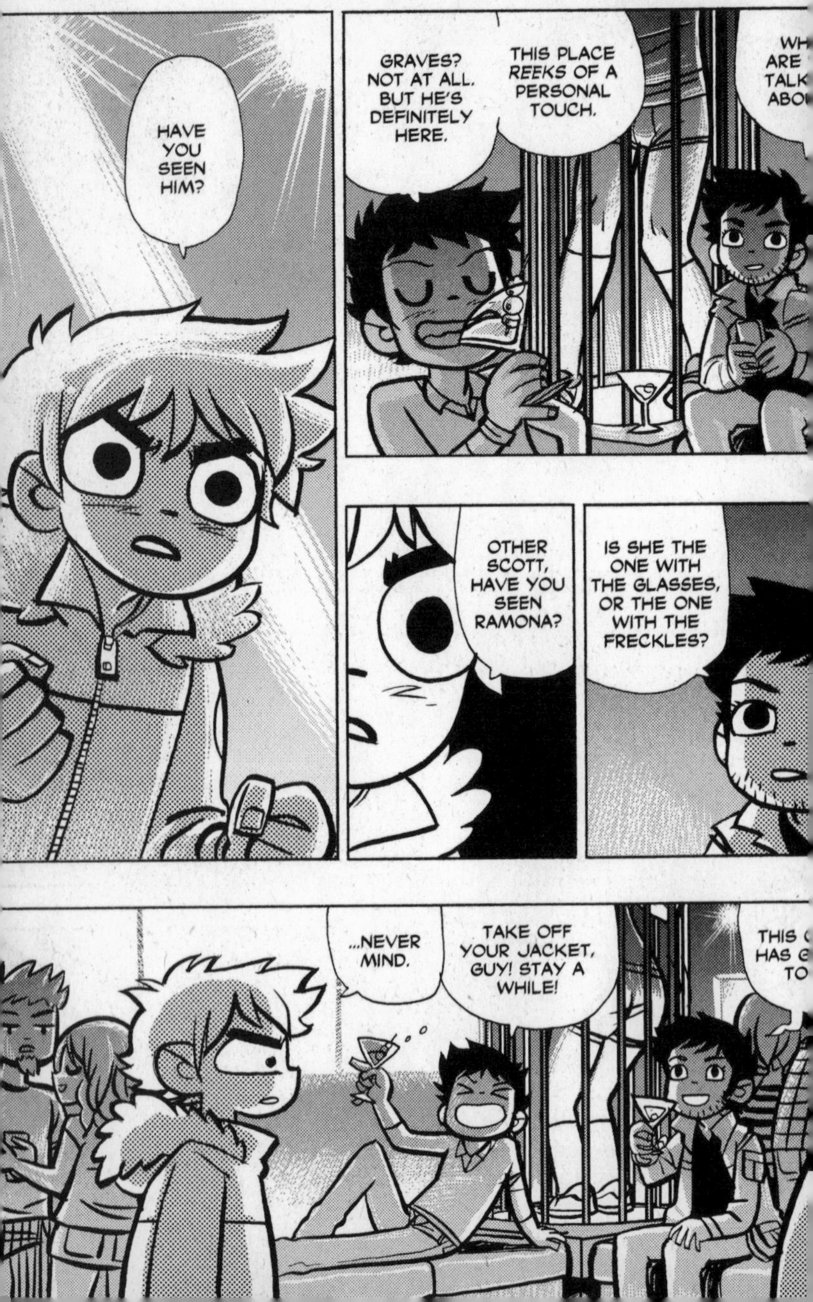

HAVE YOU SEEN HIM?
GRAVES? NOT AT ALL. BUT HE'S DEFINITELY HERE.
THIS PLACE REEKS OF A PERSONAL TOUCH.
OTHER SCOTT, HAVE YOU SEEN RAMONA?
IS SHE THE ONE WITH THE GLASSES, OR THE ONE WITH THE FRECKLES?
...NEVER MIND.
TAKE OFF YOUR JACKET, GUY! STAY A WHILE!

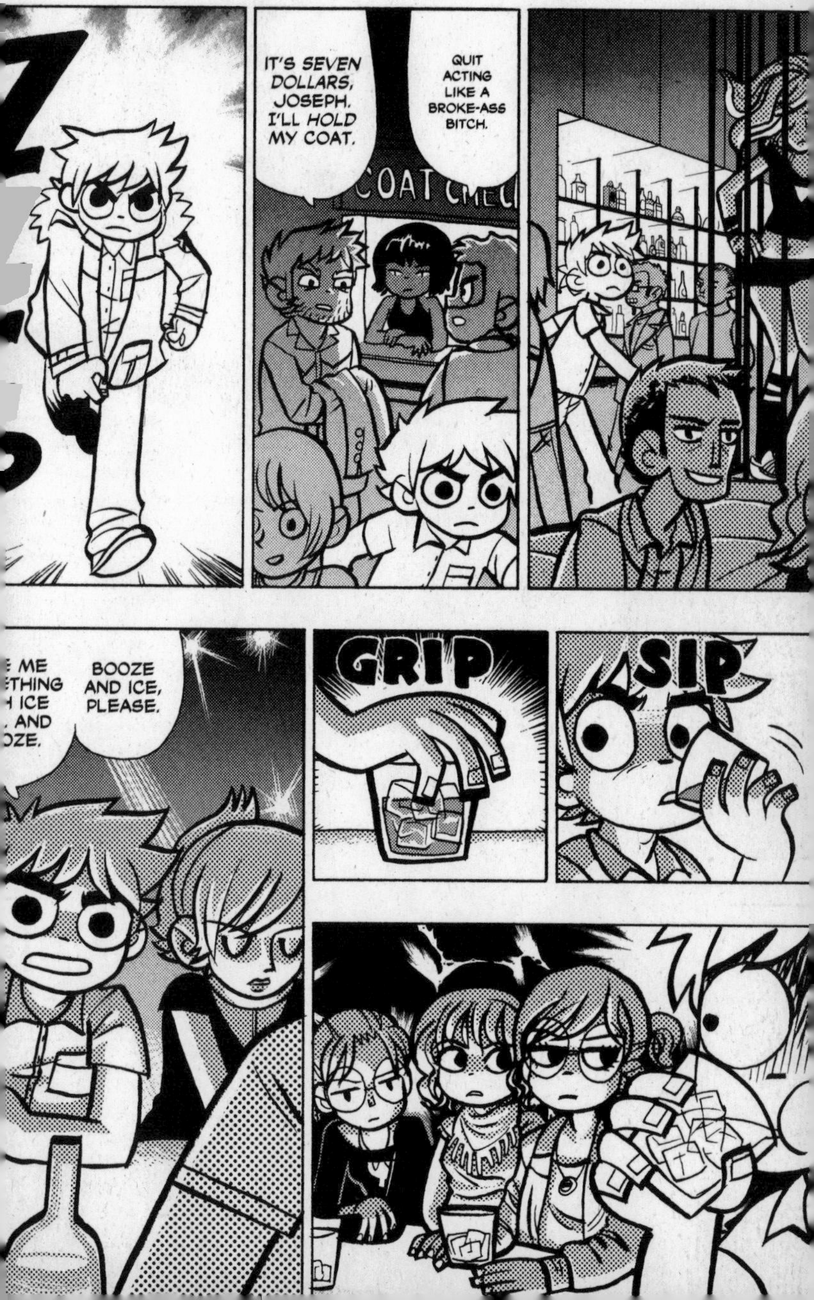

IT'S SEVEN DOLLARS, JOSEPH. I'LL HOLD MY COAT.
QUIT ACTING LIKE A BROKE-ASS BITCH.
COAT CHEC
E ME ETHING H ICE . AND OZE.
BOOZE AND ICE, PLEASE.
GRIP
SIP

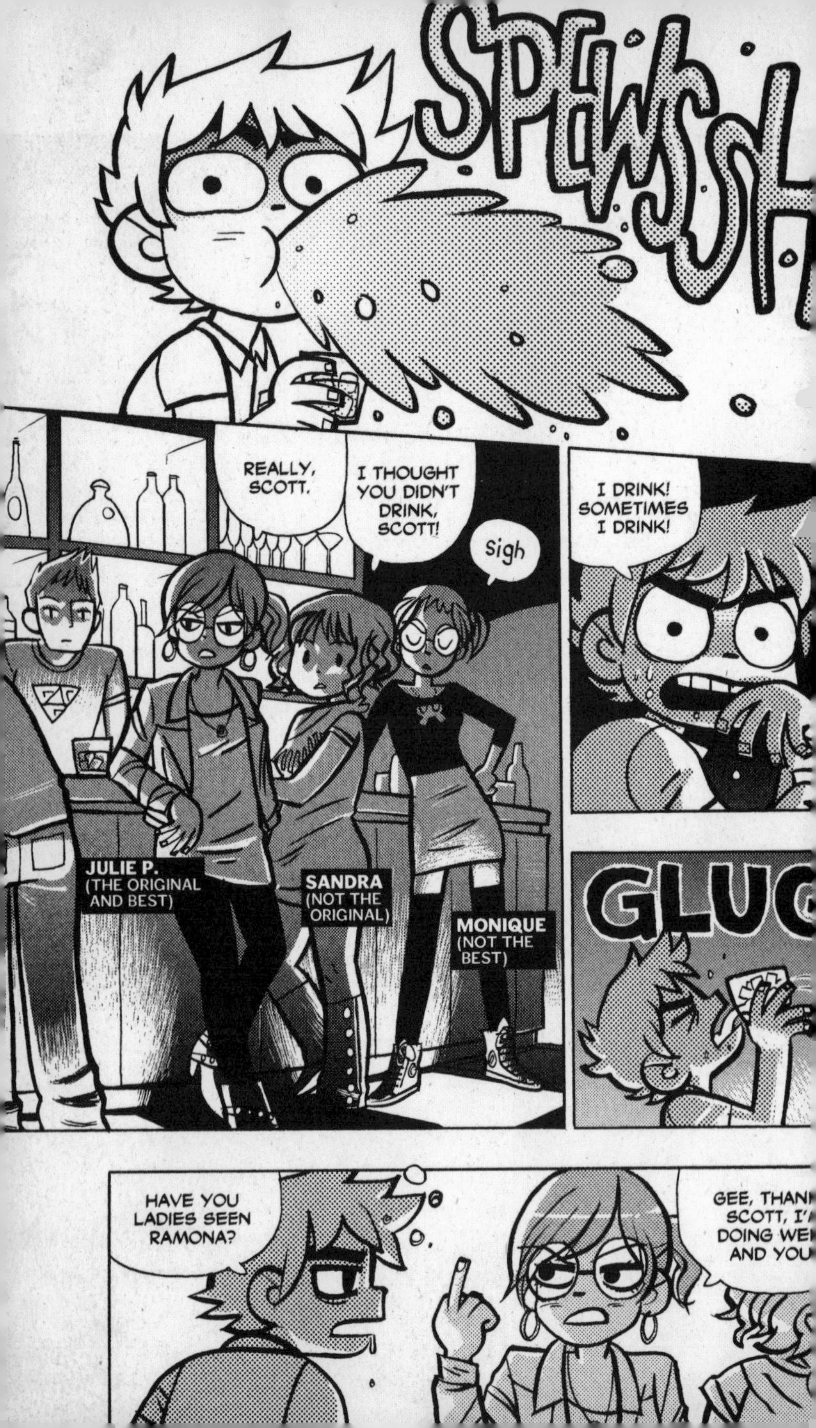

SPEWSSH
REALLY, SCOTT.
I THOUGHT YOU DIDN'T DRINK, SCOTT!
Sigh
JULIE P. (THE ORIGINAL AND BEST)
SANDRA (NOT THE ORIGINAL)
MONIQUE (NOT THE BEST)
I DRINK! SOMETIMES I DRINK!
GLUG
HAVE YOU LADIES SEEN RAMONA?

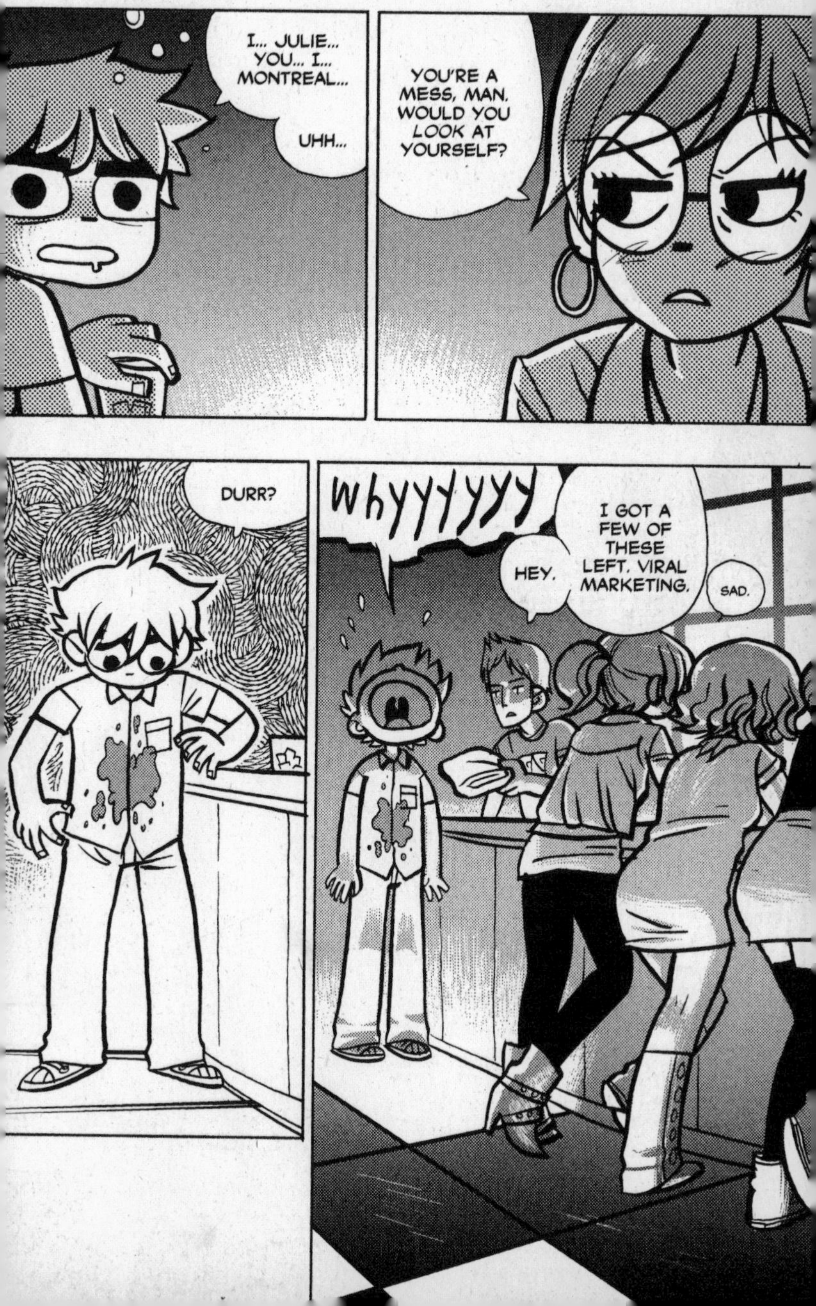
I... JULIE... YOU... I... MONTREAL...
UHH...
YOU'RE A MESS, MAN. WOULD YOU LOOK AT YOURSELF?
DURR?
whyyyyyy
HEY.
I GOT A FEW OF THESE LEFT. VIRAL MARKETING.
SAD.

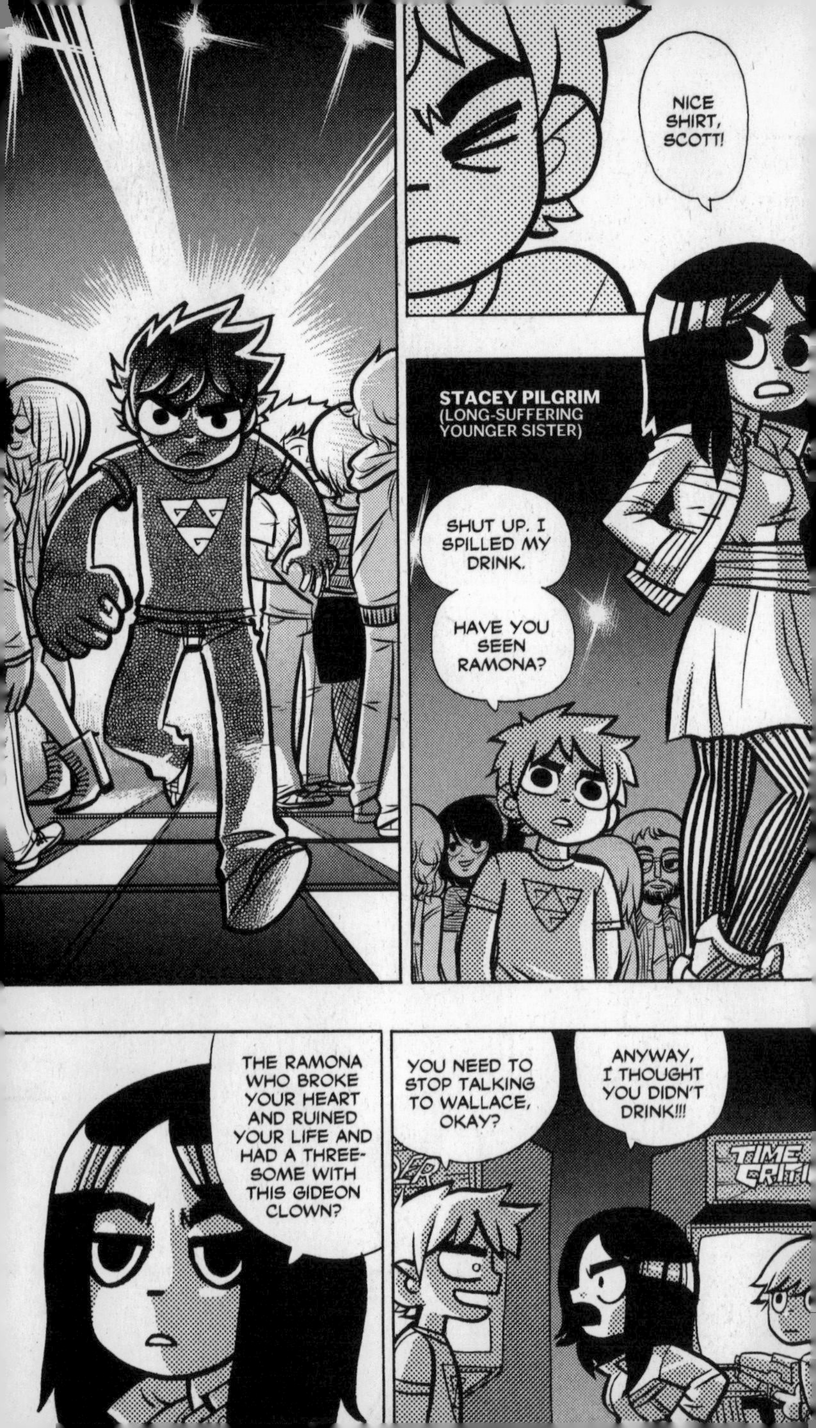
NICE SHIRT, SCOTT!
STACEY PILGRIM
(LONG-SUFFERING YOUNGER SISTER)
SHUT UP. I SPILLED MY DRINK.
HAVE YOU SEEN RAMONA?
THE RAMONA WHO BROKE YOUR HEART AND RUINED YOUR LIFE AND HAD A THREE-SOME WITH THIS GIDEON CLOWN?
YOU NEED TO STOP TALKING TO WALLACE, OKAY?
ANYWAY, I THOUGHT YOU DIDN'T DRINK!!!
TIME CRITI

OH... HEY, MAN.

UH-HUH.

PEW PEW

YOUNG NEIL

PEW

WAIT, DO YOU TWO NOT KNOW EACH OTHER? THAT'S CRAZY!

SCOTT'S SISTER, RIGHT?

NUH-UH.

PEW PEW

YEAH, HI.

STACEY, THIS IS YOUNG—

—THIS IS, UM, NEIL.

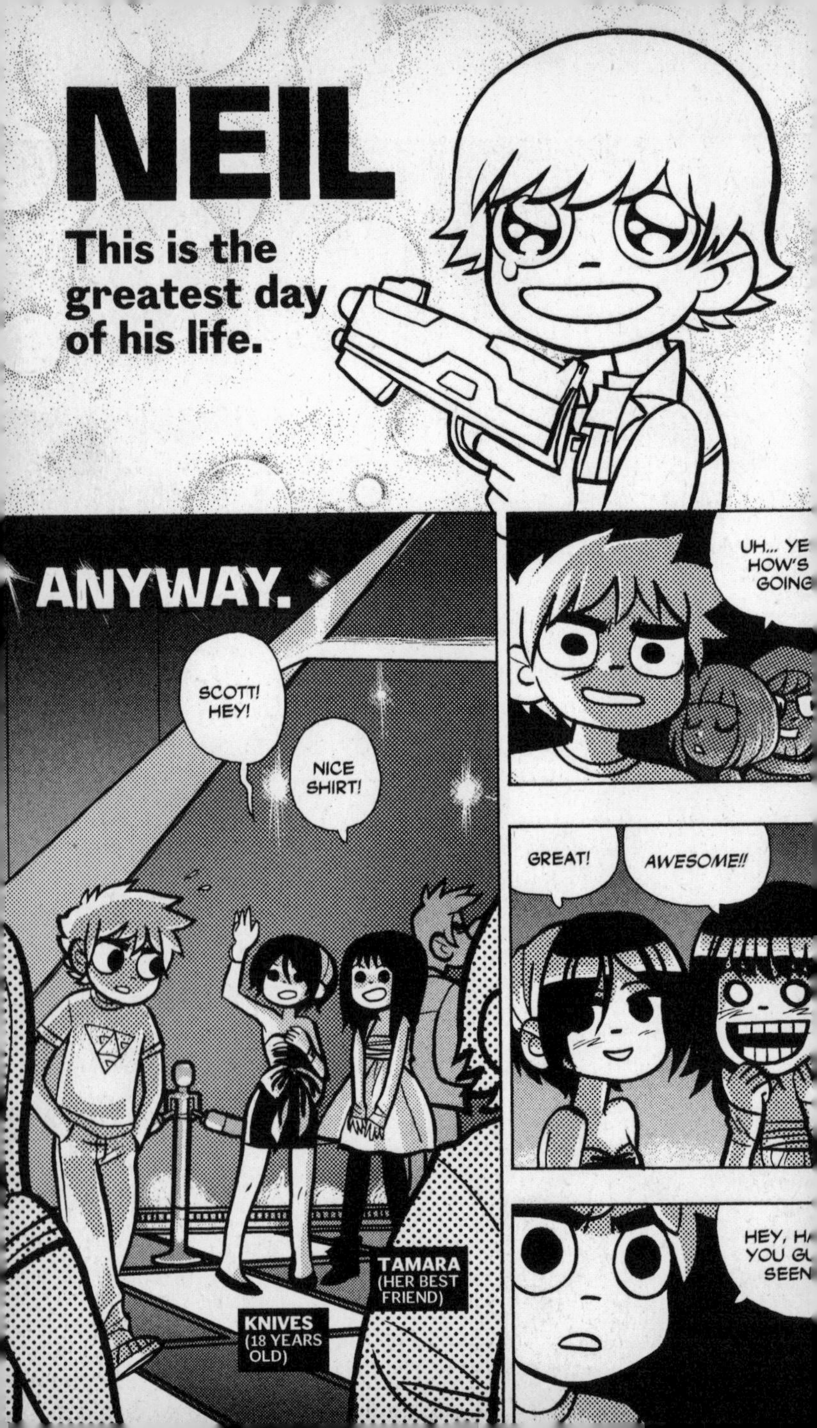
NEIL
This is the greatest day of his life.
ANYWAY.
SCOTT! HEY!
NICE SHIRT!
TAMARA (HER BEST FRIEND)
KNIVES (18 YEARS OLD)
UH... YE HOW'S GOING
GREAT!
AWESOME!!
HEY, H YOU G SEEN

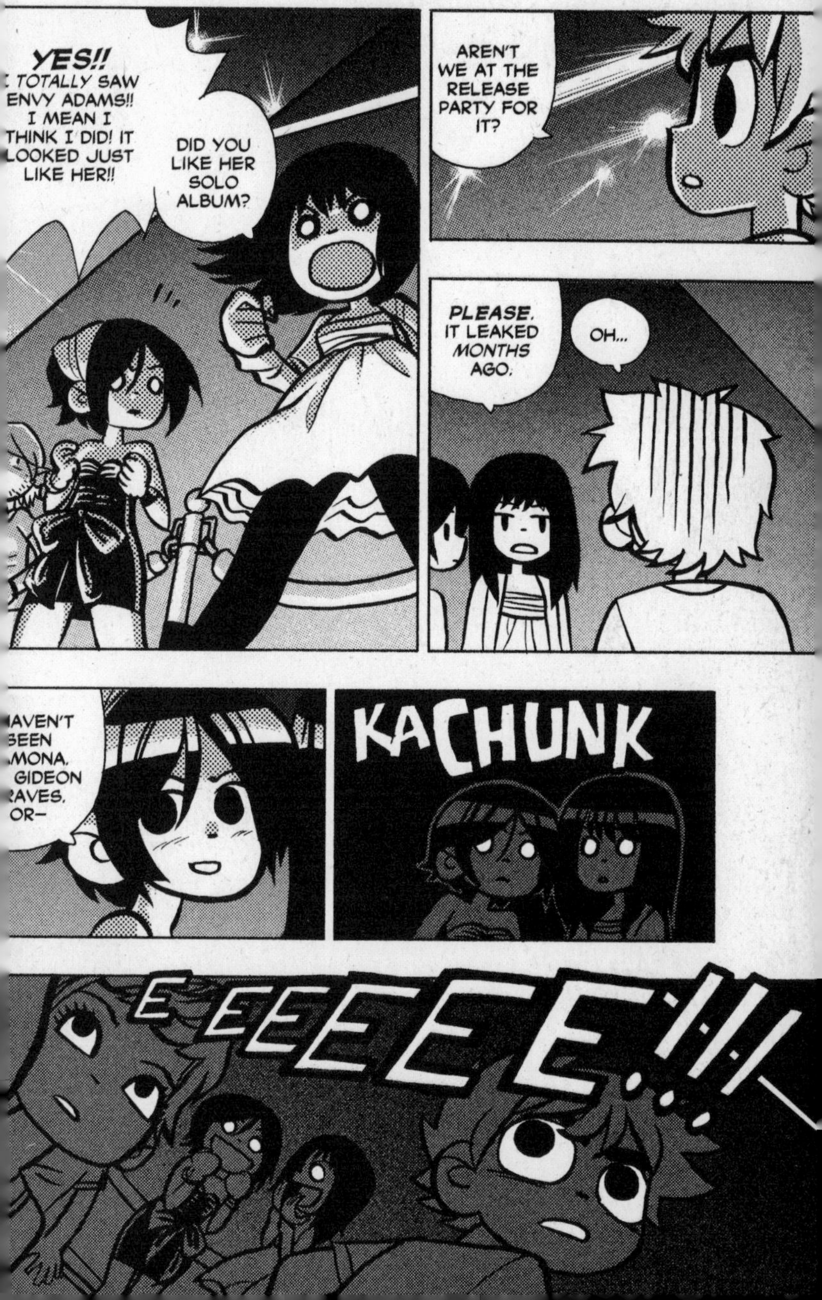

YES!! I TOTALLY SAW ENVY ADAMS!! I MEAN I THINK I DID! IT LOOKED JUST LIKE HER!!
DID YOU LIKE HER SOLO ALBUM?
AREN'T WE AT THE RELEASE PARTY FOR IT?
PLEASE. IT LEAKED MONTHS AGO.
OH...
AVEN'T EEN MONA. GIDEON RAVES. OR–
KACHUNK
EEEEEE!!!

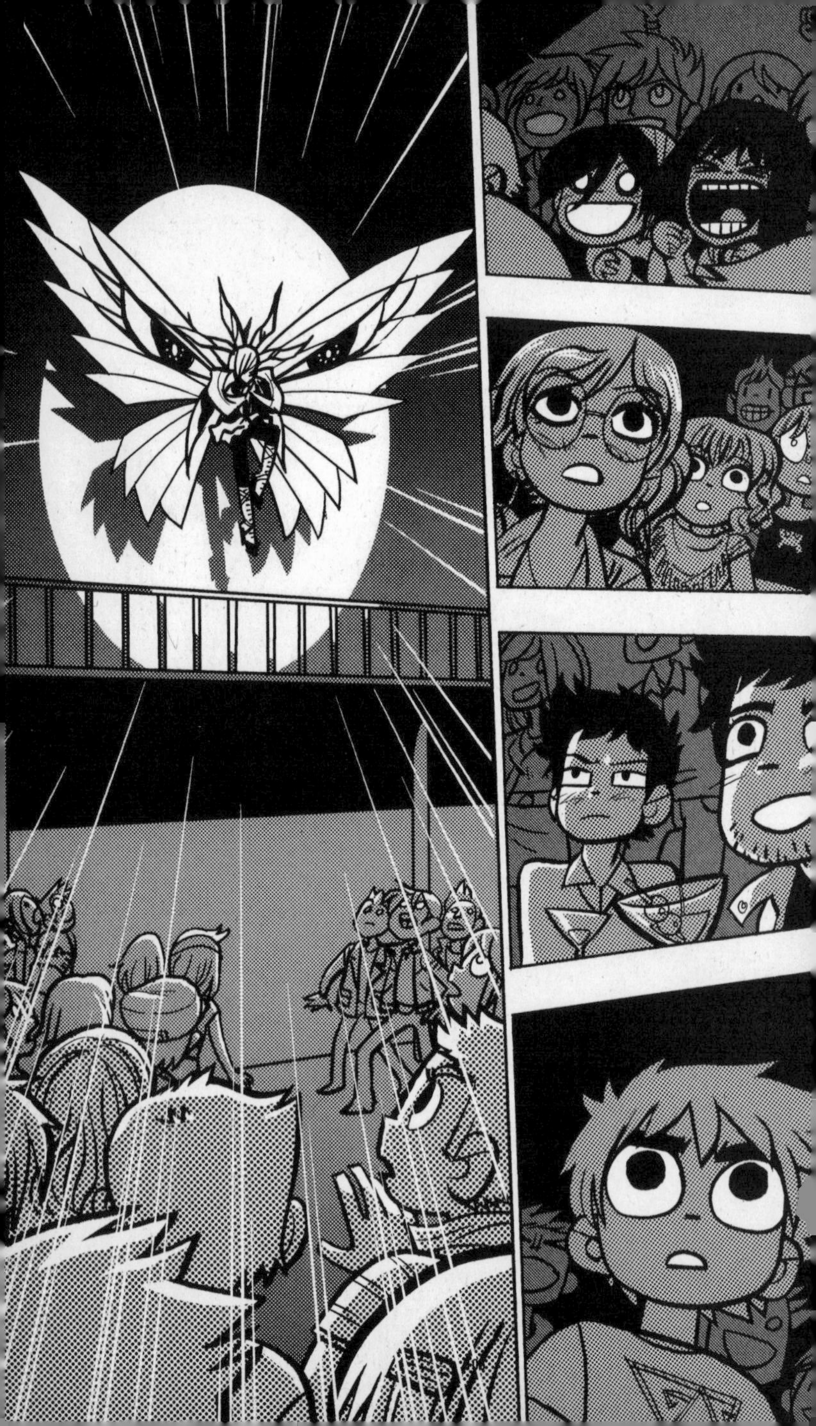

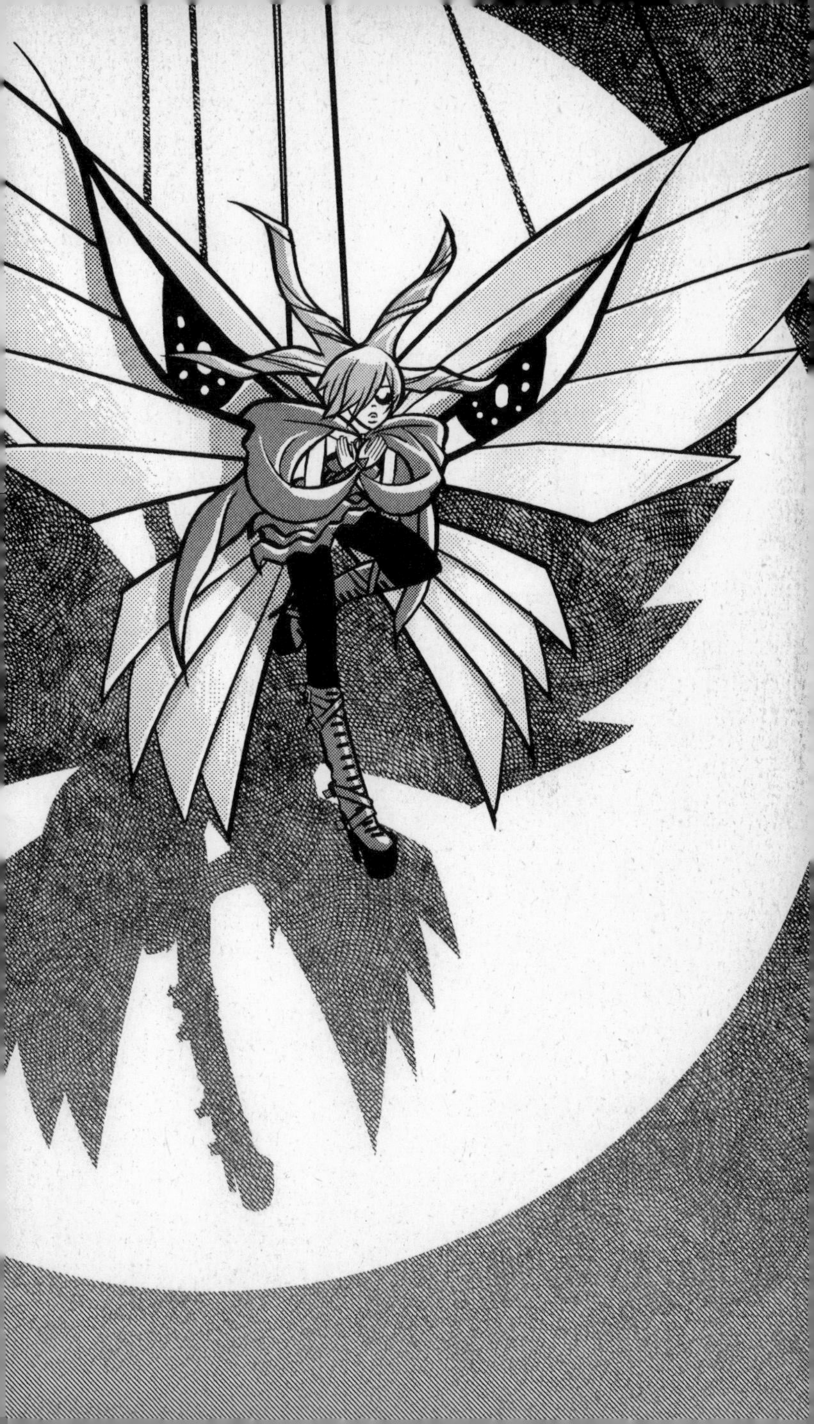

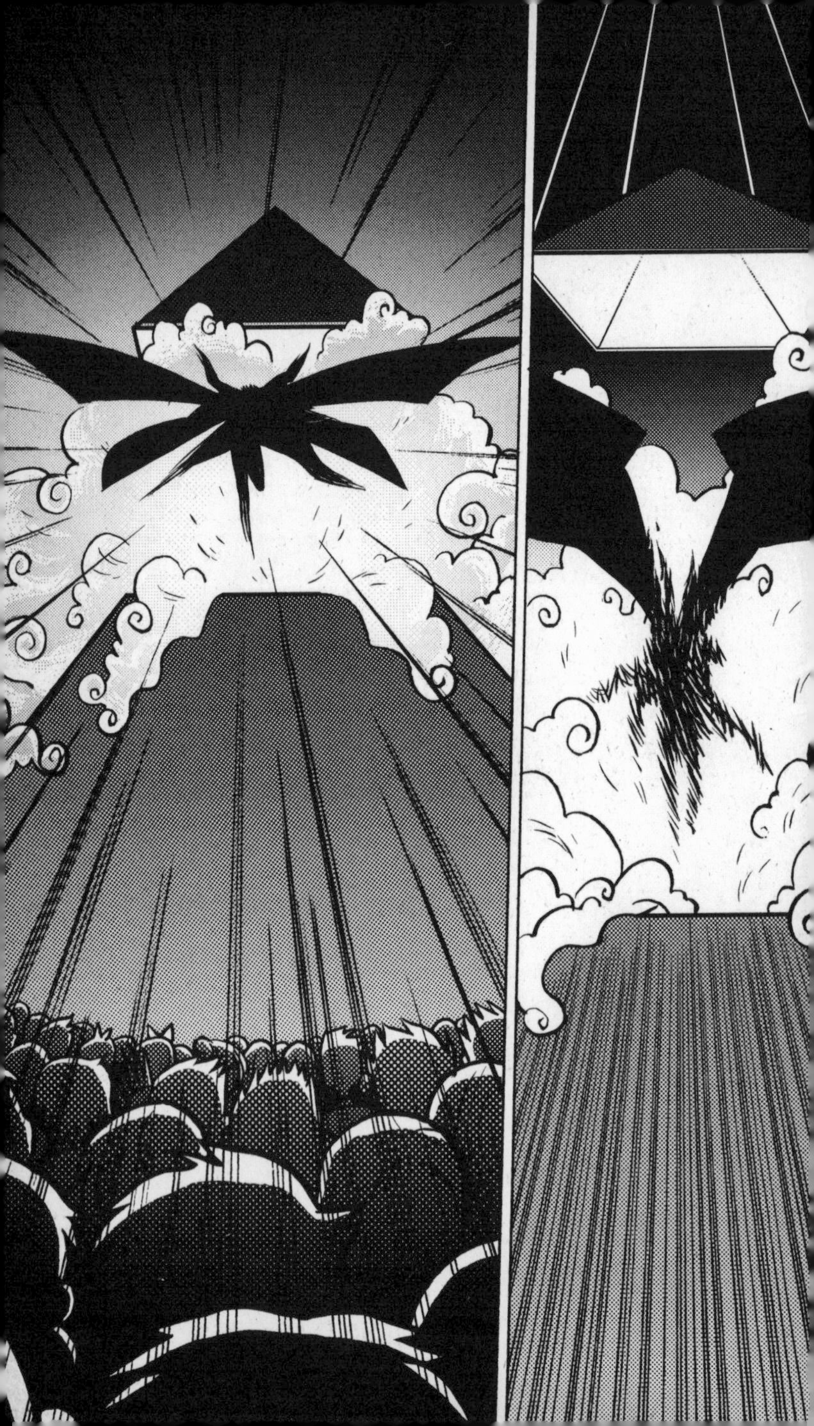

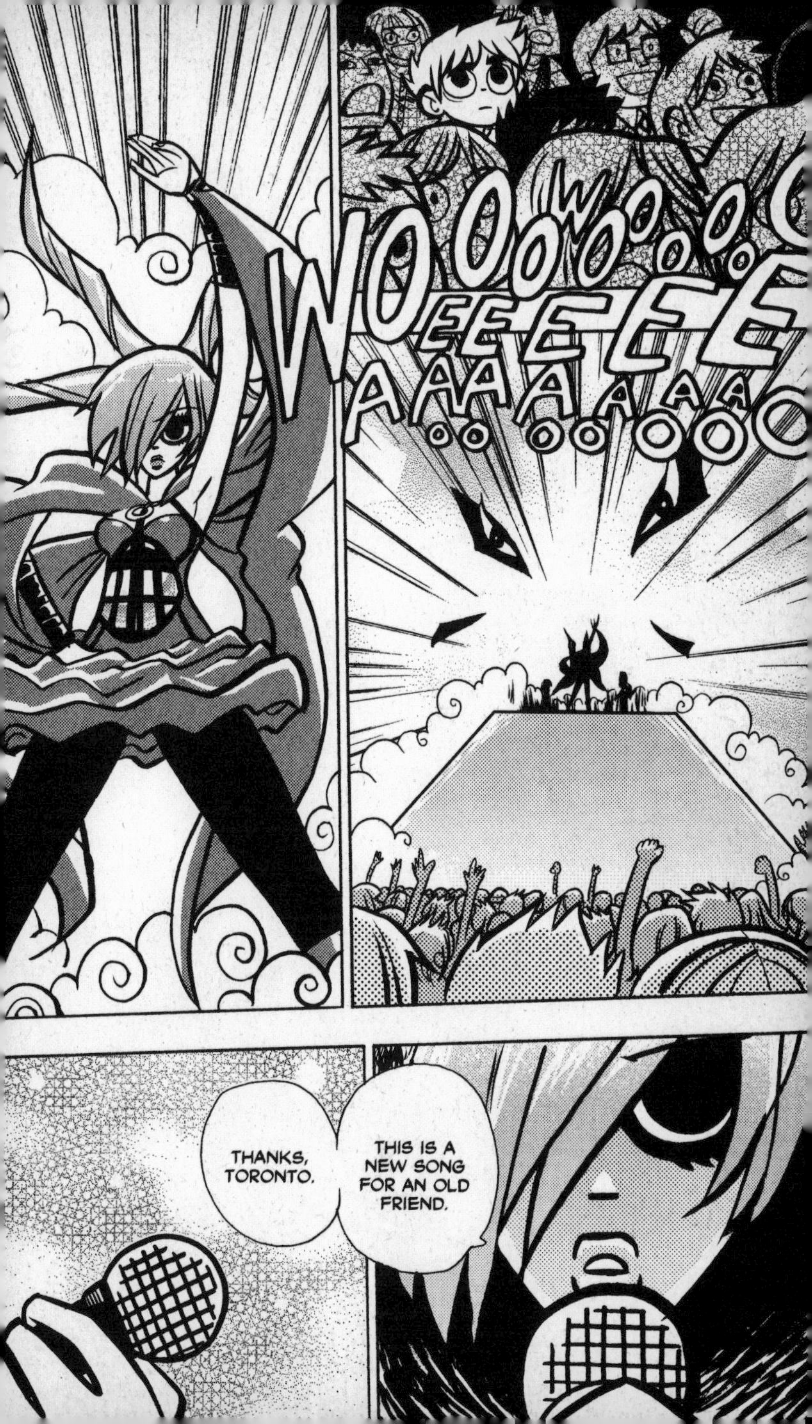

WOOOOO...O
WEEEEE
AAAAAAA
OO OOOOO
THANKS, TORONTO.
THIS IS A NEW SONG FOR AN OLD FRIEND.

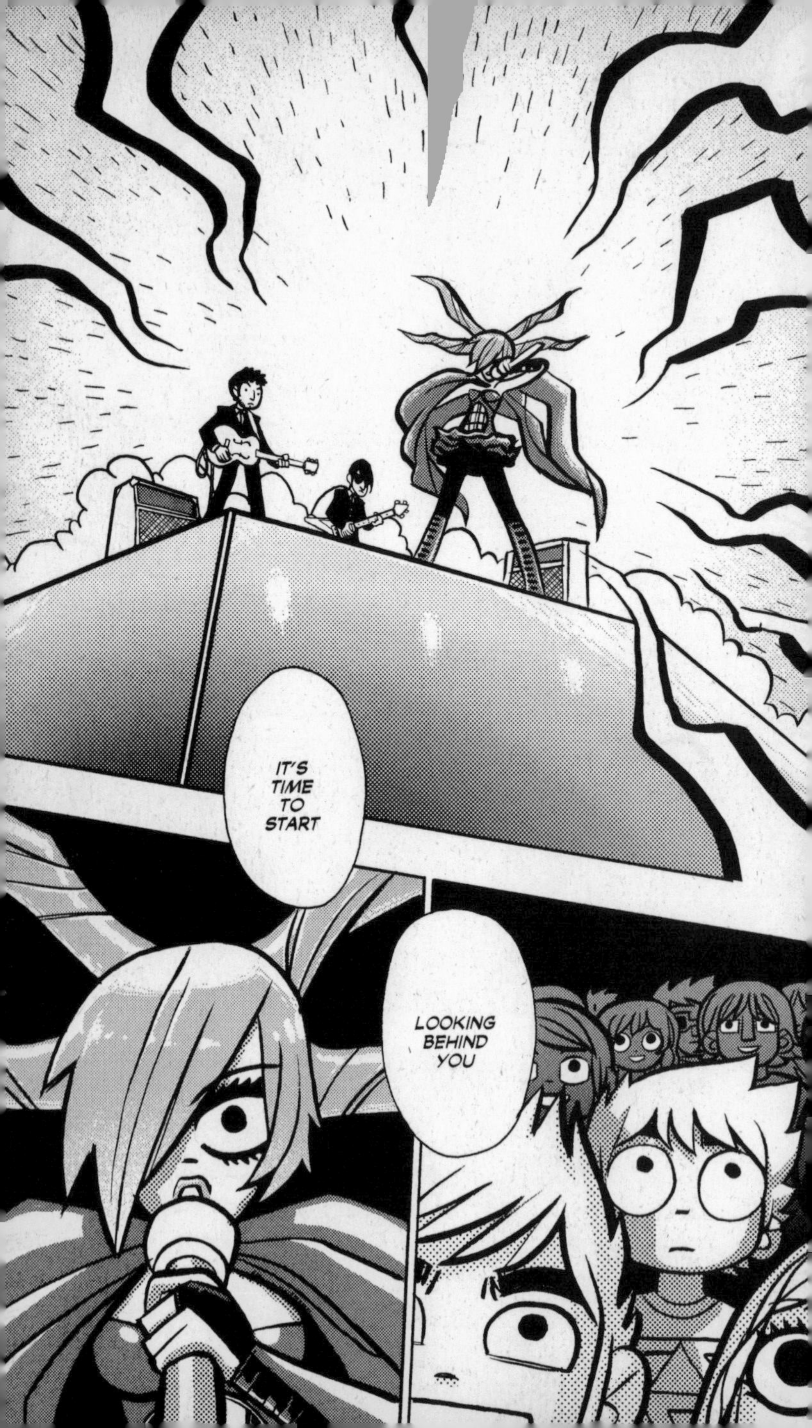
IT'S TIME TO START
LOOKING BEHIND YOU

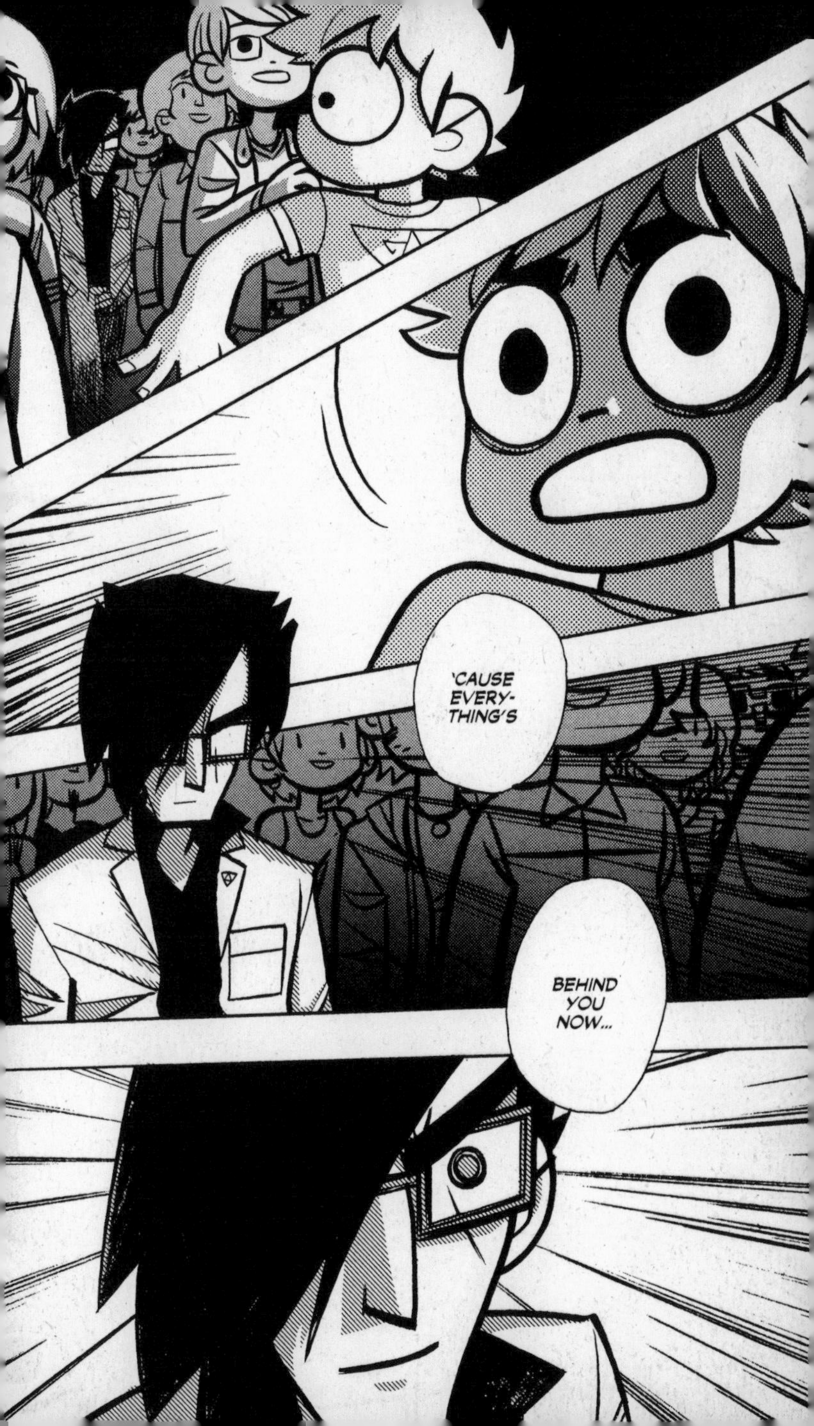
'CAUSE EVERY-THING'S
BEHIND YOU NOW...

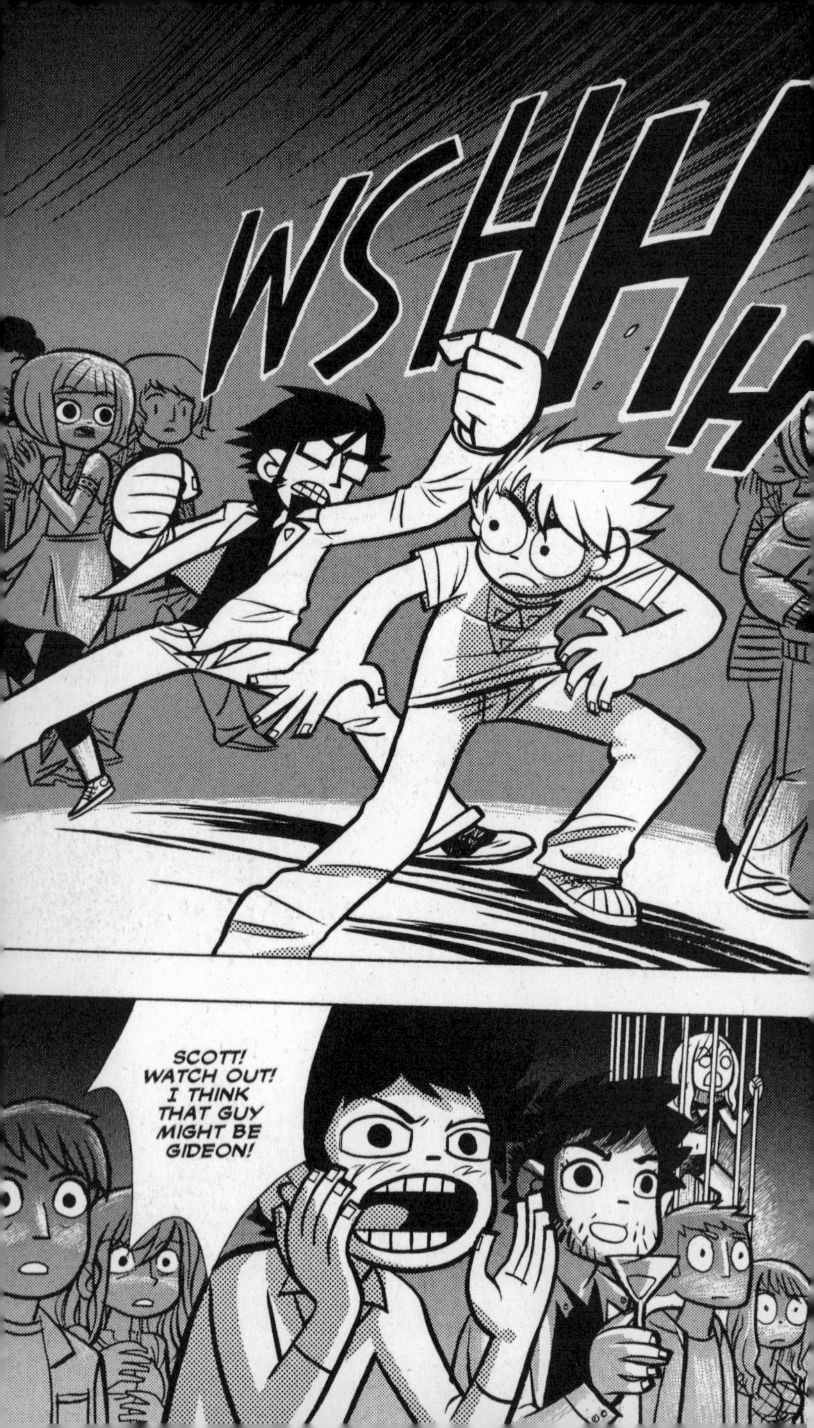
WSHHH
SCOTT! WATCH OUT! I THINK THAT GUY MIGHT BE GIDEON!

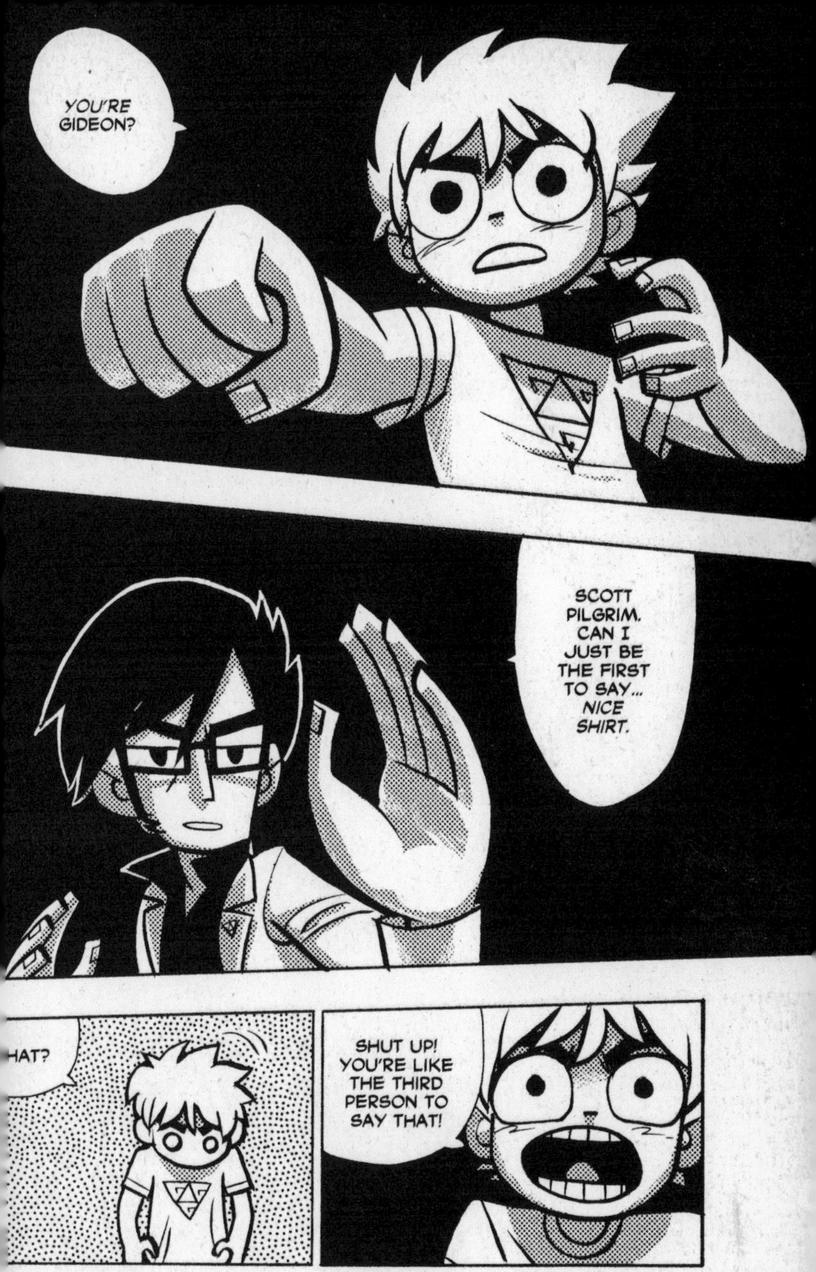
YOU'RE GIDEON?
SCOTT PILGRIM. CAN I JUST BE THE FIRST TO SAY... NICE SHIRT.
HAT?
SHUT UP! YOU'RE LIKE THE THIRD PERSON TO SAY THAT!

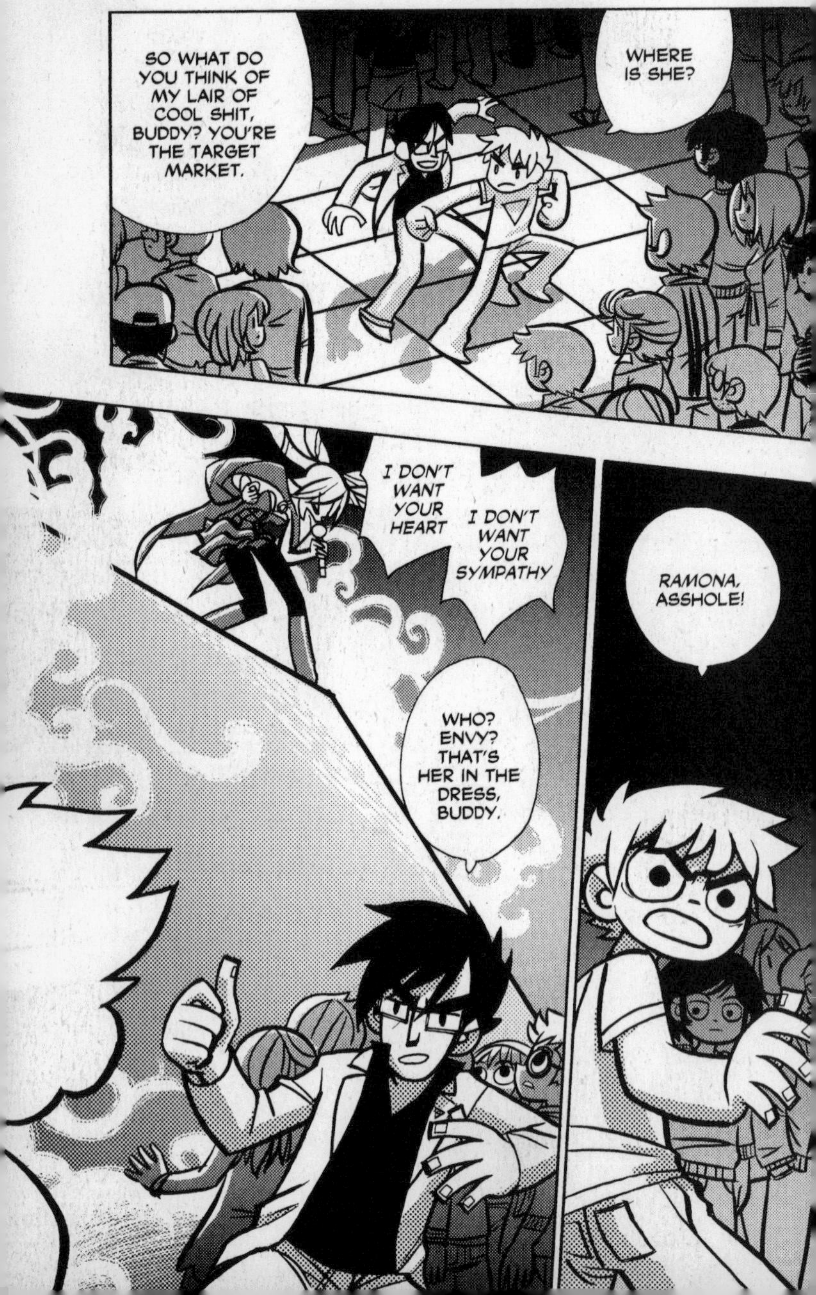
SO WHAT DO YOU THINK OF MY LAIR OF COOL SHIT, BUDDY? YOU'RE THE TARGET MARKET.
WHERE IS SHE?
I DON'T WANT YOUR HEART
I DON'T WANT YOUR SYMPATHY
RAMONA, ASSHOLE!
WHO? ENVY? THAT'S HER IN THE DRESS, BUDDY.

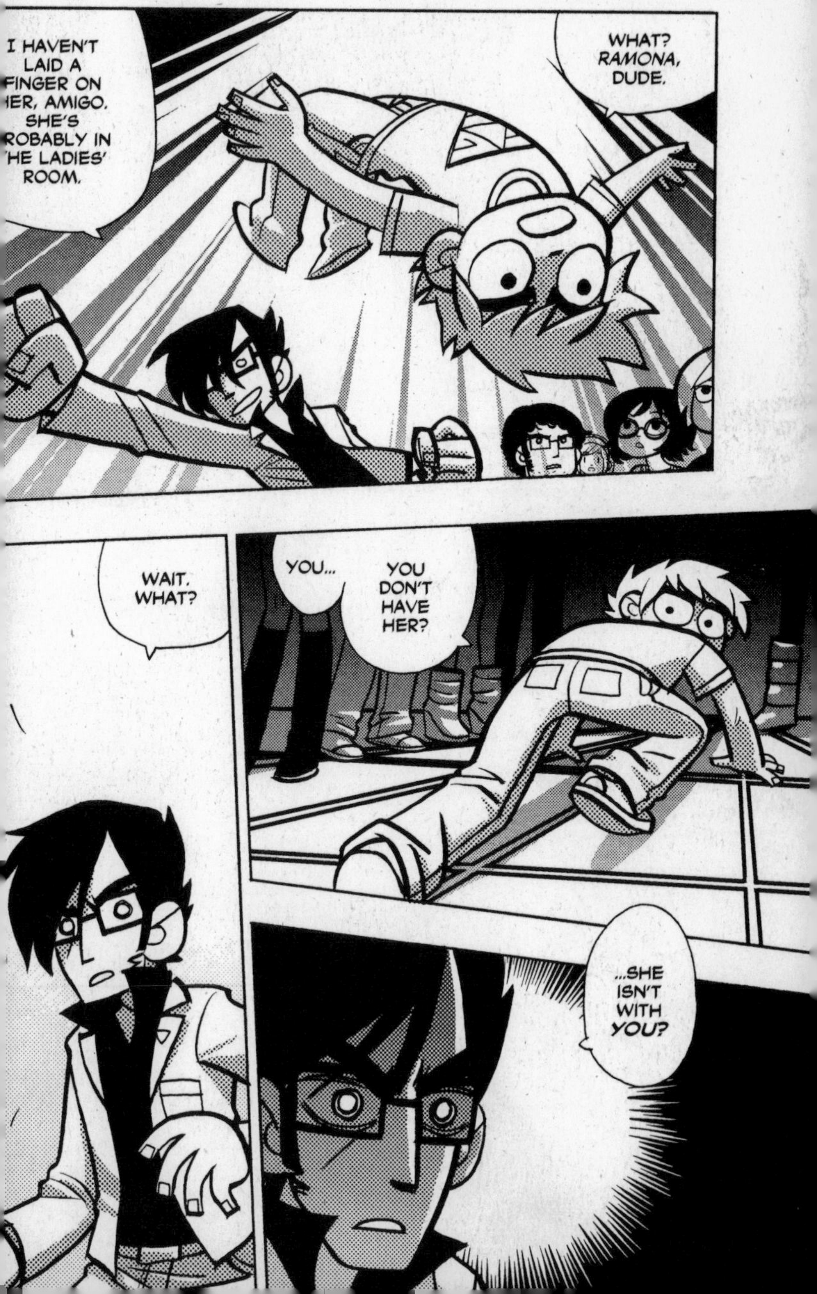

I HAVEN'T LAID A FINGER ON HER, AMIGO. SHE'S PROBABLY IN THE LADIES' ROOM.
WHAT? RAMONA, DUDE.
WAIT. WHAT?
YOU...
YOU DON'T HAVE HER?
...SHE ISN'T WITH YOU?

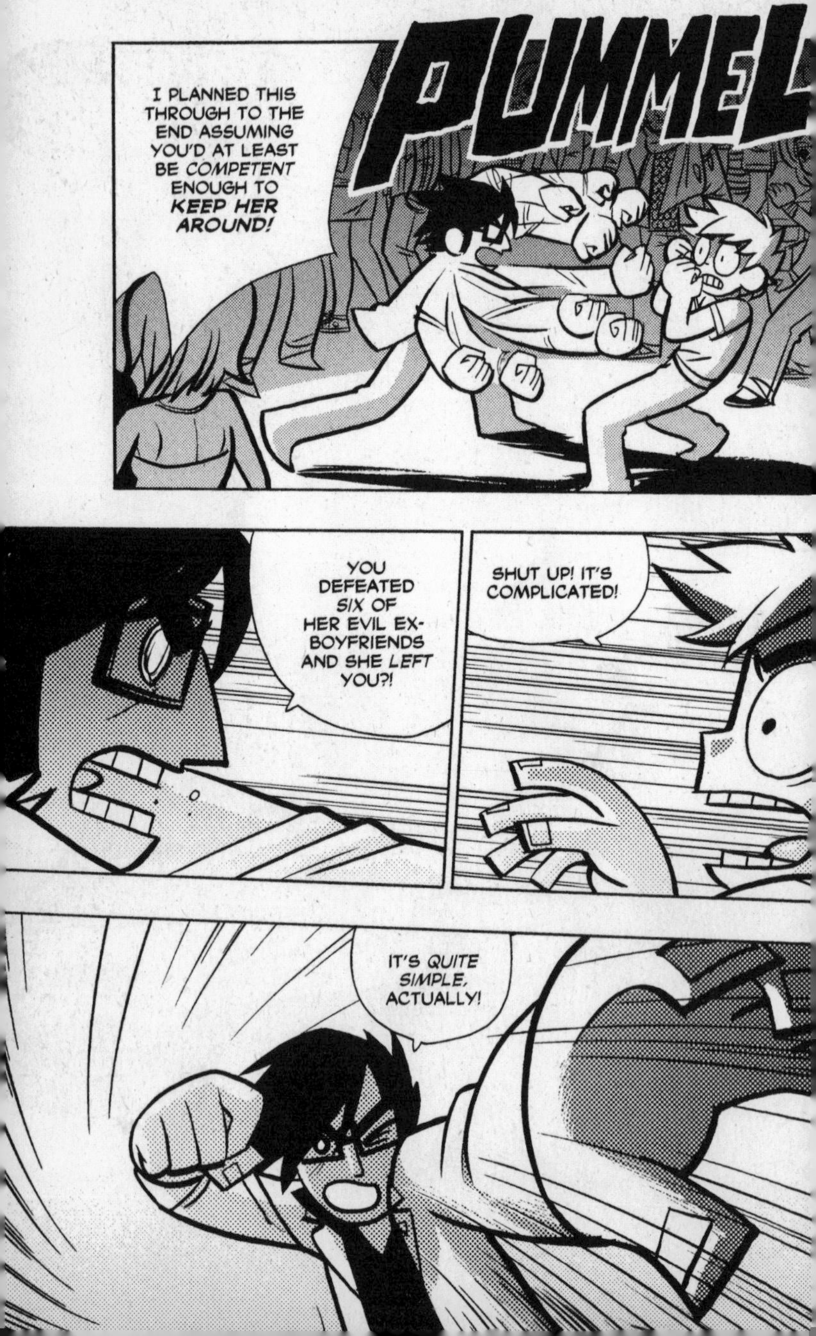
PUMMEL
I PLANNED THIS THROUGH TO THE END ASSUMING YOU'D AT LEAST BE *COMPETENT* ENOUGH TO ***KEEP HER AROUND!***
YOU DEFEATED *SIX* OF HER EVIL EX-BOYFRIENDS AND SHE *LEFT* YOU?!
SHUT UP! IT'S COMPLICATED!
IT'S *QUITE SIMPLE,* ACTUALLY!

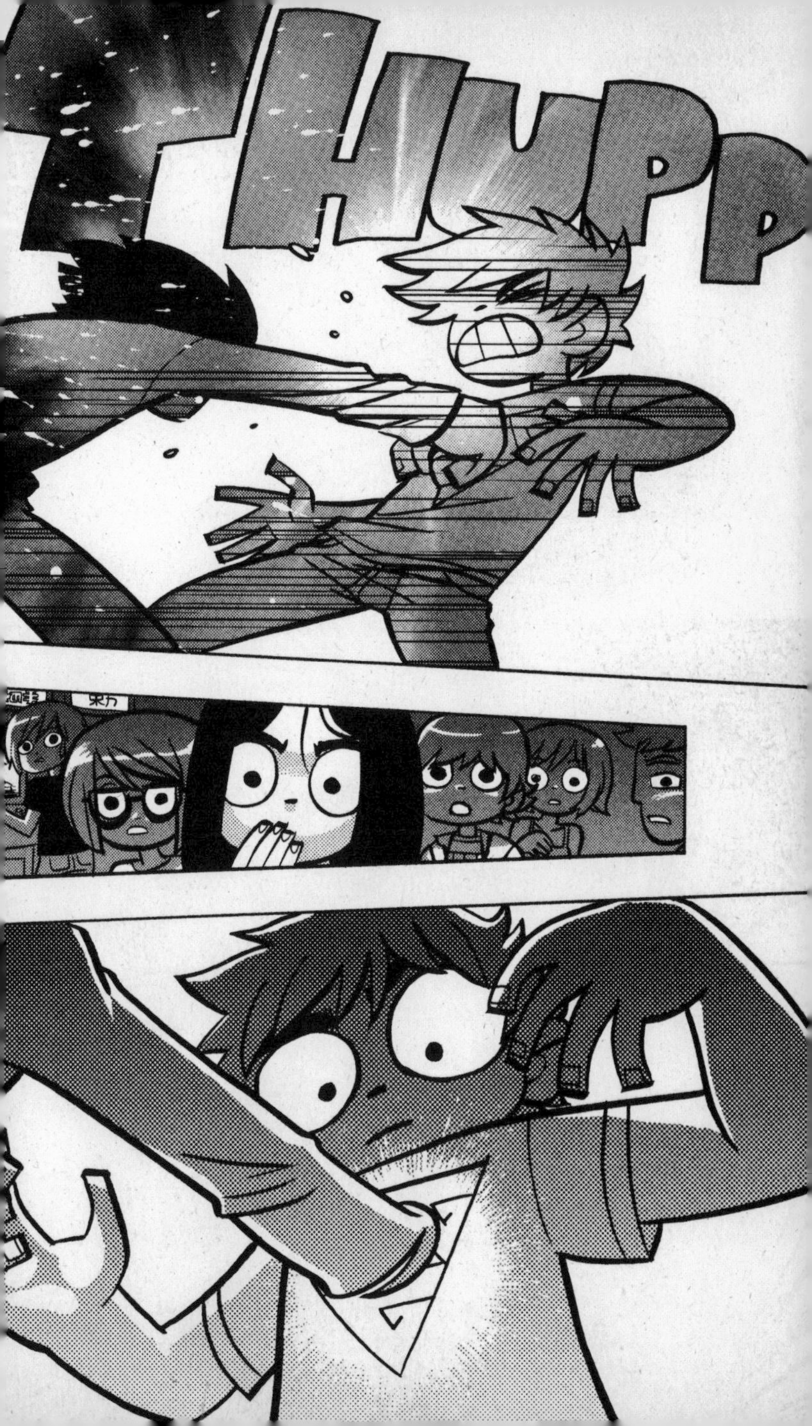
THUPP

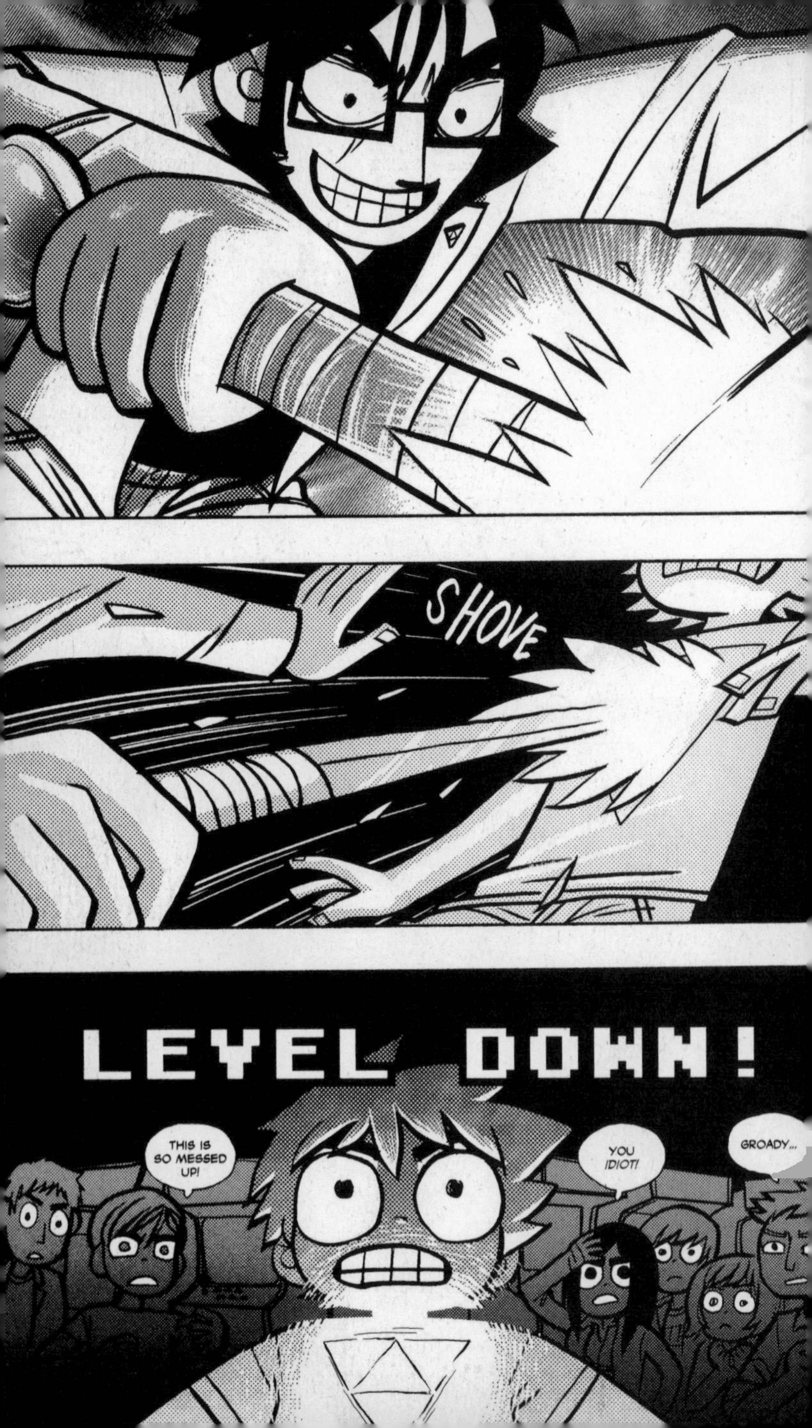
SHOVE
LEVEL DOWN!
THIS IS SO MESSED UP!
YOU IDIOT!
GROADY...

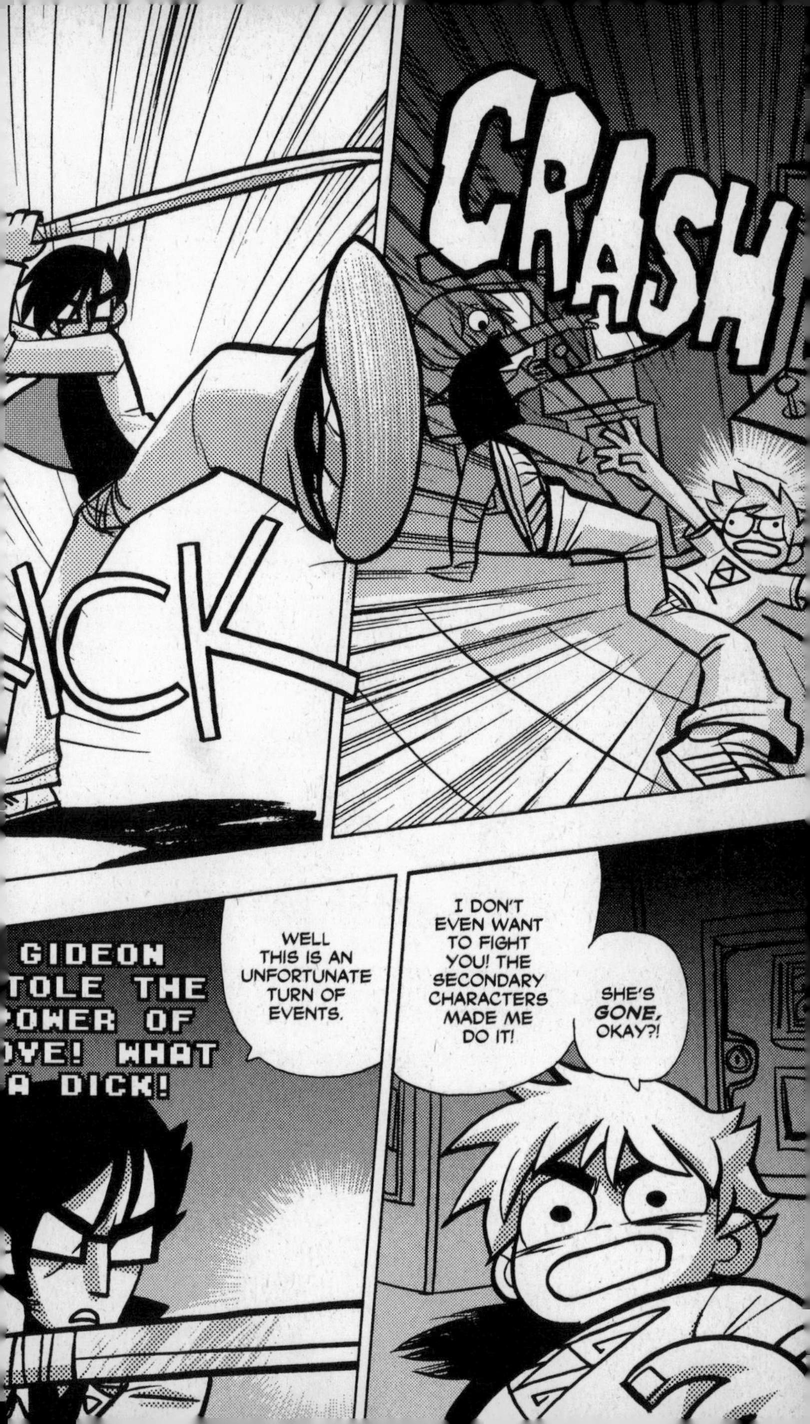
CRASH
CK
GIDEON
TOLE THE
OWER OF
OVE! WHAT
A DICK!
WELL THIS IS AN UNFORTUNATE TURN OF EVENTS.
I DON'T EVEN WANT TO FIGHT YOU! THE SECONDARY CHARACTERS MADE ME DO IT!
SHE'S GONE, OKAY?!

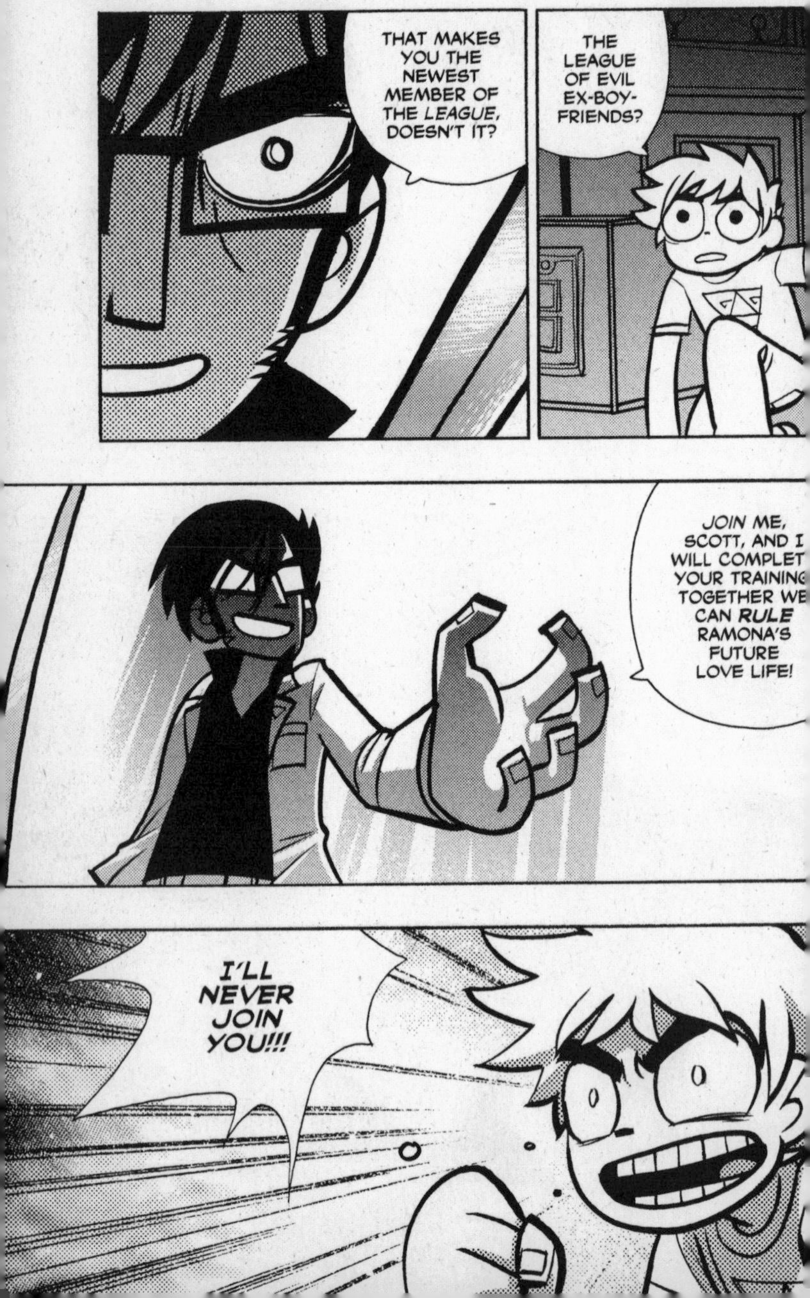
THAT MAKES YOU THE NEWEST MEMBER OF THE *LEAGUE*, DOESN'T IT?
THE LEAGUE OF EVIL EX-BOY-FRIENDS?
JOIN ME, SCOTT, AND I WILL COMPLET YOUR TRAINING TOGETHER WE CAN ***RULE*** RAMONA'S FUTURE LOVE LIFE!
I'LL NEVER JOIN YOU!!!

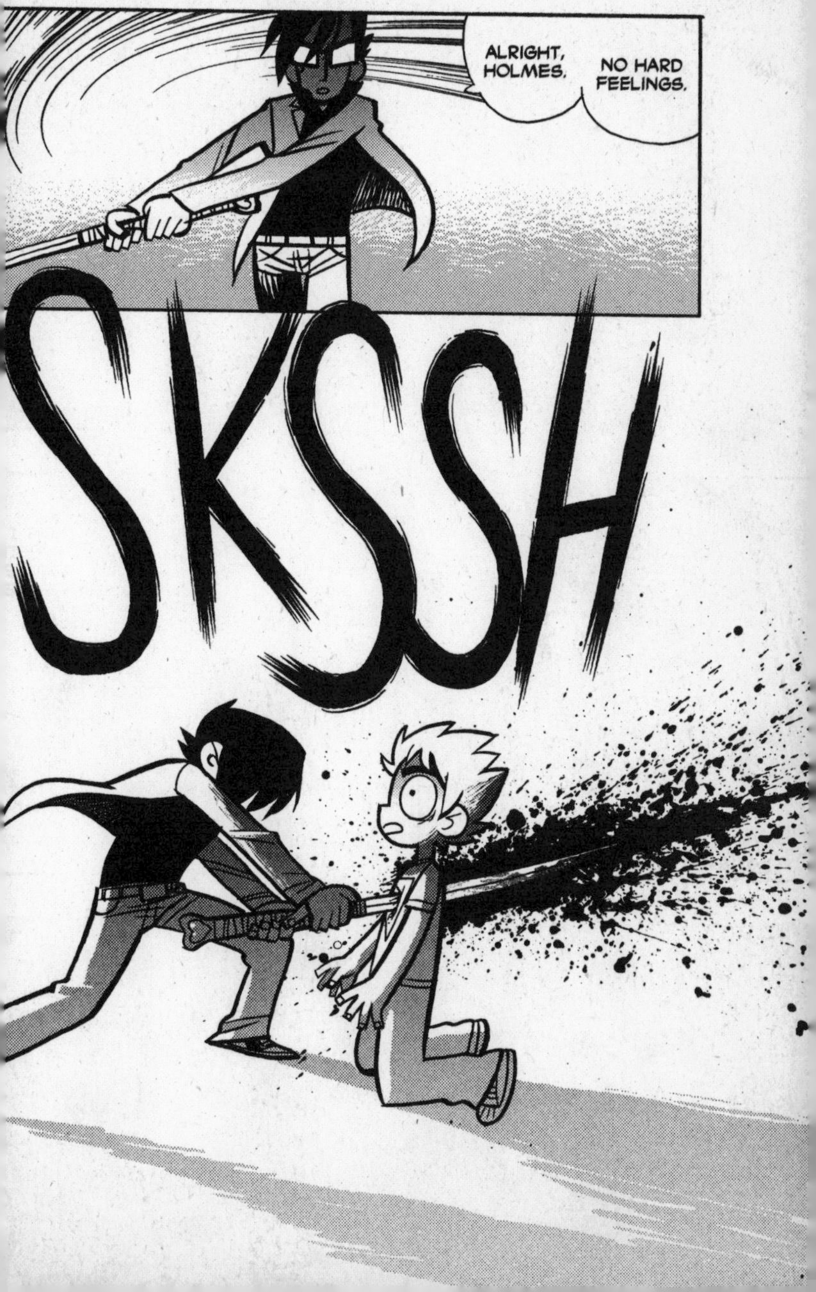
ALRIGHT, HOLMES.
NO HARD FEELINGS.
SKSSH

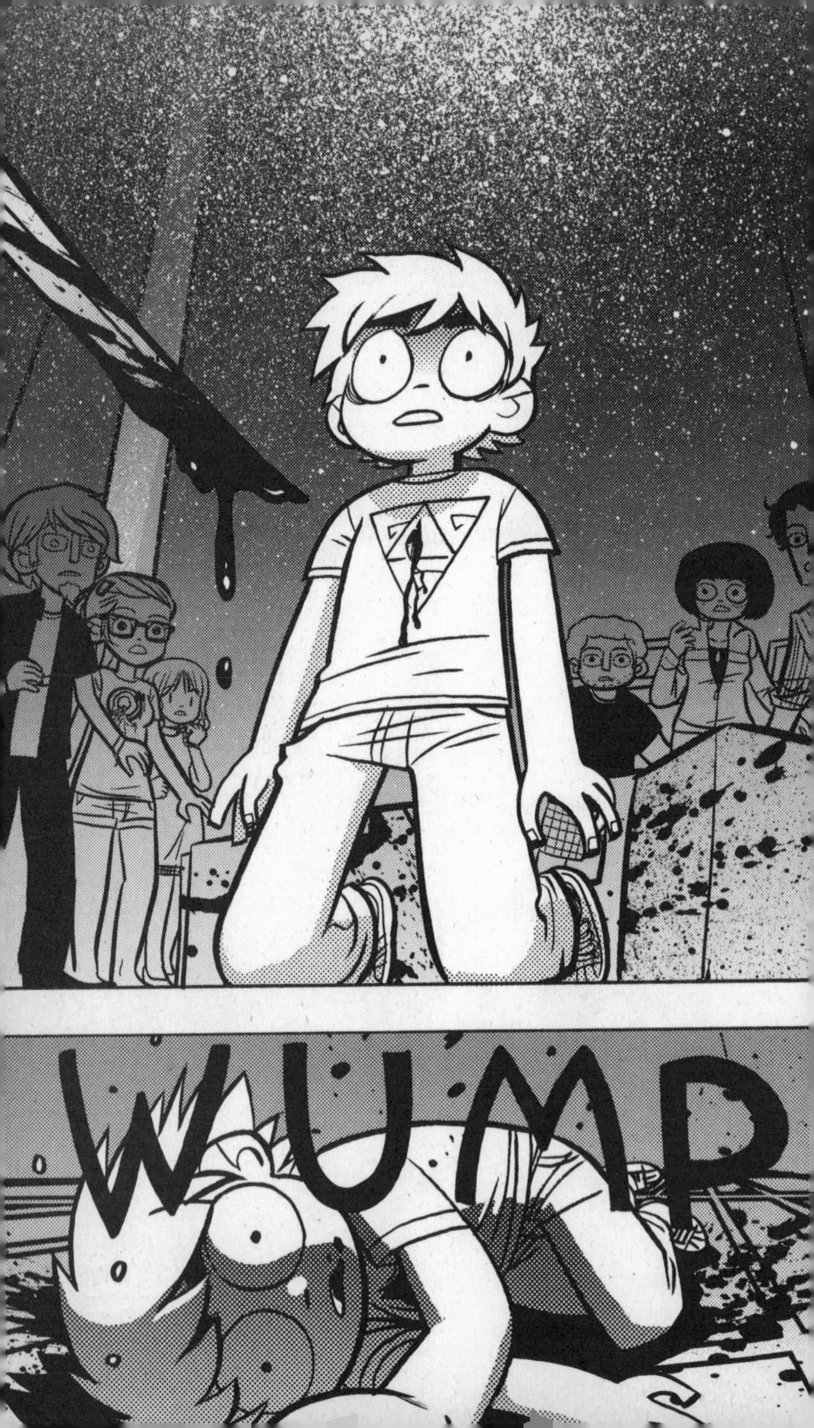
WUMP

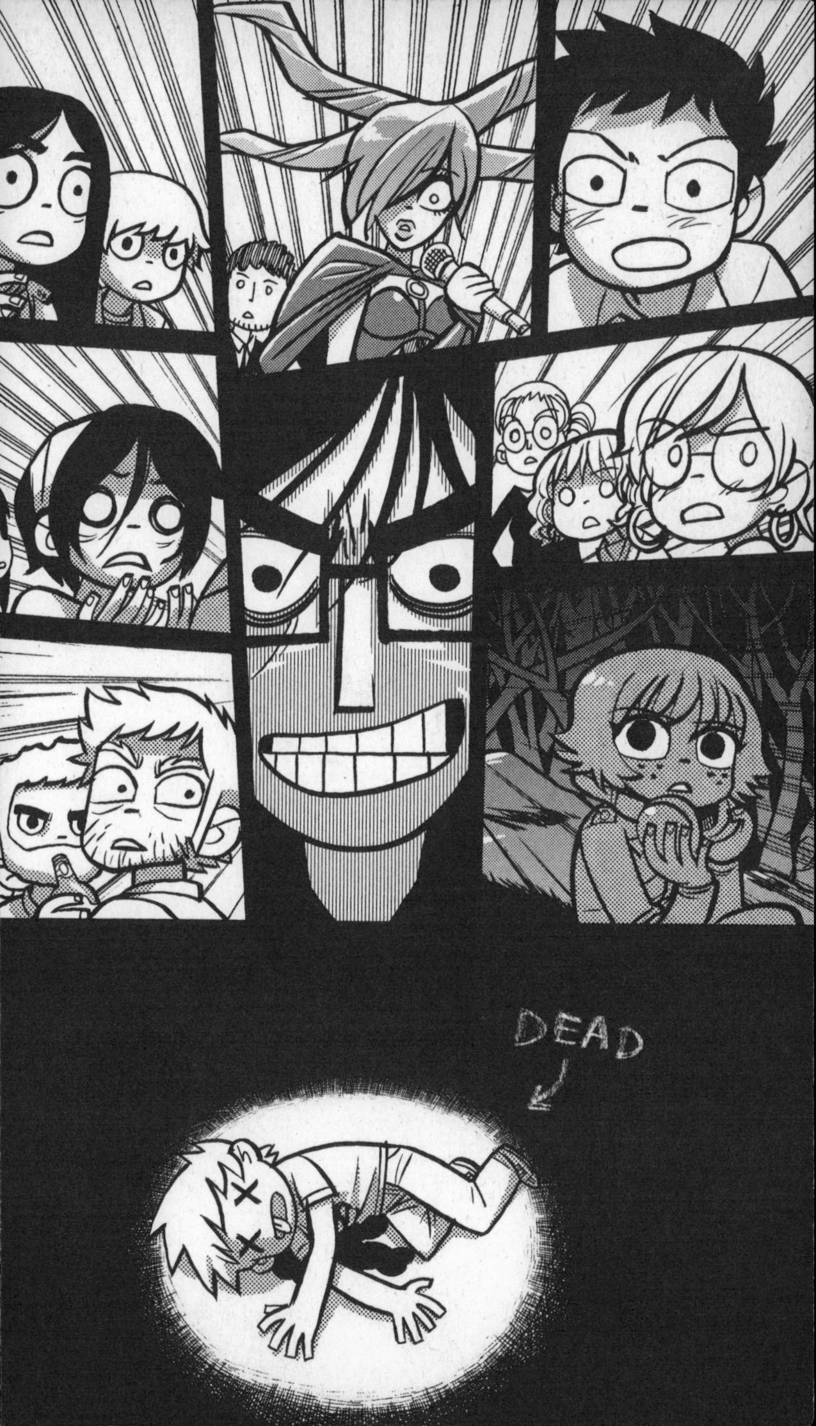
DEAD

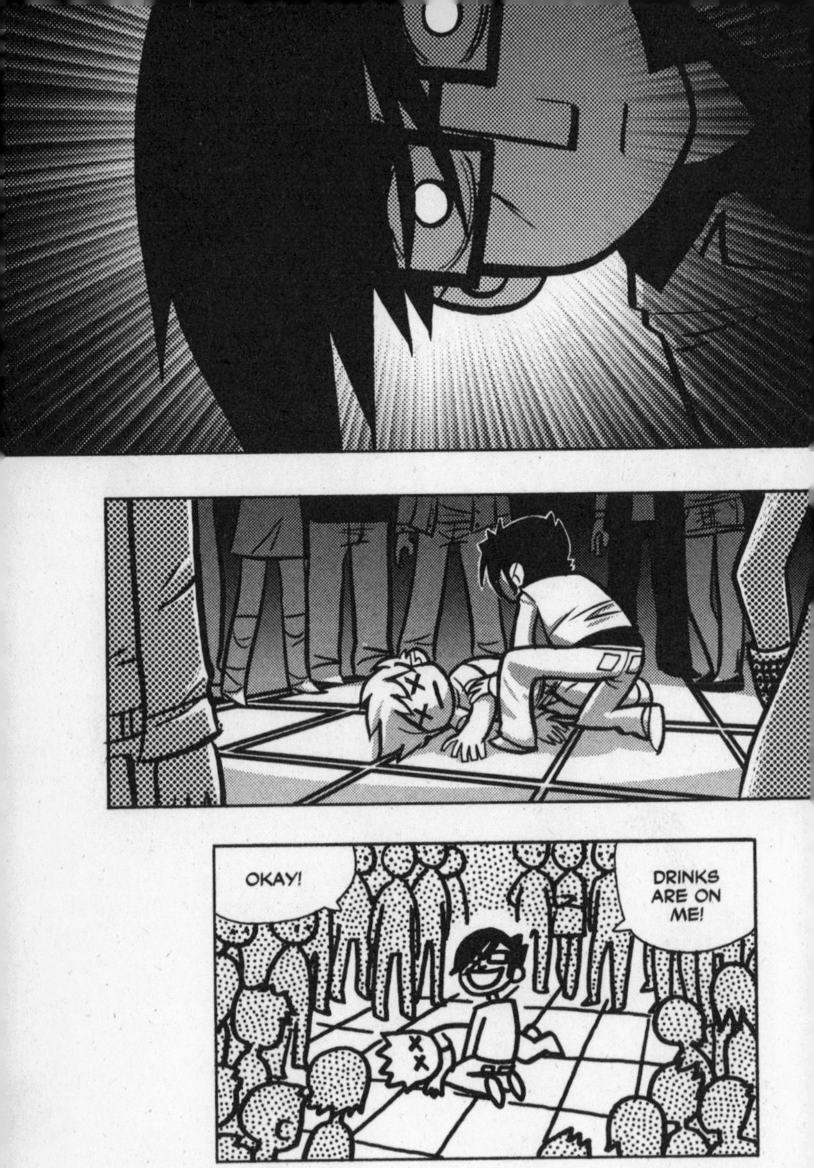
OKAY!
DRINKS ARE ON ME!

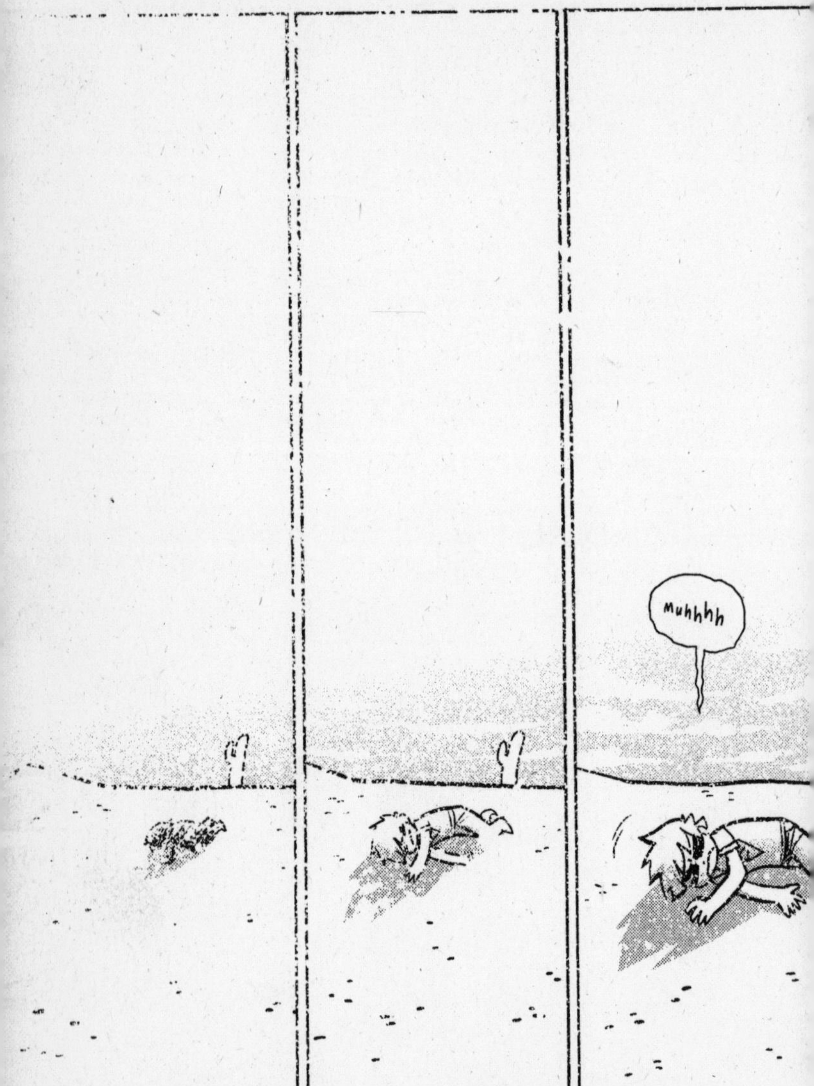
Muhhhh

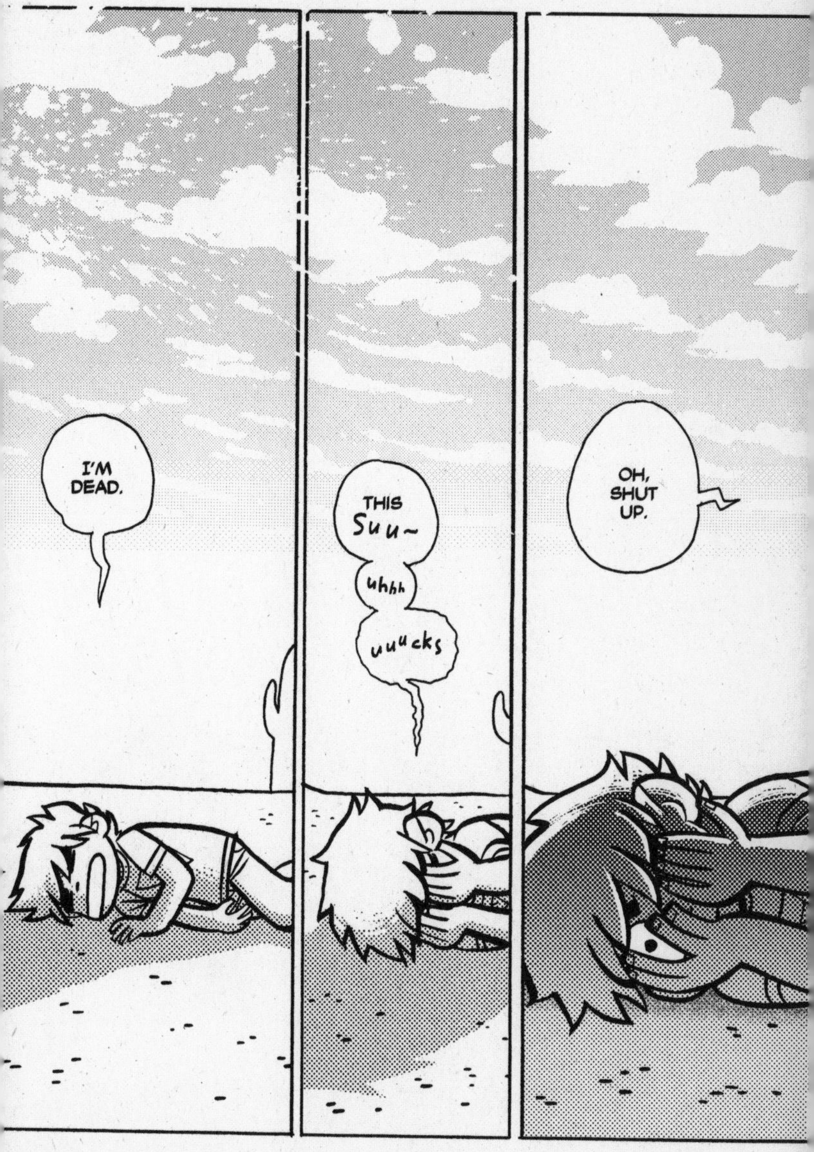
I'M DEAD.
THIS Suu~
uhhh
uuucks
OH, SHUT UP.

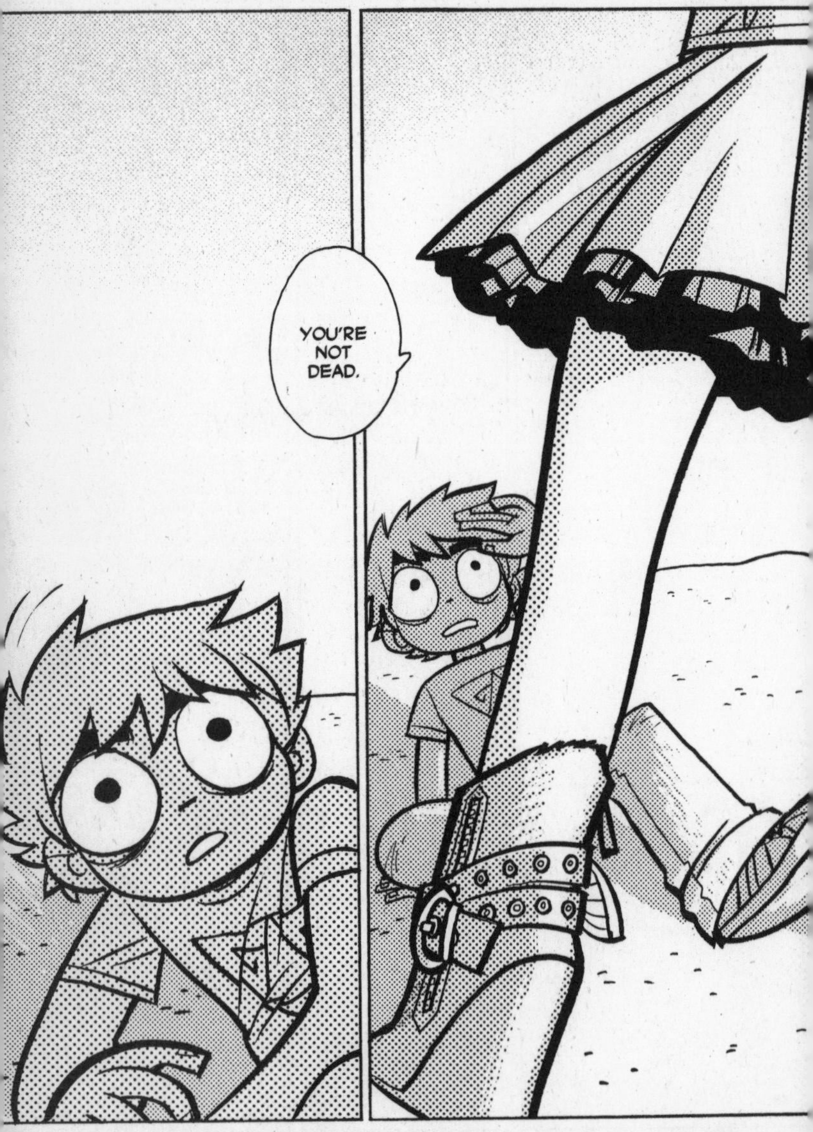
YOU'RE NOT DEAD.

36 Don't let it get you down

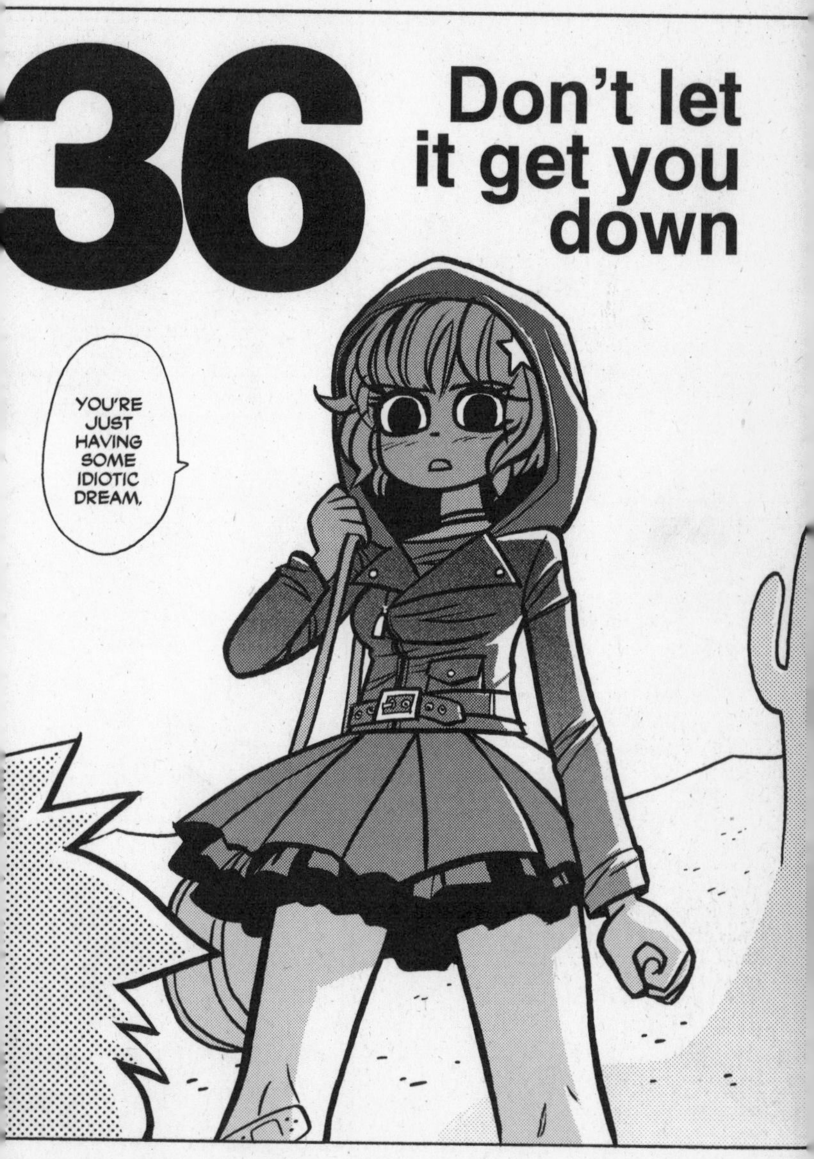
YOU'RE JUST HAVING SOME IDIOTIC DREAM.

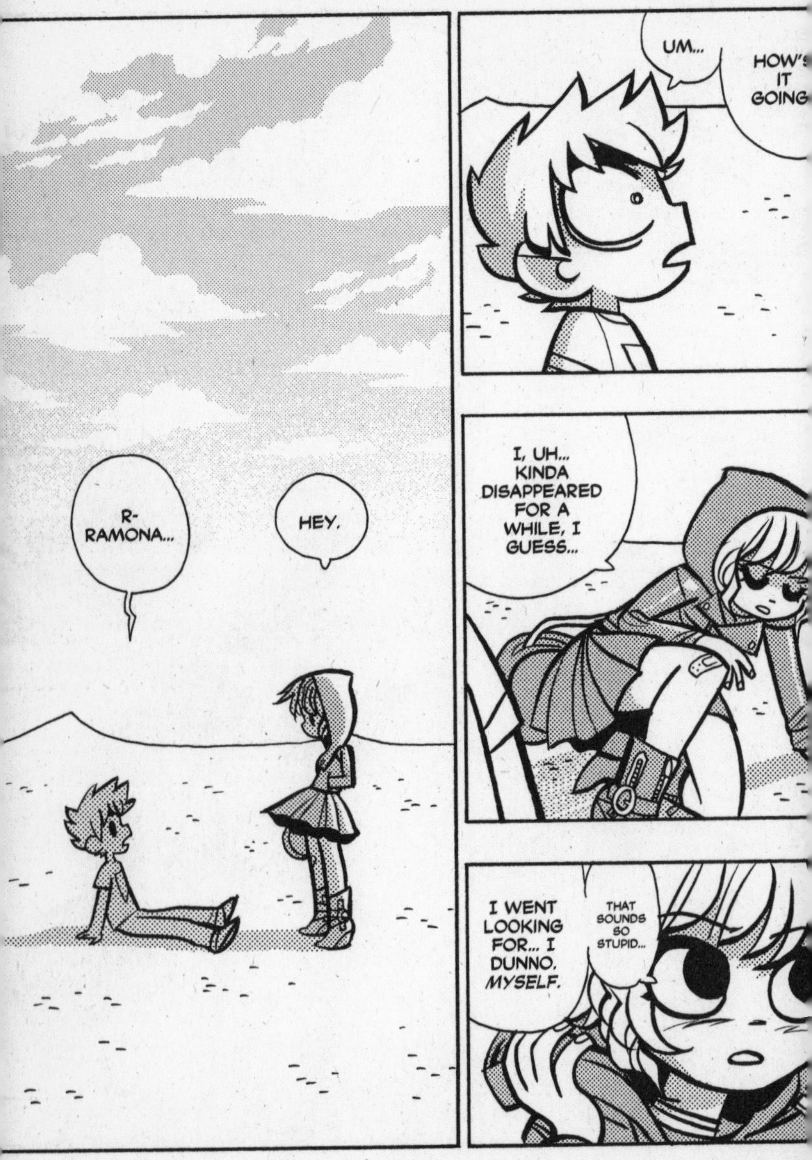
R-RAMONA...
HEY.
UM...
HOW'S IT GOING
I, UH... KINDA DISAPPEARED FOR A WHILE, I GUESS...
I WENT LOOKING FOR... I DUNNO, *MYSELF.*
THAT SOUNDS SO STUPID...

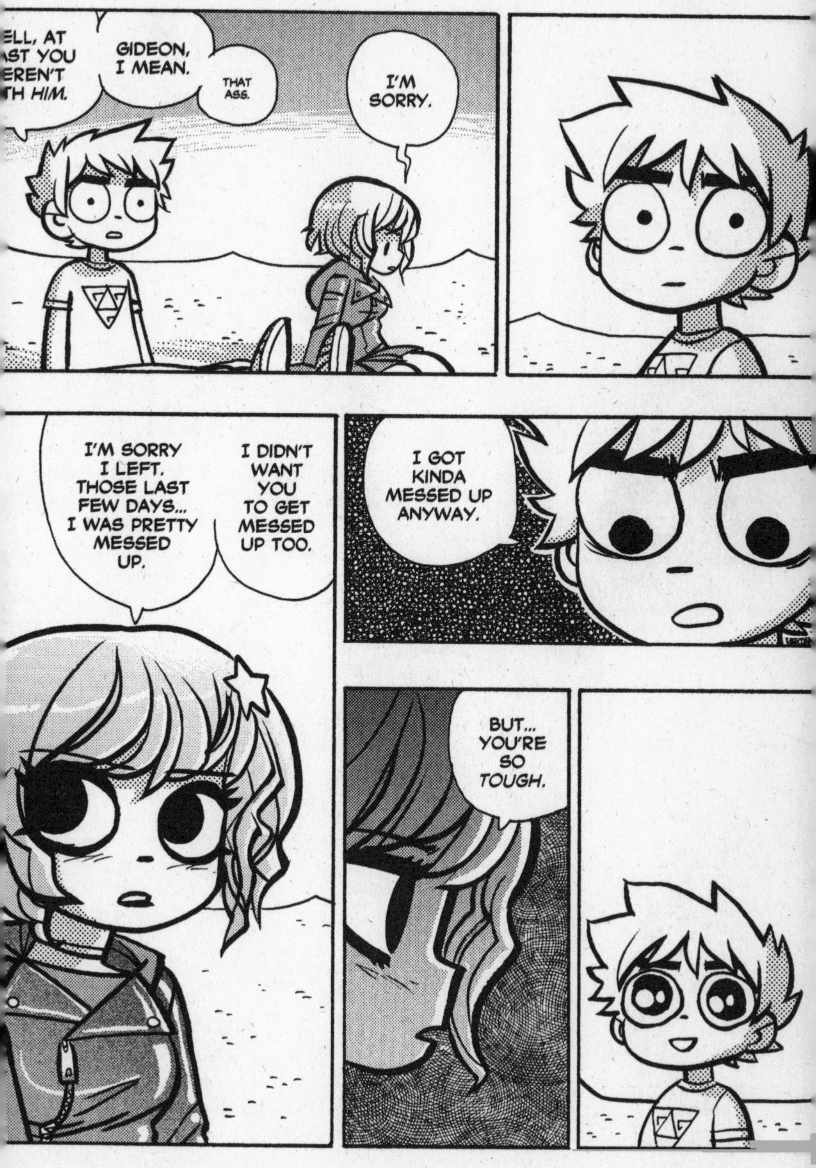

ELL, AT
AST YOU
EREN'T
TH *HIM*.
GIDEON, I MEAN.
THAT ASS.
I'M SORRY.
I'M SORRY I LEFT. THOSE LAST FEW DAYS... I WAS PRETTY MESSED UP.
I DIDN'T WANT YOU TO GET MESSED UP TOO.
I GOT KINDA MESSED UP ANYWAY.
BUT... YOU'RE SO *TOUGH*.

134

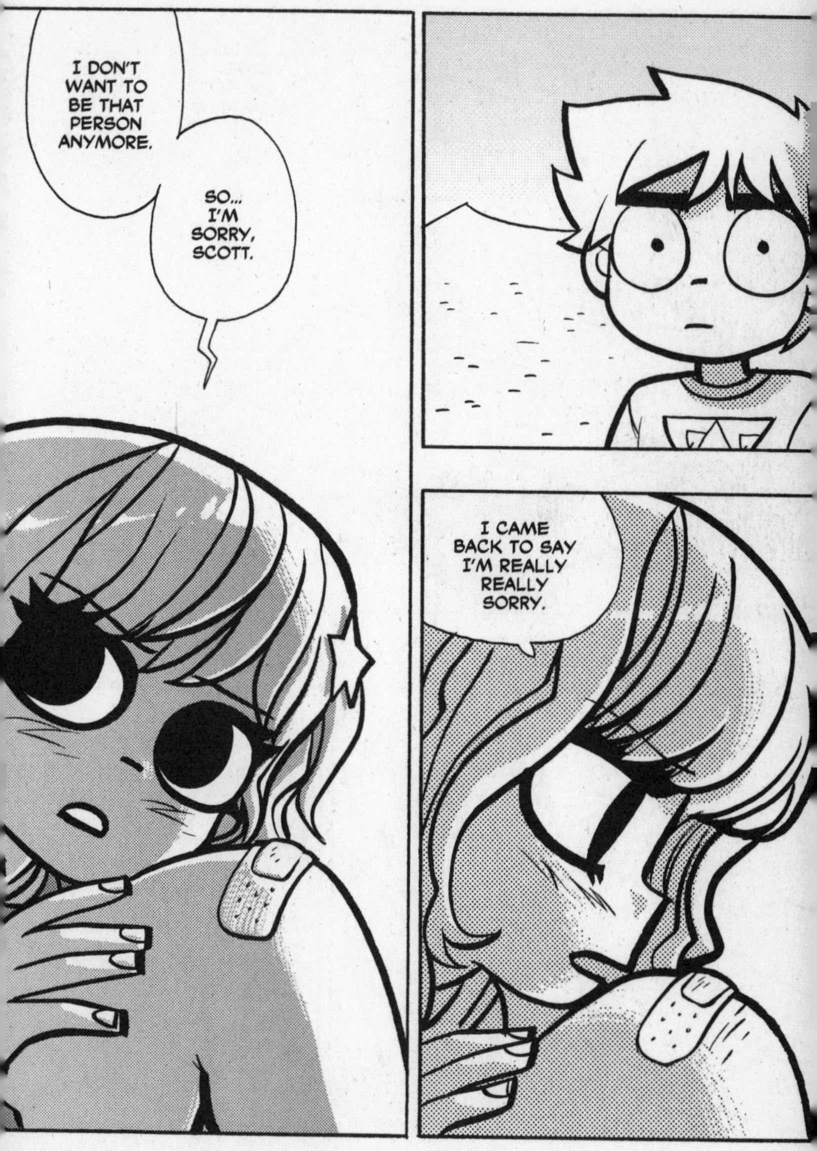
I DON'T WANT TO BE THAT PERSON ANYMORE.
SO... I'M SORRY, SCOTT.
I CAME BACK TO SAY I'M REALLY REALLY SORRY.

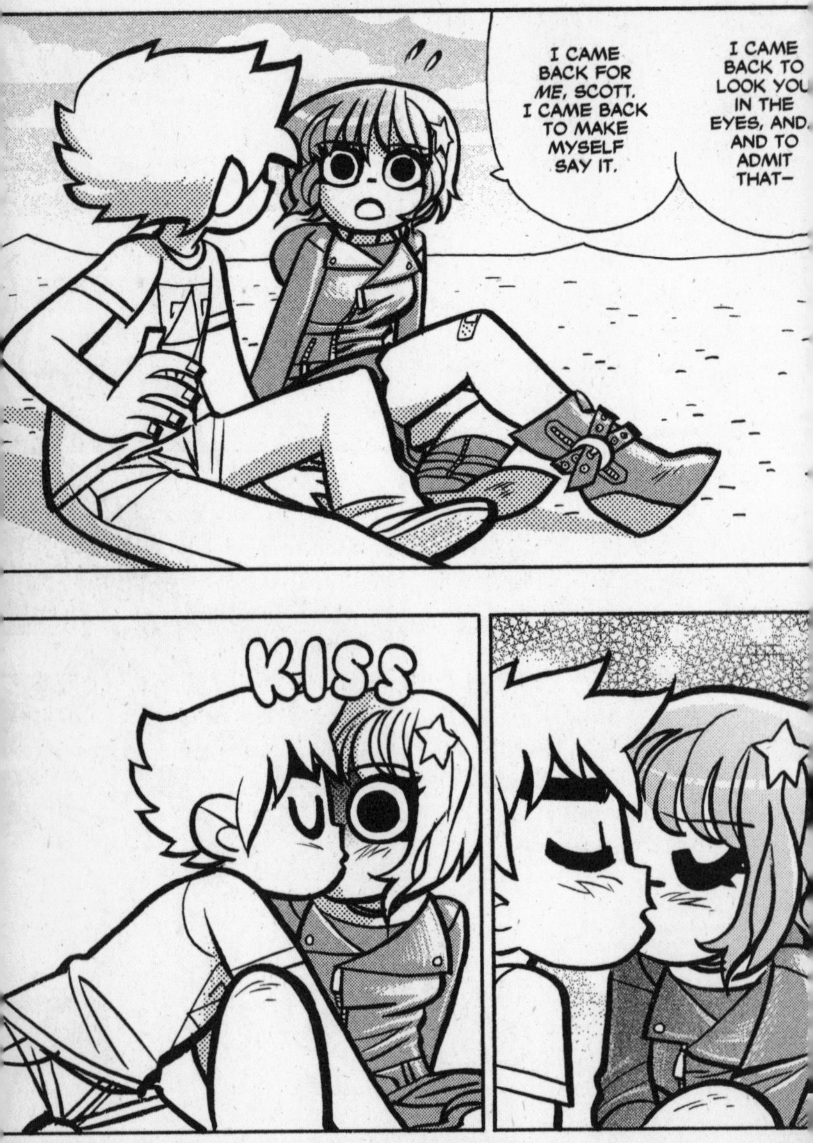
I CAME BACK FOR *ME*, SCOTT. I CAME BACK TO MAKE MYSELF SAY IT.
I CAME BACK TO LOOK YOU IN THE EYES, AND, AND TO ADMIT THAT–
KISS

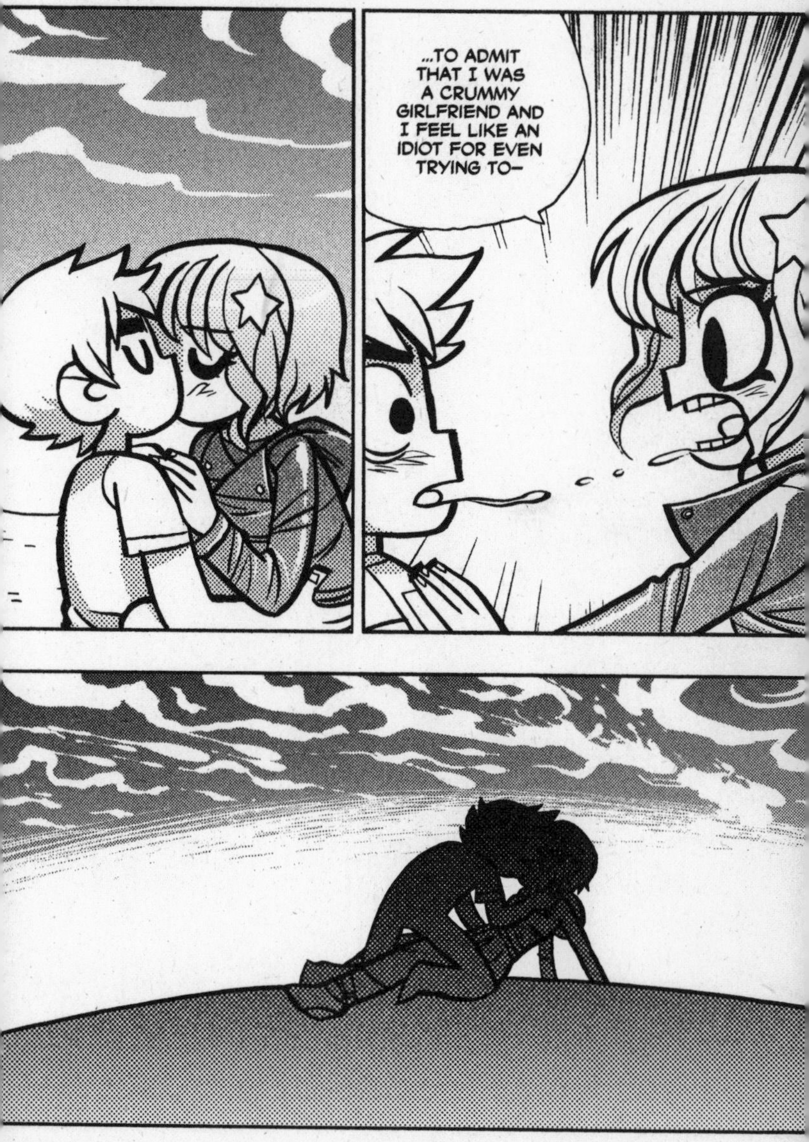
...TO ADMIT THAT I WAS A CRUMMY GIRLFRIEND AND I FEEL LIKE AN IDIOT FOR EVEN TRYING TO–

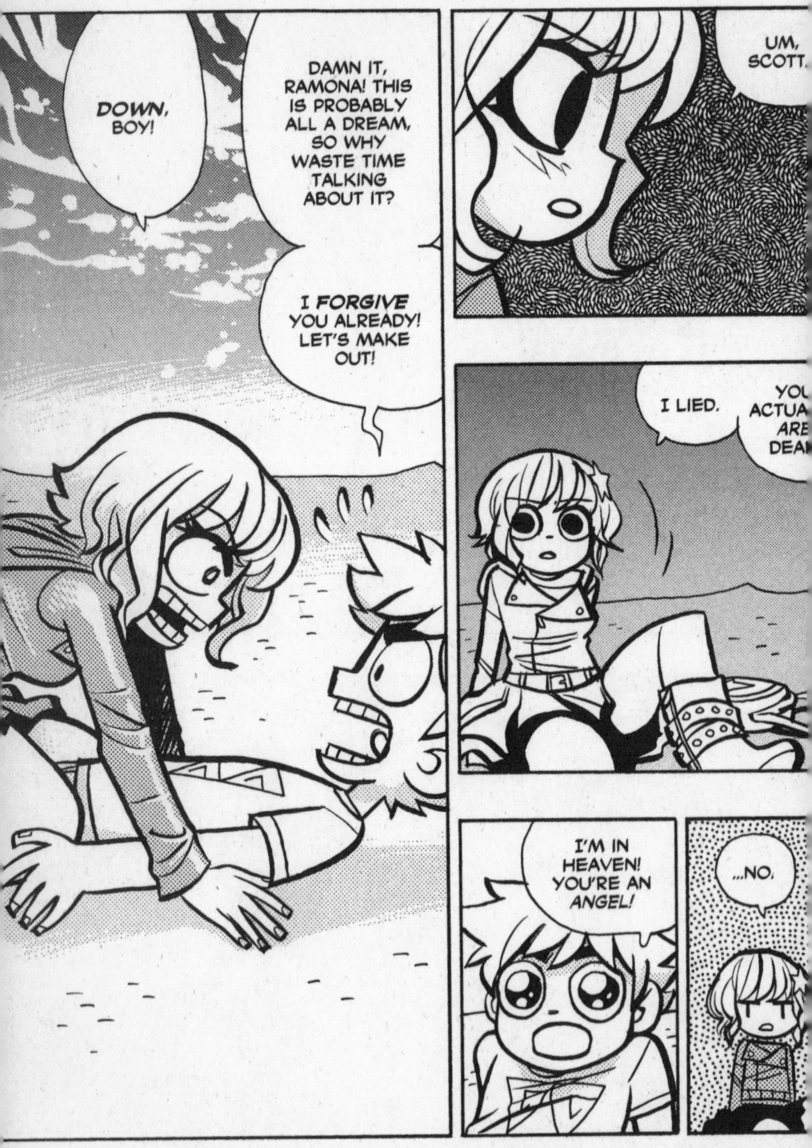

DOWN, BOY!
DAMN IT, RAMONA! THIS IS PROBABLY ALL A DREAM, SO WHY WASTE TIME TALKING ABOUT IT?
I FORGIVE YOU ALREADY! LET'S MAKE OUT!
UM, SCOTT.
I LIED.
YOU ACTUA ARE DEA
I'M IN HEAVEN! YOU'RE AN ANGEL!
...NO.

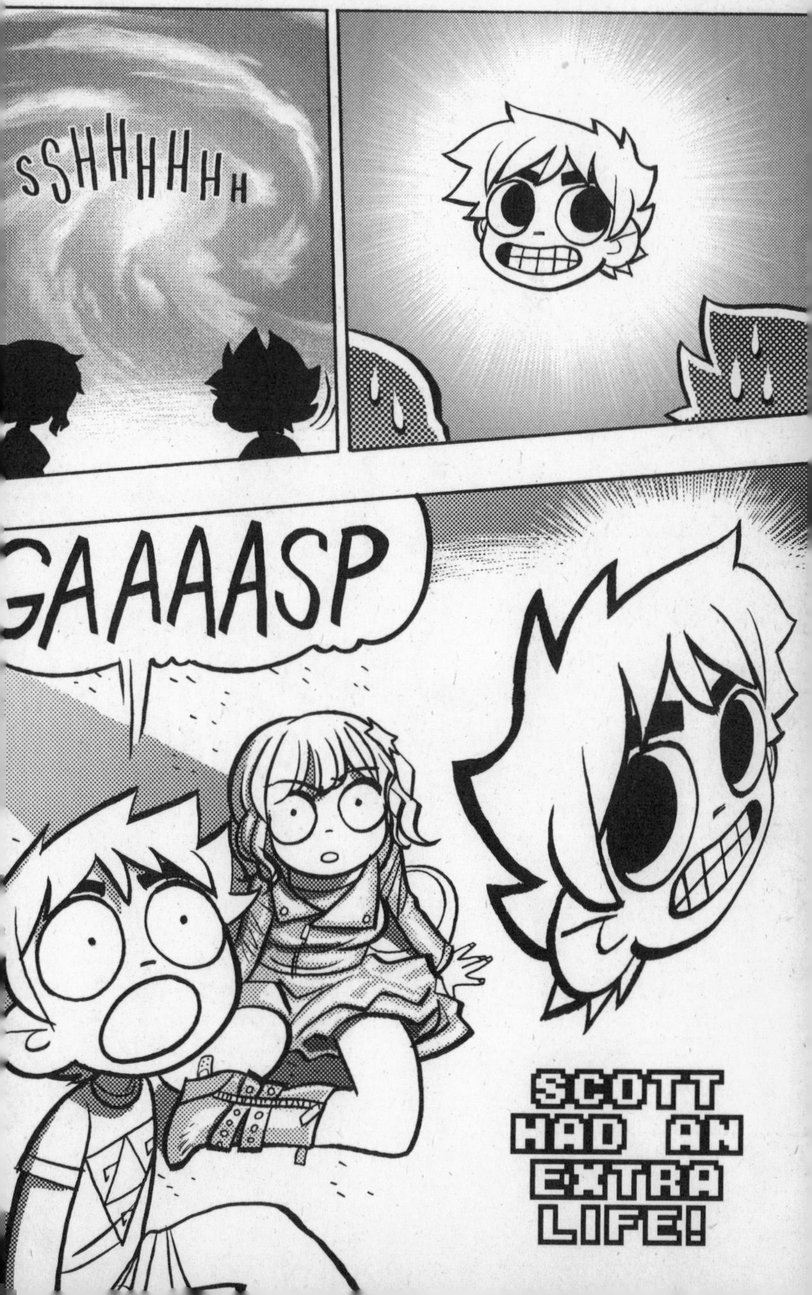
SSHHHHHHH
GAAAASP
SCOTT HAD AN EXTRA LIFE!

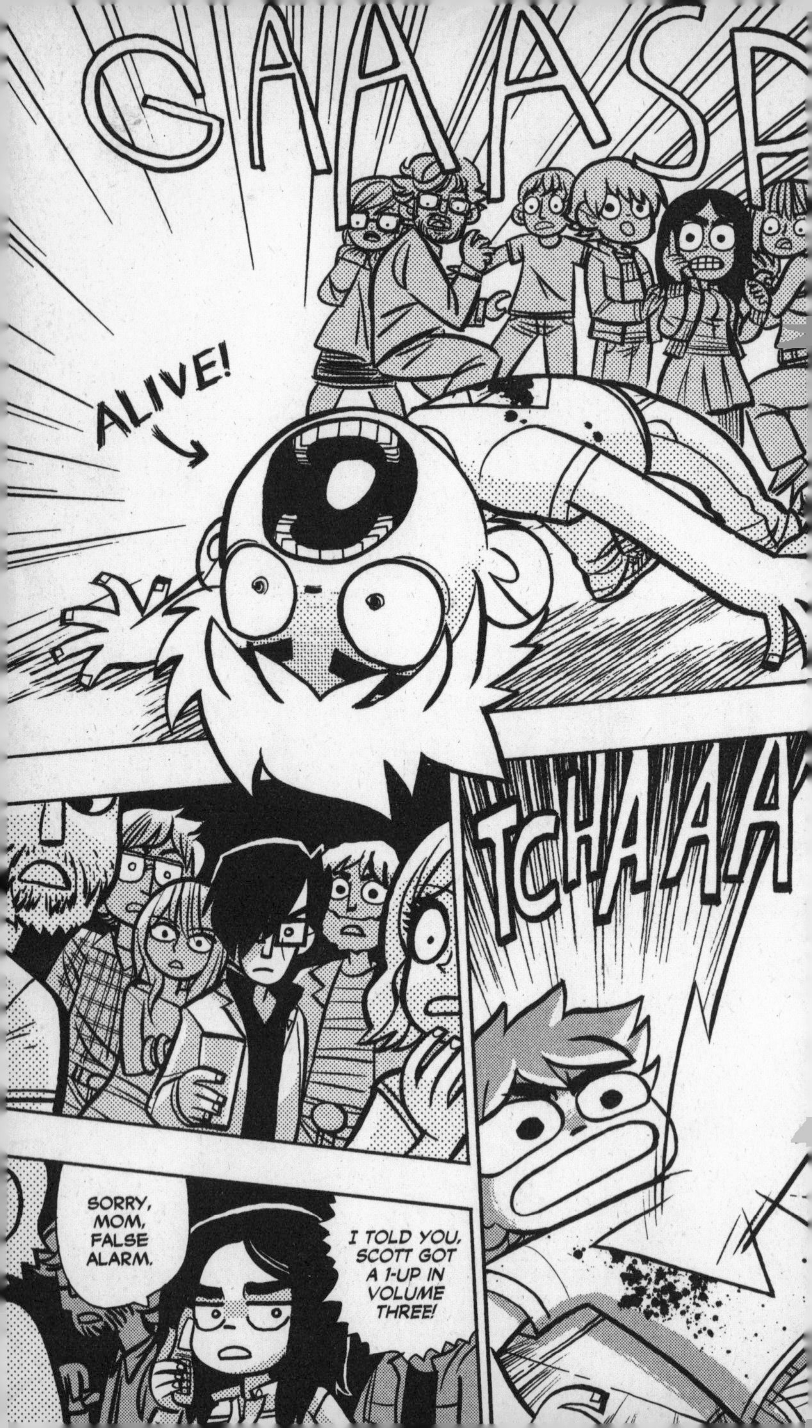
GAASP
ALIVE!
TCHAAA
SORRY, MOM, FALSE ALARM.
I TOLD YOU, SCOTT GOT A 1-UP IN VOLUME THREE!

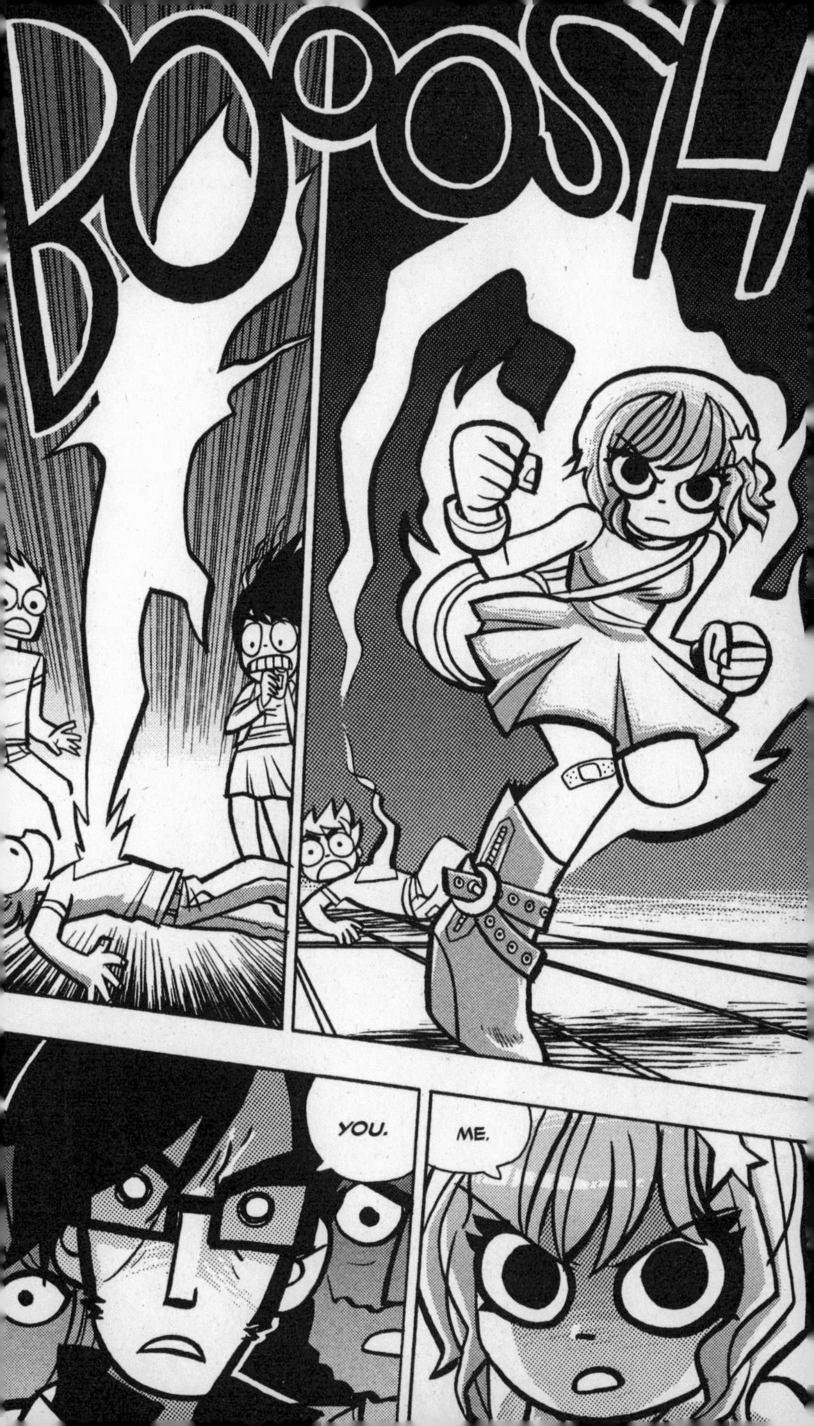
BOOOSH!
YOU.
ME.

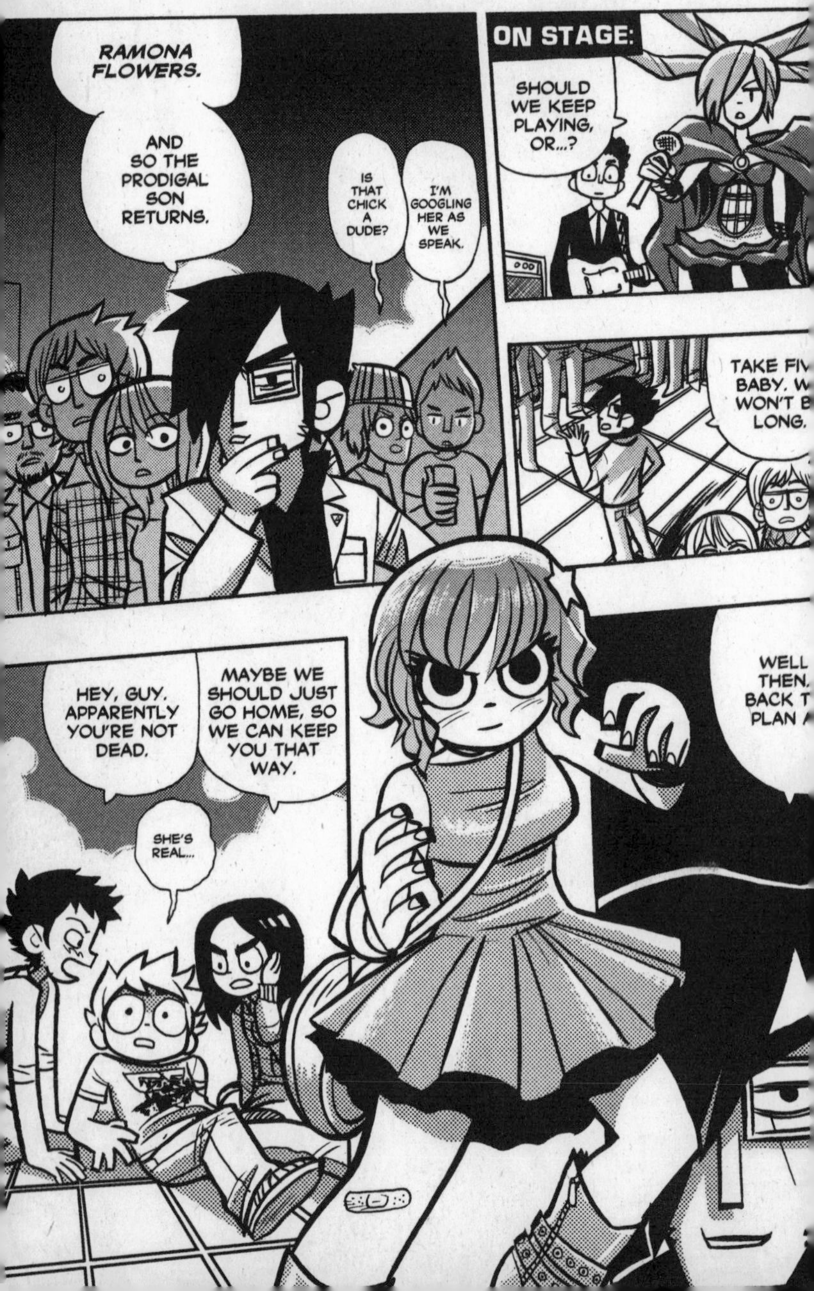

RAMONA FLOWERS.
AND SO THE PRODIGAL SON RETURNS.
IS THAT CHICK A DUDE?
I'M GOOGLING HER AS WE SPEAK.
ON STAGE:
SHOULD WE KEEP PLAYING, OR...?
HEY, GUY. APPARENTLY YOU'RE NOT DEAD.
MAYBE WE SHOULD JUST GO HOME, SO WE CAN KEEP YOU THAT WAY.
SHE'S REAL...

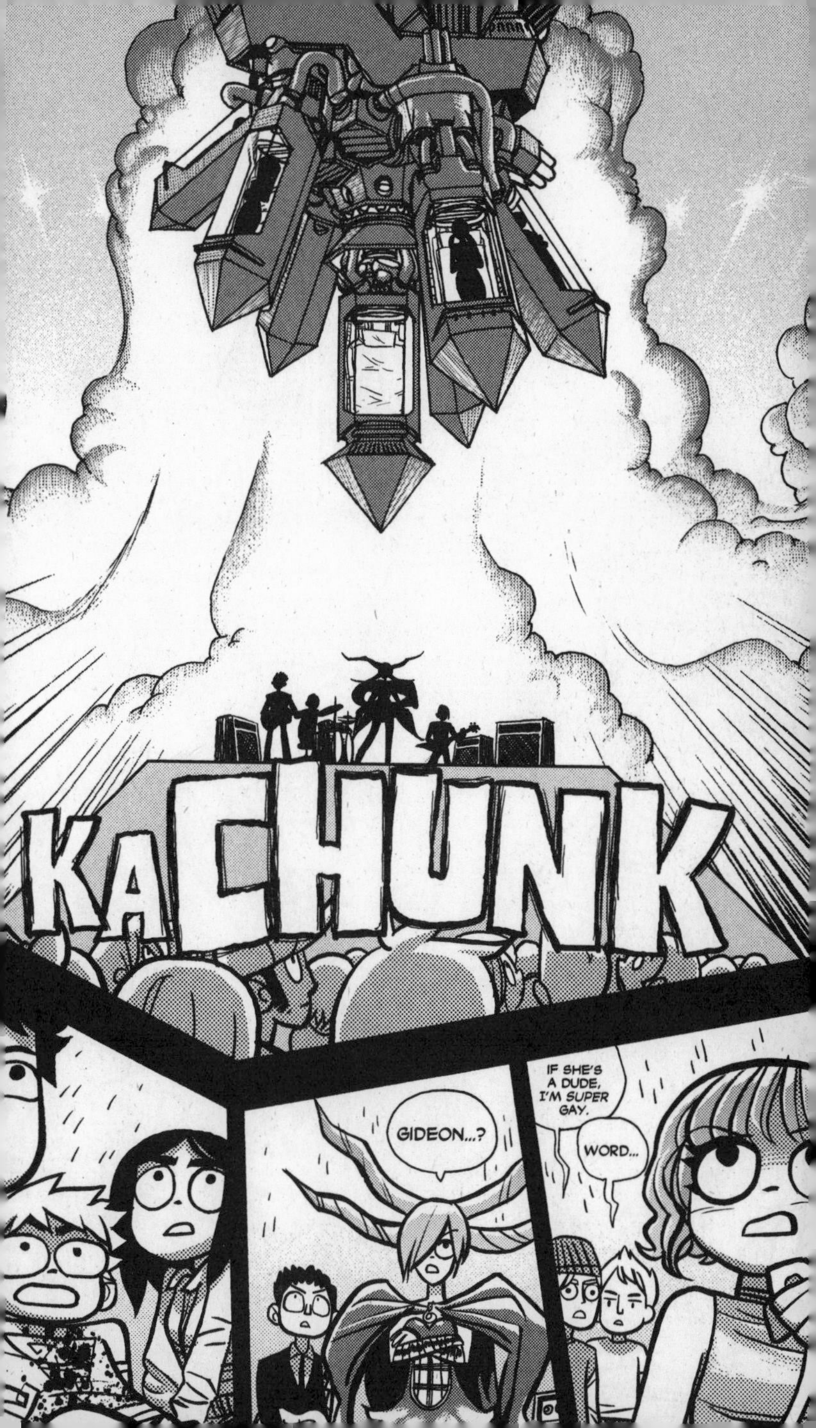
KACHUNK
GIDEON...?
IF SHE'S A DUDE, I'M SUPER GAY.
WORD...

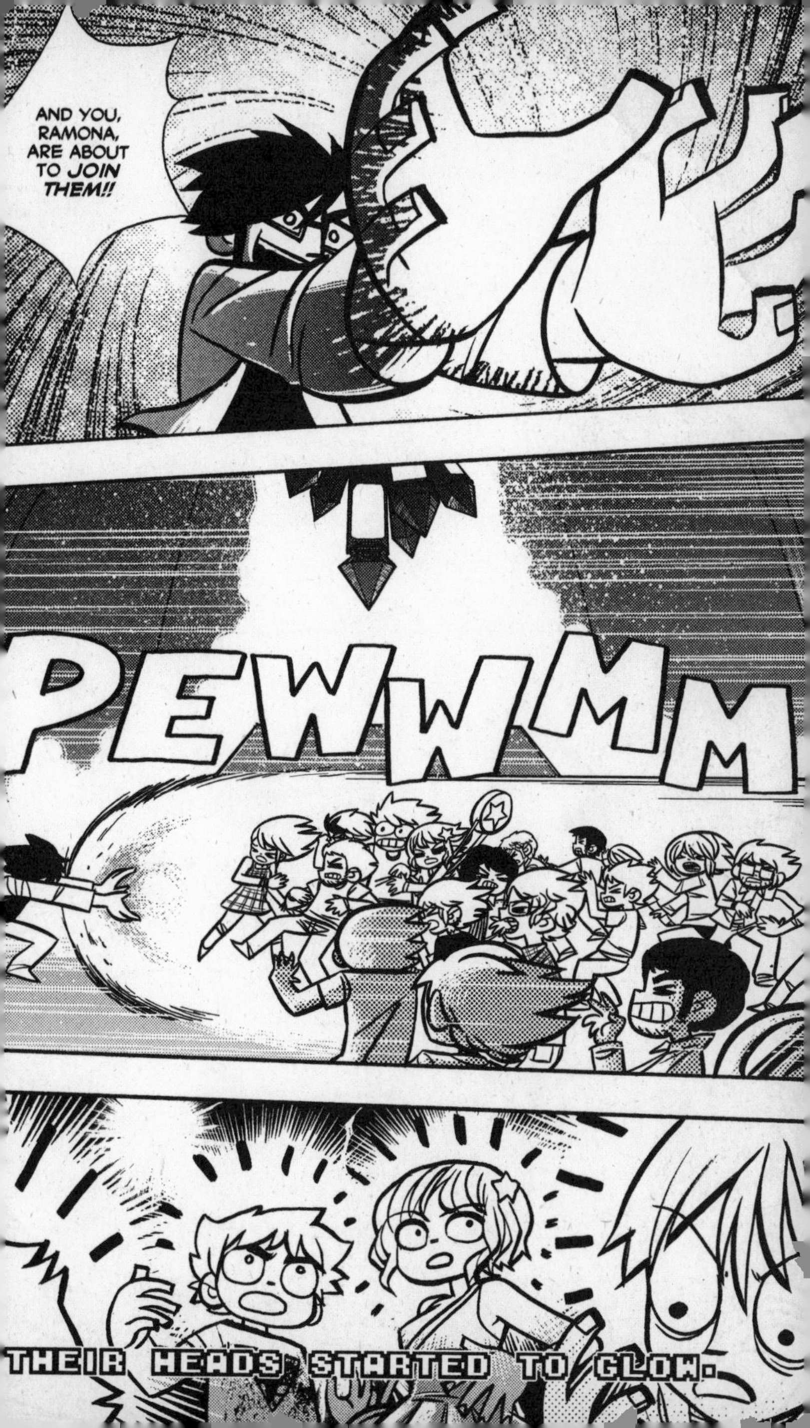
AND YOU, RAMONA, ARE ABOUT TO JOIN THEM!!
PEWWMM
THEIR HEADS STARTED TO GLOW.

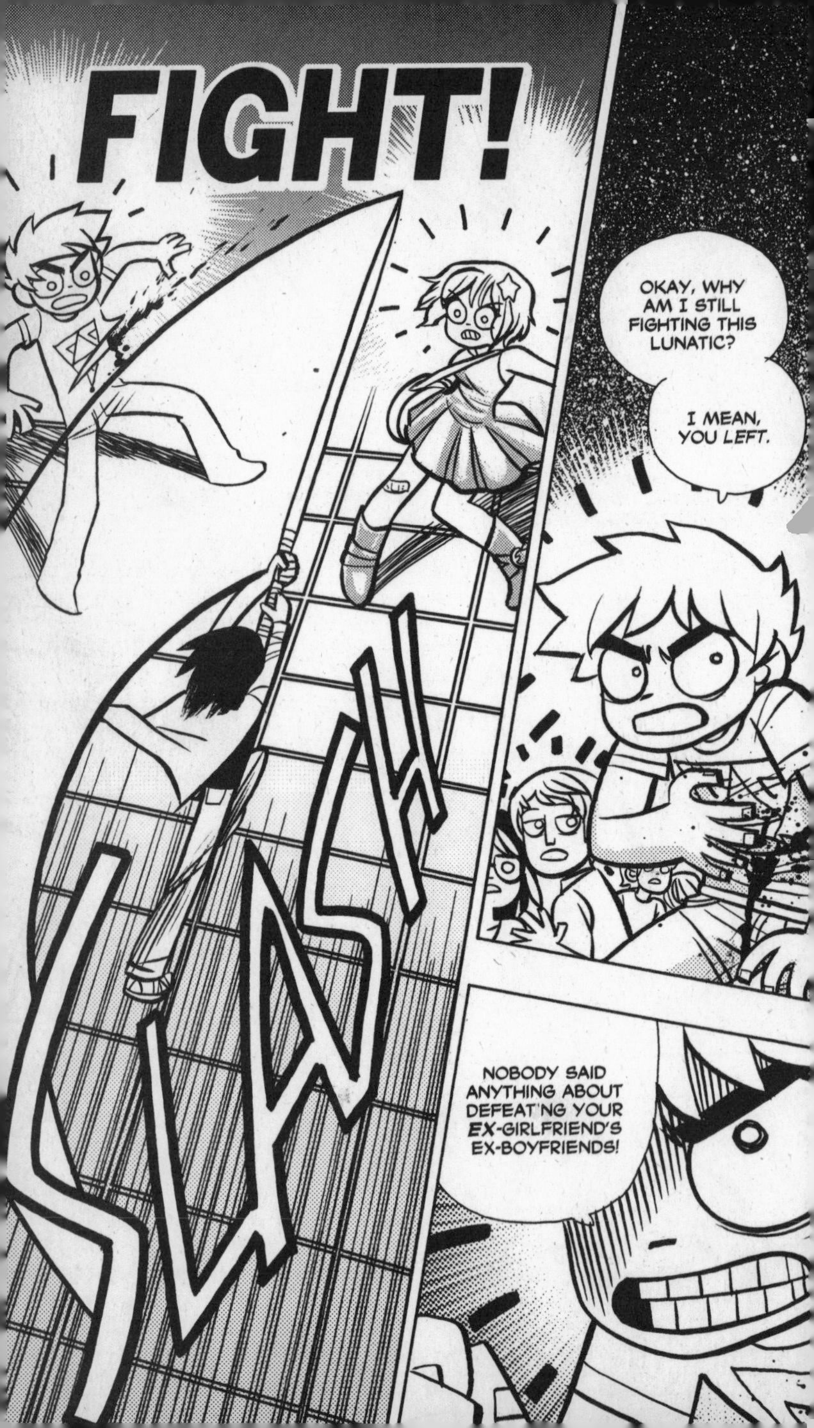
FIGHT!
OKAY, WHY AM I STILL FIGHTING THIS LUNATIC?
I MEAN, YOU LEFT.
SLASH!
NOBODY SAID ANYTHING ABOUT DEFEATING YOUR EX-GIRLFRIEND'S EX-BOYFRIENDS!

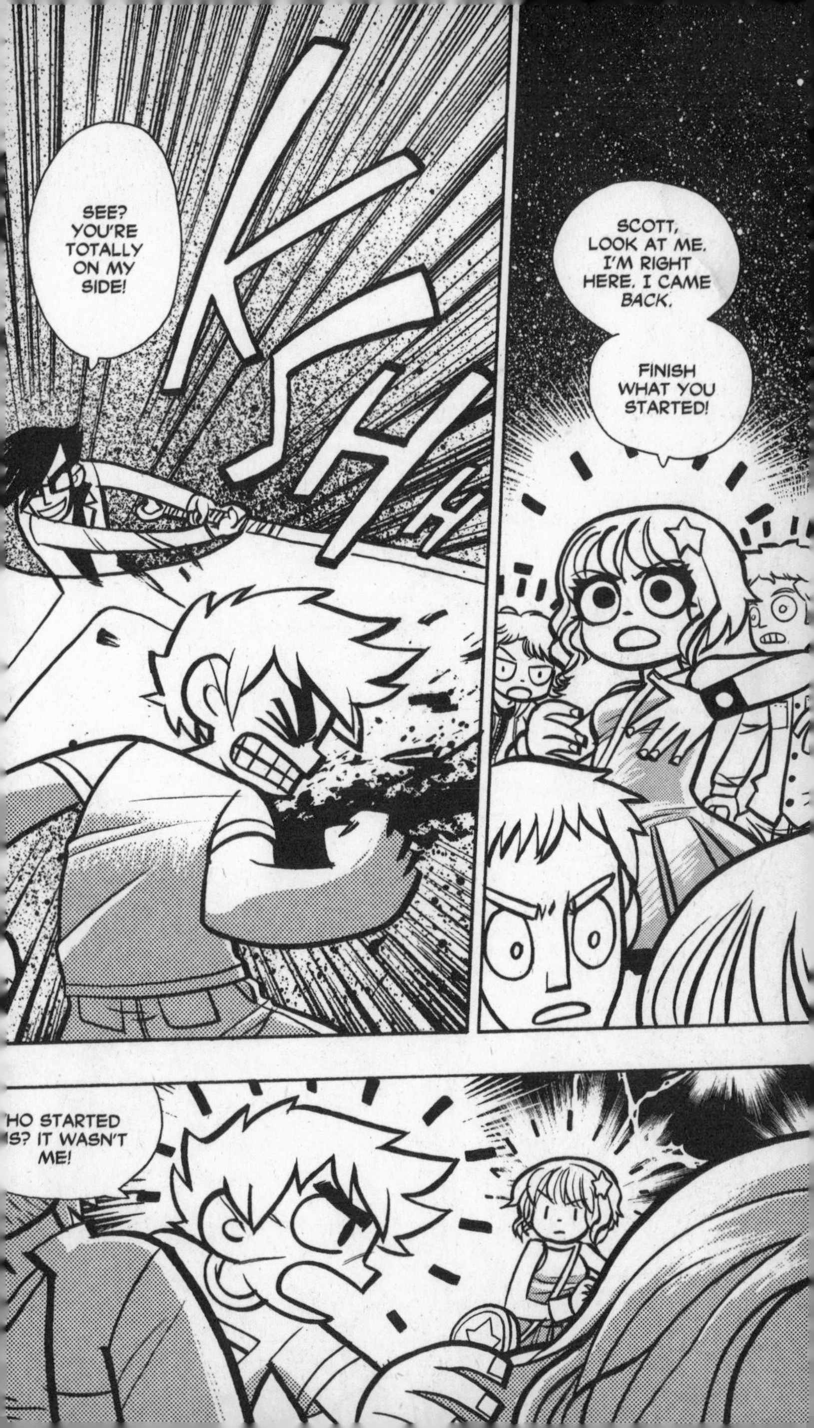

SEE? YOU'RE TOTALLY ON MY SIDE!
KSHHH
SCOTT, LOOK AT ME. I'M RIGHT HERE. I CAME BACK.
FINISH WHAT YOU STARTED!
HO STARTED S? IT WASN'T ME!

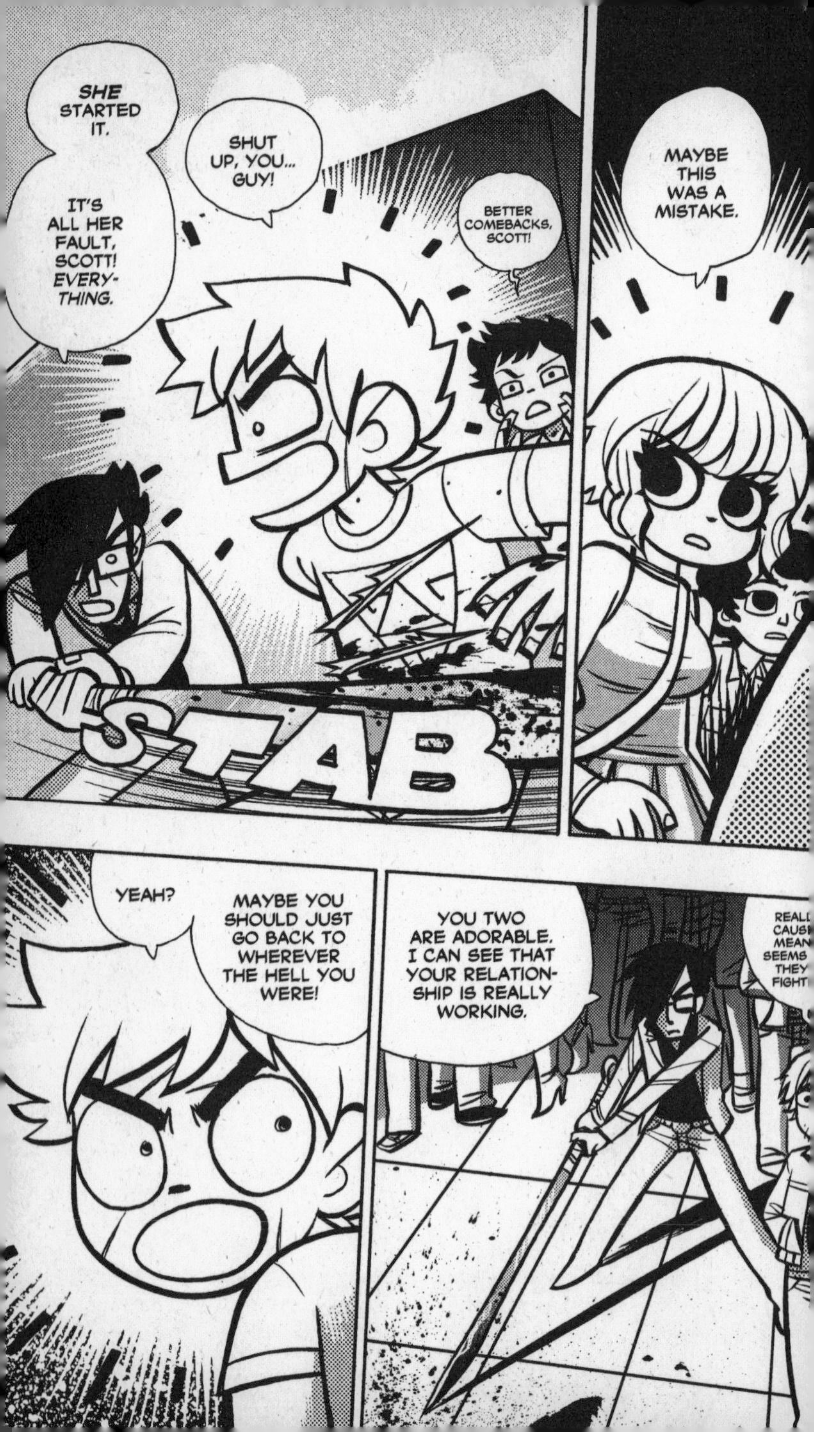
SHE STARTED IT.
IT'S ALL HER FAULT, SCOTT! EVERY-THING.
SHUT UP, YOU... GUY!
BETTER COMEBACKS, SCOTT!
MAYBE THIS WAS A MISTAKE.
STAB
YEAH?
MAYBE YOU SHOULD JUST GO BACK TO WHEREVER THE HELL YOU WERE!
YOU TWO ARE ADORABLE. I CAN SEE THAT YOUR RELATION-SHIP IS REALLY WORKING.
REALL CAUS MEAN SEEMS THEY FIGHT

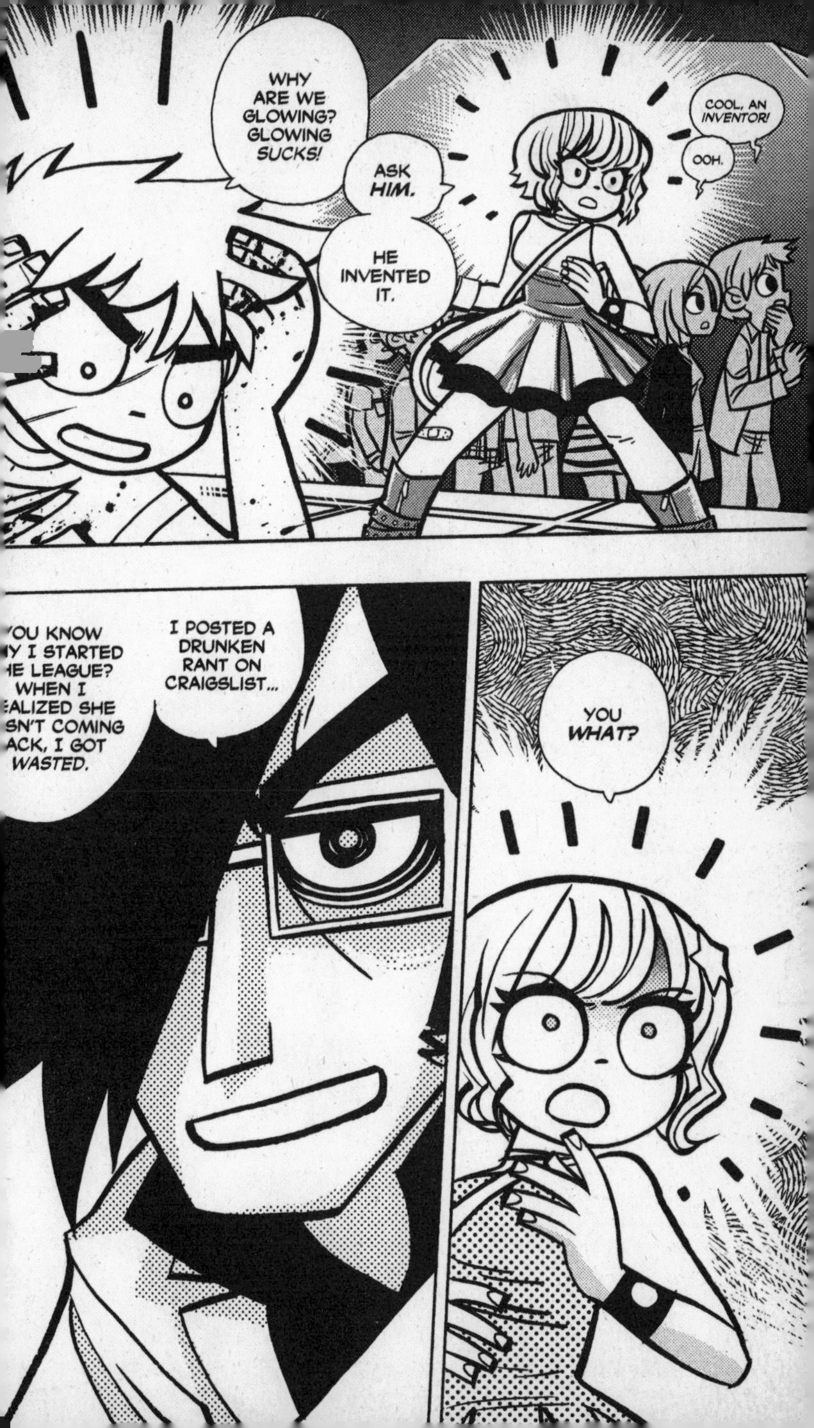
WHY ARE WE GLOWING? GLOWING SUCKS!
ASK HIM.
HE INVENTED IT.
COOL, AN INVENTOR!
OOH.
YOU KNOW Y I STARTED HE LEAGUE? WHEN I EALIZED SHE SN'T COMING ACK, I GOT WASTED.
I POSTED A DRUNKEN RANT ON CRAIGSLIST...
YOU WHAT?

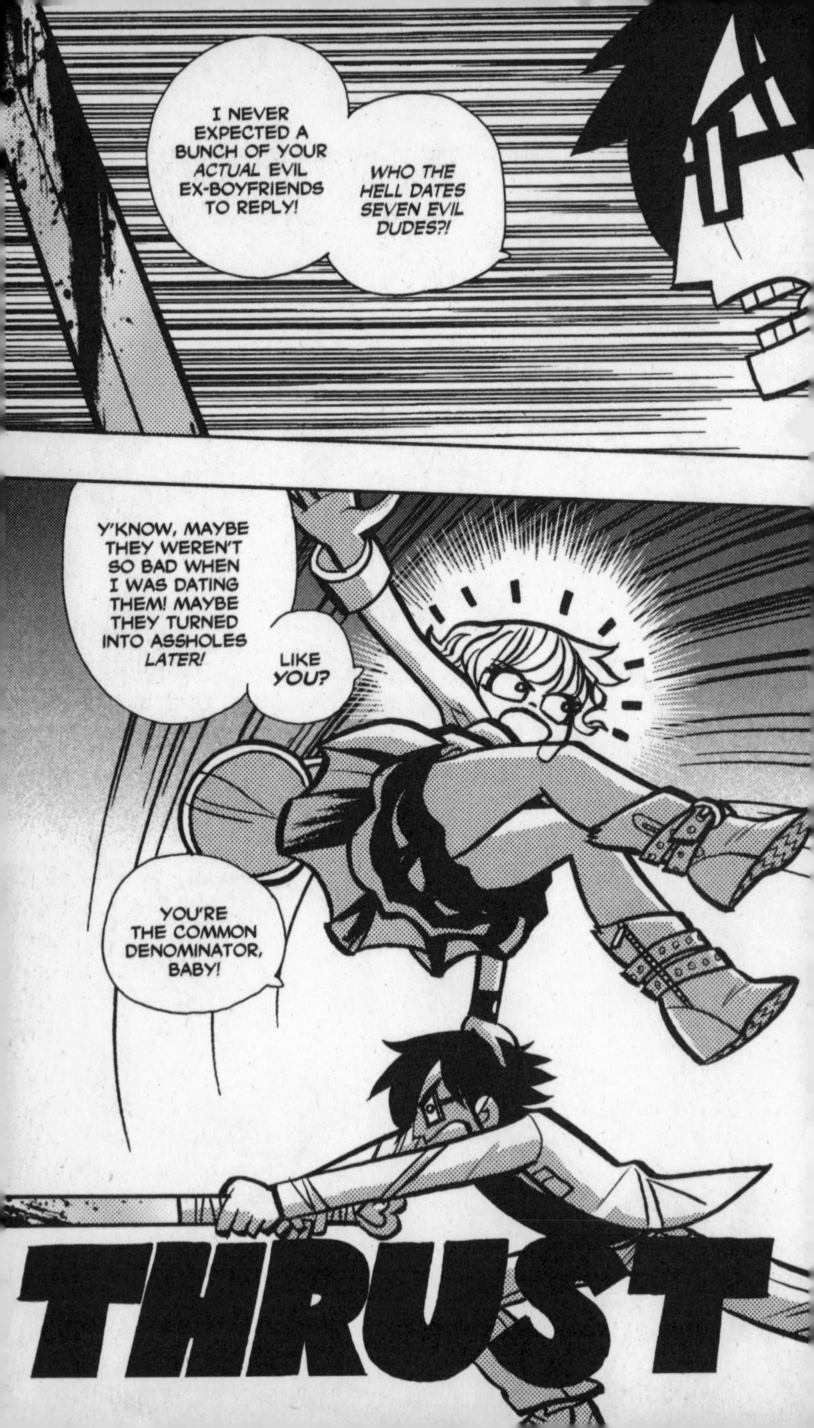

I NEVER EXPECTED A BUNCH OF YOUR *ACTUAL* EVIL EX-BOYFRIENDS TO REPLY!
WHO THE HELL DATES SEVEN EVIL DUDES?!
Y'KNOW, MAYBE THEY WEREN'T SO BAD WHEN I WAS DATING THEM! MAYBE THEY TURNED INTO ASSHOLES *LATER!*
LIKE *YOU?*
YOU'RE THE COMMON DENOMINATOR, BABY!
THRUST

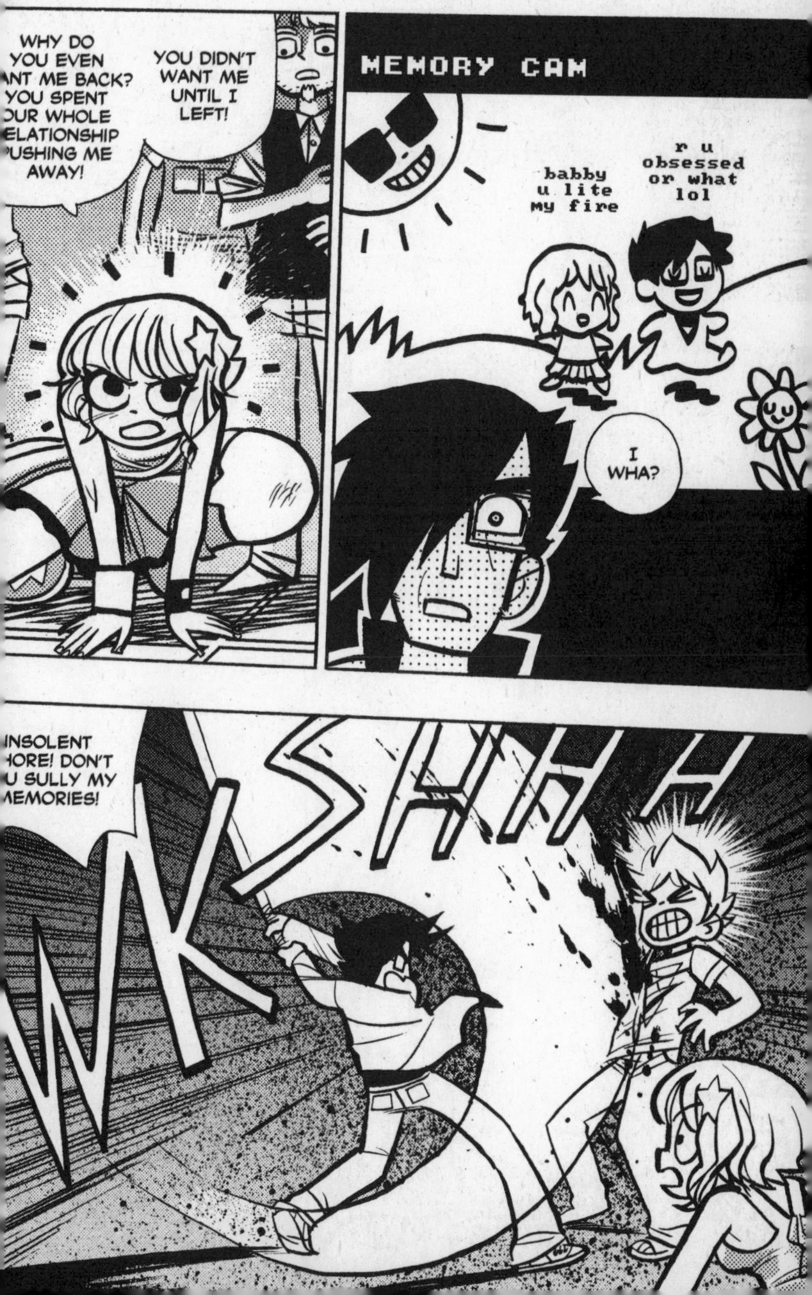
WHY DO YOU EVEN ANT ME BACK? YOU SPENT OUR WHOLE ELATIONSHIP USHING ME AWAY!
YOU DIDN'T WANT ME UNTIL I LEFT!
MEMORY CAM
babby u lite my fire
r u obsessed or what lol
I WHA?
INSOLENT HORE! DON'T U SULLY MY EMORIES!
WK
SHHH

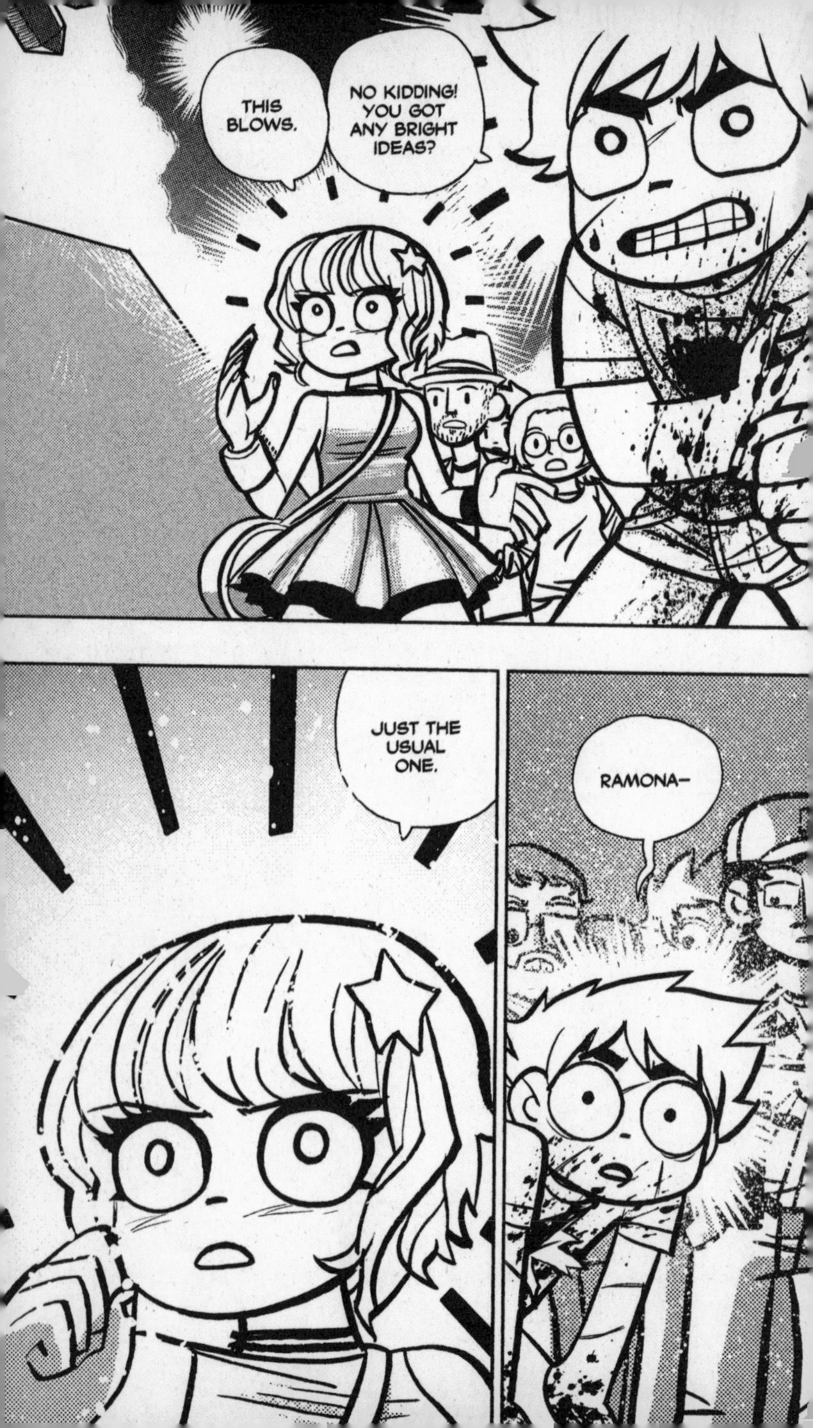
THIS BLOWS.
NO KIDDING! YOU GOT ANY BRIGHT IDEAS?
JUST THE USUAL ONE.
RAMONA—

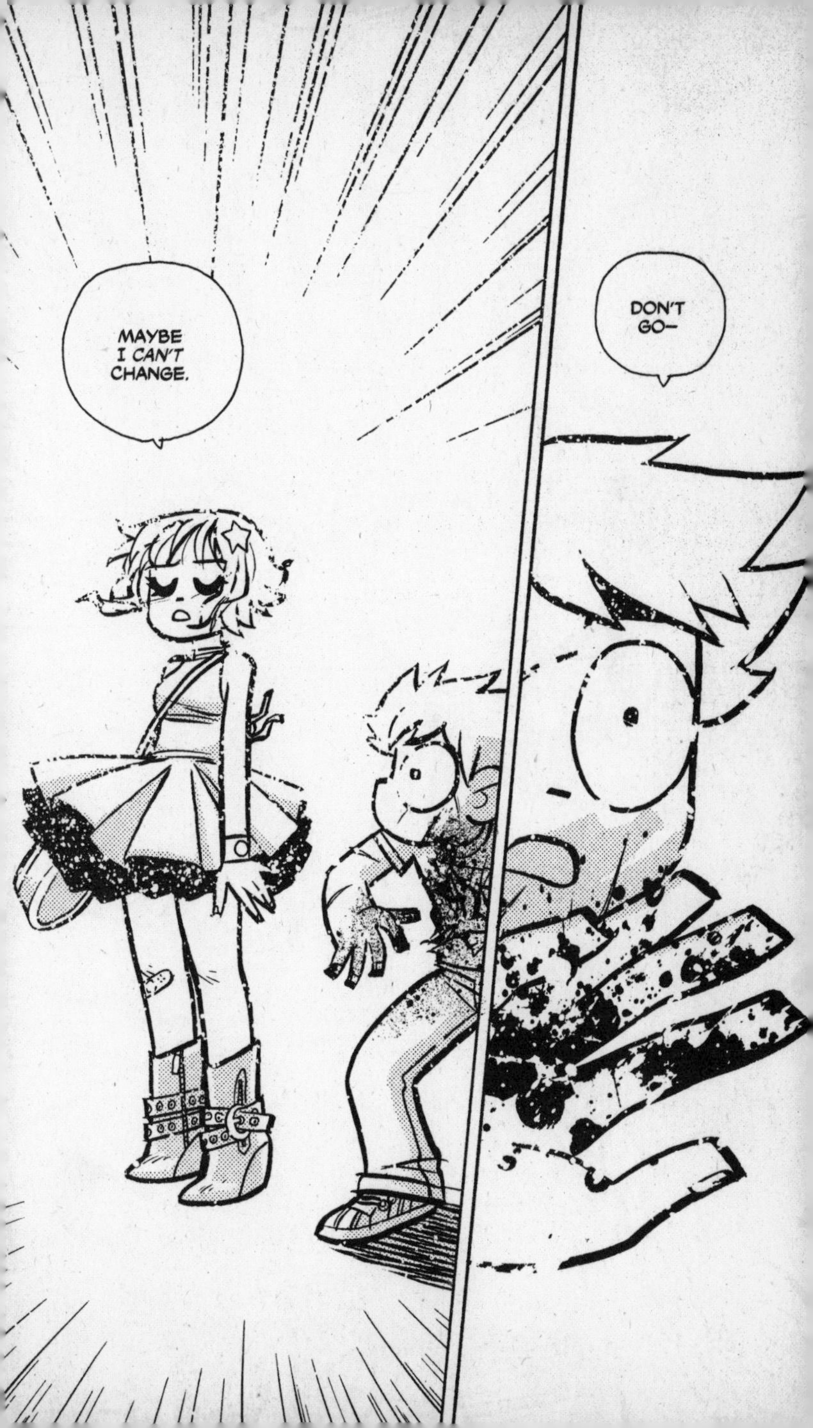
MAYBE I CAN'T CHANGE.
DON'T GO—

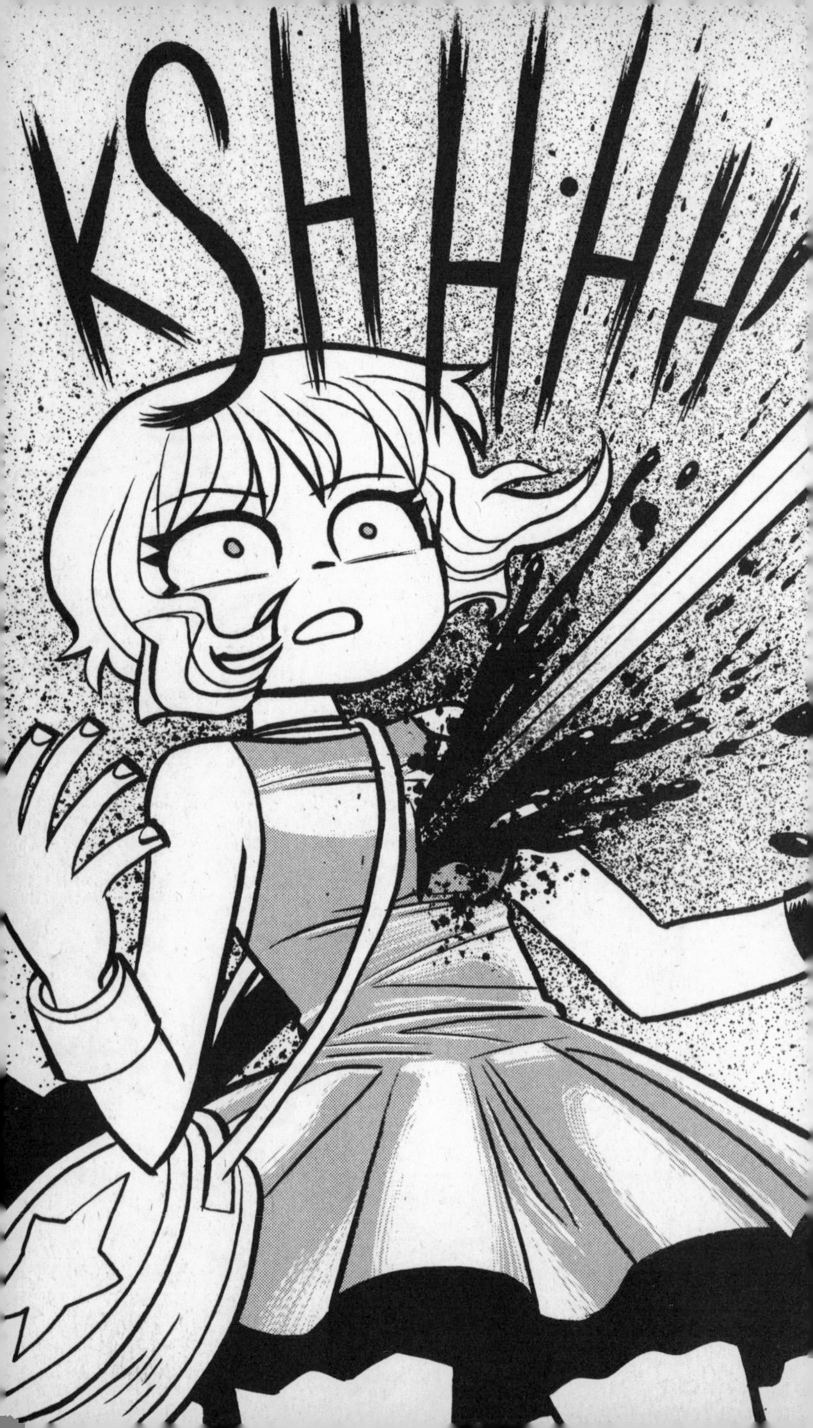
KSHHHH

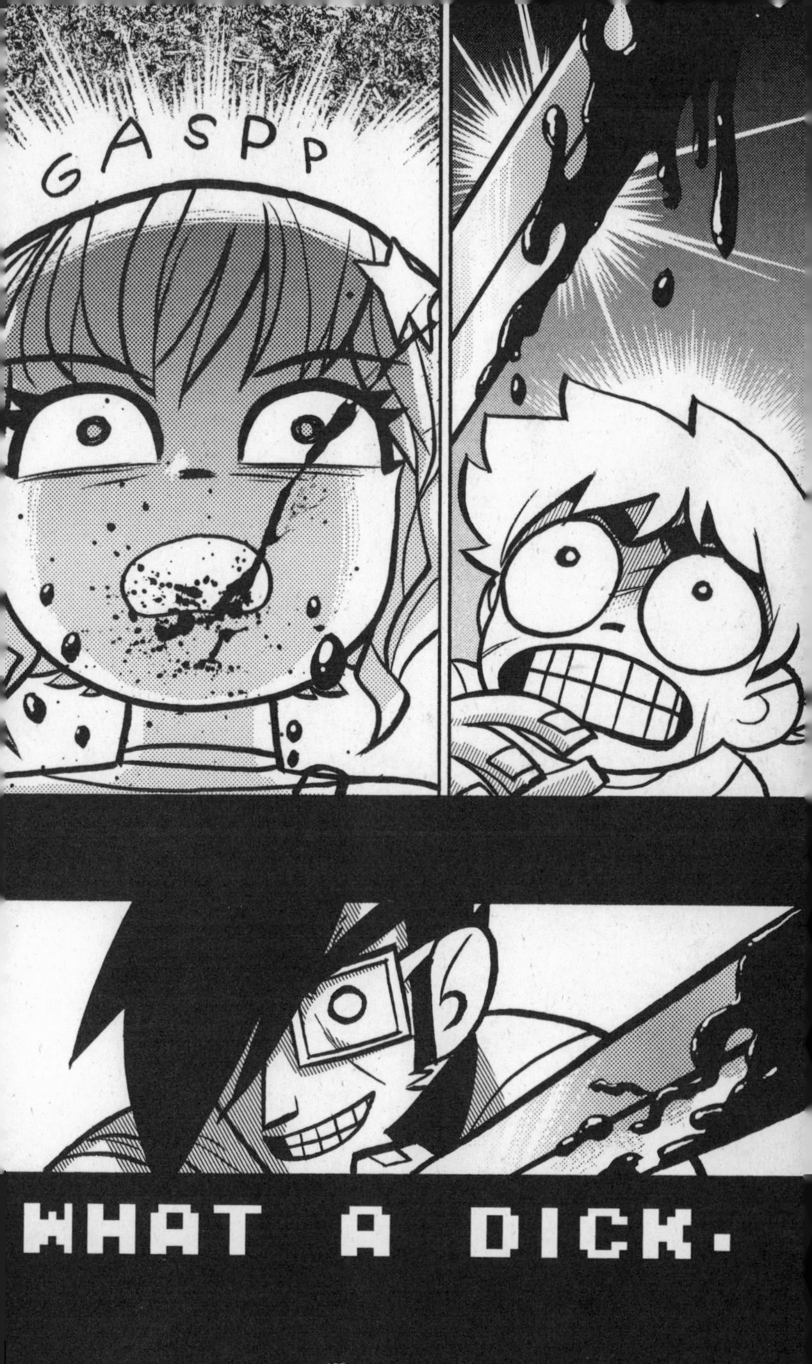
GASPP
WHAT A DICK.

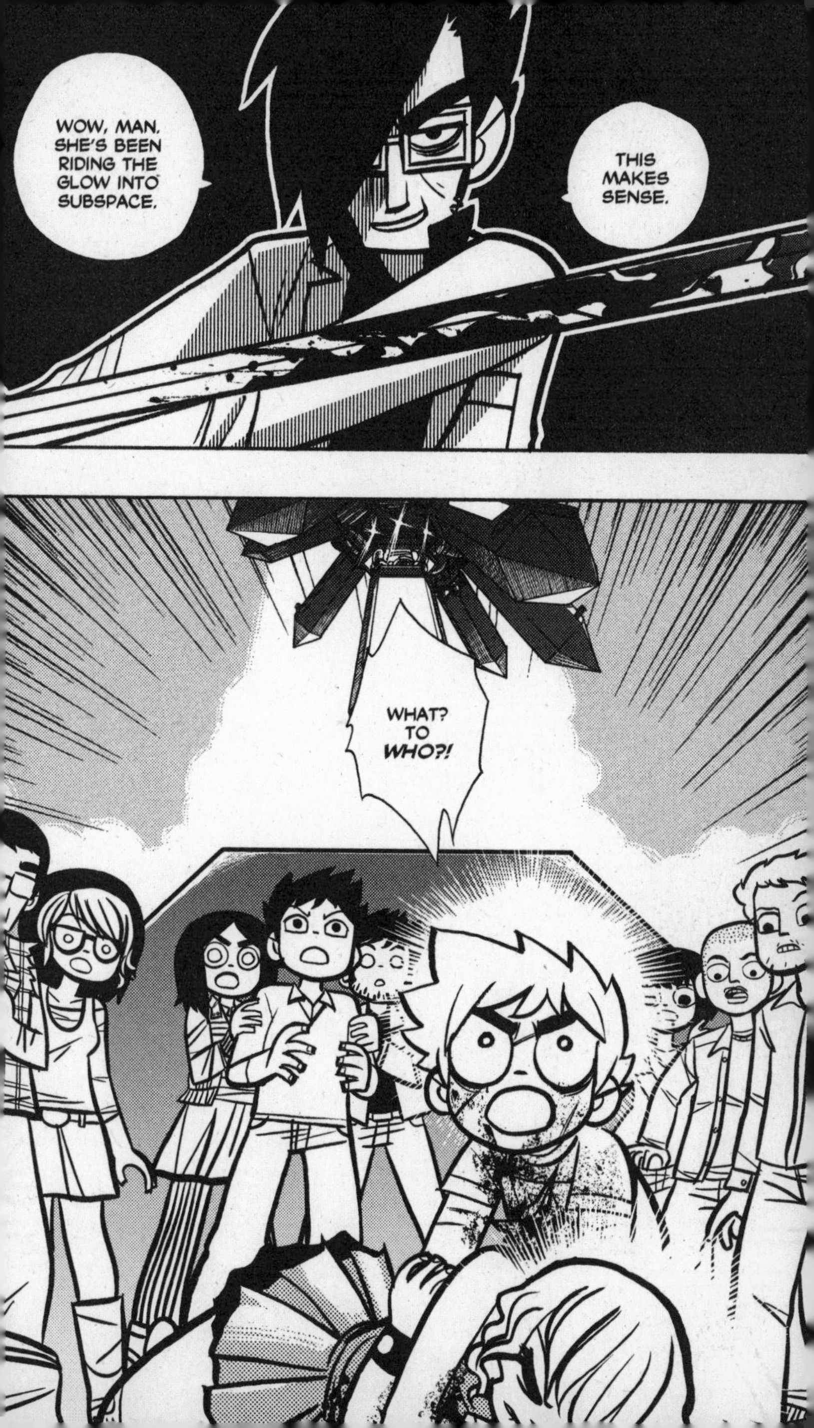
WOW, MAN. SHE'S BEEN RIDING THE GLOW INTO SUBSPACE.
THIS MAKES SENSE.
WHAT? TO *WHO?!*

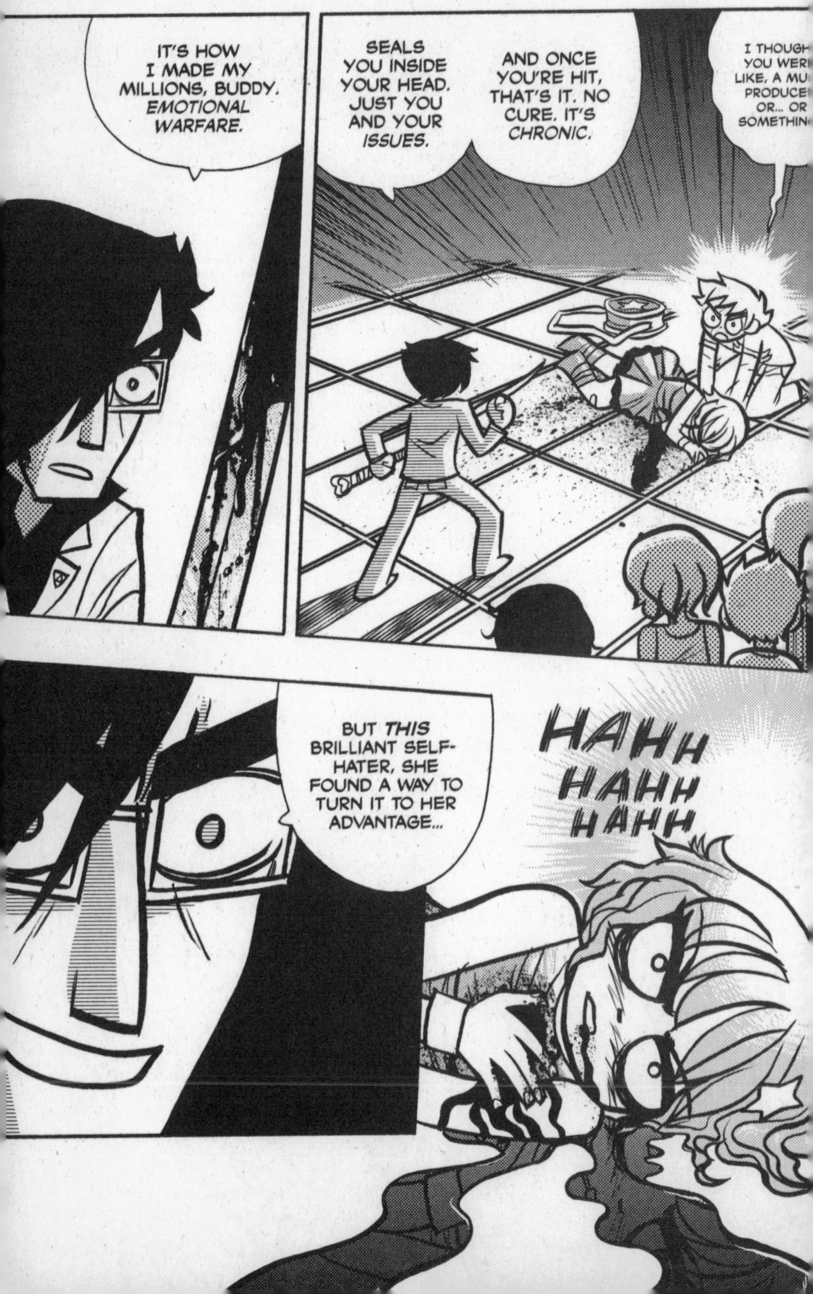
IT'S HOW I MADE MY MILLIONS, BUDDY. EMOTIONAL WARFARE.
SEALS YOU INSIDE YOUR HEAD. JUST YOU AND YOUR ISSUES.
AND ONCE YOU'RE HIT, THAT'S IT. NO CURE. IT'S CHRONIC.
I THOUGH YOU WER LIKE, A MU PRODUCE OR... OR SOMETHIN
BUT THIS BRILLIANT SELF-HATER, SHE FOUND A WAY TO TURN IT TO HER ADVANTAGE...
HAHH HAHH HAHH

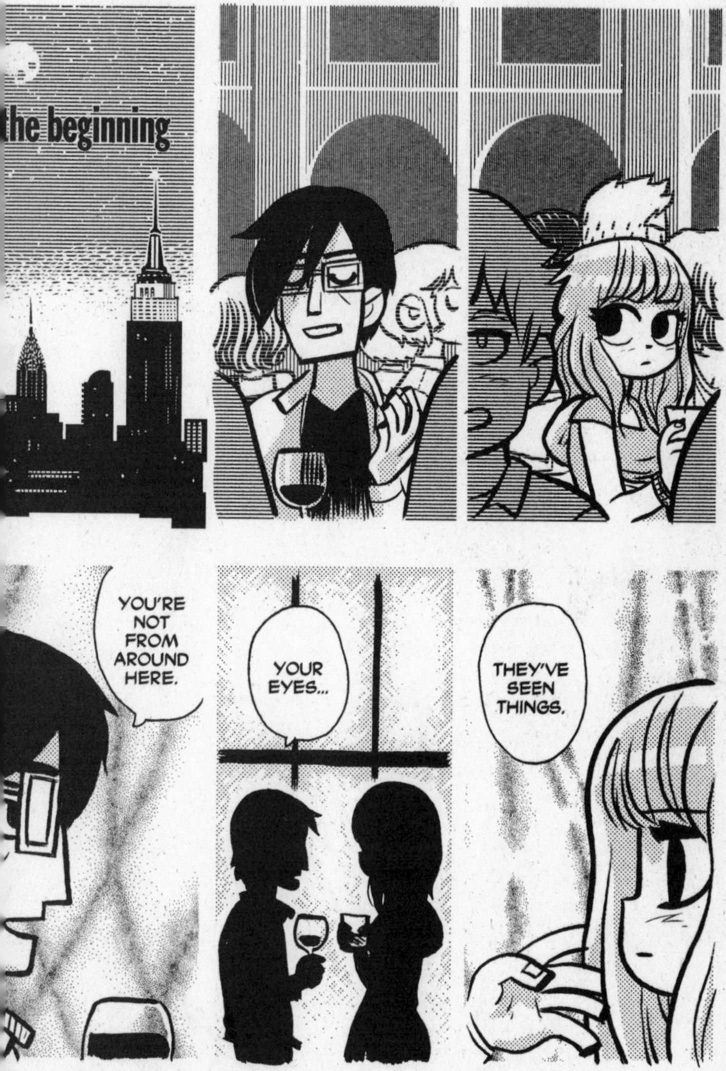
the beginning
YOU'RE NOT FROM AROUND HERE.
YOUR EYES...
THEY'VE SEEN THINGS.

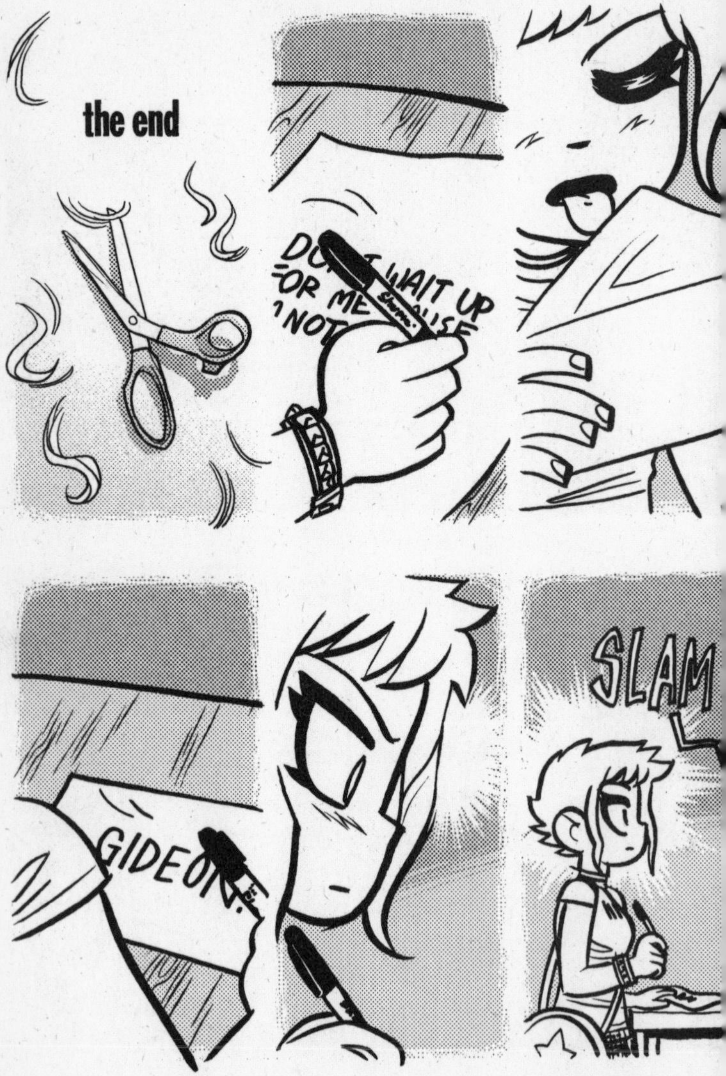
the end
WAIT UP
Sharpie
GIDEO
SLAM

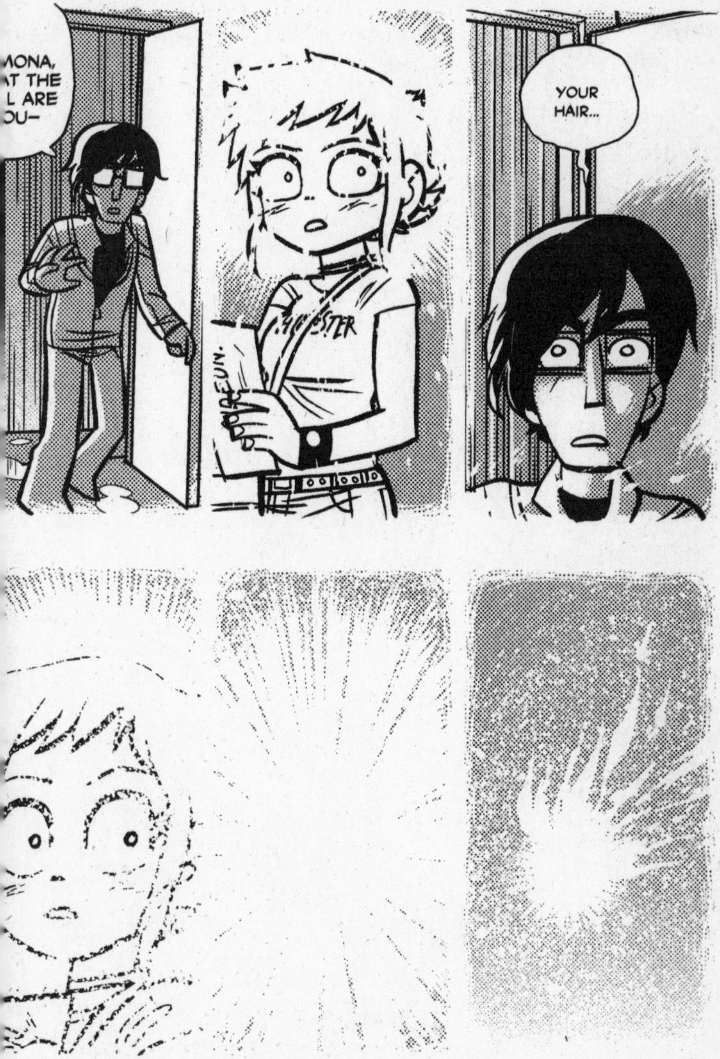

MONA,
AT THE
L ARE
OU–
YOUR HAIR...

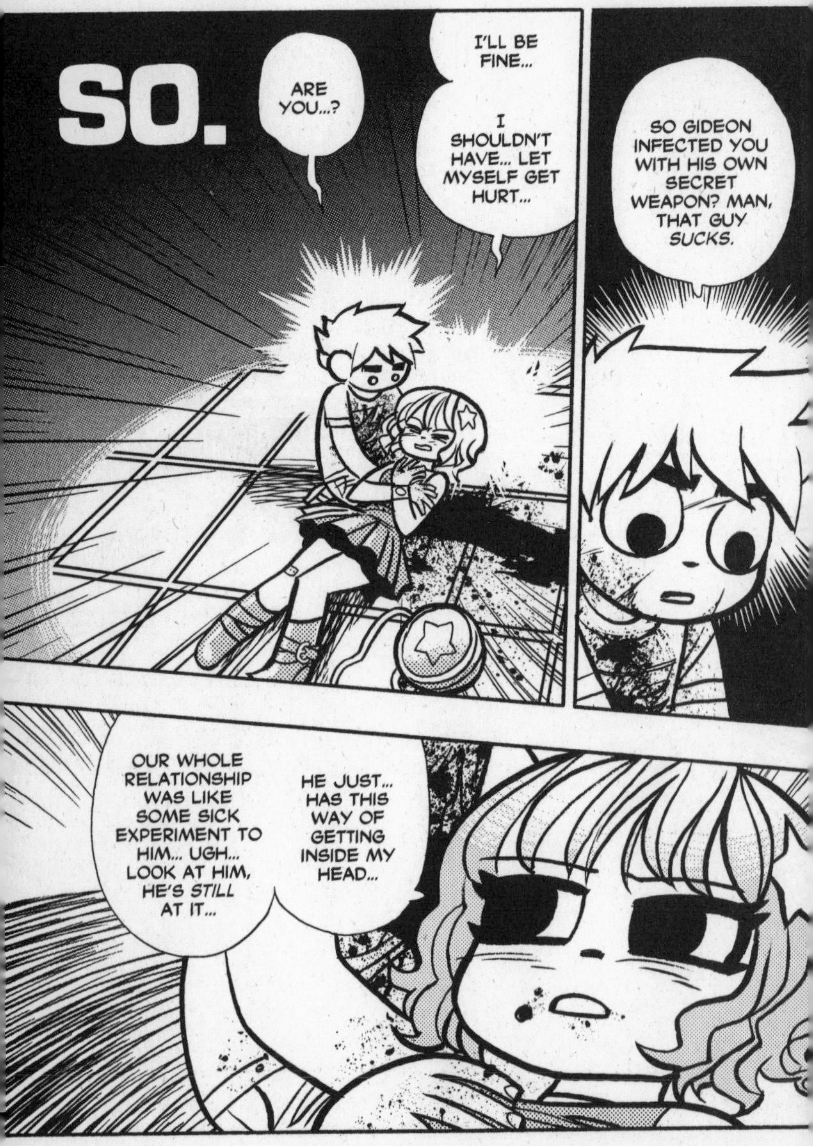
SO.
ARE YOU...?
I'LL BE FINE...
I SHOULDN'T HAVE... LET MYSELF GET HURT...
SO GIDEON INFECTED YOU WITH HIS OWN SECRET WEAPON? MAN, THAT GUY *SUCKS.*
OUR WHOLE RELATIONSHIP WAS LIKE SOME SICK EXPERIMENT TO HIM... UGH... LOOK AT HIM, HE'S *STILL* AT IT...
HE JUST... HAS THIS WAY OF GETTING INSIDE MY HEAD...

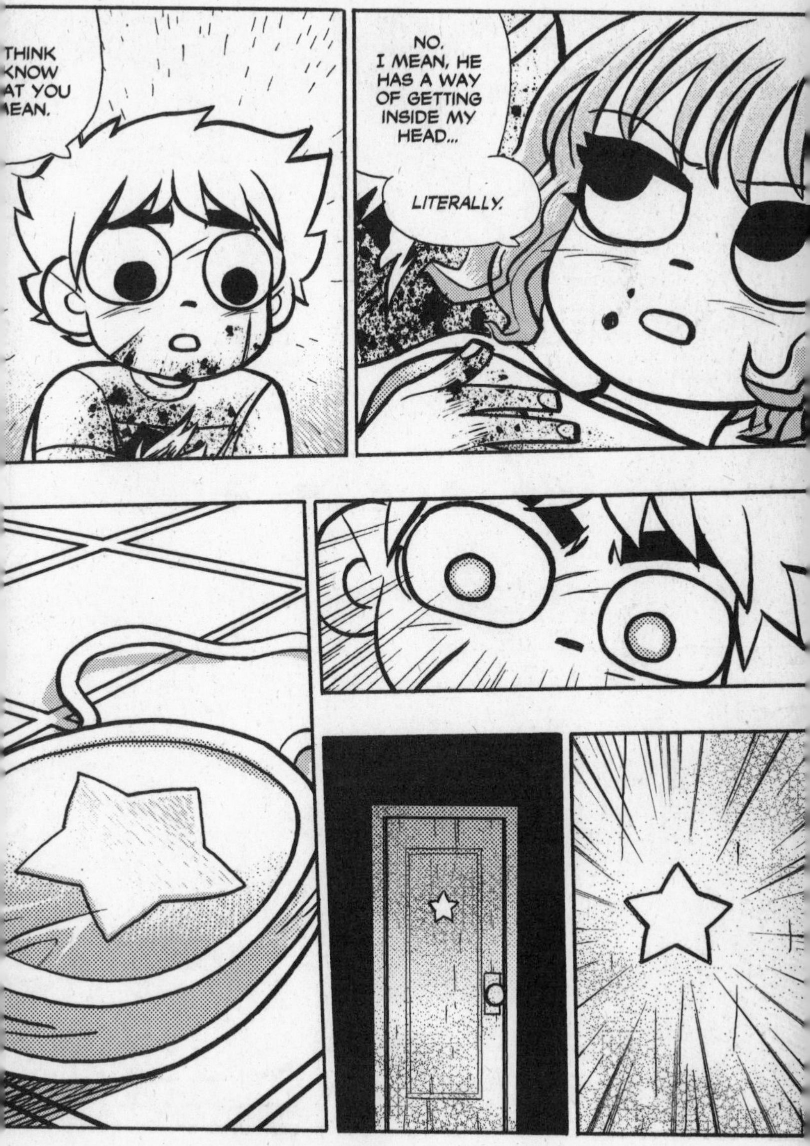
THINK KNOW AT YOU MEAN.
NO. I MEAN, HE HAS A WAY OF GETTING INSIDE MY HEAD...
LITERALLY.

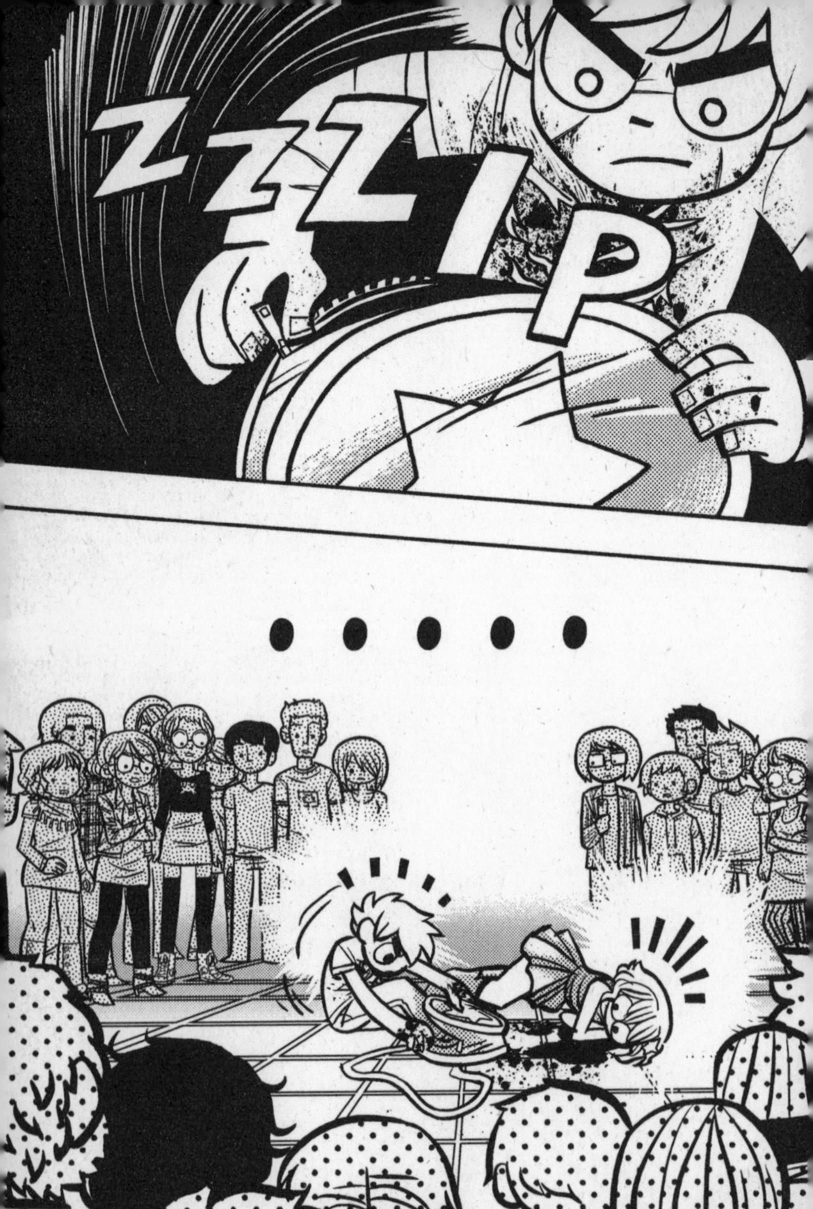
ZZZIP
.....

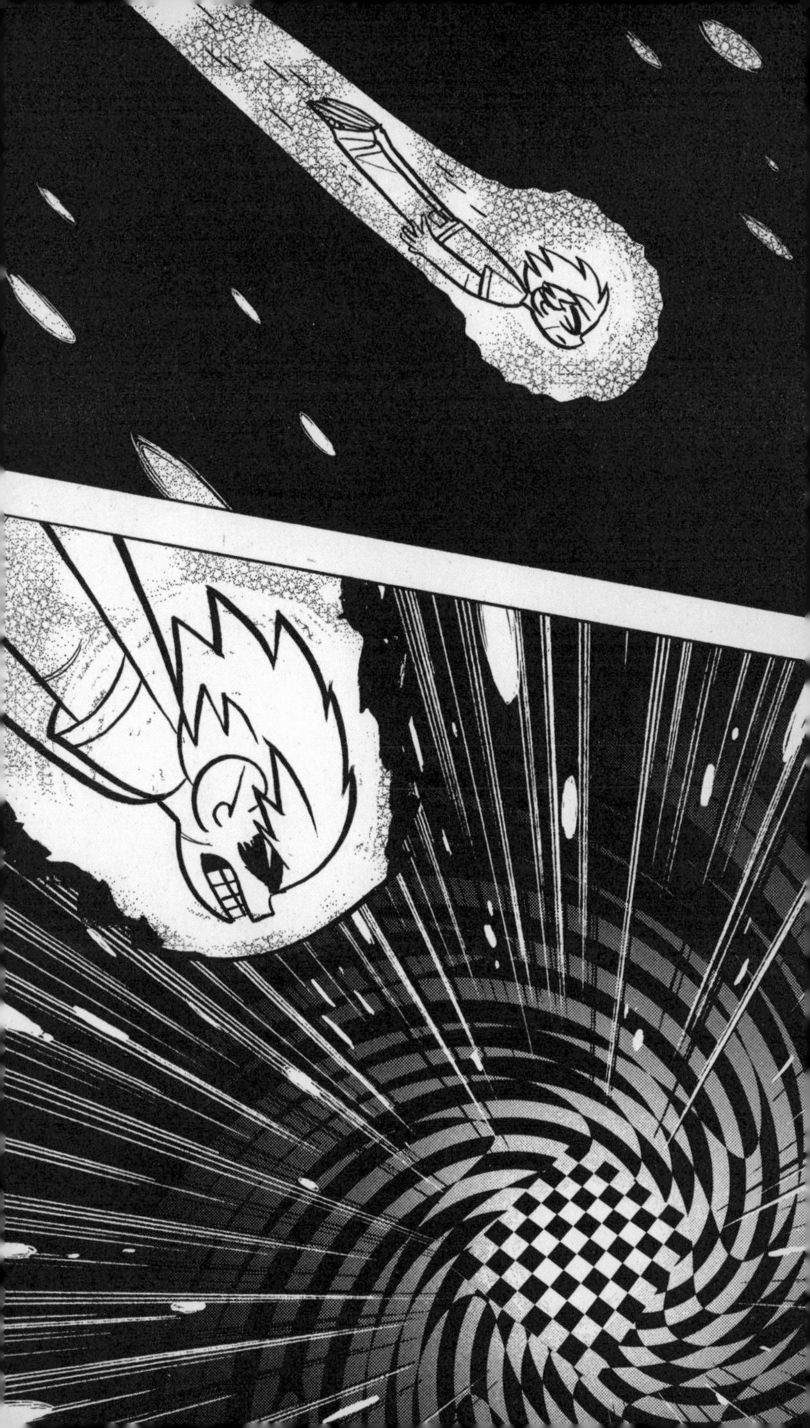

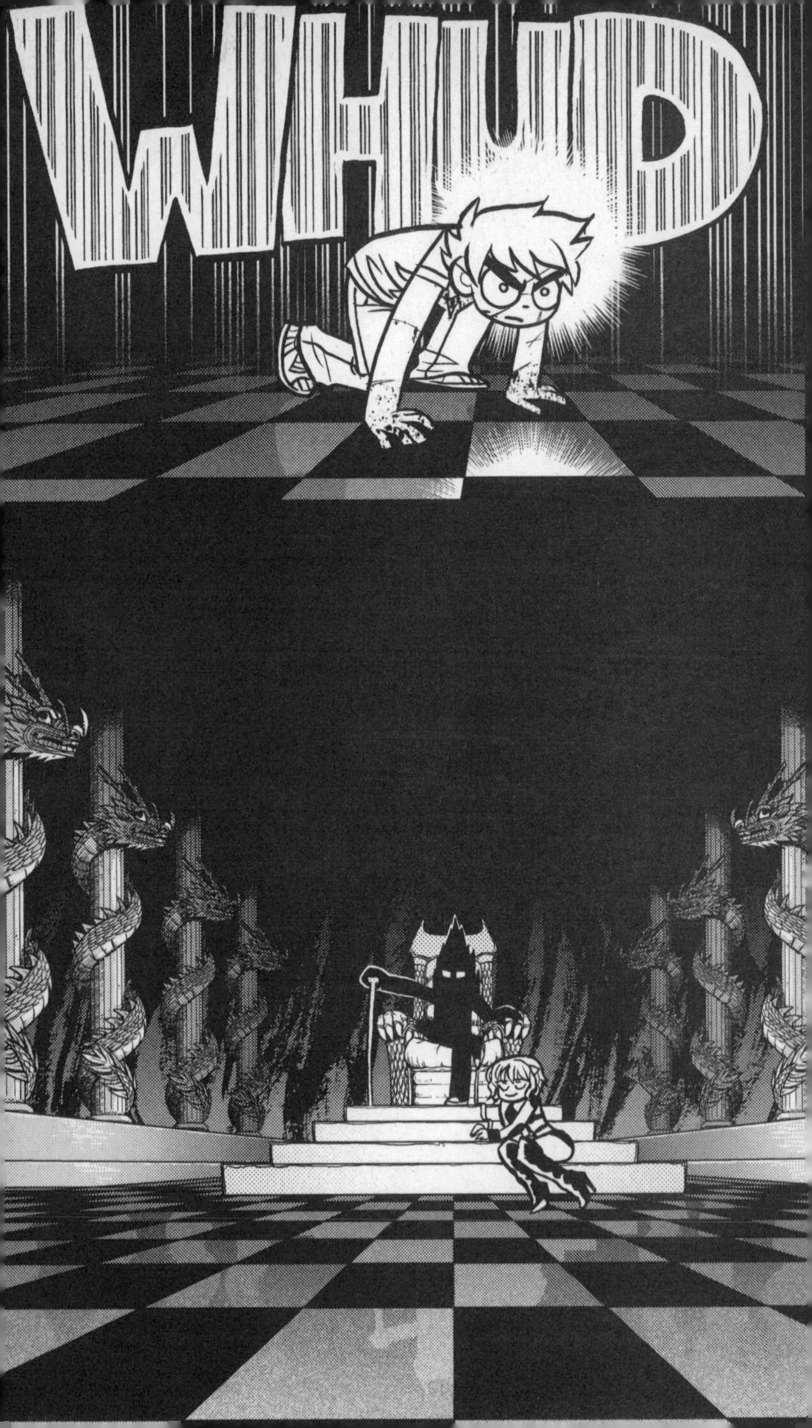
WHUD

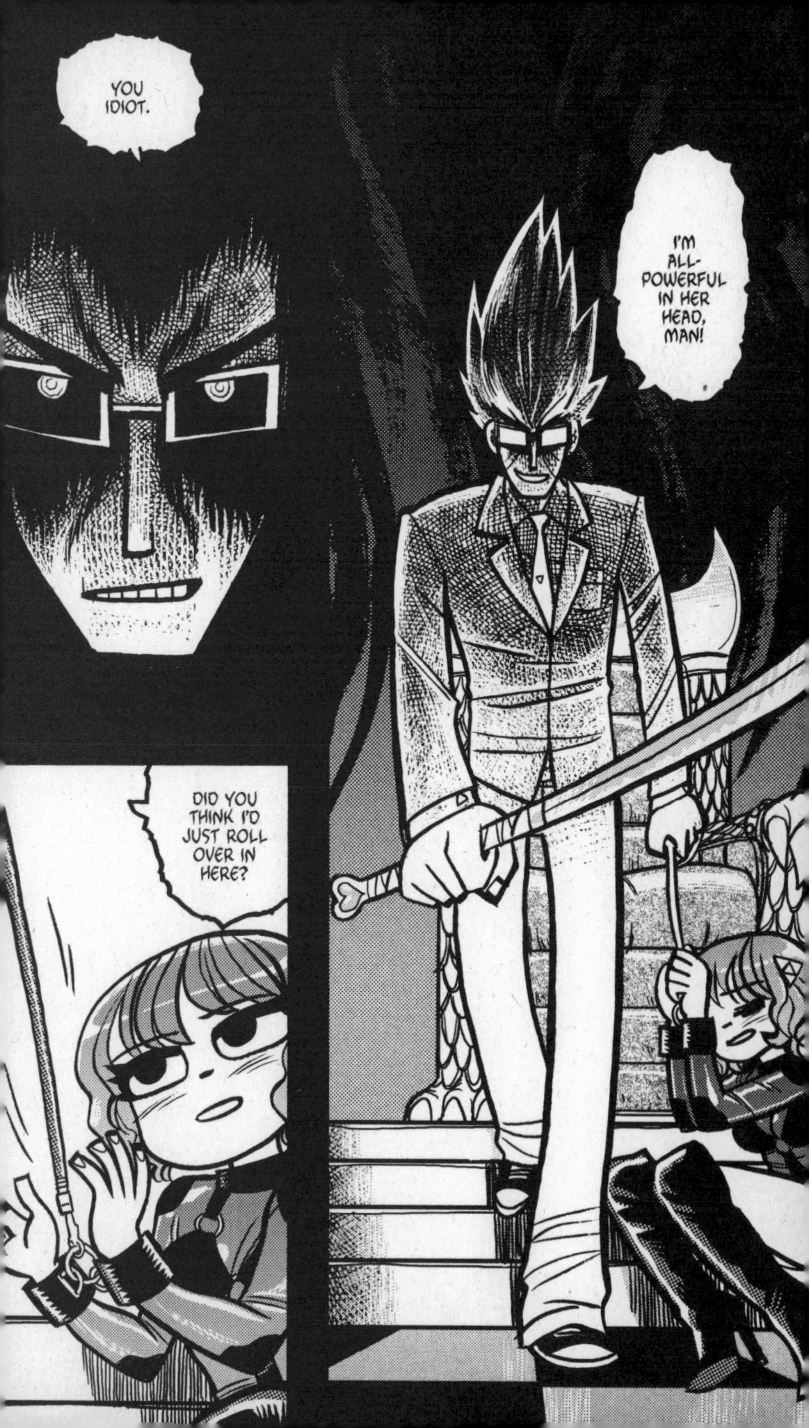
YOU IDIOT.
I'M ALL-POWERFUL IN HER HEAD, MAN!
DID YOU THINK I'D JUST ROLL OVER IN HERE?

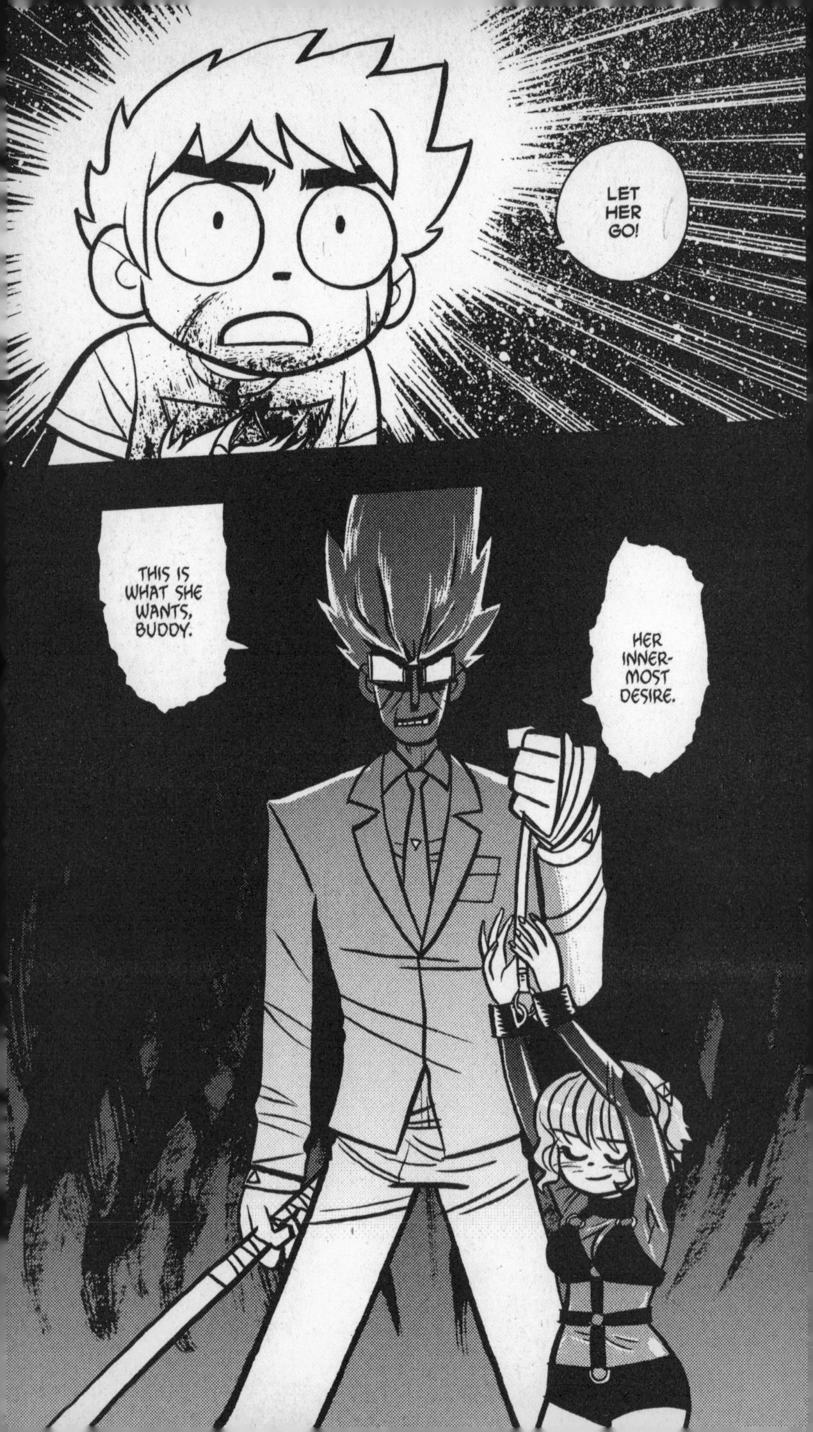

LET HER GO!
THIS IS WHAT SHE WANTS, BUDDY.
HER INNER-MOST DESIRE.

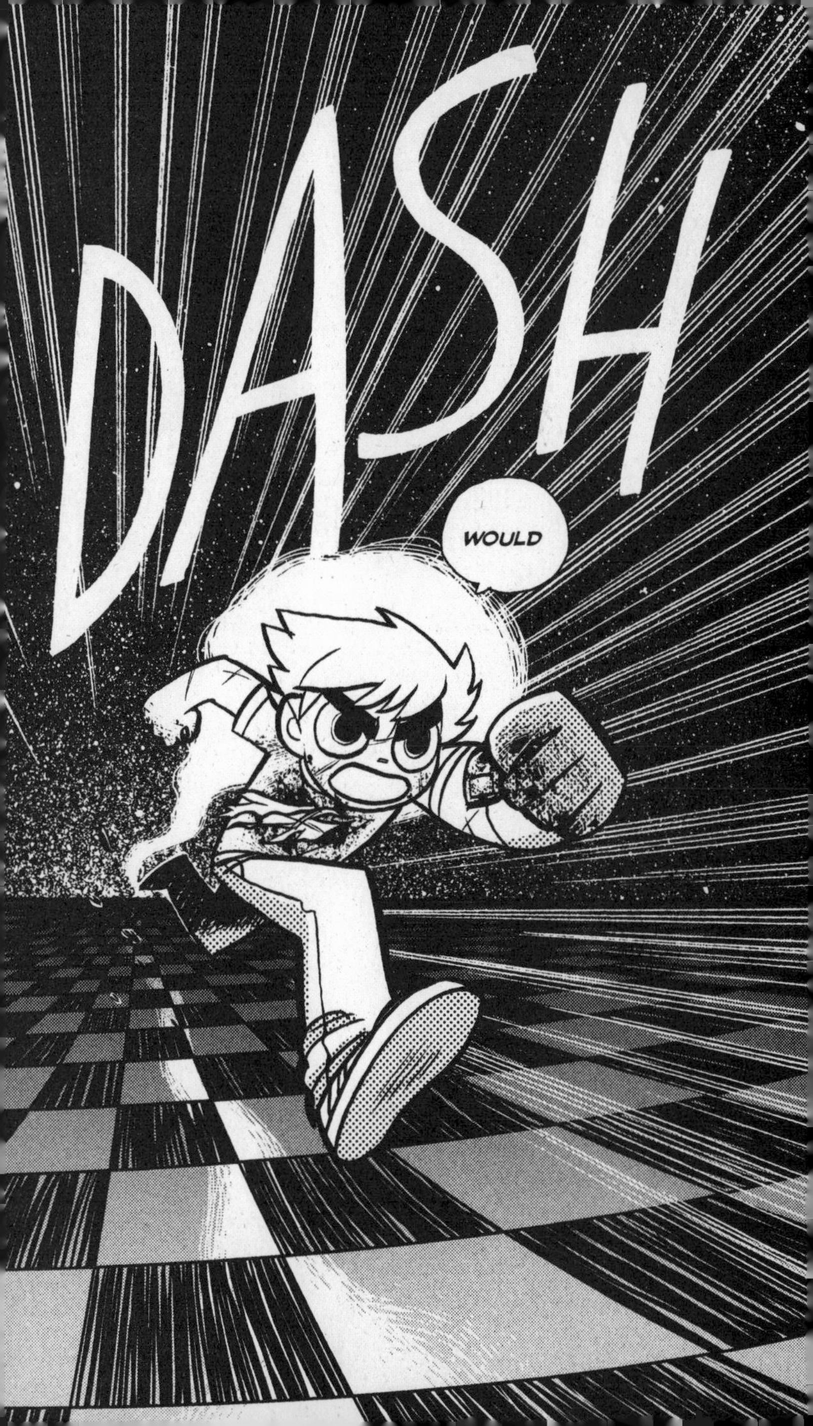
DASH
WOULD

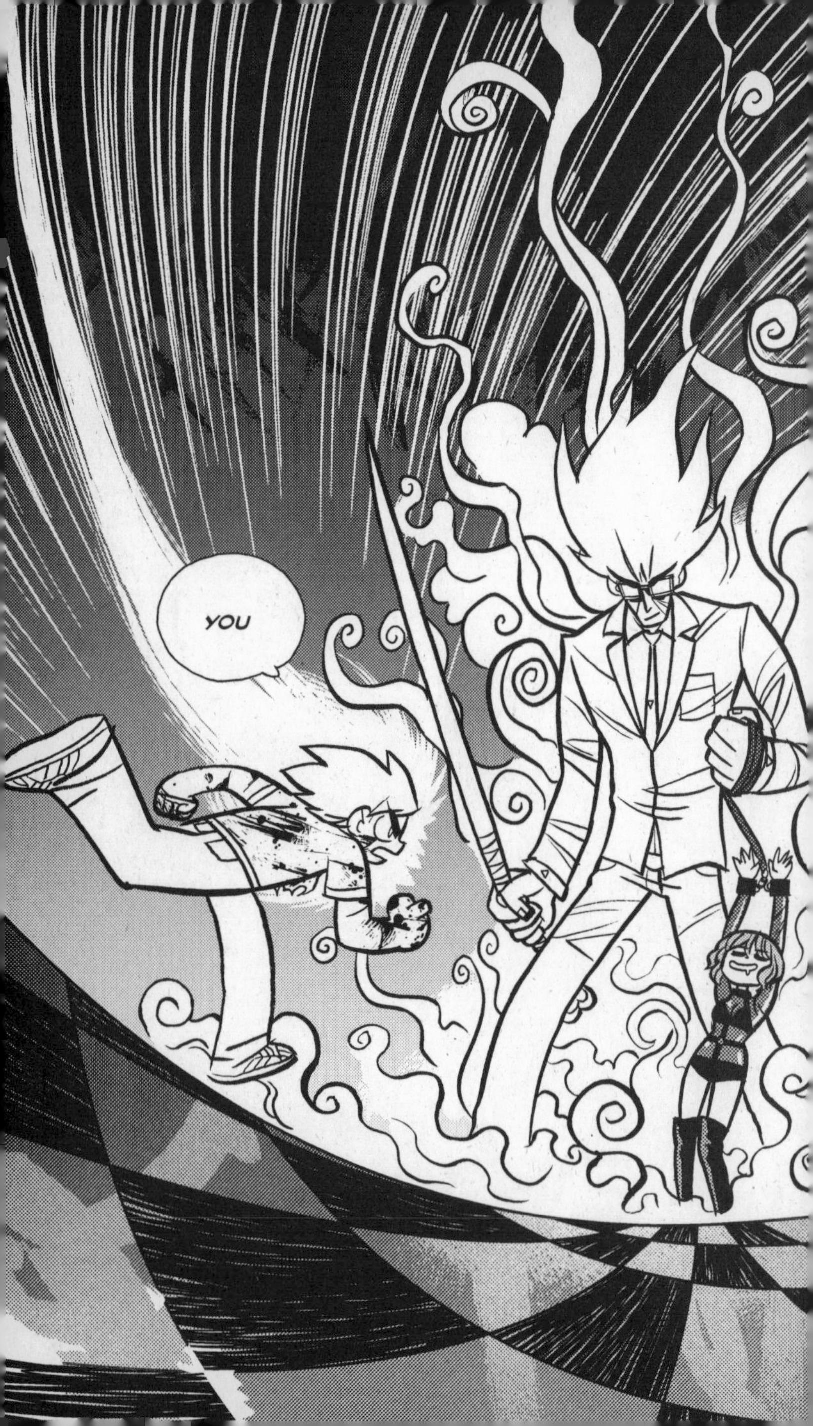
YOU

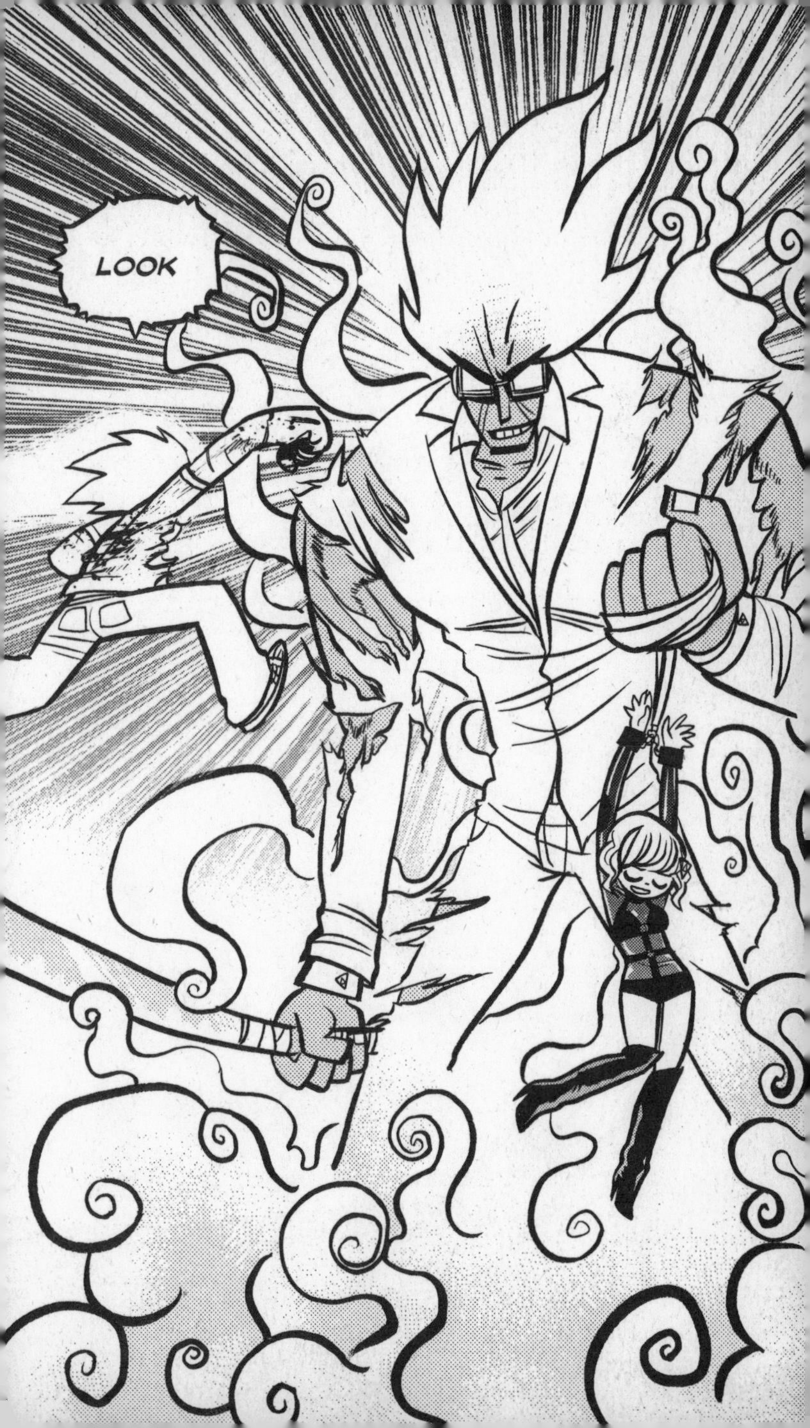
LOOK

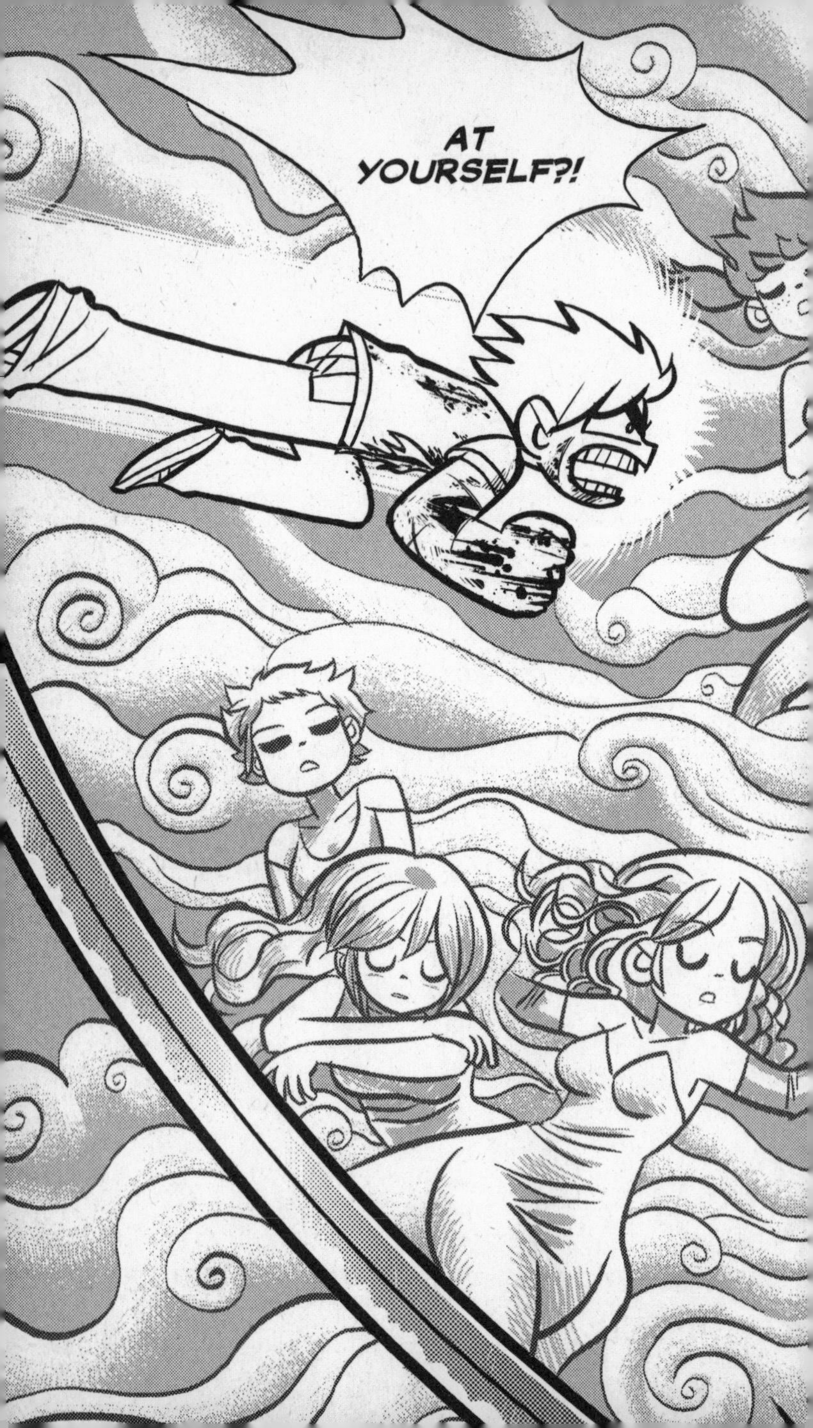
AT YOURSELF?!

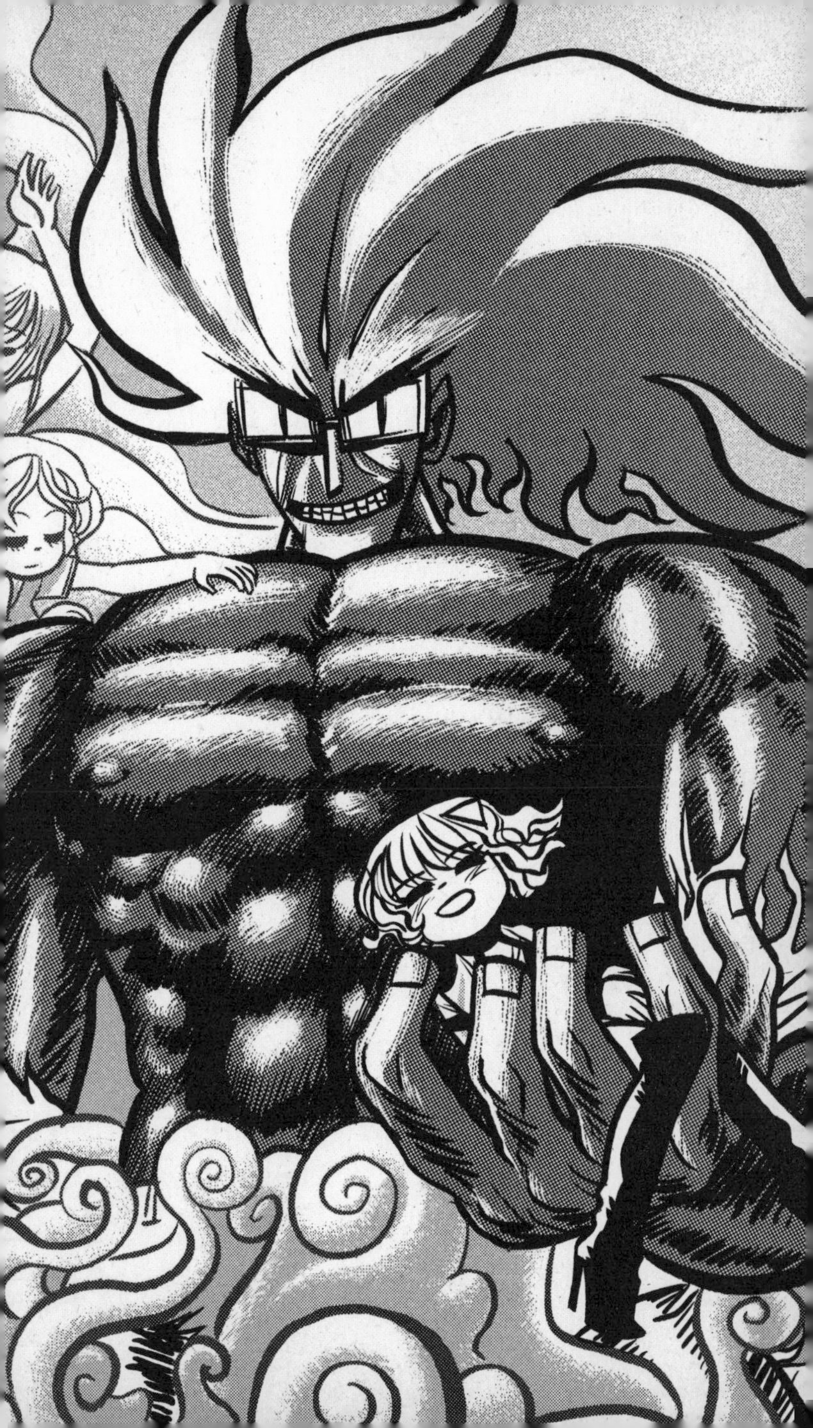

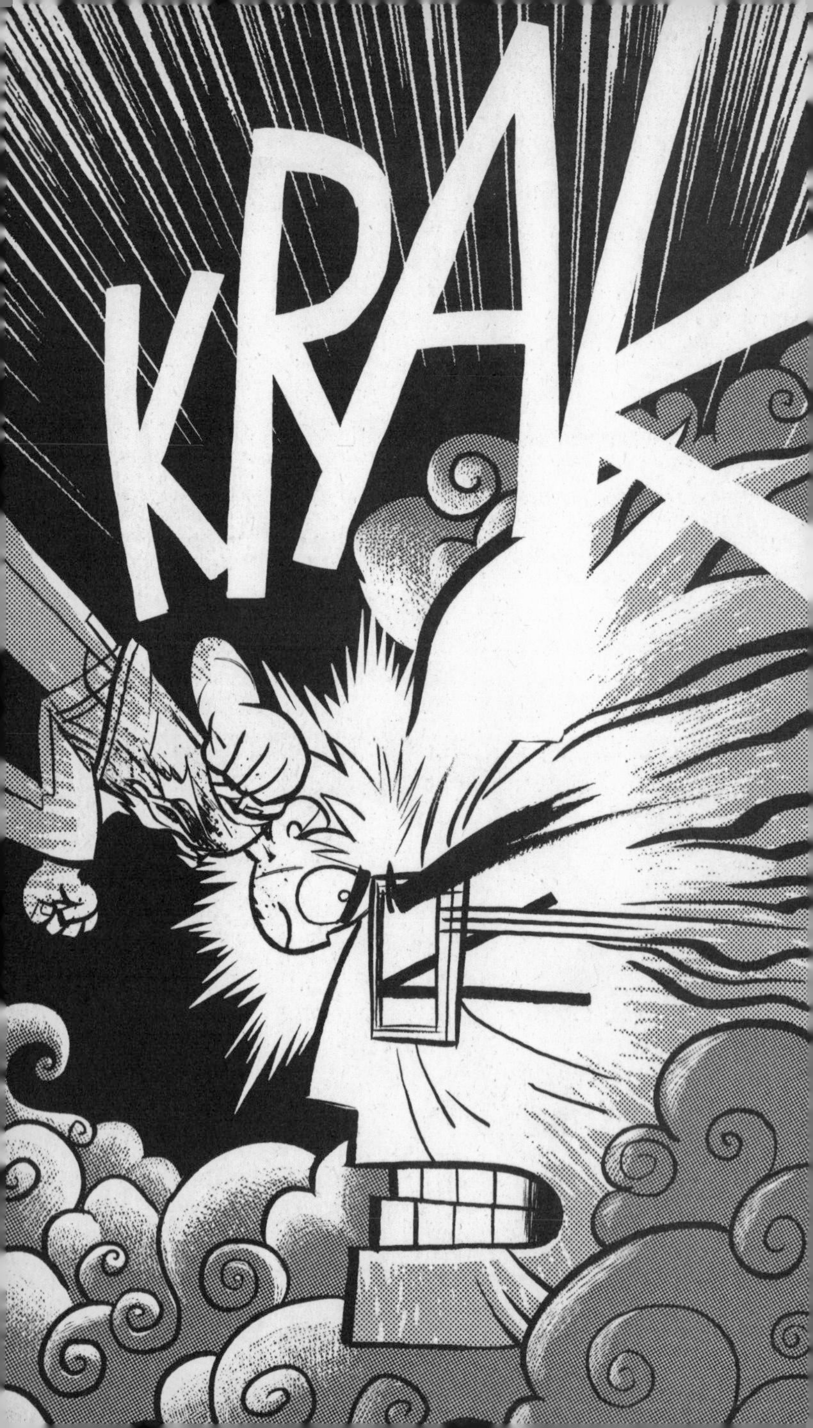
KRAK

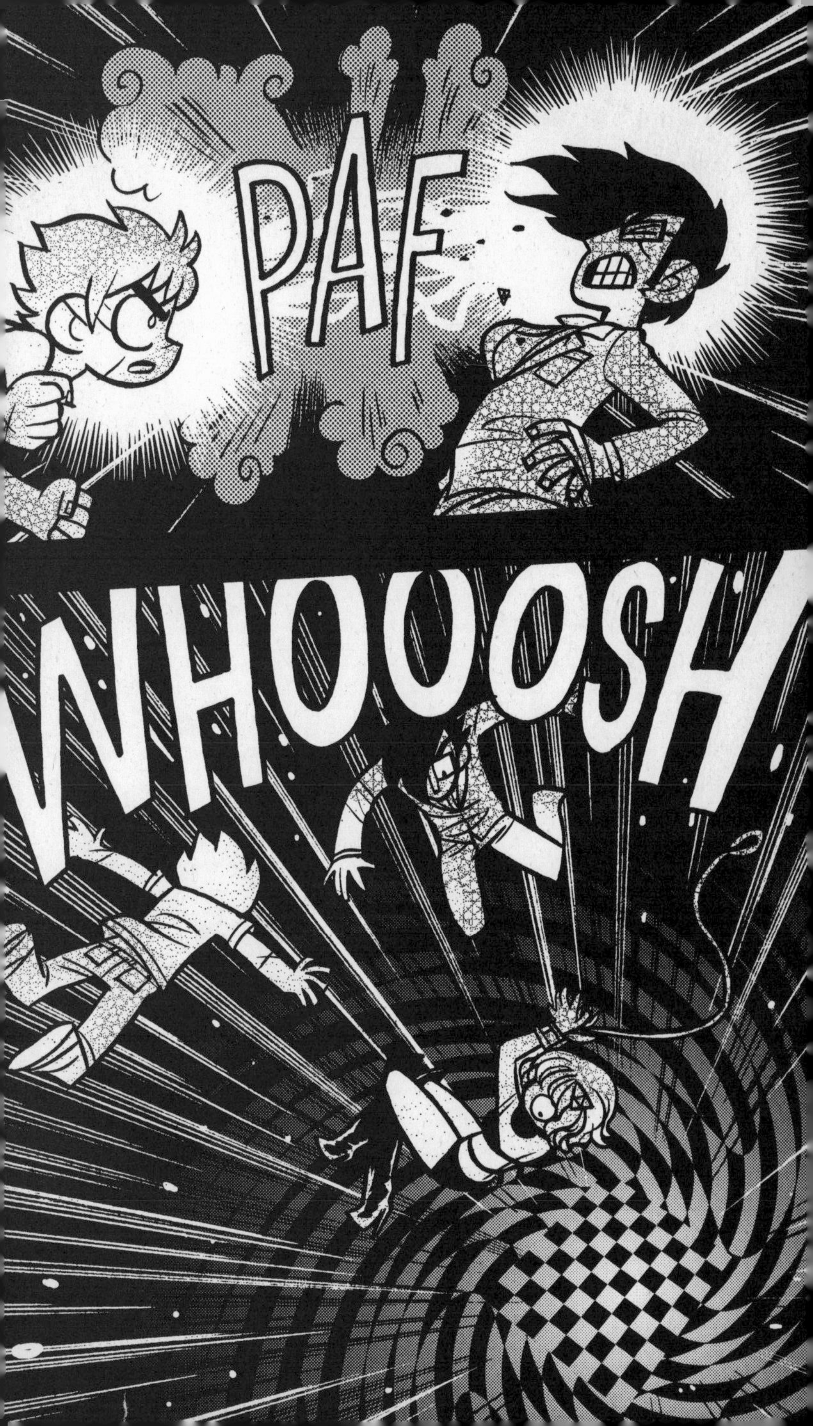
PAF
WHOOOSH

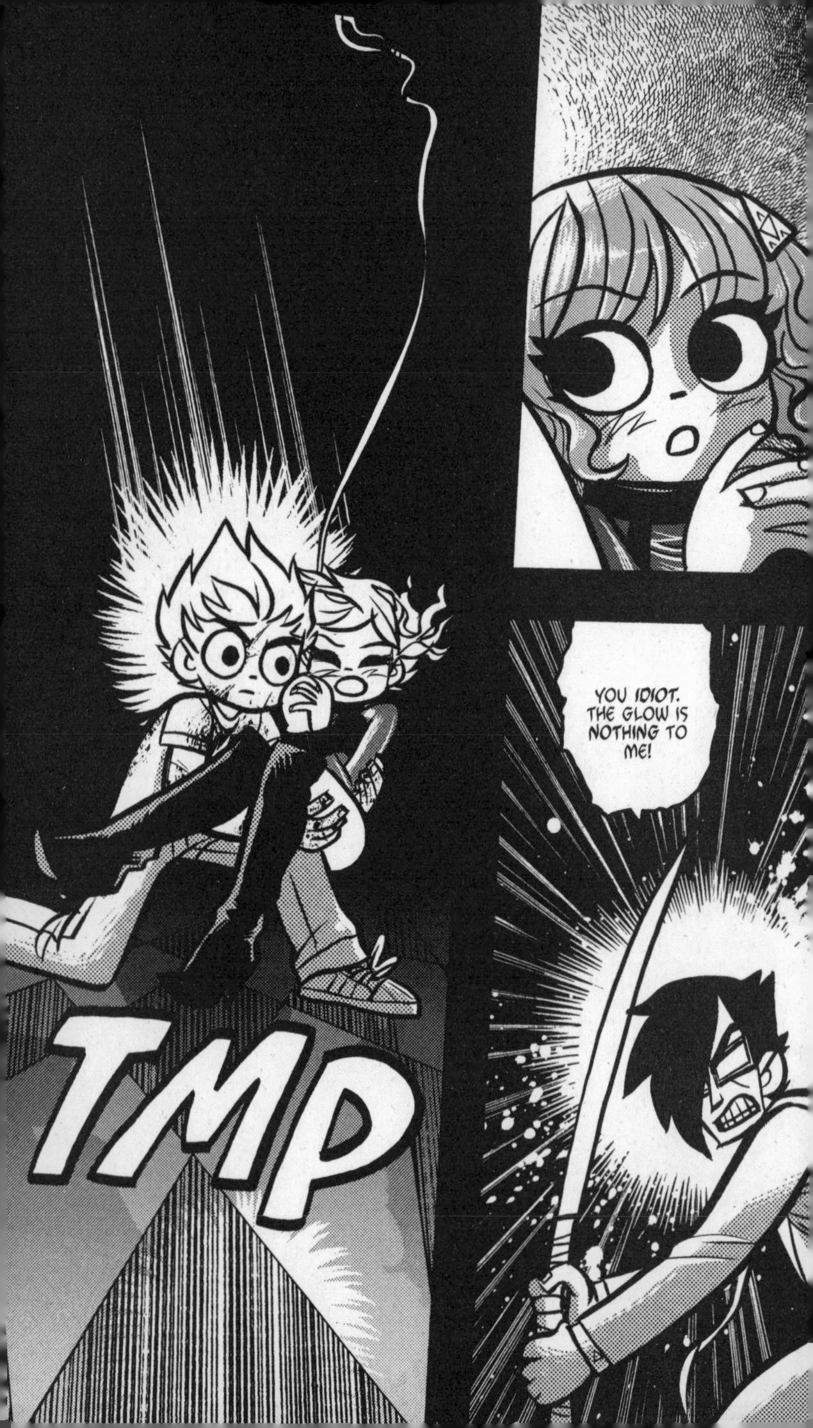
TMP
YOU IDIOT. THE GLOW IS NOTHING TO ME!

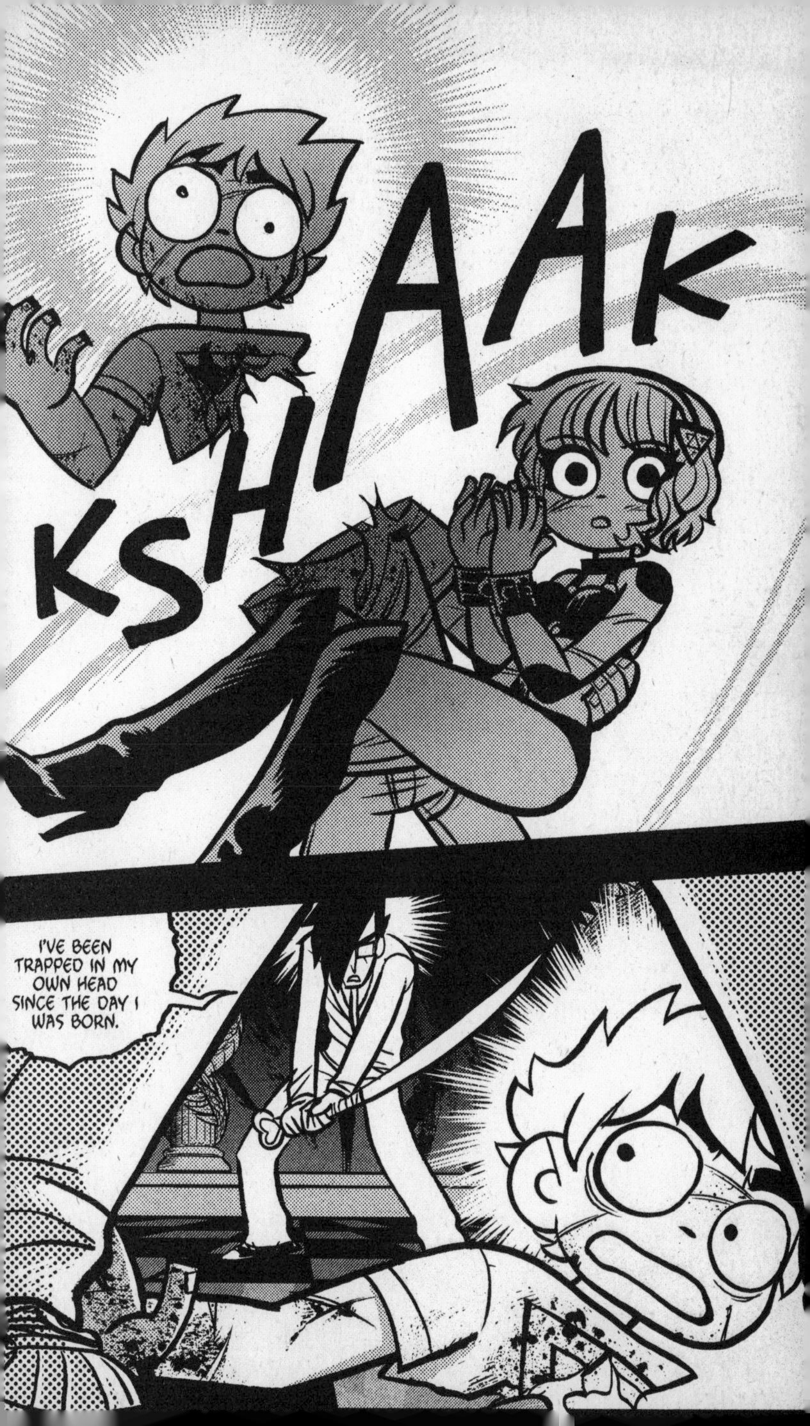
KSHAAK
I'VE BEEN TRAPPED IN MY OWN HEAD SINCE THE DAY I WAS BORN.

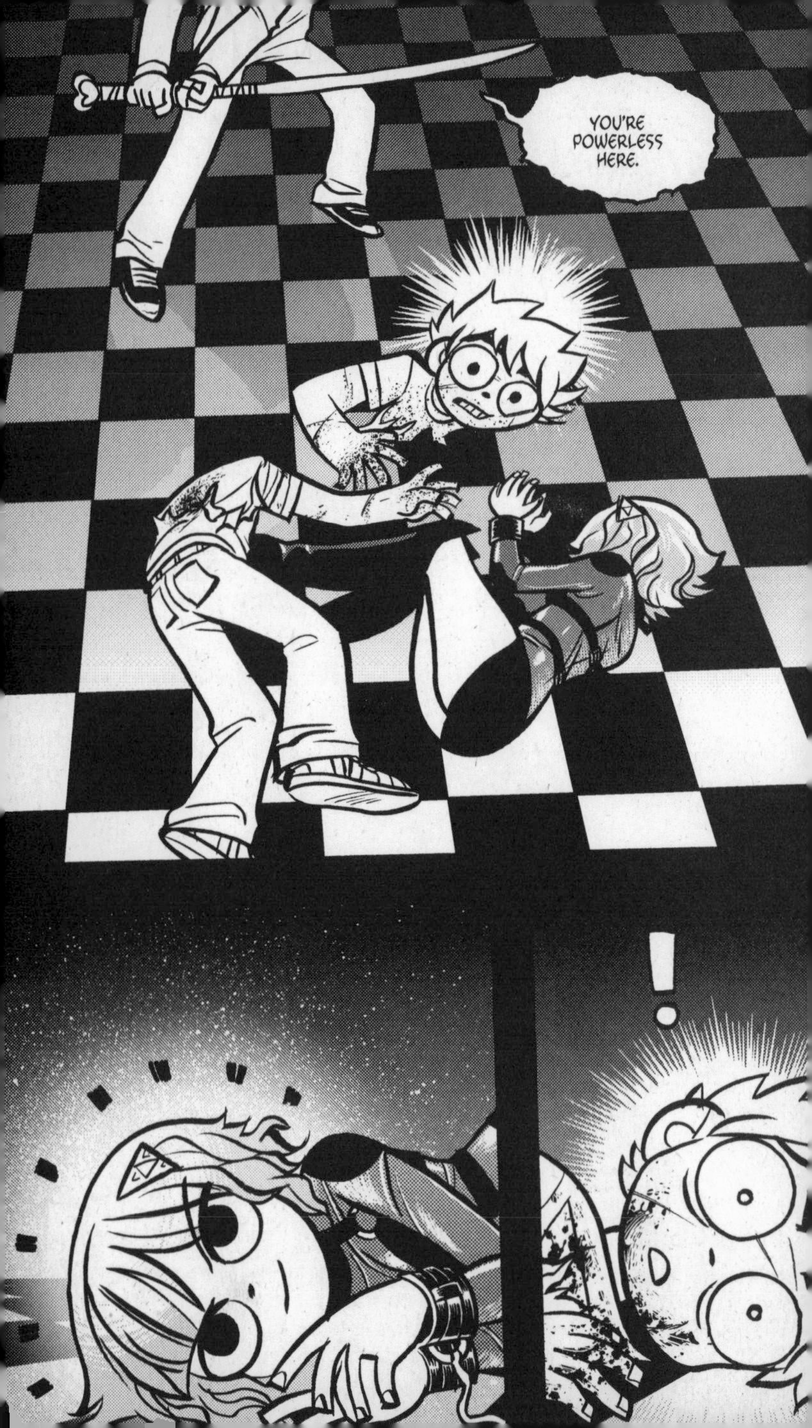
YOU'RE POWERLESS HERE.
!

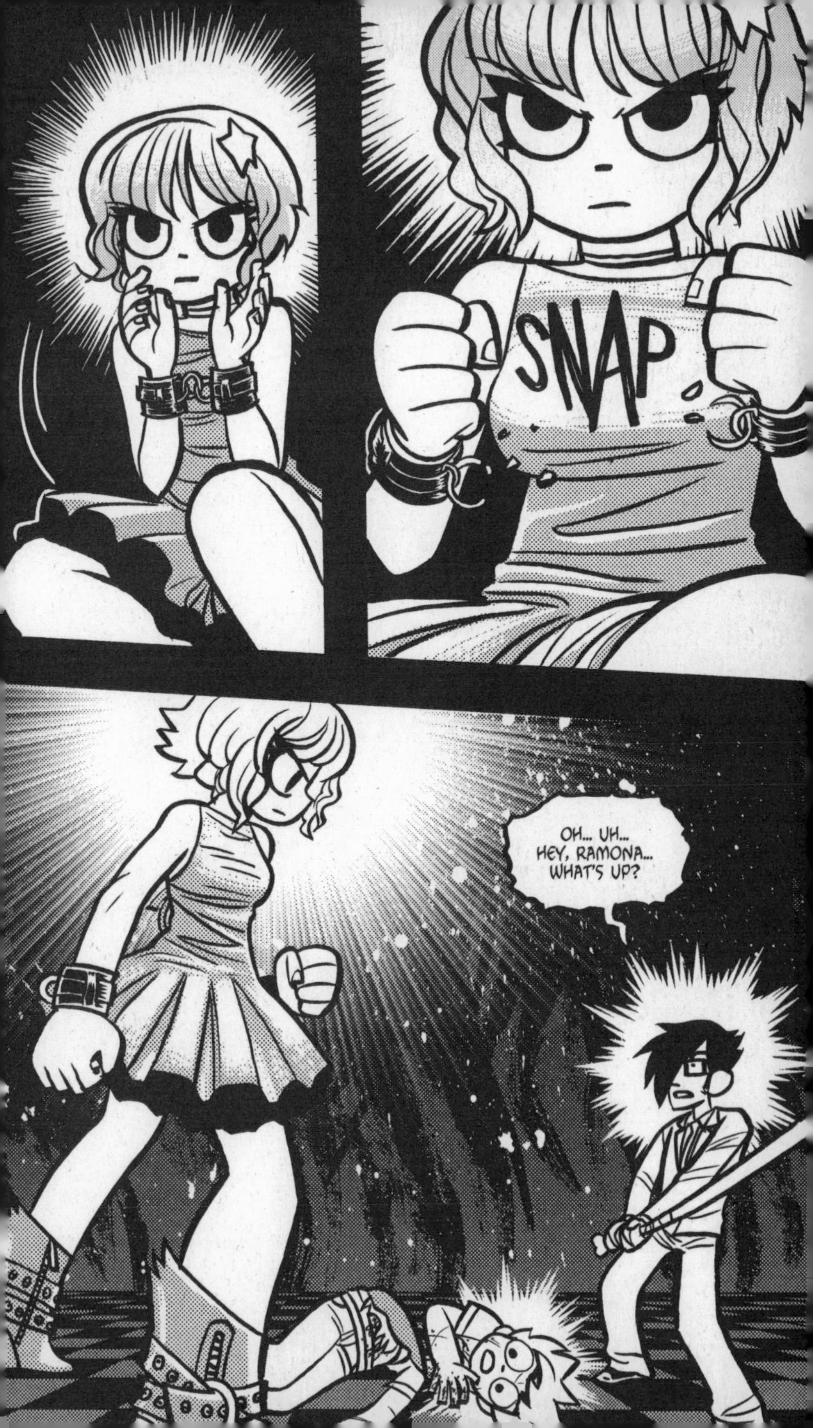
SNAP
OH... UH... HEY, RAMONA... WHAT'S UP?

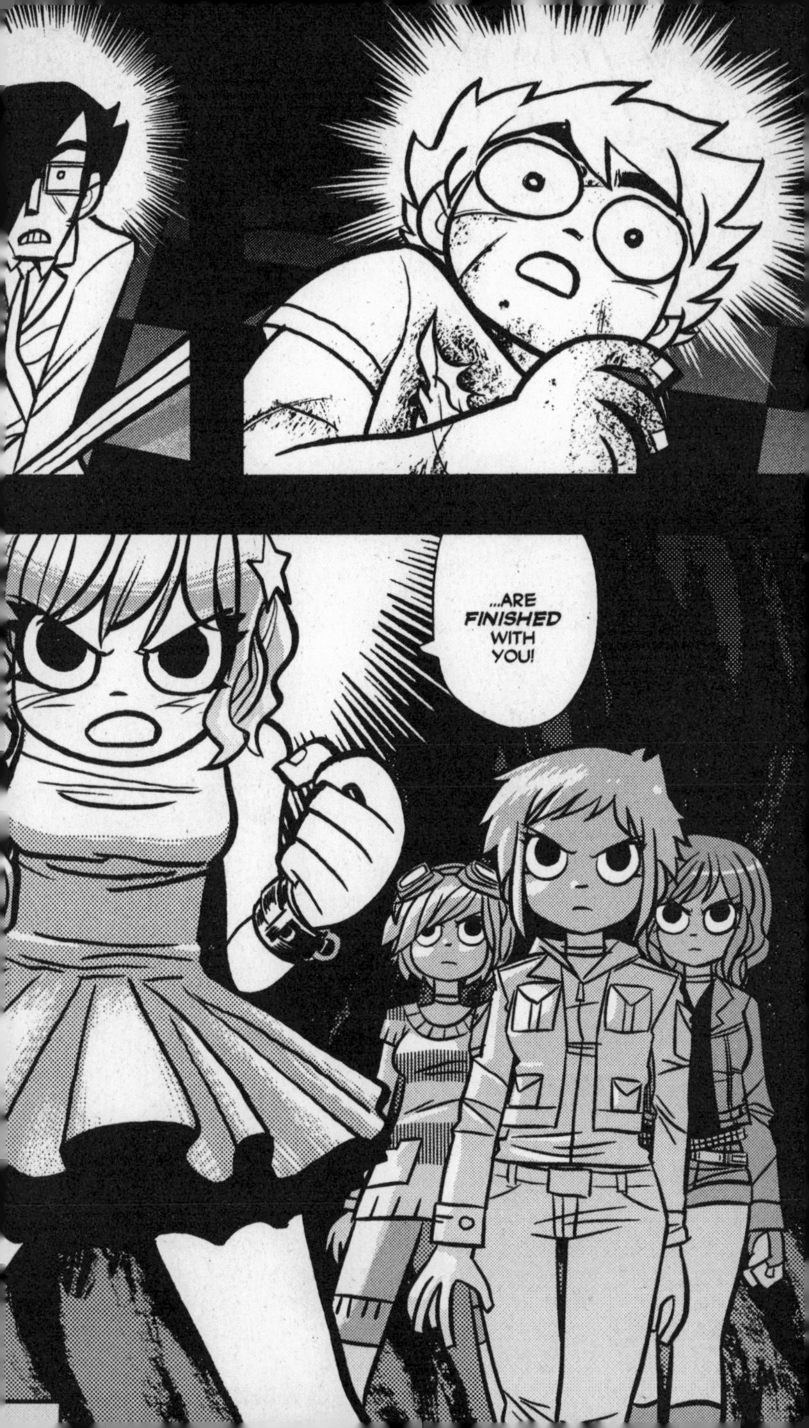
...ARE FINISHED WITH YOU!

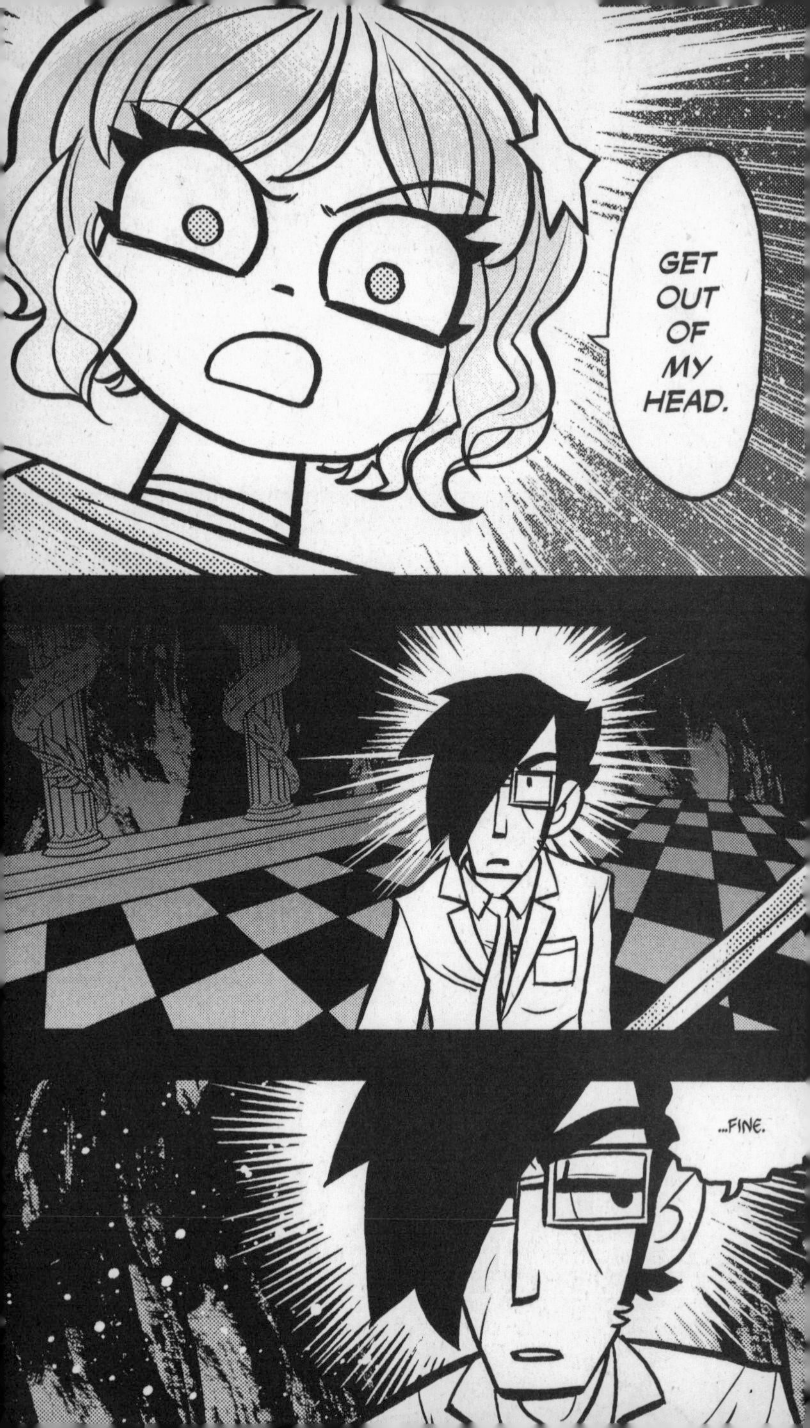
GET OUT OF MY HEAD.
...FINE.

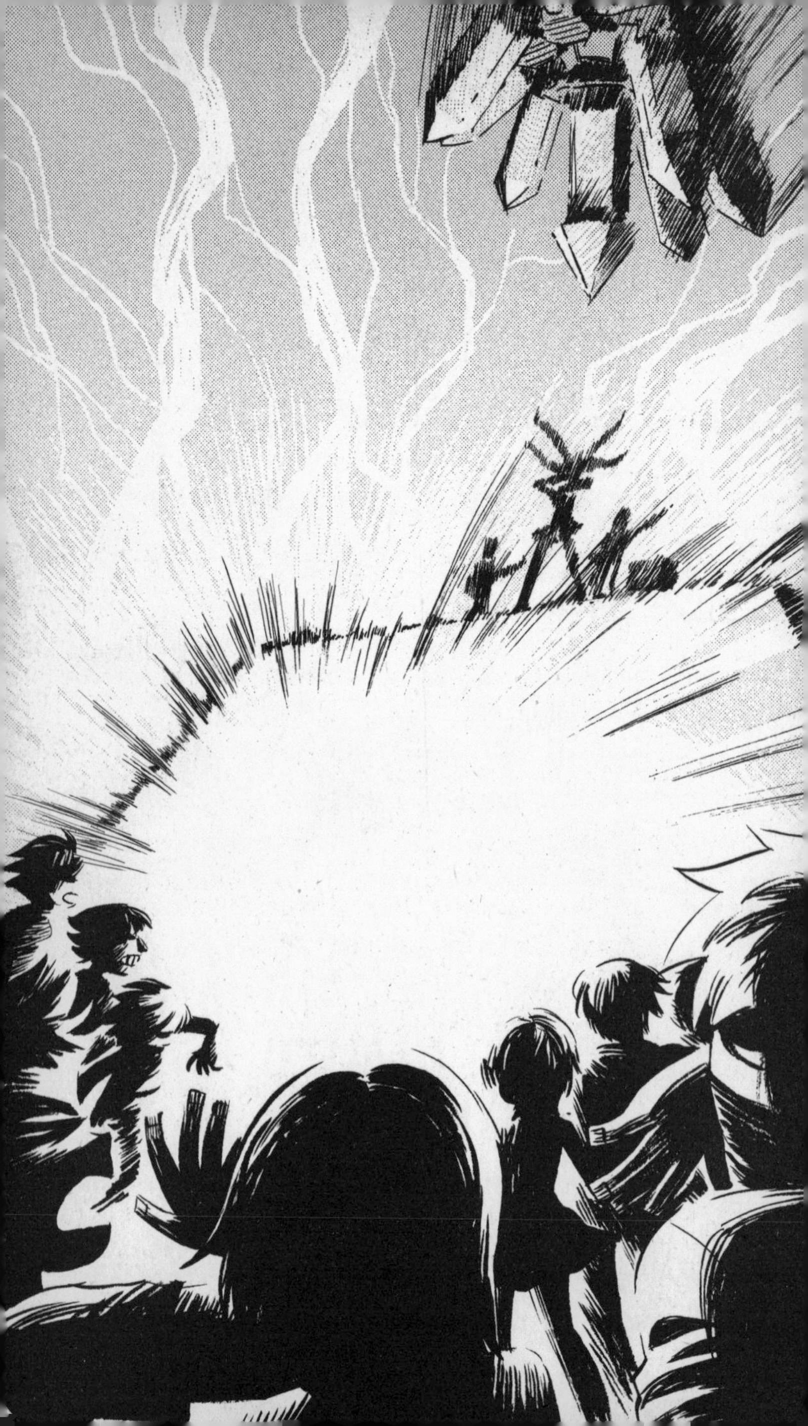

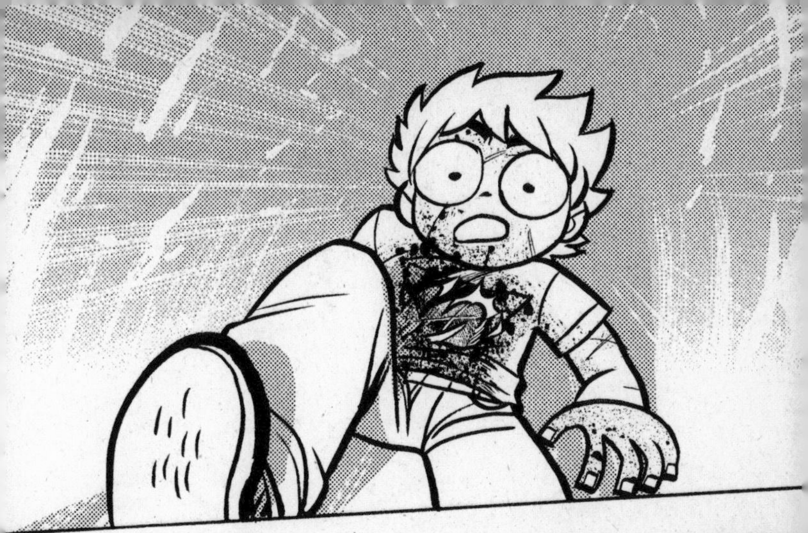

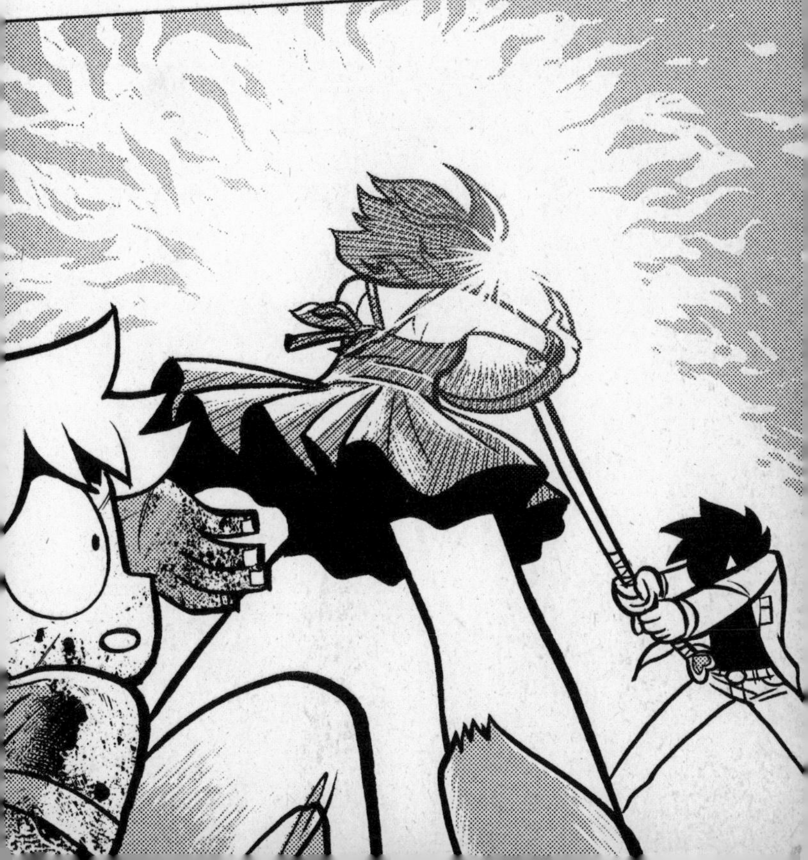

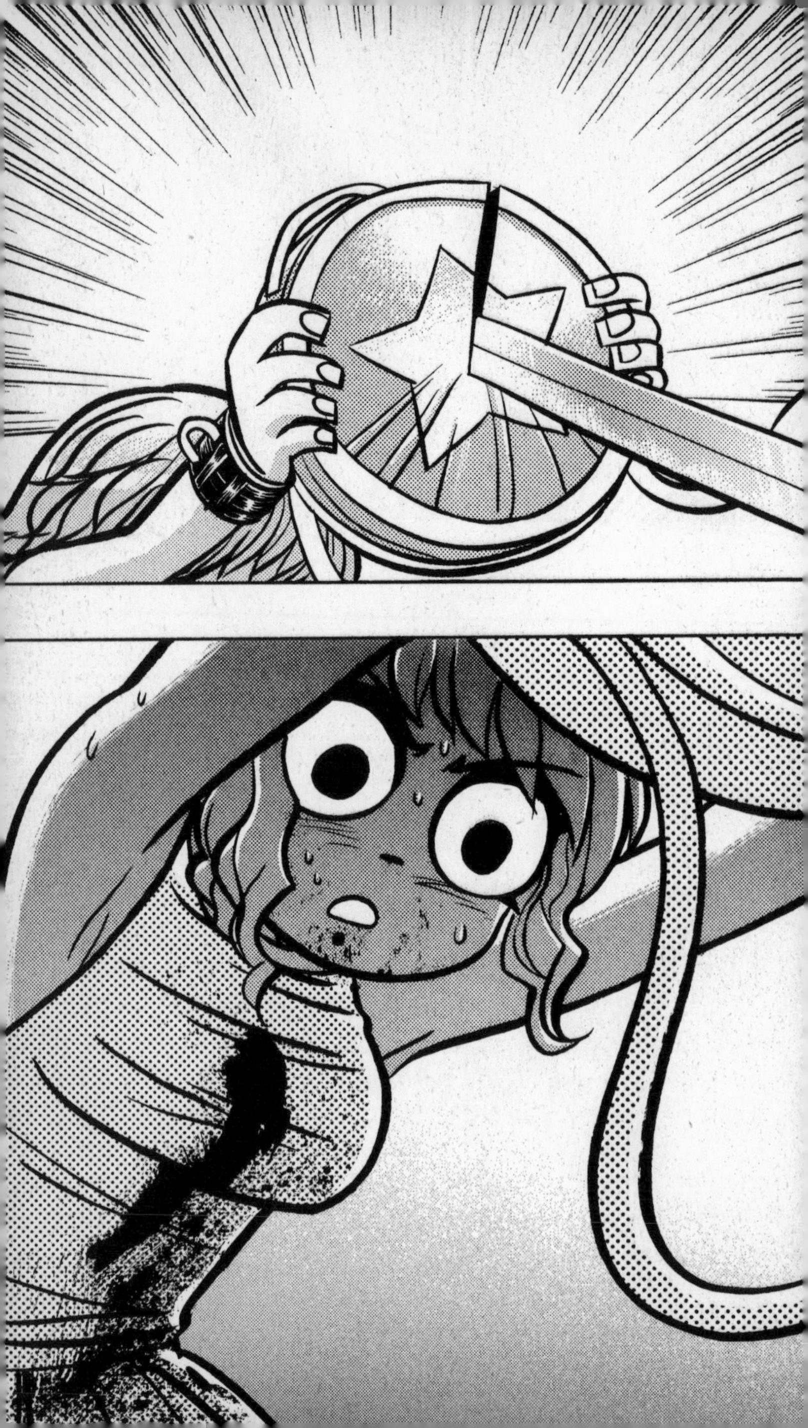

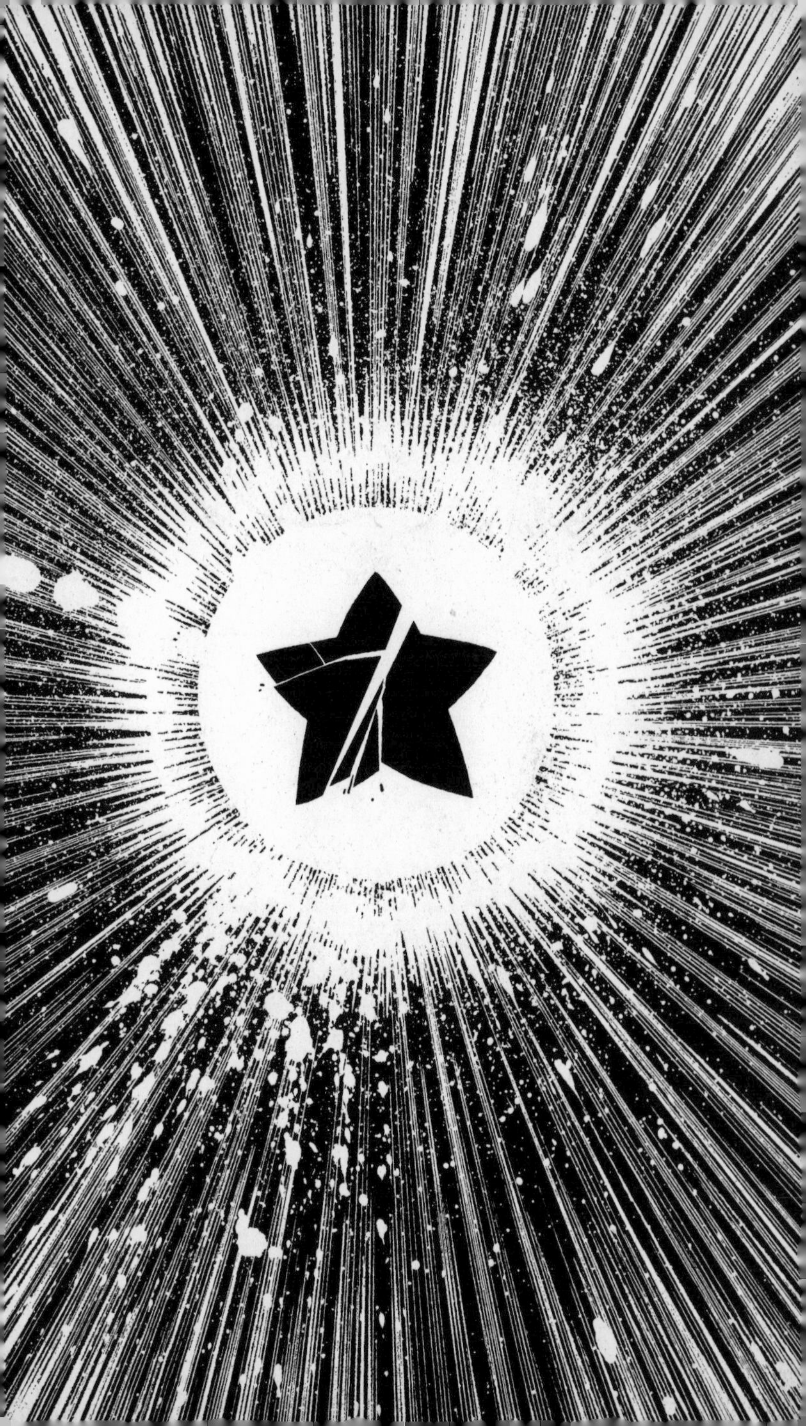

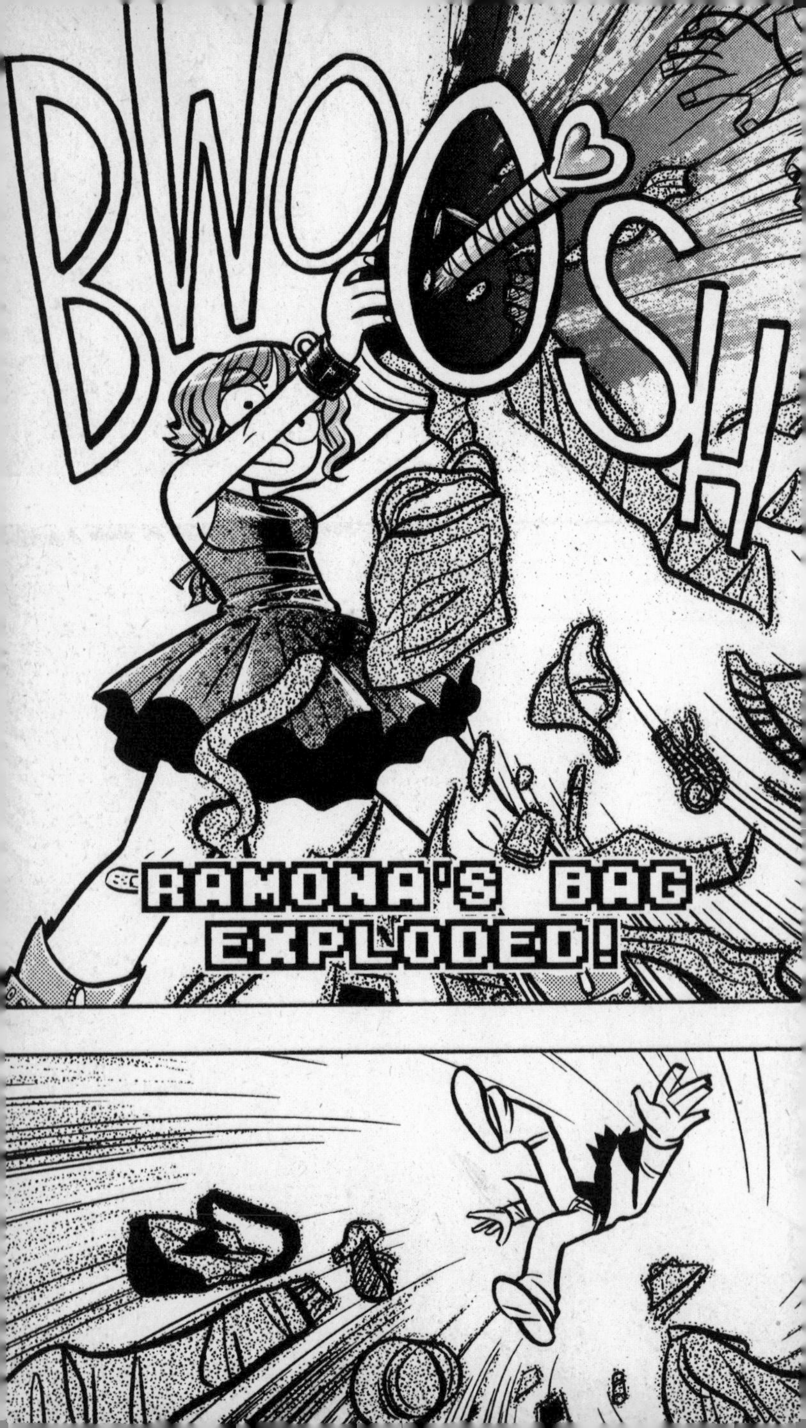
BWOOOSH
RAMONA'S BAG EXPLODED!

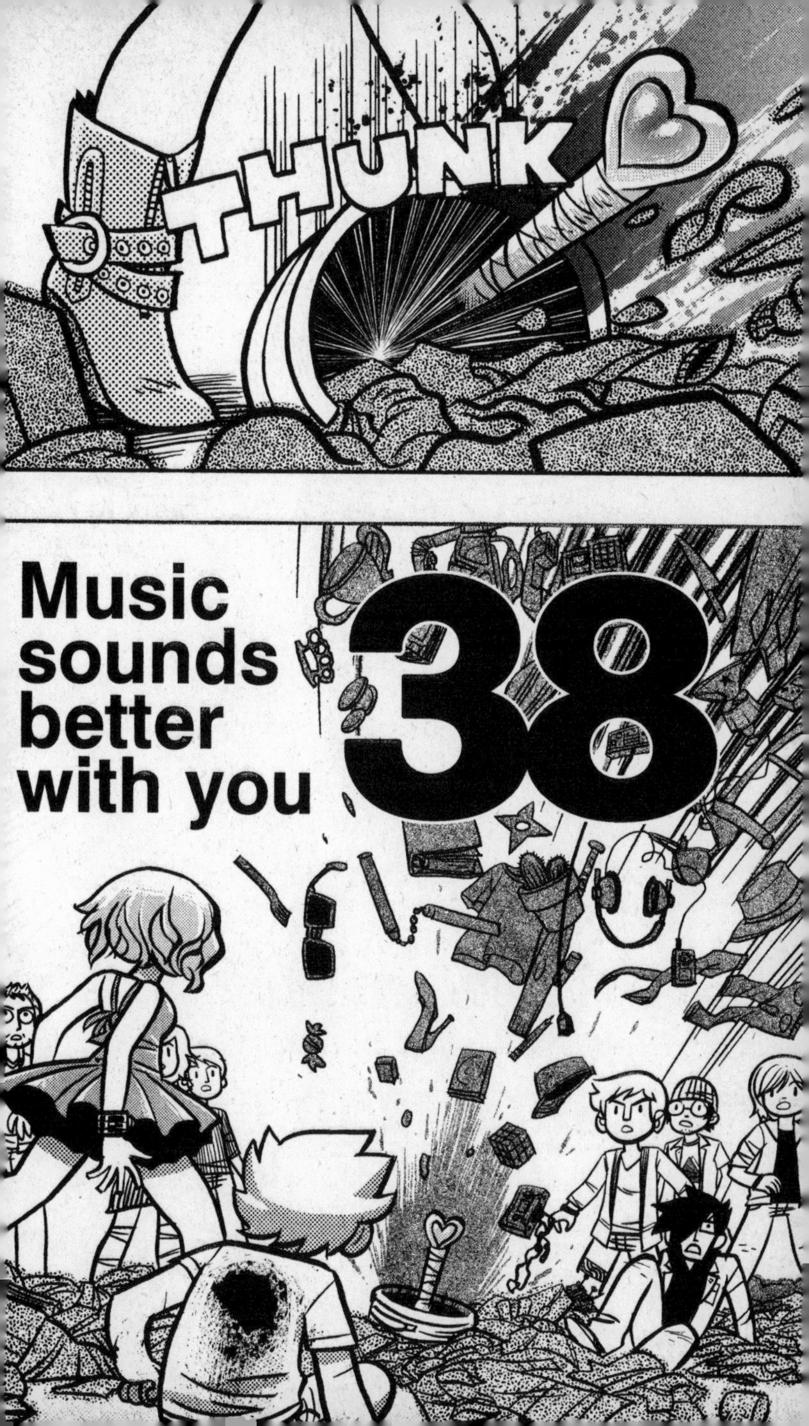
THUNK
Music sounds better with you
38

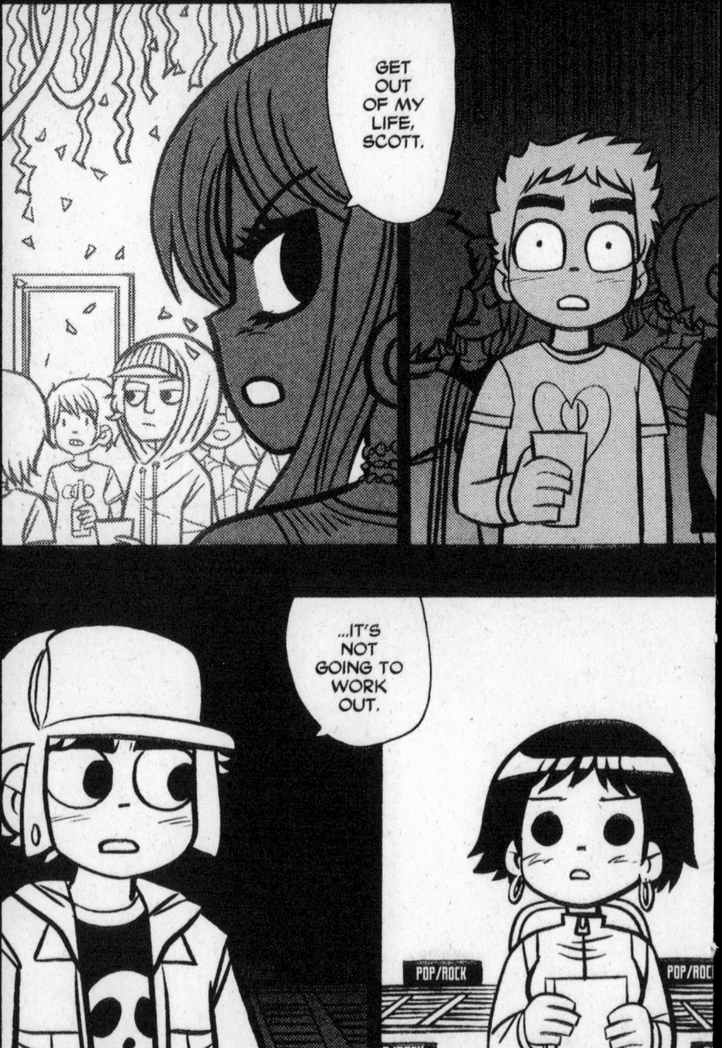
GET OUT OF MY LIFE, SCOTT.
...IT'S NOT GOING TO WORK OUT.
POP/ROCK
POP/ROCK

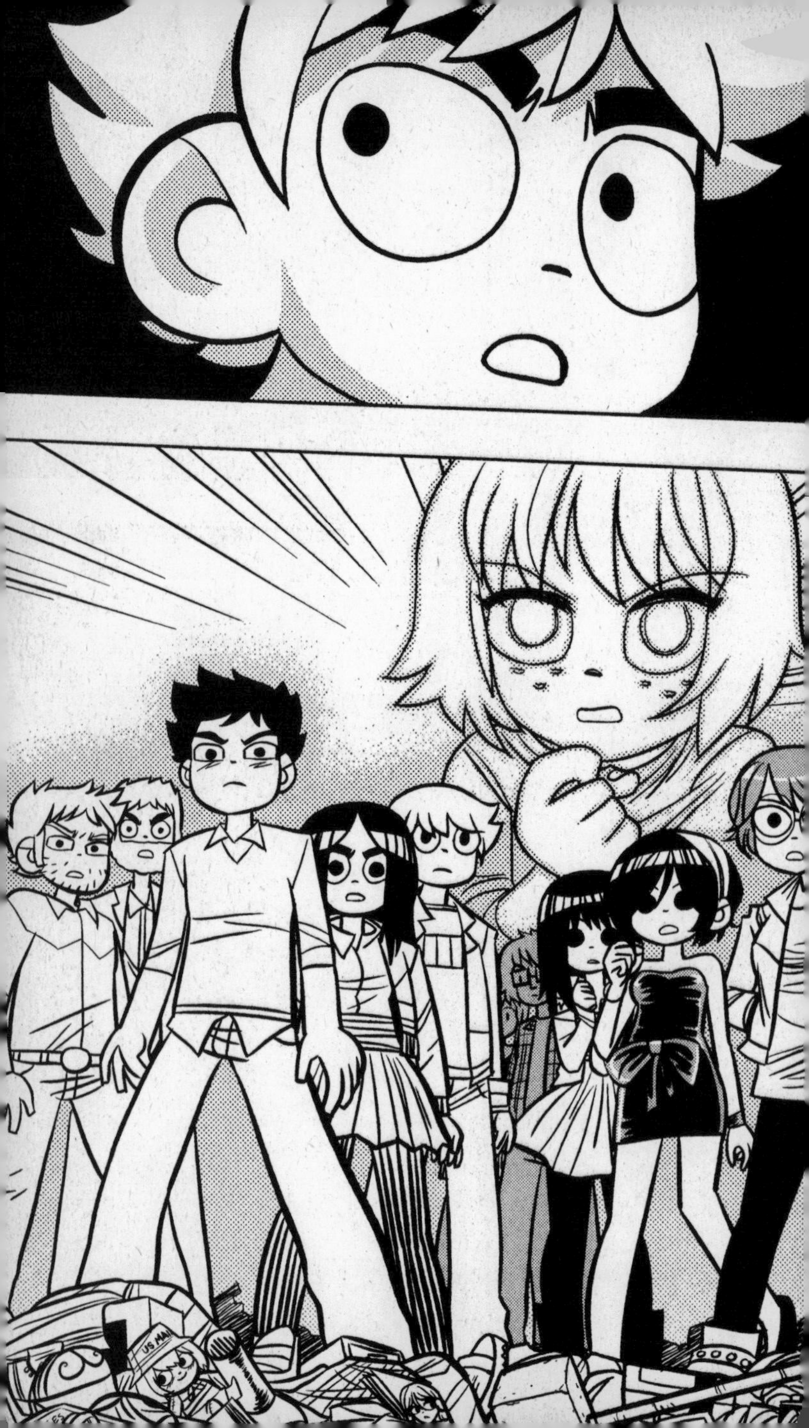

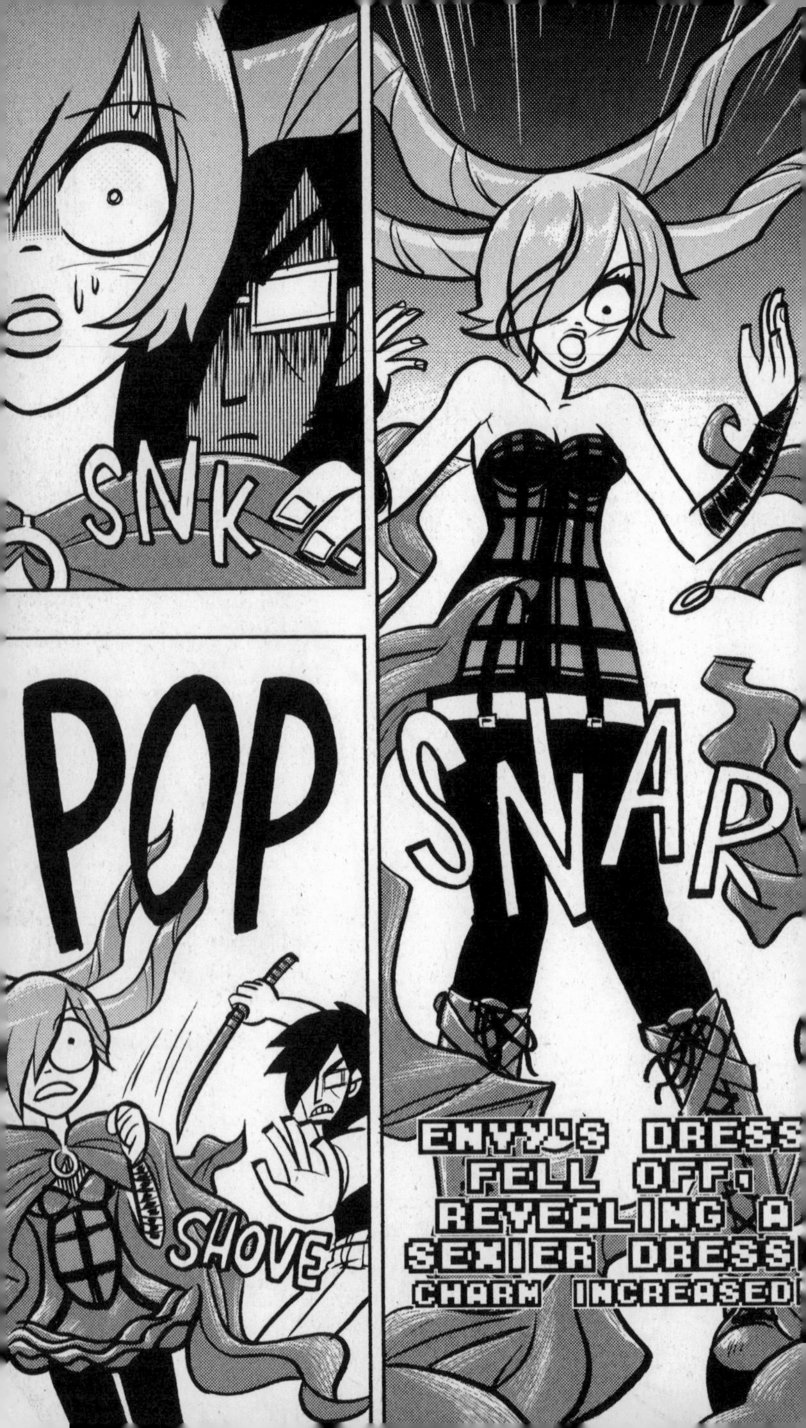

SNK
POP
SHOVE
SNAR
ENVY'S DRESS FELL OFF, REVEALING A SEXIER DRESS
CHARM INCREASED

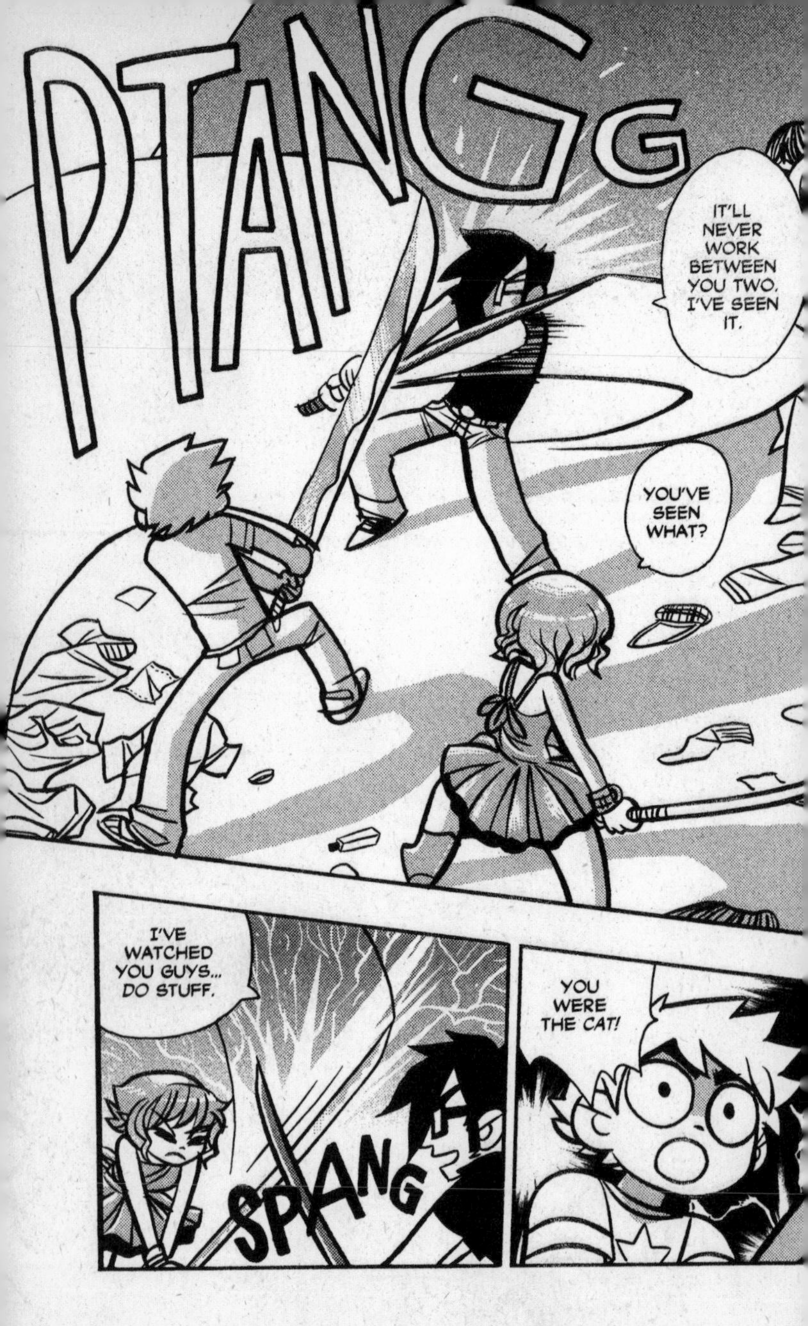
PTANGG
IT'LL NEVER WORK BETWEEN YOU TWO. I'VE SEEN IT.
YOU'VE SEEN WHAT?
I'VE WATCHED YOU GUYS... DO STUFF.
SPANG
YOU WERE THE CAT!

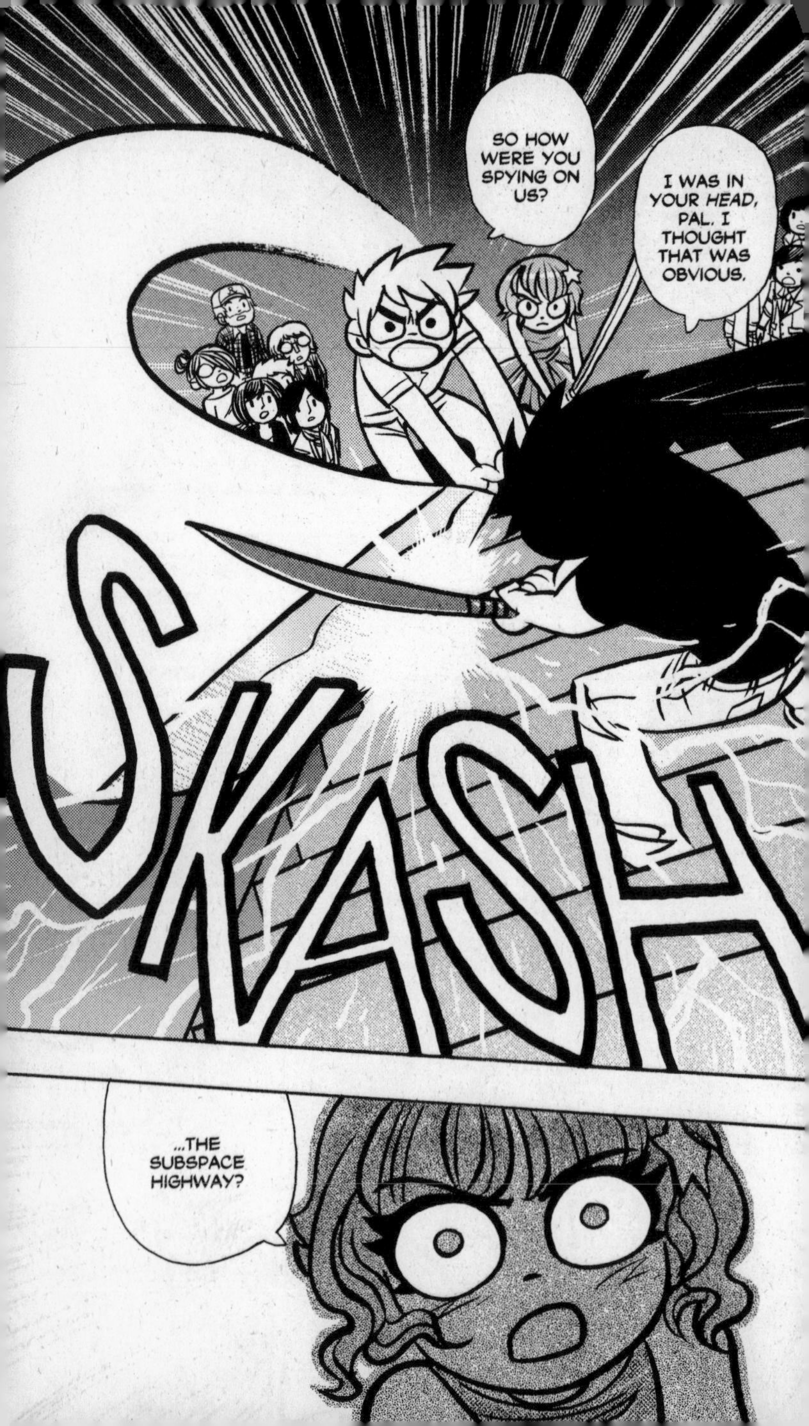
SO HOW WERE YOU SPYING ON US?
I WAS IN YOUR *HEAD*, PAL. I THOUGHT THAT WAS OBVIOUS.
SKASH
...THE SUBSPACE HIGHWAY?

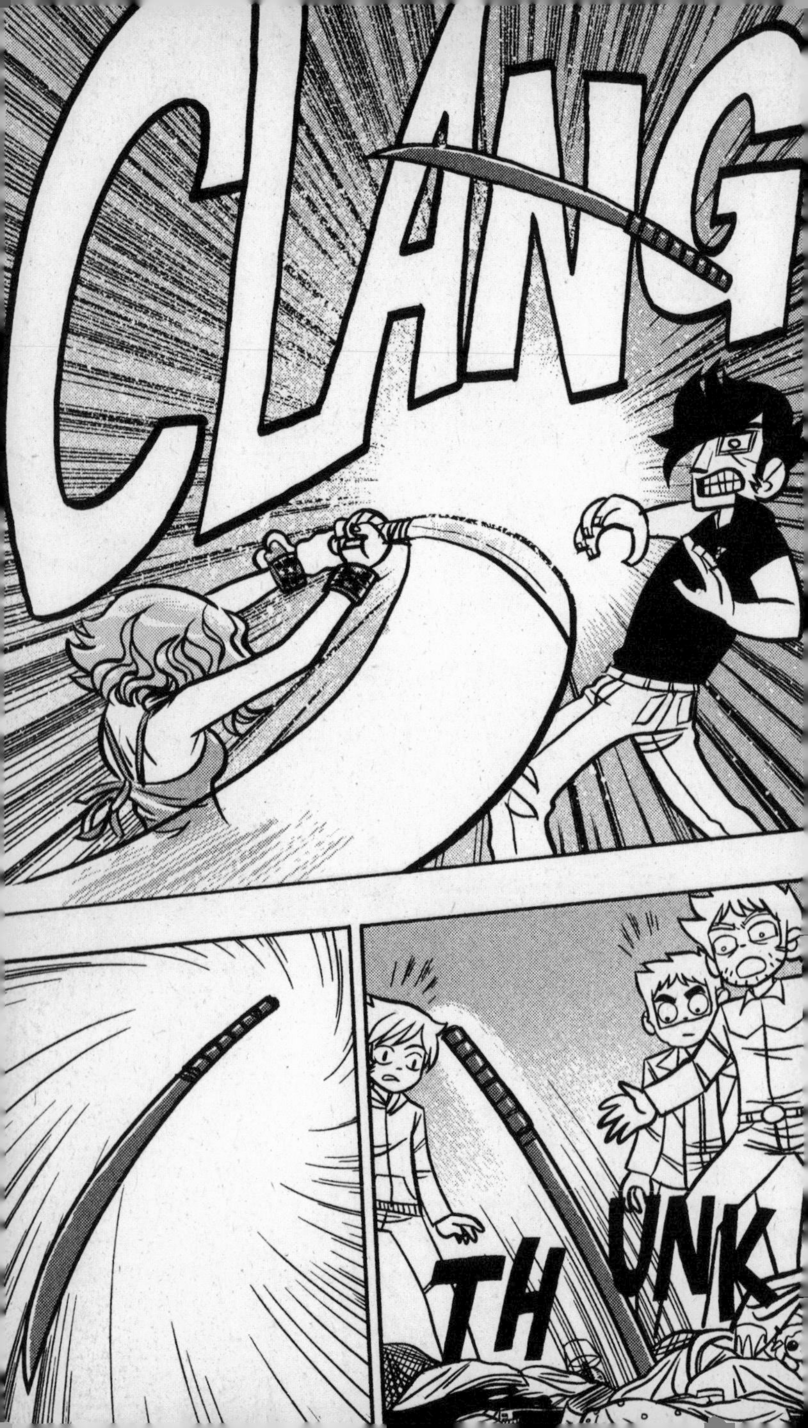
CLANG
THUNK

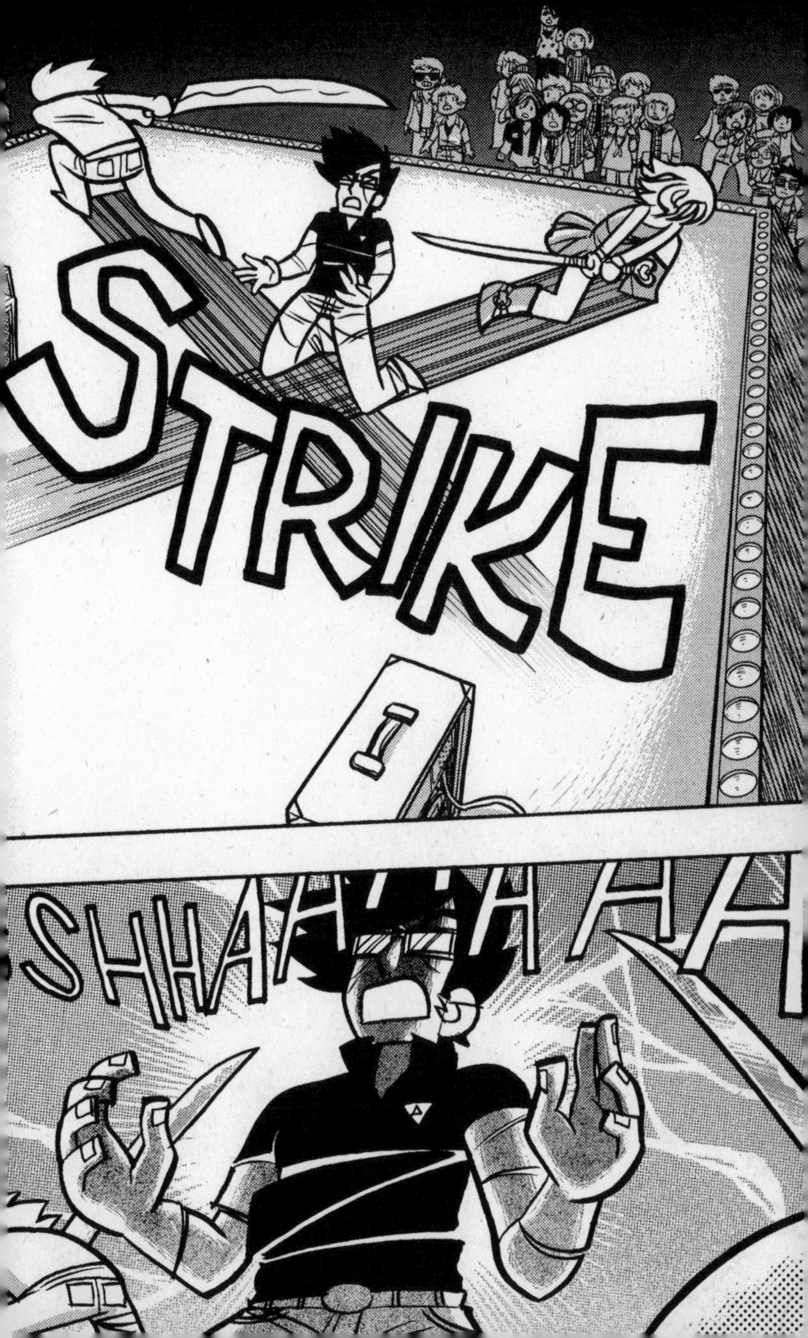
STRIKE
SHHAAAAA

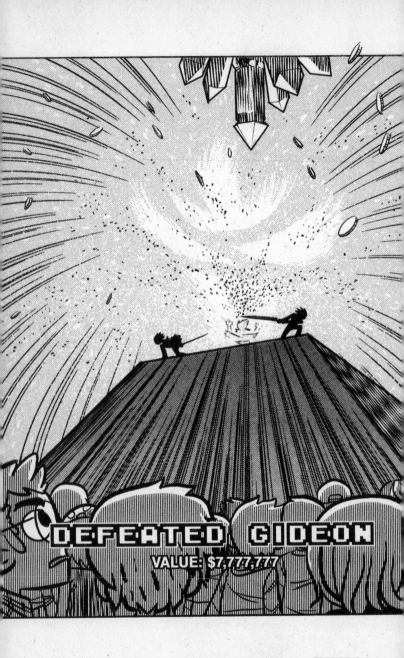

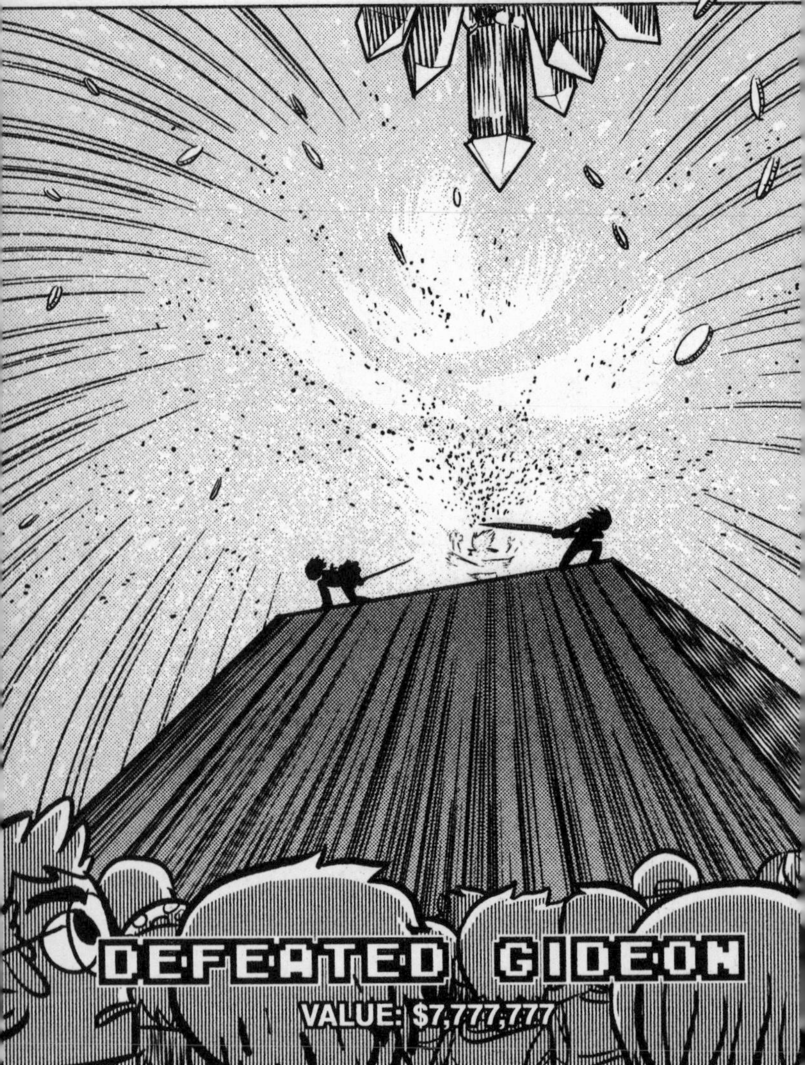
DEFEATED GIDEON
VALUE: $7,777,777

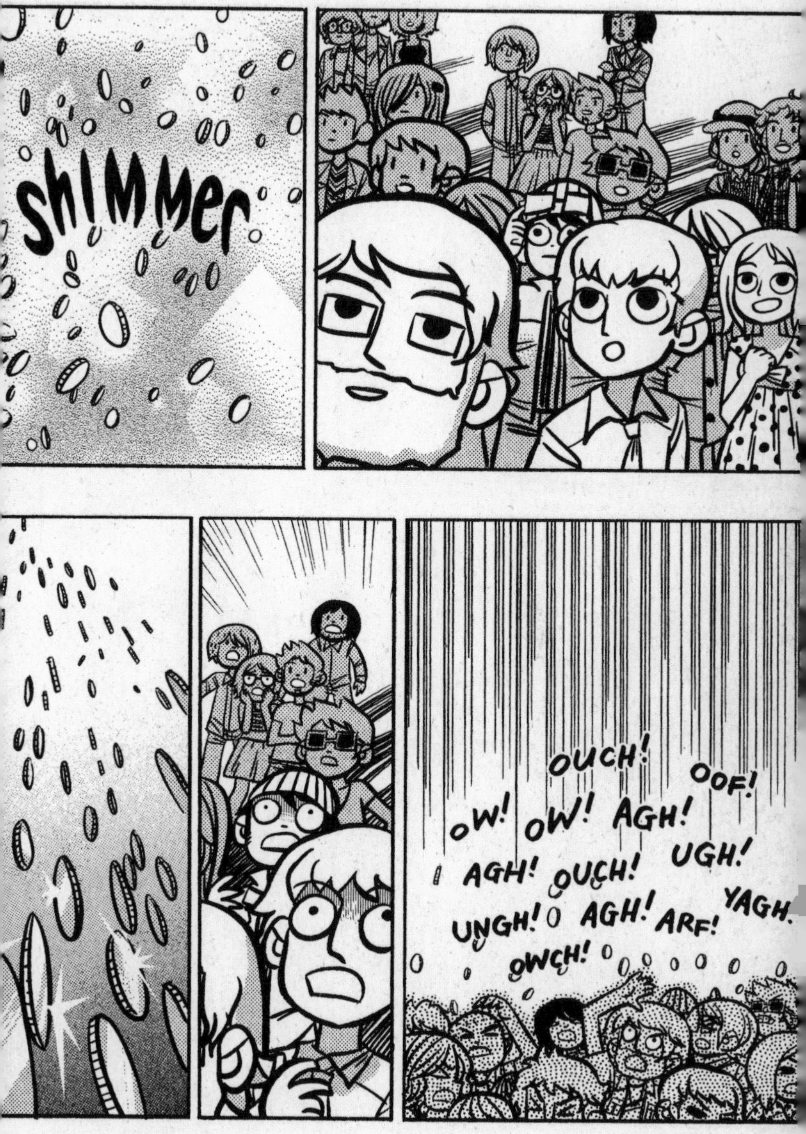
SHIMMER
OUCH!
OOF!
OW!
OW!
AGH!
AGH!
OUCH!
UGH!
YAGH.
UNGH!
AGH!
ARF!
OWCH!

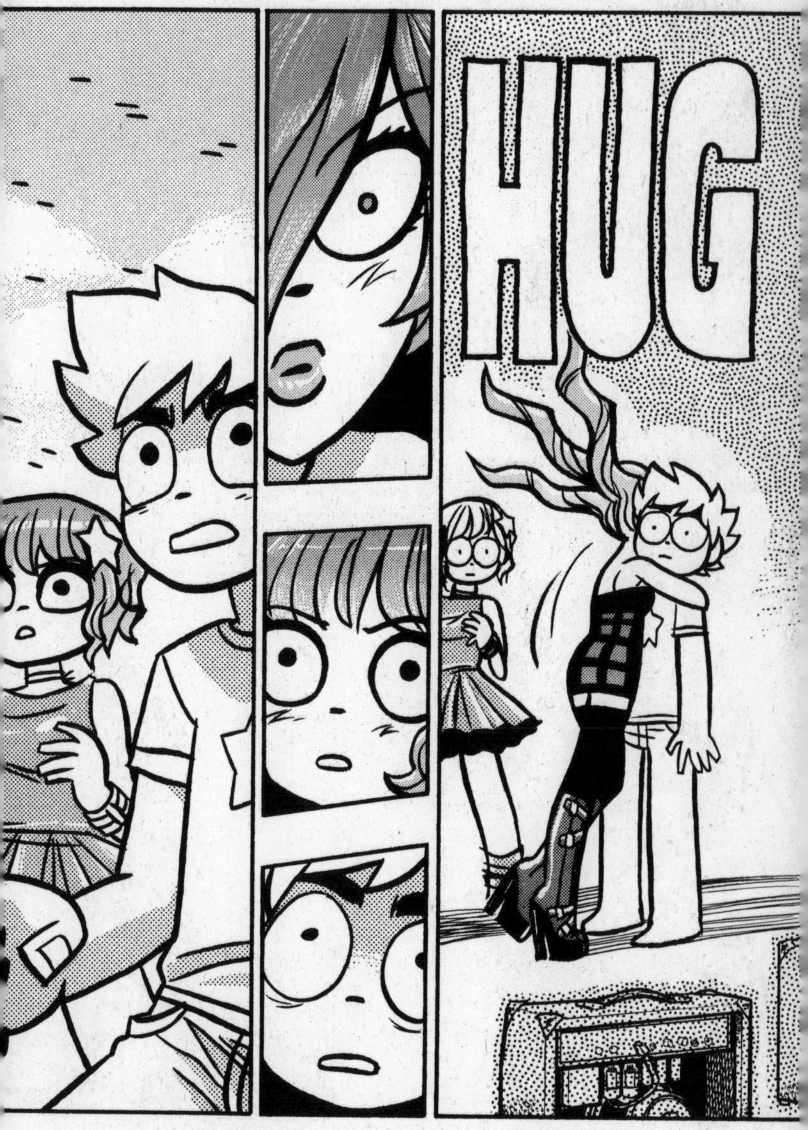
HUG

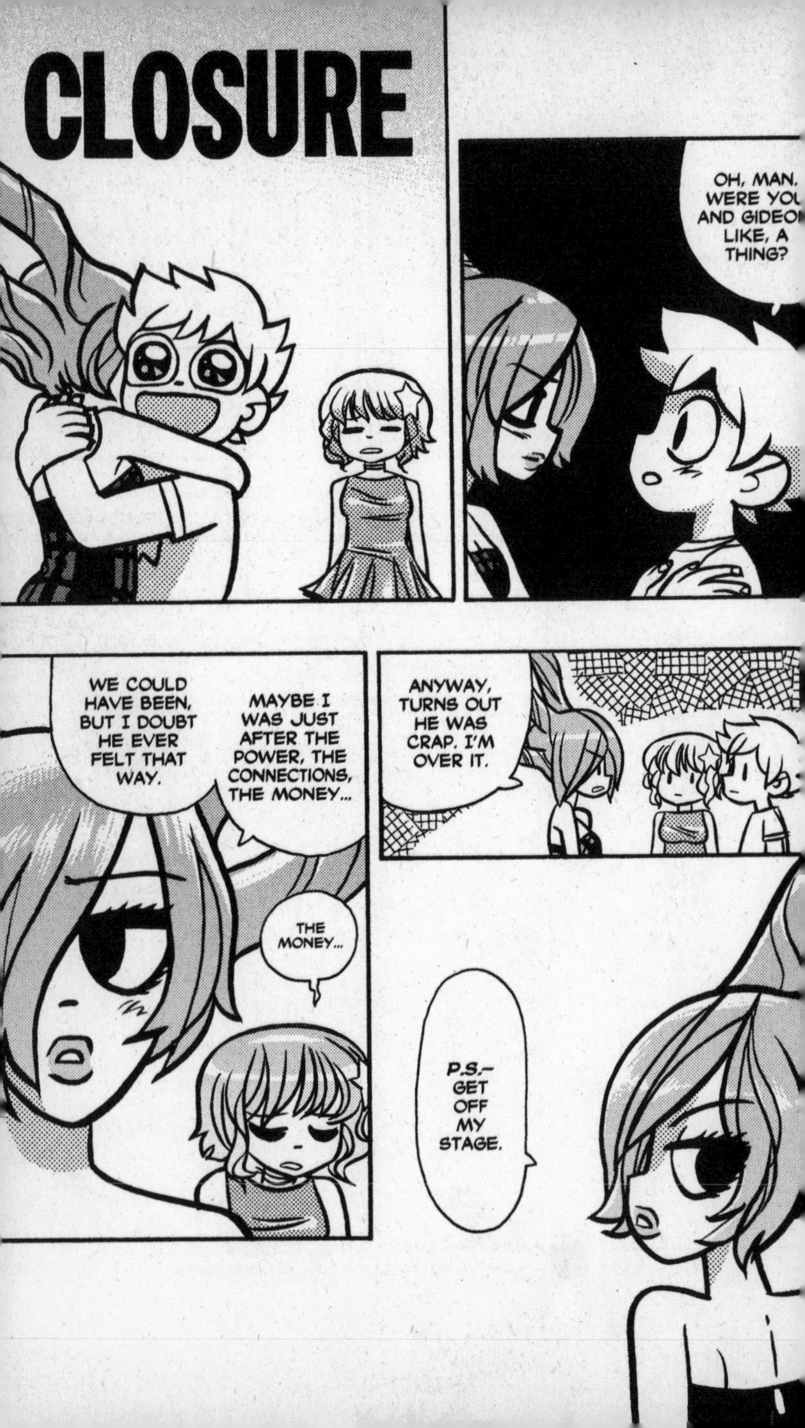
CLOSURE
OH, MAN. WERE YOU AND GIDEON LIKE, A THING?
WE COULD HAVE BEEN, BUT I DOUBT HE EVER FELT THAT WAY.
MAYBE I WAS JUST AFTER THE POWER, THE CONNECTIONS, THE MONEY...
THE MONEY...
ANYWAY, TURNS OUT HE WAS CRAP. I'M OVER IT.
P.S.– GET OFF MY STAGE.

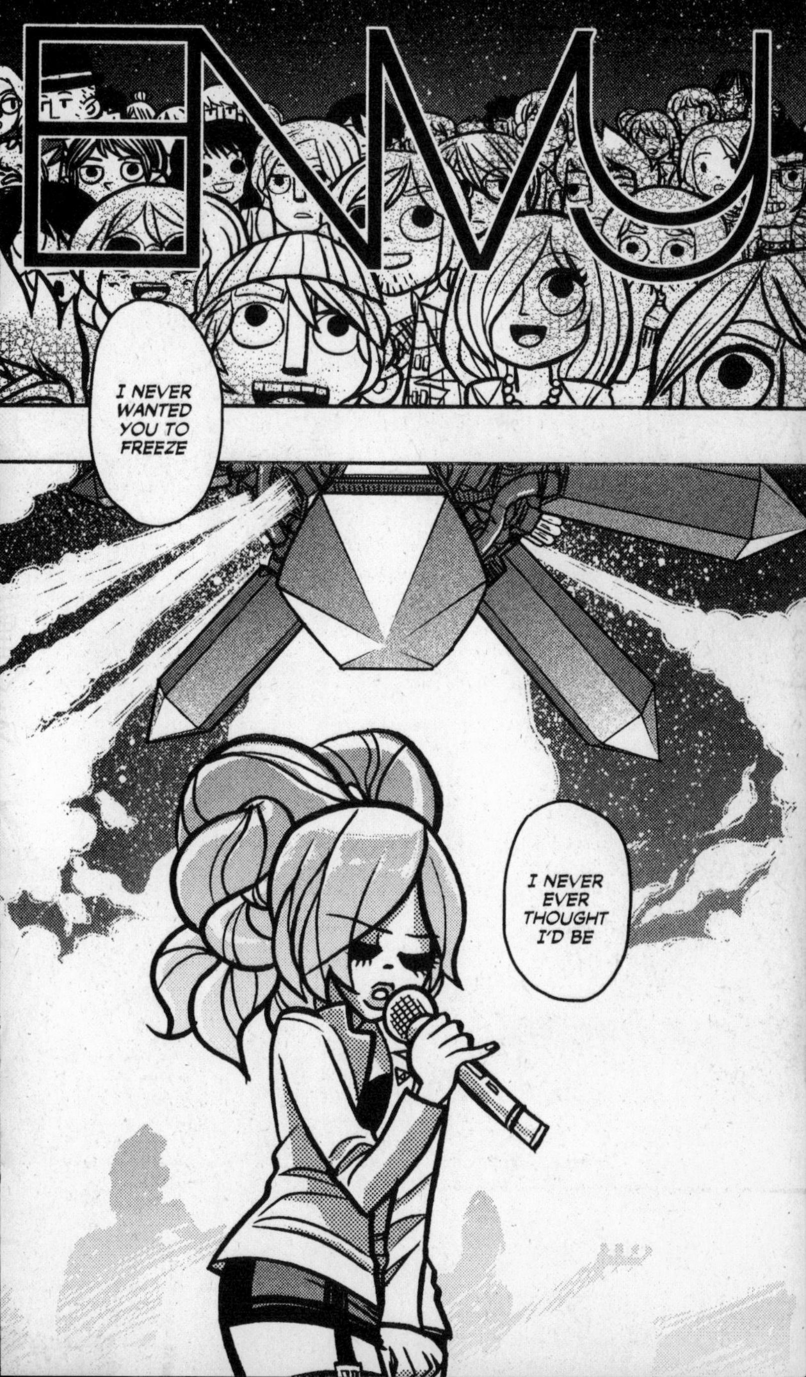
I NEVER WANTED YOU TO FREEZE
I NEVER EVER THOUGHT I'D BE

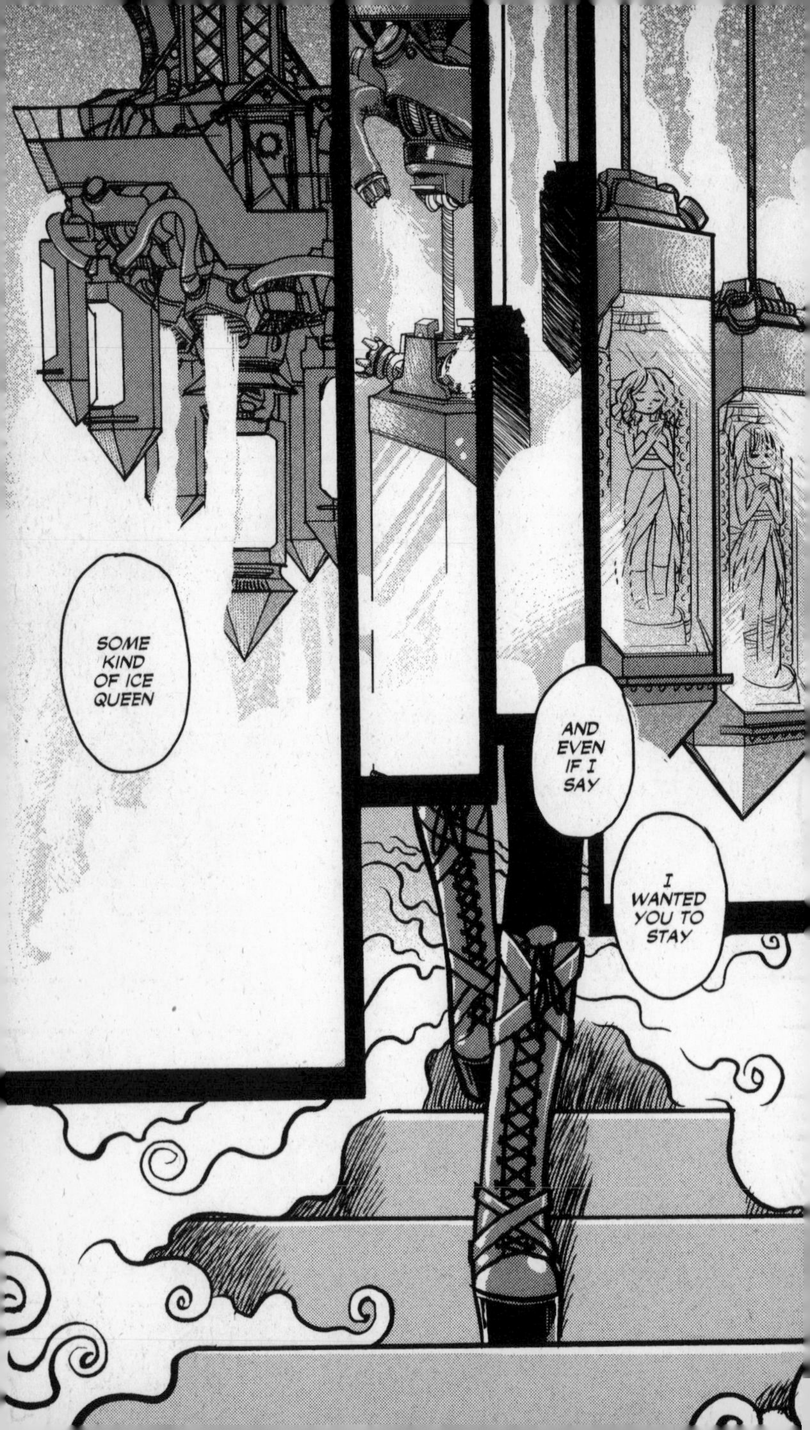
I WANTED YOU TO STAY
AND EVEN IF I SAY
SOME KIND OF ICE QUEEN

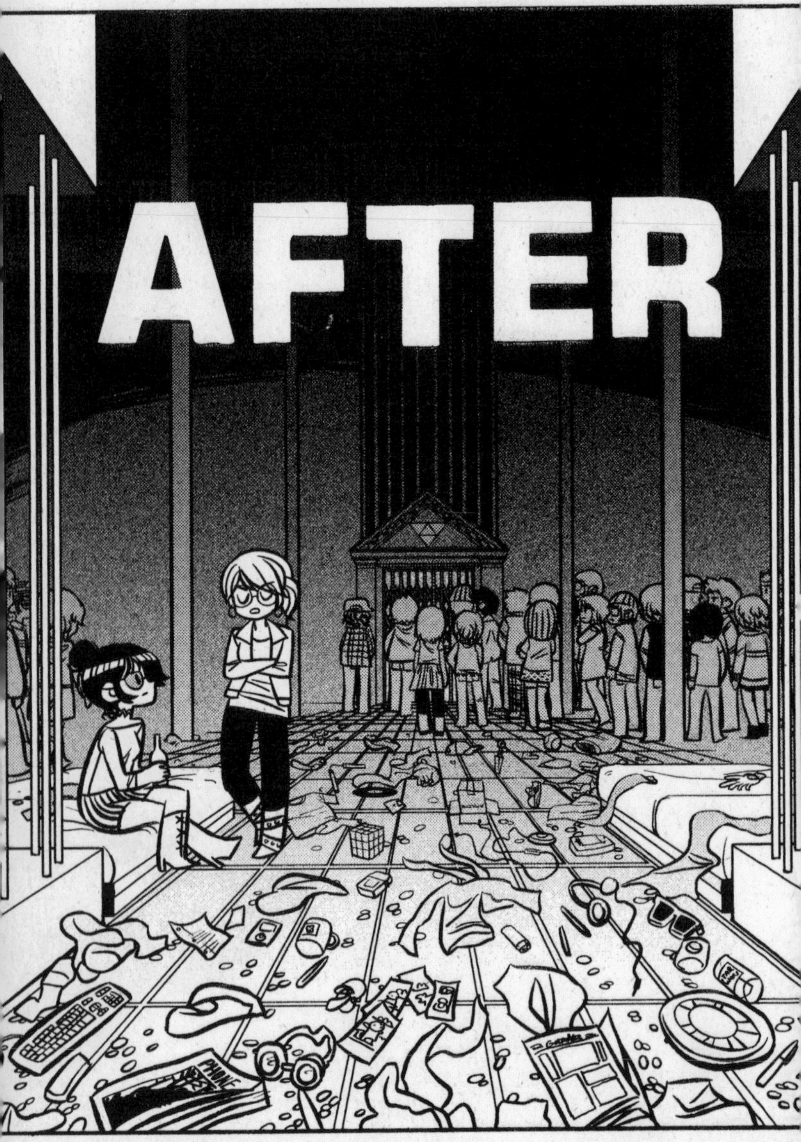
AFTER
PHONE

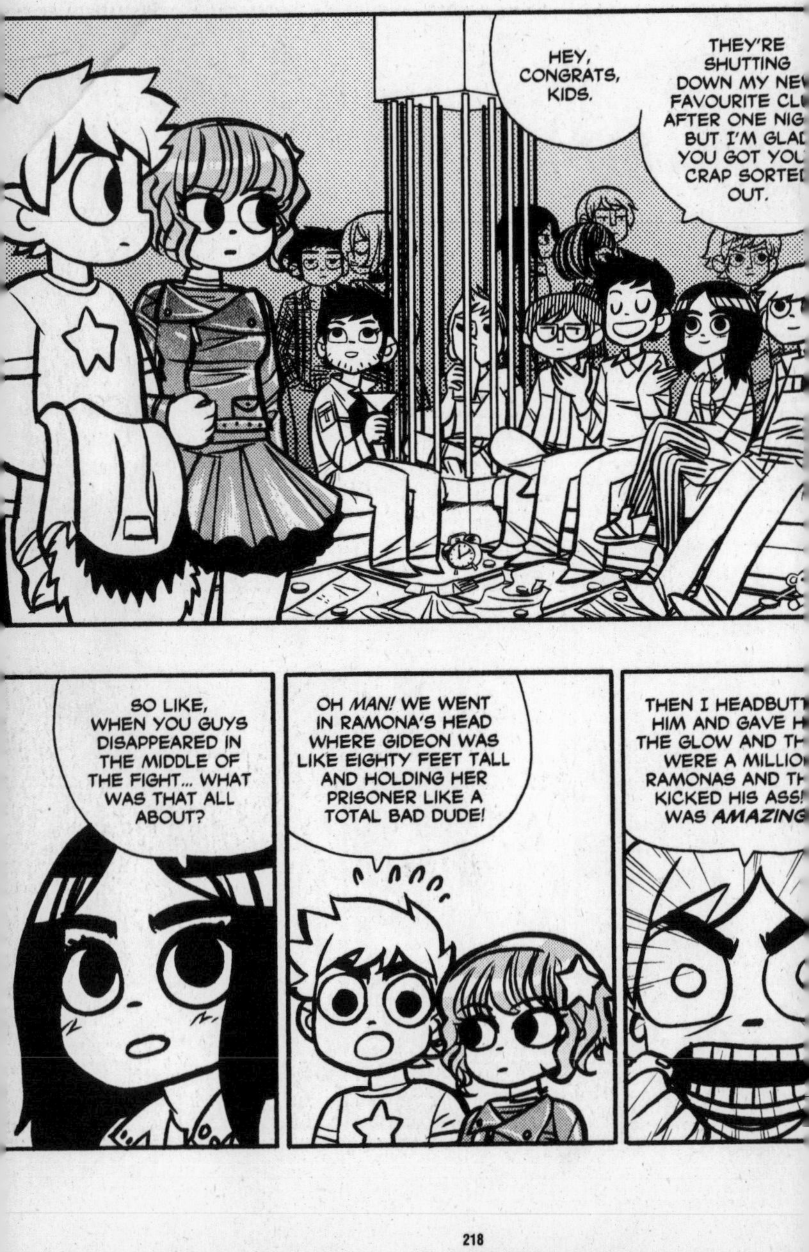
HEY, CONGRATS, KIDS.
THEY'RE SHUTTING DOWN MY NE FAVOURITE CL AFTER ONE NIG BUT I'M GLA YOU GOT YOU CRAP SORTE OUT.
SO LIKE, WHEN YOU GUYS DISAPPEARED IN THE MIDDLE OF THE FIGHT... WHAT WAS THAT ALL ABOUT?
OH *MAN!* WE WENT IN RAMONA'S HEAD WHERE GIDEON WAS LIKE EIGHTY FEET TALL AND HOLDING HER PRISONER LIKE A TOTAL BAD DUDE!
THEN I HEADBUT HIM AND GAVE H THE GLOW AND TH WERE A MILLIO RAMONAS AND TH KICKED HIS ASS! WAS ***AMAZING***

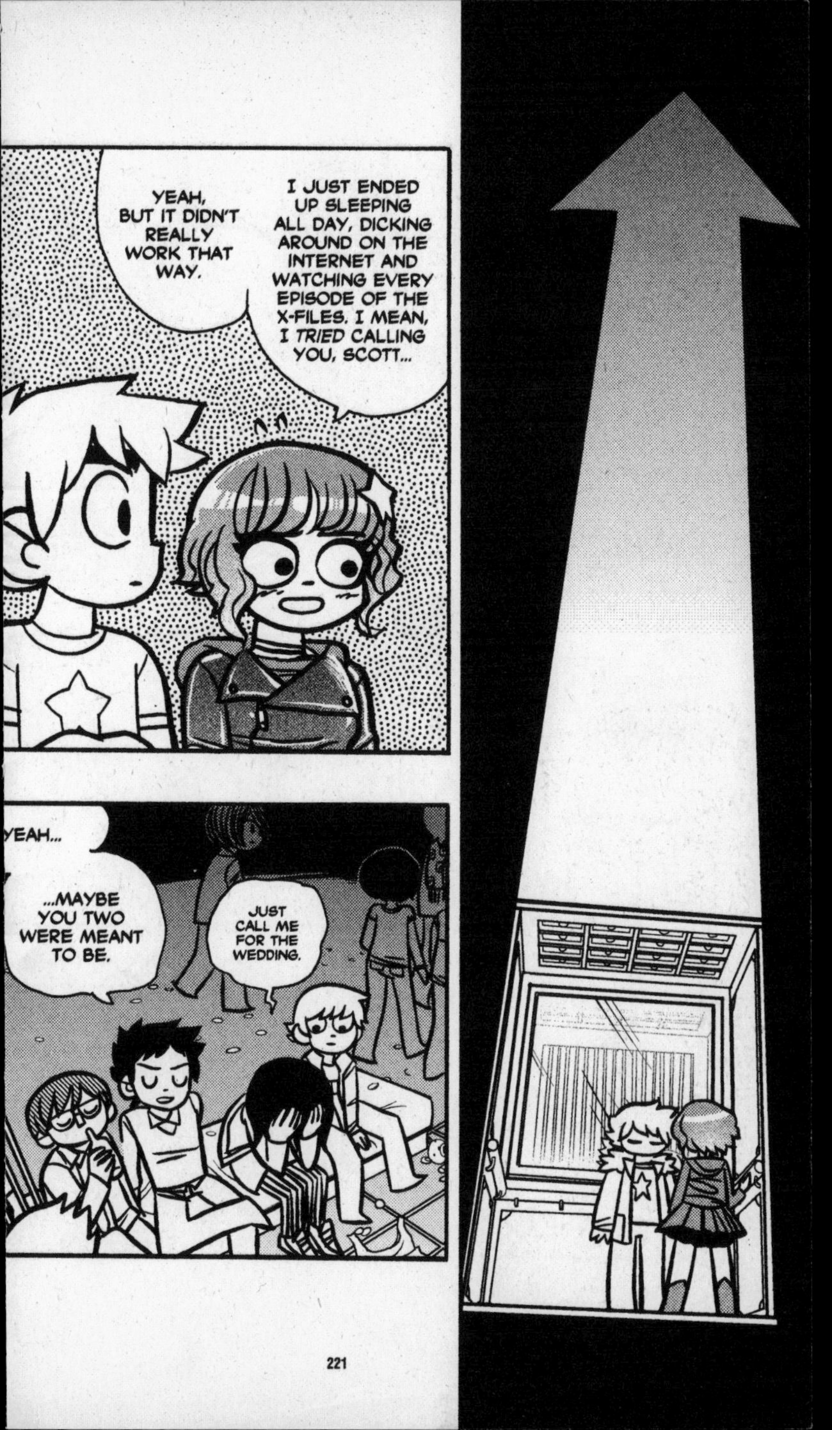
YEAH, BUT IT DIDN'T REALLY WORK THAT WAY.
I JUST ENDED UP SLEEPING ALL DAY, DICKING AROUND ON THE INTERNET AND WATCHING EVERY EPISODE OF THE X-FILES. I MEAN, I *TRIED* CALLING YOU, SCOTT...
YEAH...
...MAYBE YOU TWO WERE MEANT TO BE.
JUST CALL ME FOR THE WEDDING.

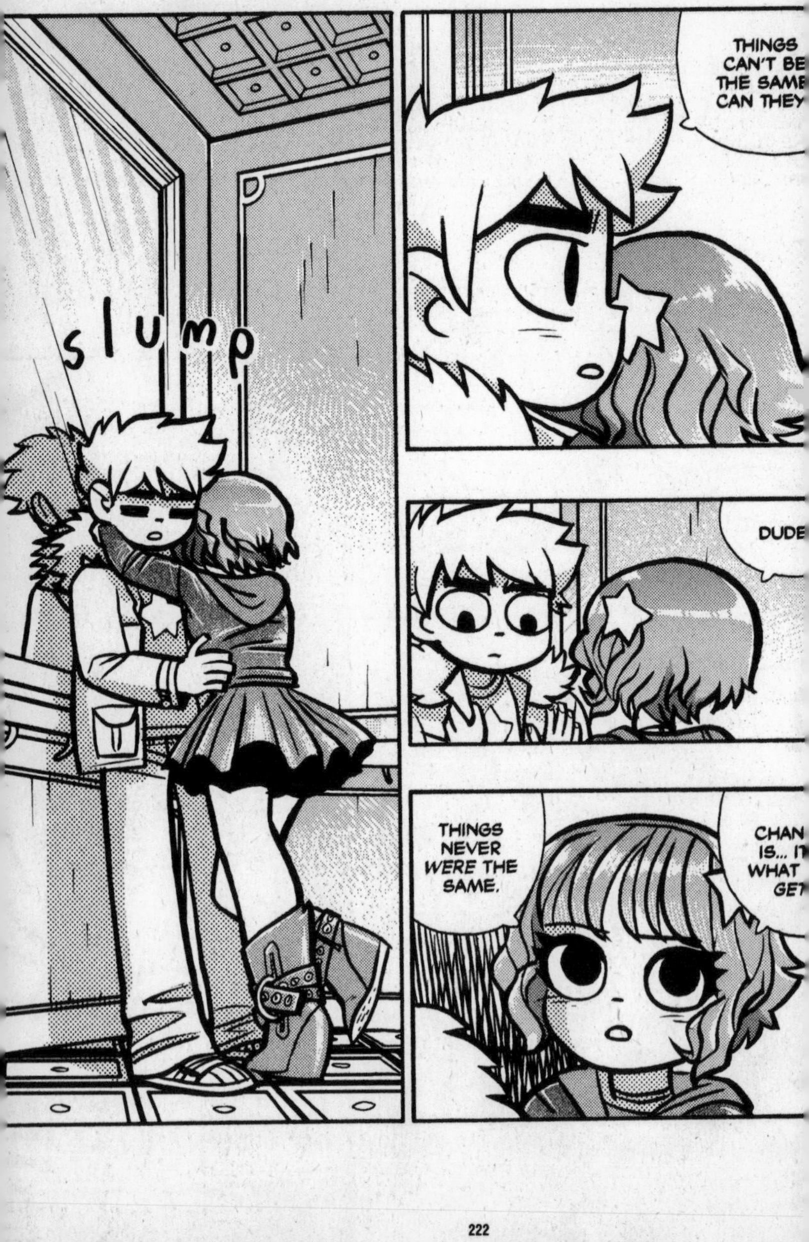
slump
THINGS CAN'T BE THE SAME CAN THEY
DUDE
THINGS NEVER *WERE* THE SAME.
CHAN IS... WHAT GET

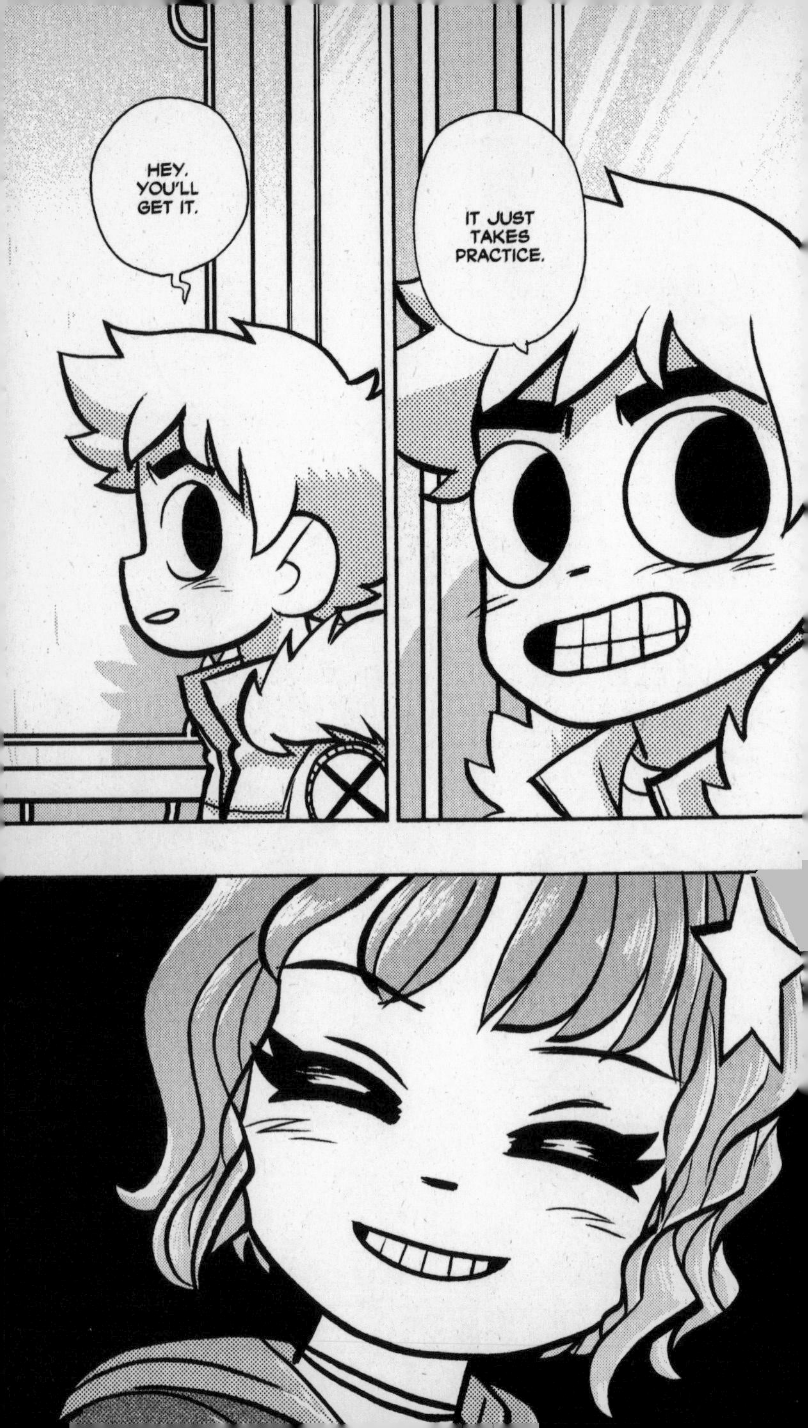
HEY. YOU'LL GET IT.
IT JUST TAKES PRACTICE.

SO
ANYWAY

STEPHEN STILLS
HEAD CHEF

SCOTT PILGRIM
WORLD'S GREATES
PREP COOK

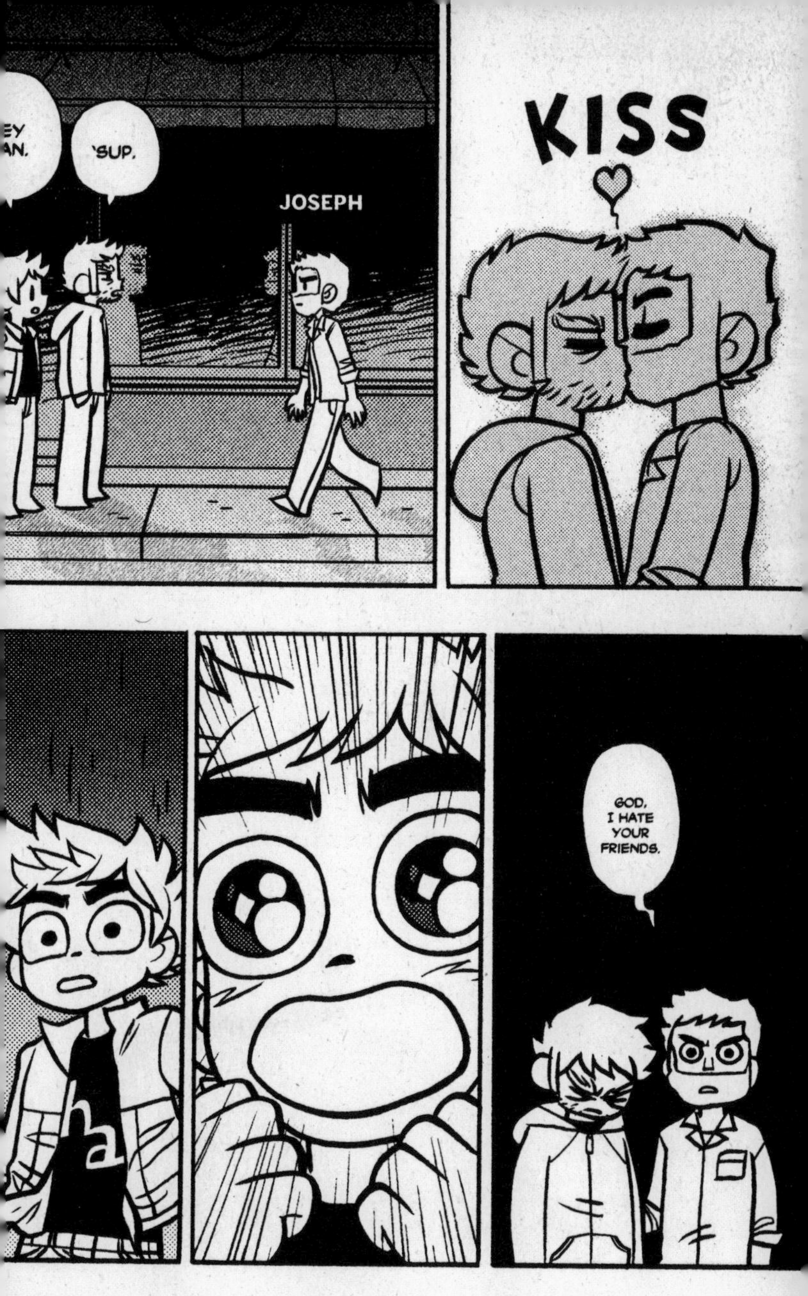
EY AN.
'SUP.
JOSEPH
KISS
GOD, I HATE YOUR FRIENDS.

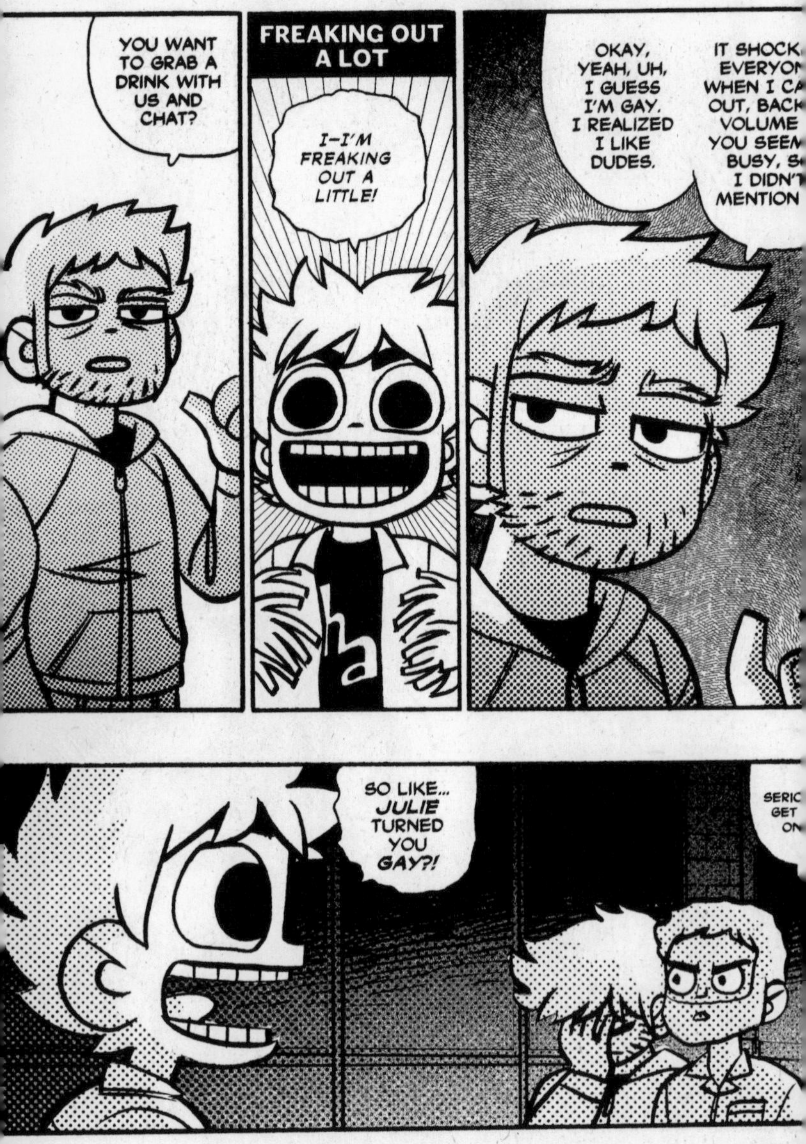
YOU WANT TO GRAB A DRINK WITH US AND CHAT?
FREAKING OUT A LOT
I-I'M FREAKING OUT A LITTLE!
OKAY, YEAH, UH, I GUESS I'M GAY. I REALIZED I LIKE DUDES.
IT SHOCK EVERYON WHEN I CA OUT, BACK VOLUME YOU SEEM BUSY, S I DIDN'T MENTION
SO LIKE... *JULIE* TURNED YOU *GAY?!*
SERIC GET ON

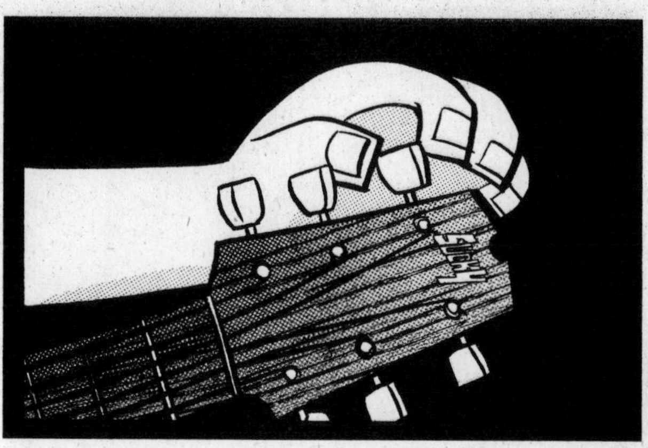
SUCKY

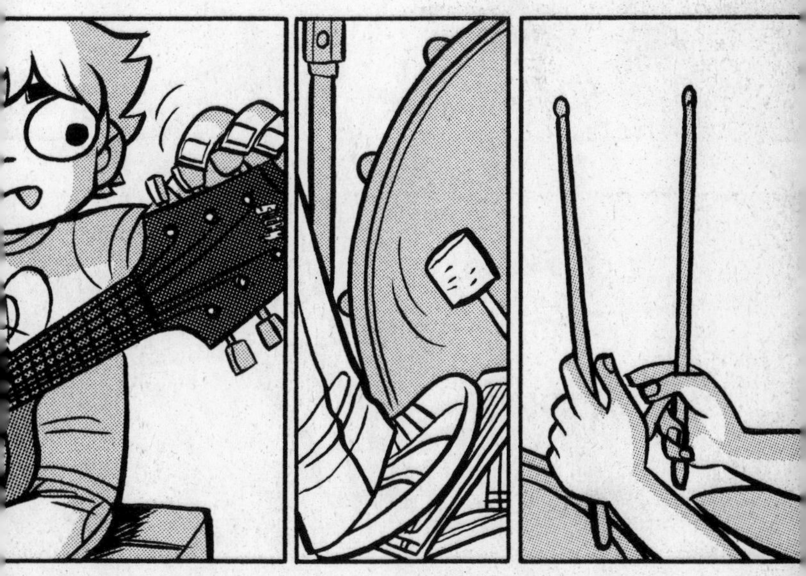

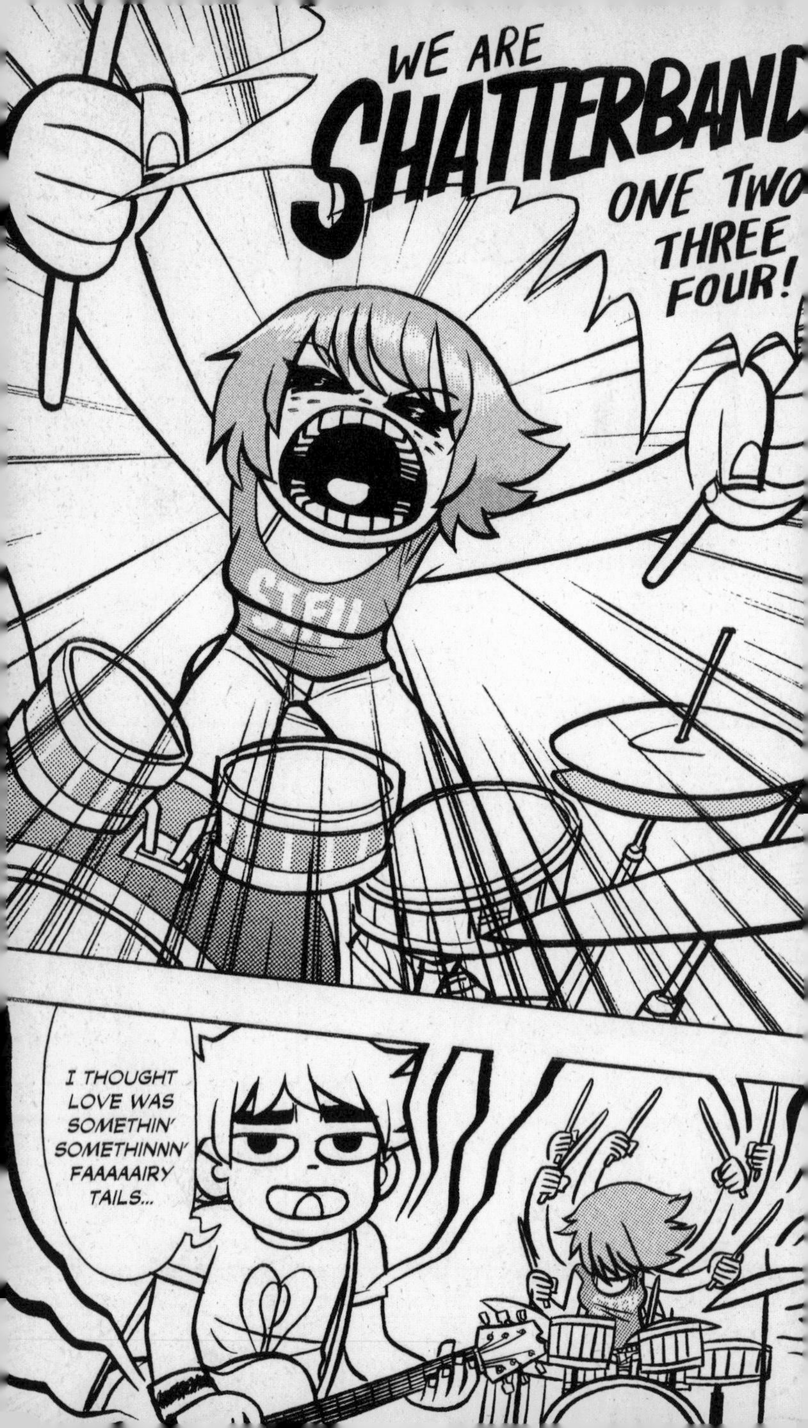
WE ARE SHATTERBAND
ONE TWO THREE FOUR!
STFU
I THOUGHT LOVE WAS SOMETHIN' SOMETHINNN' FAAAAAIRY TAILS...

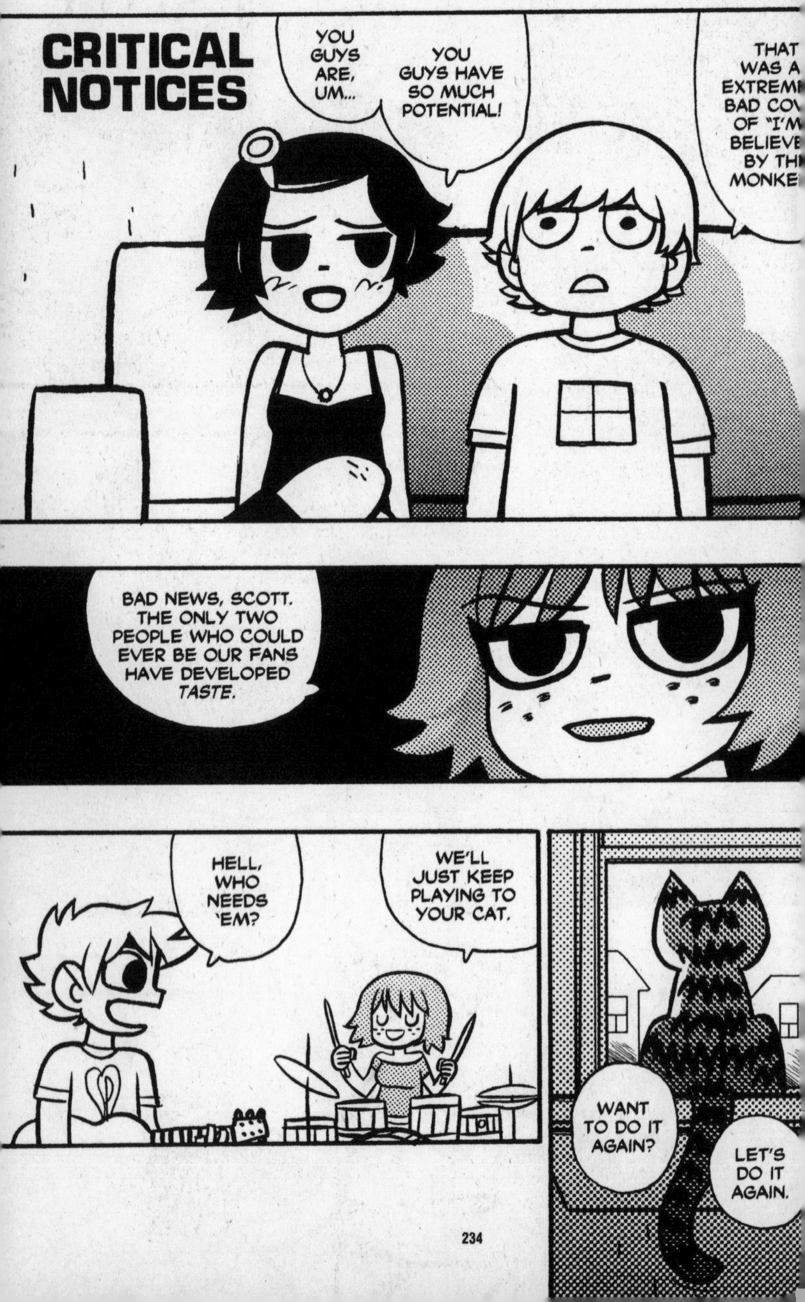
CRITICAL NOTICES
YOU GUYS ARE, UM...
YOU GUYS HAVE SO MUCH POTENTIAL!
THAT WAS A EXTREM BAD CO OF "I'M BELIEVE BY TH MONKE
BAD NEWS, SCOTT. THE ONLY TWO PEOPLE WHO COULD EVER BE OUR FANS HAVE DEVELOPED *TASTE*.
HELL, WHO NEEDS 'EM?
WE'LL JUST KEEP PLAYING TO YOUR CAT.
WANT TO DO IT AGAIN?
LET'S DO IT AGAIN.

THEN.

SO UM

I MEAN I GUESS I'LL

snff

BAWL

E ME CALL HEN RE IN WN, AY?

SCOTT...

YOU'LL ALWAYS BE MY CLASH AT DEMONHEAD.

Whatever that means.

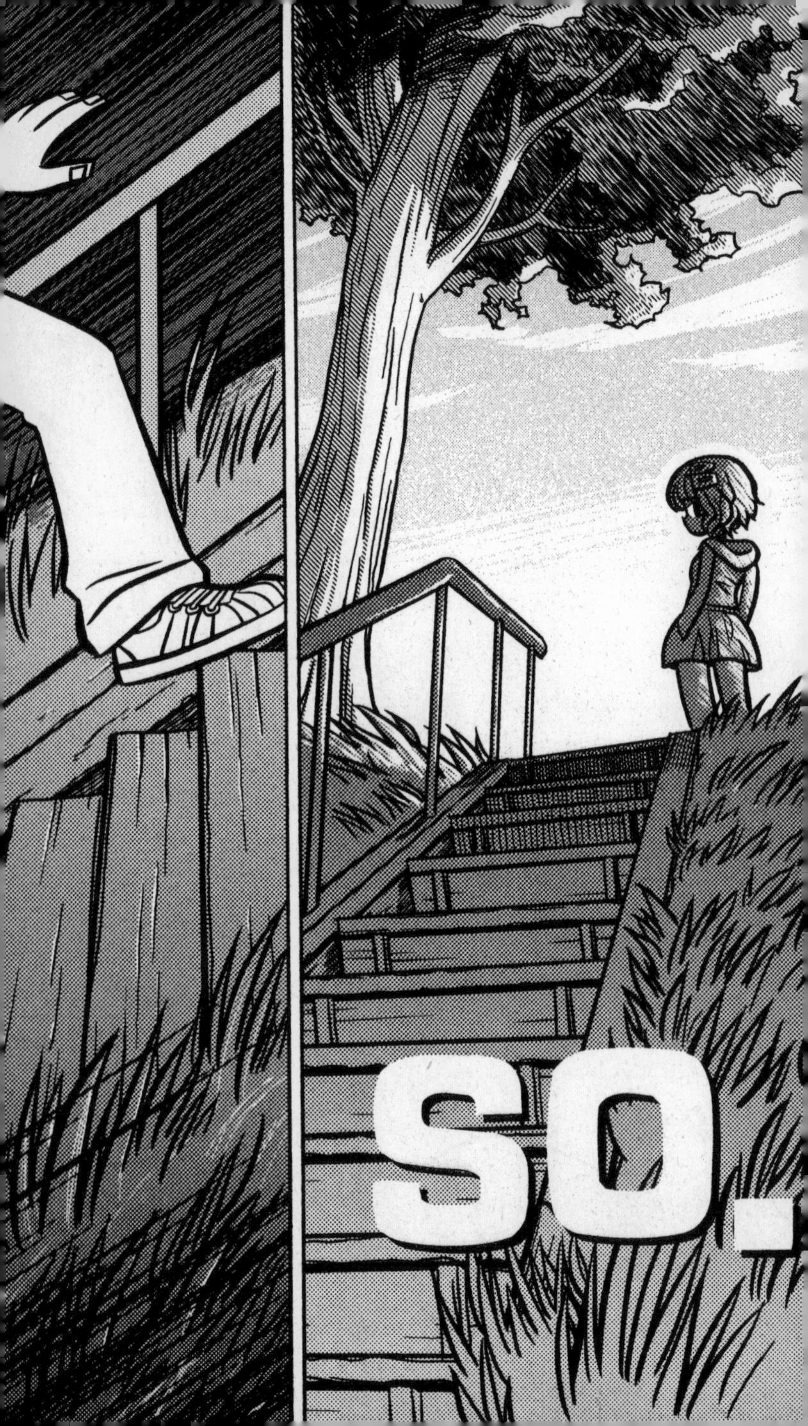
SO.

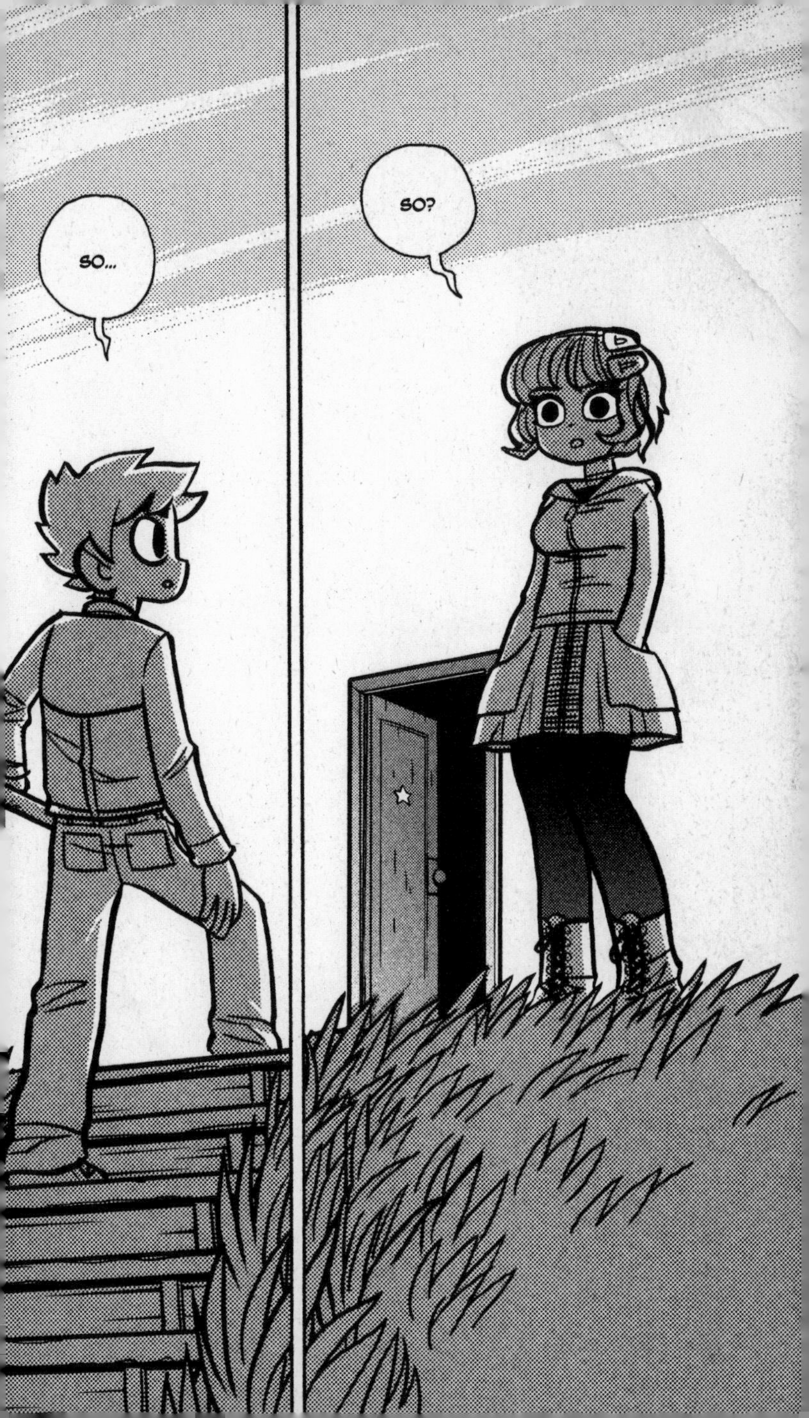
SO...
SO?

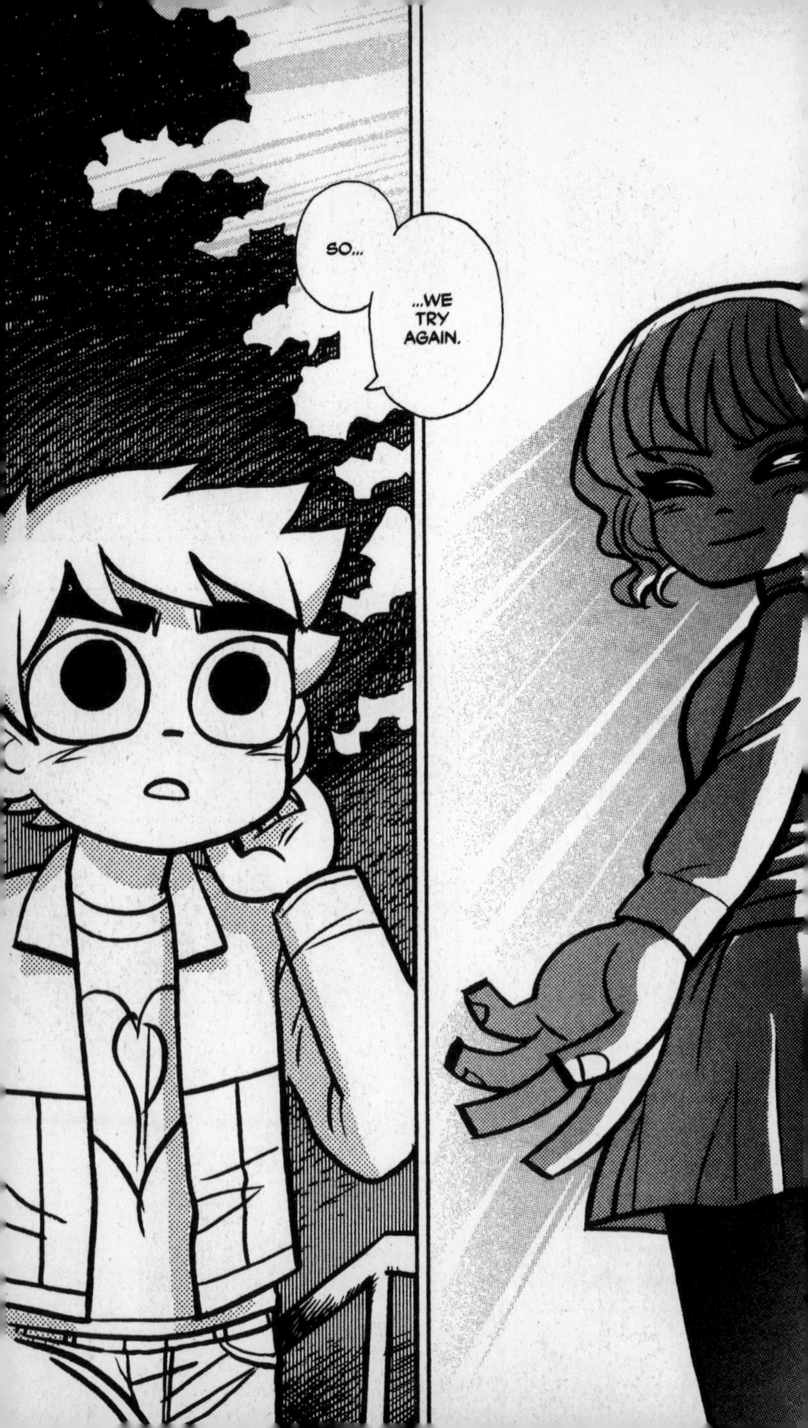
SO...
...WE TRY AGAIN.

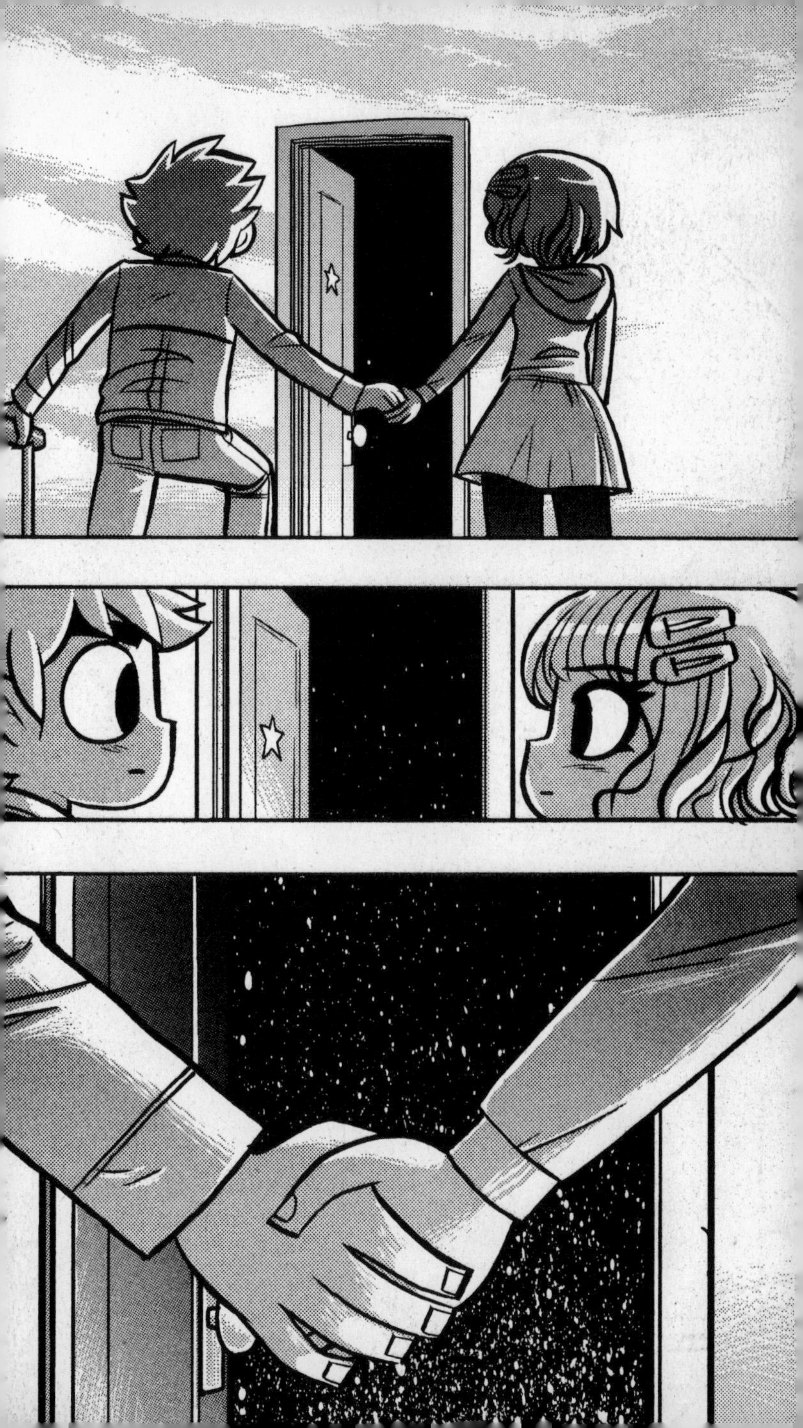

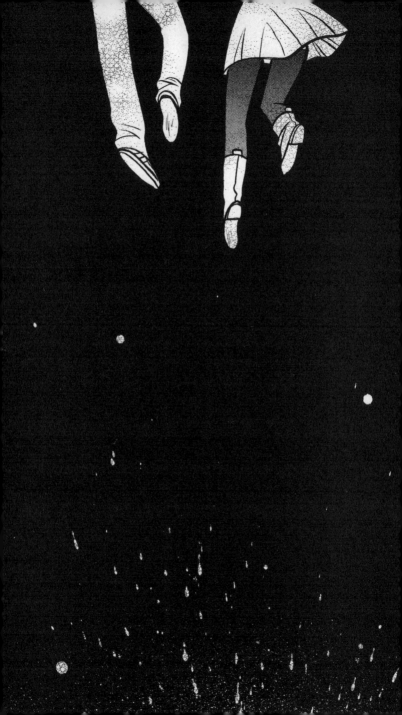

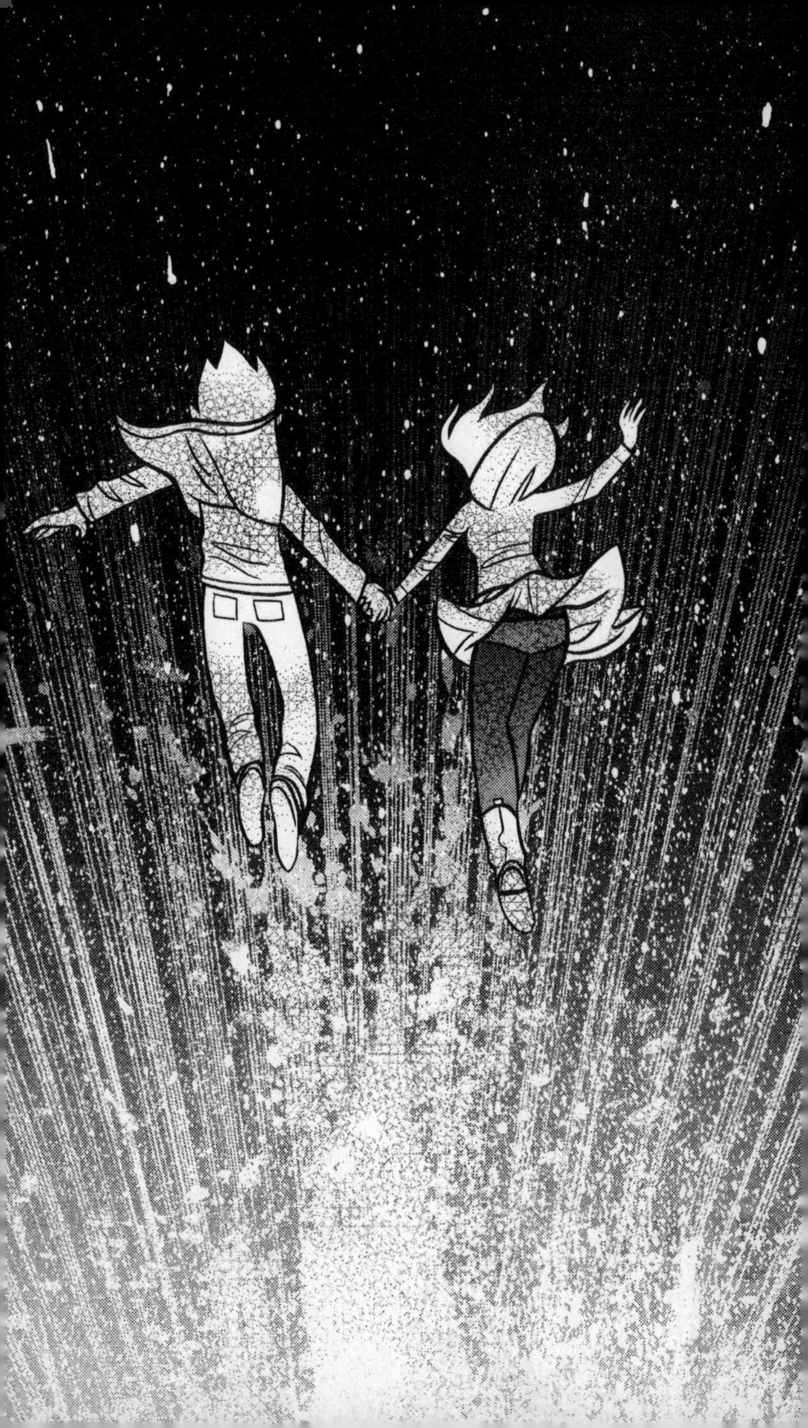

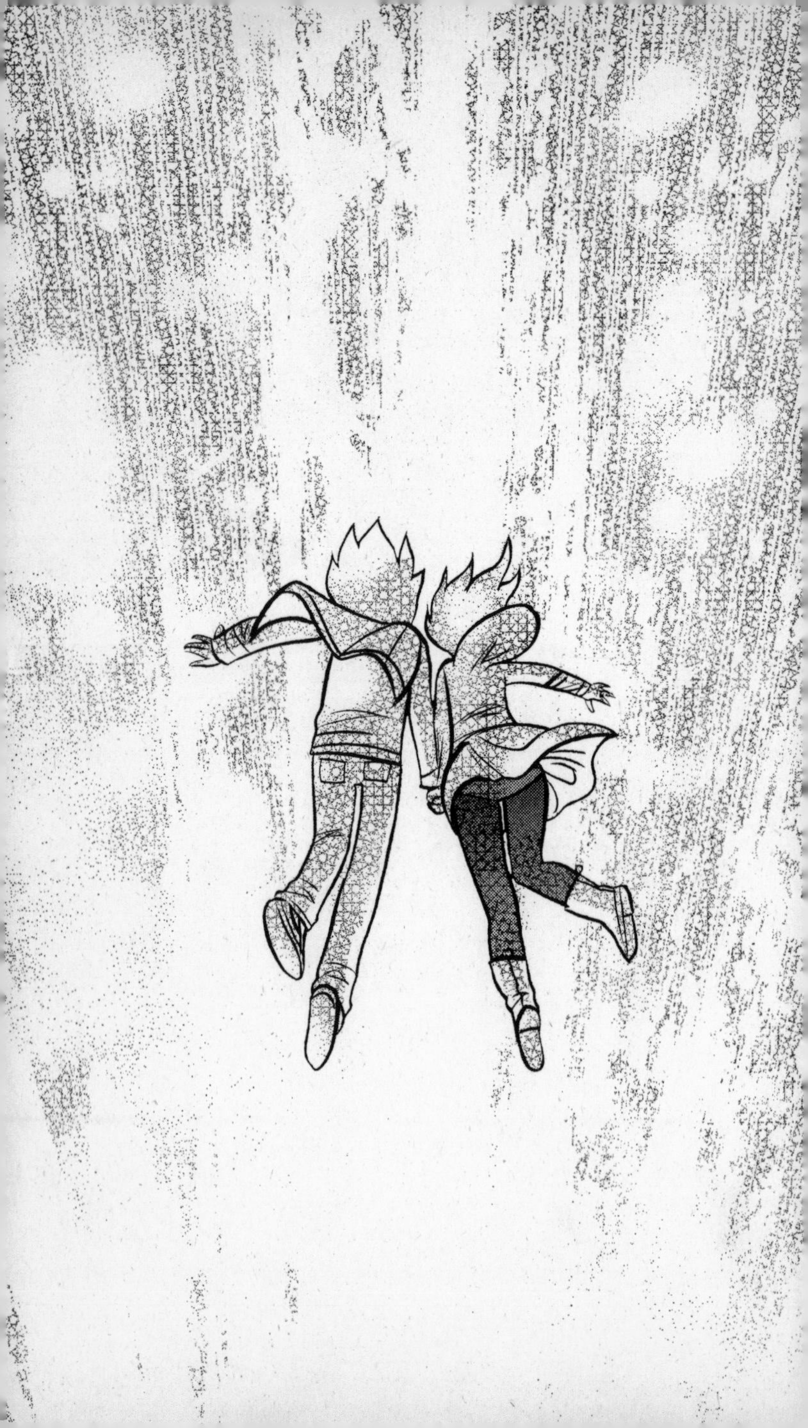

CREATED B

BRYAN LEE O'MAL
(CREATOR — 31 YEARS O

Wrote and drew the book, despite everything.

This book and all the others ar past six years and the other ye are all dedicated to Hope Lars

Thank you and goodnight.

Albums that got me through this:
The Cardigans - *Super Extra Gravity;* Annie - *Don't*
Neko Case - *Middle Cyclone;* Gorillaz - *Plastic Beac*
LCD Soundsystem - *This Is Happening;* Sleigh Bells -
Pavement - *Quarantine the Past;* and Spoon - *Trans,*

JOHN KANTZ
Screentone, background art (28 years old)
Artist, *Legends From Darkwood.*
Designed Gideon's cryogenic apparatus.
www.jackmo.com

AARON ANCHETA
Crowd scenes, inking assist (20 yea
Student at the University of Arizona
is his first published work. Drew a I
Ramonas. *www.aancheta.com*